To Mum and Dad

LAST
of the
Summer
MOËT

Wendy Holden

HEAD
of ZEUS

First published in the UK in 2018 by Head of Zeus, Ltd

Copyright © Wendy Holden 2018

The moral right of Wendy Holden to be identified as the author
of this work has been asserted in accordance with the
Copyright, Designs and Patents Act of 1988.

9 7 5 3 1 2 4 6 8

A catalogue record for this book is available from
the British Library.

ISBN (HB): 9781784977580
ISBN (XTPB): 9781784977597
ISBN (E): 9781784977573

Typeset by Palimpsest

Printed and bound in Great Britain by
CPI Group (UK) Ltd, Croydon CR0 4YY

Head of Zeus Ltd
First Floor East
5–8 Hardwick Street
London EC1R 4RG

WWW.HEADOFZEUS.COM

LAST *of the* *Summer* MOËT

Number-one bestselling author WENDY HOLDEN was a journalist on *Tatler*, *The Sunday Times*, and the *Mail on Sunday* before becoming an author. She has since written ten consecutive *Sunday Times* Top Ten bestsellers.

Find out more at wendyholden.net

LAST *of the* *Summer* MOËT

CHAPTER ONE

L aura Lake, deputy editor of *Society* magazine, returned to her desk after the daily features meeting. She felt as if she had done ten rounds with Floyd Mayweather. Glancing round at her colleagues as they slunk back to their workstations, she could tell that they felt the same.

Raisy and Daisy, the interchangeable blonde sisters who shared the job of fashion director, were looking particularly crushed. Their ideas about furry lederhosen had not got past first base, still less their suggestions for directional glittery clogs. Raisy (whose name was actually Rosie, but it had taken Laura some time to realise), was dabbing at her eyes with a sequinned Chanel hanky. The fine dark brows of Thomasella the food editor were angrily drawn as well. Her contention that Bronze Age party food – i.e. Ritz crackers and cheese hedgehogs – was back had been thrown on the same pile as the lederhosen.

Admittedly Carinthia, *Society*'s mercurial editor and Laura's boss, had always been demanding. 'The Gaze', her famous death stare, had always had the power to reduce her staff to rubble. This was all the more remarkable given that none of them could actually see it. The opaque black sunglasses Carinthia habitually wore were, alongside those of Anna Wintour of American *Vogue*, the most terrifying eyewear in journalism.

But people had respected this ruthlessness. Carinthia, they knew, demanded the best. Only the cleverest ideas made the cut, which was why the magazine was so successful. Those not equal to this quest for perfection could be summarily fired, like the style editor who had said neon-pink-sprayed midges were summer's smart garden accessory.

But of late Carinthia's demands had taken on a new, lunatic edge. Staff had been told to position their chairs exactly eight centimetres from their desk edge whether or not they were sitting in them and never, upon pain of death, hang anything on the backs. Untidy desks were photographed, named and shamed, including Laura's. Especially Laura's, the untidiest in the office.

More bizarrely still, according to Demelza, Carinthia's long-suffering PA, the editor had recently started consulting an astrologer. 'She goes up to her roof and sits under a blue plastic pyramid,' Demelza confided. 'Then she's told which days are to be avoided.'

Demelza had shown Laura the diary. Days to be avoided had been blacked out, and Carinthia didn't come in on them. There had been many black days lately, leaving Laura running the ship. While Laura enjoyed being in charge, and things tended to go more smoothly when she was, it was irritating to have the editor come back and take credit for her efforts. Or, worse, change her arrangements and cancel the features she had commissioned.

But there was one feature Carinthia would not be cancelling. One that had survived the recent meeting unscathed. Laura's coming interview with Savannah Bouche, the vastly famous and stunningly beautiful Hollywood actress and humanitarian.

Laura had set the interview up herself and was hugely proud of having done so. All *Society*'s glossy rivals had been after it too; to secure it was a coup. Laura secretly hoped she had pulled it off thanks to her growing journalistic reputation. The 'Three Weddings and a Scandal' story had shot her into the magazine stratosphere, and the adventures of the 'Luxury Press Trip', in which a billionaire businessman had been unmasked as a charlatan, had only burnished her credentials further. An in-depth report of an encounter with one of the world's most famous women would be the perfect continuation of what was promising to be a stellar career.

Sitting at her desk the regulation eight centimetres from the edge, Laura allowed this delicious daydream to continue. Carinthia's craziness notwithstanding, it was all going so well. Her dead foreign correspondent father would be proudly looking down from whatever heavenly hacks' bar he was currently standing a round in.

Even her on-off boyfriend Harry, a freelance investigative reporter with an amazing track record, would soon have to see her as more than just a glossy-mag hack. He would, Laura determined, regard her with respect instead of teasing her about seaweed wraps and sub-zero facial compression chambers.

Yes, Laura thought, absently playing with a bottle of diamond body soufflé that someone had left on her desk, this interview really was going to make her name all over again. She could hardly wait to meet Savannah, a modern Sphinx who pouted so beautifully from every magazine cover, but whose personality remained an intriguing mystery in spite of all the publicity.

What would she be like? The many interviews Laura had read in preparation had remarked on Savannah's husky voice – 'like slowly ripped velvet,' one besotted male writer had claimed. Other men had raved about her full mouth; pouty bee-stung, crushed-rose and kissable.

The flattery was not unalloyed, however. 'Her back looks like she's slept on wet newspaper,' one female writer had sniped of Savannah's famous tattoos, adding that the celebrated lips looked like 'two slugs having a spasm'.

Arrangements to meet had been complicated. A man calling himself Savannah's 'chief of staff', a nasal American called Brad Plant, had explained to Laura that the actress was 'frustrated by the whole six-star hotel penthouse interview thing'.

Laura was frustrated that Savannah was frustrated. Having never been in one before, she had been looking forward to interviewing someone in a six-star hotel penthouse. She was hoping for a six-star cup of tea.

'Miss Bouche finds it difficult to do something as trivial as chat to journalists when twenty million people live below the poverty line, y'know?' Brad Plant had gone on.

'I guess I can see that,' Laura conceded.

'So she's decided to mix it up.'

'Mix it up?'

'Yeah, do something at the same time. So you get a more interesting take on her.'

'Right.' Laura waited to hear what the something would be.

But Brad Plant was taking his time before the big reveal. 'The last person to interview Miss Bouche went to the gym with her. The one before went to a dildo show.'

Laura hoped the gym wouldn't be the chosen activity. She hated exercise.

'So where am I going?'

'I'll get back to you on that,' Brad had said, and Laura had had to be content with that even if, so far, Brad hadn't.

The morning went on. Laura applied herself to checking the page proofs of the edition about to go to press. As she did so, doubts about whether Carinthia still retained her infallible instinct for a story began to creep in. This feature here about town and country PJs, for instance. The original concept sprang from a leaden joke about PJs meaning private jets as well as pyjamas. The introduction to the piece teased *Society* readers with the idea that people had separate jets for rural and urban travel, only to reveal on the next page that the focus was actually nightwear.

'I always buy my husband's pyjamas in sets of two,' someone called Wonky de Launay had told Tatty, the goofy blonde who hoed the hard row of being *Society*'s luxury editor. 'The ones in superfine sky-blue shirting with white piping are for Chelsea, while the giant fuchsia gingham cotton ones are for the country.'

Laura shook her head despairingly. Where did one start? With the so-called joke? With the idea that a wife bought her husband's pyjamas for him? Harry would have a field day with either. To make matters worse, Wonky had been photographed in the doorway of a sleek white private jet. She was wearing the pink checked PJs, her blonde hair cascading over one tanned and narrow shoulder and the buttons undone to reveal a hint of sunkissed bosom. She was, Laura calculated, in her mid-fifties, but looked twenty years less. The country air of wherever it was must be very preserving.

She signed off the proof and picked up the arts page, whose main feature was an exhibition of giant kitchen utensils mounted in a Russian bus garage. What *Society* reader would bother to go there and see that, Laura was wondering crossly before learning that bus garage, utensils and all had been uprooted and moved to Wimbledon. 'It's a commentary on US imperialism and masculine violence,' the curator was quoted as saying.

About halfway through the morning Carinthia shut herself in her glass-walled office and noisily pulled down all the blinds. When first she had started at *Society* Laura had assumed all this crashing and swaying presaged the editor taking an important call or pondering a big idea. She knew now that what Carinthia was pondering was a bottle of white wine taken from her office mini-fridge on whose pink door her initials were embossed in Swarovski crystals.

Laura looked at her watch and whistled. Ten forty-five. Carinthia's sessions were getting earlier and earlier. On the other hand this might mean that, with the aid of a vast supply of bottled water, the editor might have vaguely sobered up by lunchtime when she was due to take out the new intern.

Interns were not usually treated to lunch with the editor. But this latest was not the usual kind of intern. The usual type of intern was skinny and drifty with swishy blonde hair that seemed to constitute their entire personality. This new girl, Wyatt, was plump and Gothic; with an all-black wardrobe and an unbrushed blue mane that descended no further than a rounded, spotty chin. Nor did Wyatt drift gracefully; she stumbled around in huge Dr Martens. Whenever she moved one of the fashion rails she sent the metal coat-hangers crashing more violently than Carinthia's blinds.

This was bad enough, causing *Society*'s highly strung staff to shy and start like nervous thoroughbreds. But what was worse was Wyatt's tendency to knock off, in her clumsy manoeuvres, the labels attached to the rails that showed what shoots the clothes were intended for. She then put them back on the wrong ones. That 'Revenge Dresses' were subsequently shot on the 'Re-Imagining the Cardigan' models was only one of the disastrous mistakes resulting. 'My aesthetic has been completely compromised!' Raisy wailed.

Normally, Wyatt would never have got within a thousand miles of Carinthia's office, were it not for the fact that her father had bid for the internship at a charity auction. Laura had not attended this glittering event. But Carinthia had been there with bells on – quite literally, in something from Daisy's shoot on cross-pollinated metallics – along with the flower of rich City bankers.

After a lavish dinner by leading chef Beowulf Borgenberg – beef aged in Himalayan salt caves served with After Eight gravy – an auction had been held. Besides the internship on *Society*, the lots had included a drawing lesson with Mary Berry, baking with Lewis Hamilton and driving tuition from Tracey Emin. It had been this version of events, heavily laced with alcohol fumes, that confirmed Laura's suspicions all was not well with her boss.

That Wyatt's father had offered more than twice Laura's annual salary for this opportunity for his daughter was something Laura took on the chin. Life wasn't fair, and life on glossy magazines less fair than most. The real question was why Wyatt's father had bothered. His daughter had never, from the moment her solid AirWear™ sole had first made contact with the *Society* carpet, shown the least interest in the workings of a glossy magazine. Perhaps Wyatt was simply shy, Laura thought, glancing over to the fashion department and spotting the intern shoving a rail of gossamer ballgowns marked 'Vietnam Chic – #TravisBickle' into the fashion cupboard.

At quarter to one, Laura shot a look at the still-drawn blinds of the editor's office. Would Carinthia be sober enough to take Wyatt out? Normally she would offer to lunch the intern herself, especially as, according to Demelza, the booking had been made at L'Esprit, an extremely smart and chic restaurant much frequented by the rich and famous.

But Laura was having lunch with her best friend Lulu, who was getting married and for whom she was being a bridesmaid. Lulu had chosen to meet at Umbra, a restaurant Laura had not heard of before.

'Ees last thing!' Lulu had enthused on the phone. 'Latest thing,' Laura effortlessly translated, accustomed by now to her friend's mispronunciations. Lulu's mixed international accent – a little bit Russian, a little bit French, perhaps with something Arabic in there too – had once been unflatteringly compared to the well-trodden carpet of a first-class airport lounge. Laura knew that beneath the glittering outer shell of the designer-clad heiress beat a warm and loyal heart. But that didn't stop the world from trying to exploit her and her wealth. This restaurant would doubtless be some dreadful new place that the kindly Lulu had been persuaded to book by a desperate PR. As she stood up to leave and positioned her chair according to the rules, Laura wondered what the place would be like.

CHAPTER TWO

Umbra, the fashionable new restaurant where Lulu had chosen to meet, seemed to have had a power cut. Or so Laura assumed, entering from the brightly sunlit street into an interior of intense black. As the door behind her clicked shut, the last slice of daylight disappeared. Darkness pressed in all around. It was like being in the deepest of caves; nothing at all was visible. There were sounds, however; the murmur of conversation, the clink of cutlery on china, the occasional tinkle of laughter.

'Hello?' Laura called, disconcerted.

A small point of light now came towards her, like a torch beam. It was a torch beam, and above it was a face. The face was young, male and smiling as if the situation could not have been more natural. 'Madam has booked?'

'My friend has,' Laura told him. 'But she won't be here

yet.' Lulu was always half an hour late for everything. 'And hopefully when she is the lights will be back on.'

'Lights?' The smiling face above the torch beam looked puzzled. 'But, madam, Umbra does not have lights. That is the point. It is dark on purpose.'

Laura laughed. There was surprise in her laughter; London waiters, in her experience, were not great exponents of irony. But as the torchlit face changed from puzzled to irritated, she realised the assertion was serious. Her own amusement gave way to astonishment. 'Dark? But why?'

'To heighten our clients' sense of taste, madam. To give them the ultimate flavour experience.'

'You serve people in the pitch blackness and that makes the food taste better?'

'And the wine, madam.'

'I suppose,' Laura allowed, 'it brings a whole new meaning to "blind tastings".'

The waiter did not bat an eyelid. Not so far as Laura could see, anyway. 'Absolutely, madam. Shall I show you to your table?'

Laura followed the torch beam as it shone along a length of hideous swirled carpet. But of course there was no need to decorate a blacked-out restaurant in the latest expensive designer style. The proprietors of Umbra could well be on to something. She groped her way to her seat. The invisible chair and table seemed light and plastic, like very cheap garden furniture.

She sat there for what seemed like a very long time. Behind her and around her, the conversation flowed as it might in any high-end Mayfair eaterie at lunchtime.

'Everyone who's anyone lives there,' a woman behind her was saying. 'But no one's ever heard of it.'

Laura was instantly on the alert. She was desperate to find a new lead for Selina the travel editor, who, encouraged by the new, crazed Carinthia, was currently putting together a piece about trekking in the Arctic whilst living on reindeer blubber and lining your clothes with tinfoil. This luxury enclave being discussed was far more the thing. Where was it? Connecticut? Puglia?

The woman's companion was speaking. 'They say Great Hording's the most expensive village in the UK.'

Village? The *UK?* Laura was so surprised she wobbled the table and a number of unseen things fell to the floor where, fortunately, the briefly glimpsed hideous carpet cushioned the impact. She was memorising the name of this fortunate place – Great Hording, Great Hording – as a small point of light flashed on her accompanied by an excitable voice with a strong foreign accent.

'Laura! Is so lovely to see you!'

Lulu obviously had night-vision glasses. Or else ate a lot of carrots.

Laura reached out to give her friend a hug but felt her lips, in the dark, make contact with an unshaved and bristly cheek. In the meantime, Lulu's 'mwah, mwah' could be heard being bestowed some distance away.

'Is you I kiss, Laura, yes?' Lulu sounded doubtful.

'I wouldn't worry about it.'

Laura wondered who she had kissed herself. The waiter? One of the women behind them? They could now be heard receiving the bill. 'Shall we go Dutch? I'll just get my bag, I put it down here. . .'

'You like this restaurant? Is original, no?' Across the flimsy table, Lulu sounded to be shuffling off something squeaky, possibly leather or crocodile.

'It's definitely that,' Laura had to agree.

'Is where comes everyone to see and be seen,' Lulu asserted.

'Where's my bag?' The voice behind had a sharp, panicked edge. 'I can't find it!'

'Me neither!' Her companion joined in the chorus of alarm.

Something heavy was now put on the table, accompanied by a tinkle. Laura pictured one of Lulu's vast designer totes, rattling with gold decoration. 'Is making table fall over,' Lulu murmured as the flimsy surface lurched alarmingly sideways. 'I put bag on floor.'

'I wouldn't,' Laura said quickly. Possibly another of Umbra's advantages was that it made expensive handbags ripe for the picking. 'Hang it on the back of your chair.'

'Would you like to see the menu?' The waiter's voice came suddenly out of the darkness.

'Is it in Braille?' Laura asked.

The waiter ignored her remark. 'Today's specials are *pâté et saucisson en sauce tomates* and *haricots blancs en sauce tomates sur pain grillé ,*' he announced coldly.

They ordered one of each. 'And two champagne glasses,' Lulu added. It was her signature drink.

'With champagne in them, madam?' the waiter asked sardonically.

'Moët,' confirmed Lulu. It was her favourite brand. Laura loved champagne too but it always went straight to her head. With regret she remembered the office. 'Not for me. I have to work this afternoon.'

Lulu groaned from across the table. 'So I will drink both glasses. Has been heavy morning.'

Laura braced herself for the news that the wedding plans

were in difficulty. Lulu was marrying the successful rapper and hugely wealthy businessman, South'n Fried, famous for his aggressive lyrics, for wearing several expensive watches at once and having a whole Knightsbridge house for his collection of designer trainers. The pair had bonded over their shared love of handicrafts – a guilty passion that South'n Fried had kept hidden from his manager and fans for years, lest it ruin his reputation as the poster boy for urban discontent.

Their first months together had been a secret idyll of wildflower-pressing in Wiltshire and tie-dying in Tintagel. But all too soon South'n Fried had been torn away to begin his 'Bust Yo Ass' world tour. This had left Lulu with the wedding arrangements, which, in line with the expectations of South'n Fried's fanbase, had initially been envisaged as a three-day extravaganza on the French Riviera. This had slowly changed focus and was now a strange hybrid of the simple boho ceremony the couple would secretly have preferred and the high-octane spendfest traditionally associated with celebrity rapper weddings. Jewelled hessian tablecloths and 'found' glass milk-bottles rolled in diamond dust had been some of the uneasy compromises so far suggested.

There were more, as Laura now heard.

Finding a gold-plated tractor to convey Lulu and South'n Fried to their chosen little country church was proving a headache. To further complicate things, the farmer who owned the barn upon which Lulu's heart was set for her simple rural celebration was objecting to the inside being gutted and fitted out with a hot tub, underlit dance floor and an enlarged entrance for the twenty-tier, thirty-foot home-made lemon drizzle cake.

'And vicar not like helicopter either,' Lulu mourned, as

she sipped her brace of champagnes. If indeed champagne it was. Waiting for her Coke to arrive, Laura had accepted her friend's offer of a sip. It had tasted suspiciously like elderflower fizz to her.

'Helicopter? I thought you were arriving in a tractor.'

'Helicopter is to scatter flowers on guests. For picturesque rural touch outside church. Vicar say disturb bats in tower. But why old ladies in tower in first place? Hmm?'

The food arrived. Laura, who had chosen the *pâté et saucissons en sauce tomates*, tasted it gingerly. Would it be the flavour sensation Umbra seemed to pride itself on?

'Is good, no?' Lulu, from the darkness across the table, spoke through a mouthful of *haricots blancs en sauce tomates sur pain grillé*.

Laura hesitated. The waiter, bestowing the dish with impressive accuracy on the table, had waxed lyrical about tomato *coulis* bursting with southern Italian sunshine, circular rings of pasta hand-rolled by *nonnas* in Naples and tiny sausages from a village near Ferrara which made them only at particular times of the year. But what it reminded Laura of more than anything else was tinned spaghetti hoops and sausages. She decided not to say so, however. Lulu, whose choice Umbra had been, might be hurt.

'How's yours?' she asked. Lulu's dish had arrived with a similar fanfare about beans gathered in a glowing Tuscan dawn placed with loving precision on a slice of bread made with a century-old culture.

Lulu, in the darkness, seemed to be hesitating. 'This flavour, you know? Remind me something but can't put my foot in it.'

'Put your finger on it,' Laura translated.

'Make me think of toast on beans at my finishing school, hmm?'

Laura, remembering the vast bill which the neighbouring ladies had been unable to pay due to the disappearance of their handbags, could only admire the chutzpah of Umbra's owners. Across the table, Lulu continued to talk about the wedding. A fiddler was to lead the guests from the church to the barn. 'How lovely,' said Laura, charmed as well as surprised at what seemed a genuinely simple rural touch. 'Very Thomas Hardy.'

'Very Harry Winston,' corrected Lulu, explaining that the fiddler's Stradivarius was encrusted in priceless diamonds and the fiddler herself was Simon Rattle's favourite soloist.

They moved on to the wedding dress, which was as simple and rustic as anything designed personally by Karl Lagerfeld could be, and Lulu's tiara, which was to feature hand-dived Hebridean pearls in a nod to South'n Fried's apparent Scottish ancestry.

'How is Vlad?' Laura asked eventually, deciding she had heard enough and turning the subject to her friend's Estonian butler. She was very fond of Vlad, who ran with military efficiency Lulu's designer-logoed Kensington mansion.

'Vlad is addict of harchas,' was the alarming news.

Addict? Laura stiffened with alarm. Harchas?

'Me too now,' Lulu said. 'We do it every Sunday morning in kitchen.'

Laura tried not to panic as she imagined the two of them steadily consuming this mysterious narcotic amid Lulu's Chanel saucepans as the bells of nearby Kensington Church called the faithful to prayer. 'But. . . what is it?'

'Seriously? You don' know harchas?' Lulu sounded

astonished. 'But you must! You catch up double-decker bus.'

The *Archers* omnibus, Laura realised. Lulu had become a devotee of the radio soap and had the last two months' worth backed up on her iPod in preparation for a long flight. She was going to Miami the following day to join South'n Fried on the latest leg of the 'Bust Yo Ass' tour. 'Love Roger Oldridge,' she added. 'Remind me of Donald Trump.'

This was more than enough. Laura rose to her feet in the blackness. 'I've got to go back to work.'

Emerging from the tenebrous hole of the restaurant was like coming out of a dark prison. The sunshine was painfully strong; for Laura, at least. Lulu was unaffected; like Carinthia, she wore oversized black sunglasses at all times.

Lulu's appearance was always startling but it was doubly so after being in a black cave for an hour. Looking at her was a bit like looking directly into the sun. Everything blazed and shone, from the big blonde hair which reared from her forehead before tumbling to her waist, to the white teeth framed by glossy pink lipstick glowing in the plump brown oval face. Lulu's figure, curvaceous rather than skinny, looked more pneumatic than ever in a tiny white leather quilted biker jacket festooned with gold zips. Tight pink leather trousers strained over her generous hips and the look was rounded off with matching pink suede ankle boots whose blocky heels were studded with crystals.

Lulu was, like her, twenty-three – or so Laura calculated; one could never be entirely sure – but their personal styles could not be more different. Beside her exuberant friend, slim and dark in her unvarying outfit of dark jeans, tight black blazer, close-fitting navy shirt and ankle boots, her black hair swept up into a working ponytail, Laura felt like Night next to glorious Day.

She kissed her friend's warm, scented cheek in farewell. 'Give my love to South'n Fried. Ring me when you get back.'

CHAPTER THREE

Laura walked quickly back to work, her mind filling with all the different tasks to be completed. Nailing down the location/activity for the Savannah Bouche interview was the priority. Tomorrow was Saturday and no one would be working. If she was to climb Ben Nevis, go to Sainsbury's or visit A&E in the company of the actress, she needed to be told now.

Her eyes had not yet fully adjusted to the glare of the London sun as it bounced off the spotless Bond Street pavements and ricocheted off the diamonds in the jewellers' windows. The gleamingly clean glass panes reflected her lean figure as she walked along. She remembered how drab she had felt next to Lulu, but then, the latter's label-cluttered look wasn't really her thing. 'You are not a billboard,' her Parisian grandmother, Mimi, always told her. 'Initials are for the optician's chart.'

Laura's label-free thing worked, anyway. Brought up in Paris on a budget narrower than her trousers, she had been surprised and pleased to find that glossy-mag London aspired to the French-girl look she had adopted mainly from necessity. In Britain, gratifyingly, it was regarded as the height of chic. Even her hair, cut in a blunt fringe just above her brows, the rest flopping in a shining black mane on her narrow shoulders, was admired, although Laura stopped short of admitting that its gamine chop was due to kitchen scissors and the shine came from the home-made beer rinse that Mimi, now ninety-four, had used all her life.

Society's office was located in a gracious eighteenth-century square whose gracious eighteenth-century houses had long been replaced by more utilitarian Edwardian and twenties buildings containing movie corporations, retail offices, social media empires and the headquarters of the British Magazine Company. The Art Deco block of Society House took up the south-east corner of the square, its name carved in gold capitals above a silver metal revolving door which turned constantly to admit and release a stream of visitors and staff.

Delivery boys yanked their trolleys past helmeted motorbike couriers bearing clipboards from which pens swung like metronomes. The boom and pouf of boxes being thrown into the open-doored backs of vans was counterpointed by the swift clack of kitten heels as magazine staff in oversized designer glasses hurried in and out clutching smartphones and expensive handbags.

A slim woman with punky hair, a black asymmetric skirt and towering black high heels stood on the pavement looking indignantly about. An editor expecting a taxi, Laura knew. She would be unable, quite literally, to move a foot otherwise. That the taxis and the shoemakers round here worked in tandem was something Laura had long suspected. Not that the editors put up much of a fight. 'I've never really seen the point of walking,' Carinthia had once airily declared. 'Just putting one foot in front of another – why bother?'

As she neared Society House Laura drew a deep, satisfied breath, relishing the familiar scent of perfume mixed with petrol fumes. She looked up at the building's flat white façade, taking delight, as ever, in spotting the sixth-floor window nearest to her desk and noting, as she did so, the line of bigger windows on the floor above it, where Christopher Stone, CEO of the British Magazine Company, had his lair.

Laura loved the feeling of belonging here, of being part of this exclusive, glossy world. Fitting in had not been easy, but her first year at *Society* had ultimately been a triumph. The 'Three Weddings and a Scandal' story had simultaneously elevated her professional stock to gilt-edged status and got rid of her worst office enemy, the vicious Clemency Makepeace.

Approaching the revolving door, Laura smiled. It was bliss to enter the office building in the knowledge that Clemency was no longer there, plotting against her with her glossy red hair and glassy green cat's eyes that could look so innocent but conceal such evil.

Carinthia and Wyatt had not returned from lunch, nor had Brad Plant returned any of her calls, or answered any of her emails. Possibly, as it often went with big celebrities, the whole interview was off and he had not yet bothered to tell her. Perhaps – ghastly thought – he had gone with one of *Society*'s rivals. The idea gnawed unbearably at Laura, who was compulsively competitive, especially over any feature that had been her idea. This determination to protect her journalistic territory came, she was sure, from her father.

A new set of proofs waited on her desk and Laura started diligently to work her way through them. As she did so, the conviction she was reading a parody of *Society* magazine returned. The feature was a set of short profiles of 'London's Hottest Totty', which seemed both outdated and offensive.

Carinthia routinely countered such objections with the claim that *Society* was simultaneously ironic and above political correctness. She prided herself in her intolerance of such social advances as breastfeeding in public and gender-neutral toilets, although had learnt not to say so before Laura, who, with Vlad in mind, defended the latter in particular against the editor's contention that it was liberalism gone mad.

And anyway, Laura thought, reading on, wasn't liberalism, however mad, infinitely preferable to such 'hot totty' as Lady Squiffy Farte who took her maltipoo daily to Harrod's pet spa for claw polishes, blow-dries and a blueberry face mask? Or society artist Rupi von Rumtopf, here described as 'the best thing out of Austria since Mozart', whose art involved taking photos of pieces of priceless porcelain a split second after he'd blown them up.

Imagining Harry reading all this, Laura cringed. They were meeting later, to see the new Bond film. This starred Laura's friend and sometime lover Caspar, a formerly struggling actor who had shot to fame last year. She had vaguely hoped Harry might be a bit jealous, but he had been characteristically taciturn on the subject.

As Carinthia had still not showed, Laura thought about bunking off early and tidying up her flat in advance of

Harry's visit. Not being subject to the same name-and-shame regime as her desk, it habitually looked as if it had been burgled. Most of the rest of the staff had gone anyway, the few, that was, who came in on the last day of the week and weren't Friday-to-Mondaying at someone's country house. Laura had been surprised, when she started at *Society*, just how many of the staff spent their weekends hunting, shooting or attending elaborate balls amid ancestral acres. For some people it was as if the twentieth century had never happened.

A sudden disturbance at the door now made her look up. Carinthia came staggering in, her clothes awry, her sunglasses skew-whiff on her face, her usually smooth brassy bob sporting a distinct hedge-backwards aspect. She looked as if she had either been hit or had fallen over.

Laura sprang to her feet. 'What's the matter?'

Carinthia did not answer but rushed, gasping, past Laura's desk and slammed into her office. The blinds fell down and crashed agitatedly against the windows; the rattle of wine bottles could be heard. Laura turned to Wyatt, who trailed in the editor's wake. Beneath the blue hair her large white face looked shell-shocked. 'What happened?'

Wyatt sighed. 'There was kind of, a riot?'

'A *riot*?' But the lunch had been at L'Esprit, haunt of the rich and powerful. Riots were not its business; rather, casually expensive food served amid plutocratic calm. 'What happened?'

'Well, we were put at the back, which I thought was fine but Carinthia didn't like.'

Laura could imagine. Where one sat in L'Esprit was crucial. Favoured and important clients got the tables towards the front while tourists and non-regulars were put at the rear. If Carinthia had been thus relegated, it could only mean that L'Esprit's famously smooth-but-firm *maîtresse d'* had had enough of her histrionics.

'And this woman was there breastfeeding, and, um. . .'

A cold feeling went through Laura. 'Surely Carinthia didn't ask her to. . . stop?'

Wyatt's unkempt blue head moved up and down. 'She was pretty drunk, she'd been adding her own vodka miniatures to her Bloody Mary.'

'What did the breastfeeding lady say?'

'That she'd breastfeed where she liked and Carinthia was a fascist.'

'Oh dear.'

'So Carinthia yelled that she was a nipple-flashing Nazi. . .'

Laura covered her face with her hands.

'. . . and started screaming that if that was how things were she'd get her tits out as well. . .'

'You're joking!'

'. . . and kind of ripped off her blouse. . .'

'NO!'

'And the *maîtresse d'* said could she just stop it because there was a journalist from the *Evening Standard* at the very next table and—'

'Seen this?'

The voice was Demelza's and the sound was that of a tabloid newspaper landing with a thud on the desk. The front page was worse than Laura's worst nightmare. 'NIPPLES AT DAWN' was the headline above a breathless account of the scene at L'Esprit. The accompanying picture, presumably from the journalist's smartphone, showed Carinthia, who the piece described as 'the last of London's legendary glossy magazine editors', drunken, shouting and exposing a pair of skinny breasts to tables of outraged men in pinstripes.

Laura rose to her feet but just then a powerful waft of expensive aftershave announced the arrival of Christopher Stone, the British Magazine Company's CEO and ultimate boss of everyone present. The few staff members still around stood sharply to attention, but Stone, a dapper figure with a pink handkerchief in the jacket of his grey Savile Row suit, ignored them. He glided swiftly in his Jermyn Street brogues towards the closed door of Carinthia's office. The signet-ringed hand below the expensive if understated watch was holding a copy of the *Standard*.

Laura's phone now rang, and while she meant to ignore it in the face of this latest twist in the drama, her screen told her that this was, at last, the elusive Brad Plant. The representative on Earth of Savannah Bouche was finally getting in touch.

'Buckingham Palace,' he snarled in his nasal American tones.

'What?' Laura was confused.

'Buckingham Palace? You know it? Big building at the top of the Mall?' He pronounced it 'maul'.

'Of course I do. What about it?'

'Miss Bouche wants to go on a tour of it. With you. While you interview her.'

Laura only half heard. Her attention was on Carinthia's office door. Christopher Stone had closed it behind him, and nothing could be heard from within. What was going on?

'You still there?' snarled Plant from the other end.

Laura forced herself to concentrate. 'Buckingham *Palace*? She wants to meet there?'

Was there a worse option in the whole of London? Buckingham Palace had famously huge queues. There would be crowds of mobbing tourists. There had to be a better alternative. 'What about a pod in the London Eye?'

'Miss Bouche wants the Palace,' Brad cut in. 'We've arranged a private tour.'

Oh, what did any of it matter, Laura thought. Carinthia was almost certainly being sacked, at this very moment. Which meant that, as her deputy, she would be next.

Not for the first time since coming to *Society* she was facing the prospect of being fired for no fault of her own. What was unusual was that this time Clemency Makepeace had nothing to do with it.

'Okay,' she said to Brad Plant.

And so it was arranged. Laura – presuming she was still in gainful employment – was to present herself at the Palace main entrance at ten o'clock on Monday morning.

She put the phone down at the precise moment Christopher Stone emerged from Carinthia's office. His lightly tanned face wore its usual calm expression, but there was a clench to his jaw and a light to his eyes that made Laura fear the worst.

Her heart sank as, in his gleaming hand-made shoes, he rapidly traversed the black carpet tiles between them and stopped before her desk. Laura shot to her feet at the precise moment that Christopher Stone placed a pair of lightly tanned knuckles down on the table and leant over towards her. The collision was sharp and violent.

'Ow!' howled the CEO of the British Magazine Company, reeling away and clutching his smoothly shaved chin.

Laura was rooted to the spot, buzzing with the horror of having headbutted the man described in a recent piece by the *Financial Times* as the most powerful man in magazine publishing. That really was it, then. Whatever slim chance there had been had evaporated. She was surely finished now.

Stone turned back towards Laura. He was still holding his chin, and his watering eyes glittered coldly. She cringed inwardly, expecting marching orders of the most vehement persuasion.

'Carinthia is leaving,' Stone told her.

Laura bowed her head.

'Arrangements are being made for her to enter a rehabilitation facility,' Stone went on, in the light, clipped voice that belied the heft of the power he wielded. He paused and looked Laura keenly up and down. She waited to be informed that her services were no longer required either.

'You will edit *Society* until she returns.'

CHAPTER FOUR

T hat evening, Laura could not concentrate on the Bond
film. Even the fact that her friend had the star part
did not stop her thoughts wandering to her new,
completely unexpected promotion.

She was editor of *Society* and could do anything she liked
with the magazine! It was a heady prospect, a glittering
opportunity that she was determined to make the most of.
Carinthia would not, as the *Evening Standard* had declared,
be the last of London's great glossy-magazine editors. Laura
Lake, the new generation, would take the torch forward.

Laura had already decided that she would make *Society*
more relevant to its readership. Research had shown that
a great many young working women read it, but there was
little in its pages that reflected their lives. Perhaps a fashion
shoot on the perfect job-interview outfit? She would get
Raisy and Daisy on it first thing Monday morning.

Annoyingly, printers' deadlines meant that a feature about the correct way to eat caviar (off the back of your hand) had gone through. But it would, Laura was determined, be the last of the old-school *Society*. She would retain its wit and glamour, but not the articles which risked pushing it over the edge into self-parody.

Laura was absolutely determined that the interview with Savannah Bouche would send out a strong signal about her editorship. It would be far from the usual unctuous celebrity profile. Most reporters just sat there in fawning silence while Savannah issued a stream of statements about ending every war, empowering every woman and valuing every human life. None of these statements were ever challenged. Laura planned to challenge them.

What did Harry think about Savannah? Laura wondered. There had been no time to ask him yet. She slid him a sidelong glance. Harry's tall, sprawling frame had, for the past three hours, been constrained by the small cinema seat next to her. Very possibly it was the longest they had ever sat anywhere together. Harry seemed unable to stay in the same city as her, even the same country, for very long.

Part of her liked this air of mystery; the way he would arrive in the night after weeks without a word, only to disappear in the morning. But it was also frustrating. He sometimes spent all weekend asleep in her flat, evidently exhausted, with only his worn, suntanned face to hint where he might have been. Still, there were compensations. Harry was exasperating, but the one thing he wasn't was boring.

And the other thing he wasn't, she now realised, was awake. Harry was sunk in his seat, completely asleep. As her gaze lingered on his lean, intelligent face with its high cheekbones, level brow and rumple of dark hair, she felt a backwash of tenderness. She rarely saw the ever-watchful Harry with his guard down. He looked like a little boy.

The long mouth smiled; he was watching after all. Like Brer Rabbit, with one eyelid ever so slightly open.

The film was finishing. James Bond's mouth was locked on the lips of a beautiful blonde. The camera panned back, revealing the couple to be lying on the top deck of a blazing white superyacht in the middle of a brilliant blue sea.

Monty Norman's four-note motif struck up, and the words 'JAMES BOND WILL RETURN' rolled up the screen, followed by thousands of fast-moving credits. At the top was:

JAMES BOND.....................CASPAR HONEYMAN

Laura stared, still unable to quite believe it. As the new 007, Caspar was now a fully fledged celebrity, living in a Malibu mansion next door to Cher, or so he claimed. 'You should come over,' he had added in a casual, unconvincing tone which reminded Laura of what a terrible actor Caspar actually was. That her friend had reached such heights of fame and fortune was astonishing. As a suave and steel-nerved superspy, moreover. The idea of Caspar being loyal to Queen and country, or to anyone apart from himself, was hard to believe.

The credits kept rolling, sheets of them. Did Caspar actually know who the second grip in the Chilean crew was? Almost certainly, if she was a woman. This first film for the franchise, *The Caucus Imperative*, had been filmed in locations all over the world and in the few conversations Laura had had with him, he had declared himself 'shagged out'.

Some of the shagging had certainly involved Merlot

D'Vyne, the socialite niece of a famous nineties It girl. She was playing Bond girl Prudence Handjob and it was her arms in which 007 had been left atop the yacht. Laura wondered how the real-life relationship was going.

She struggled to her feet. Her legs in their tight dark jeans felt stiff. She stretched her arms in their navy shirt and flipped out her long mane of straight dark hair. Harry, from his seat, was watching her appreciatively.

As they shuffled out through the foyer, crunching popcorn into the carpet, she glanced up at the illuminated posters advertising *The Caucus Imperative*. The film's designers had done their best to make Caspar look cool in the trademark Bond manner. But there was still something bulging and manic about his round brown eyes.

Laura smiled. She could remember as if it were yesterday those eyes rolling in despair as Caspar bewailed his lack of acting success. His big Bond break had been wildly unexpected; so down on his luck had he been at the time he had been reduced to being a Prince Harry impersonator. She herself had been so desperate she'd been living in a magazine fashion cupboard.

What a difference a year made. Now she not only had her longed-for job as a journalist, she was actually acting editor! Even Harry had been impressed when she told him, once he had stopped laughing at the story of Carinthia, the nipple-flashing fascist.

They emerged into a London whose sky glowed dirty orange above a road shining with rain, car headlights, the yellow signs of taxis and brightly lit shops. Night had fallen while they had watched Caspar running over rooftops and leaping from helicopters.

'What did you think?' she asked Harry. He remained

rather annoyingly unmoved by the fact she had once gone out with James Bond.

'I liked that bit when he got clubbed and shoved in the vat of baked beans,' Harry replied. 'Shame he came round before he got to the canning machine.'

Laura smiled. Perhaps Harry was jealous after all. The baked beans episode had reminded her of the horrible flat where Caspar had lived at his lowest ebb. The loo had lacked a seat and the only utensil had been an unwashed spatula that the four or five residents – all male – shared to eat beans straight out of the tin. 'Do you think that sort of thing really happens?' she asked.

'What – a protocol that could destroy the world with poison gas from contaminated baked beans?' Harry gave an incredulous snort.

'Well, all of it. The spy thing.'

Harry grinned. 'If you're asking me whether James Bond is an accurate reflection of the security services. . .'

'Which I could be,' Laura returned. Harry was always infuriatingly elusive about what he knew of MIs 5 and 6. But he had to know something. All Harry's exposés involved international miscreants, and it seemed unlikely he investigated them without official help. Their first date had been at the Not Dead Yet Club, a place awash with foreign correspondents and diplomats. That Harry was a spy himself did not seem out of the question. Perhaps he, not Caspar, was the real James Bond.

'. . . the answer is. . .' Harry went on.

'Yes?'

'That I really wouldn't know. Shall we get a chicken katsu curry?' Laura, who had been brought up on a diet of French classics by her Parisian grandmother, shuddered.

She found Harry's lack of interest in food both baffling and appalling. His idea of Sunday lunch was a bag of steak ridge-cut chips followed by a packet of Skittles.

Inside the takeaway, Laura tried not to wince as she watched the server ladle the curry gloop over what had been a perfectly respectable chicken escalope. 'I don't know how you can eat that stuff,' she said as they walked out, Harry's dinner in a plastic bag.

'Boarding school,' he replied easily. 'The food was horrendous. Dead Man's Leg and Nun's Toenails.'

'Oh God, yes. We had this thing called Skeleton Stew. . .'

Only after offering up her own memories of school food did Laura realise he had steered her off the subject of spies completely, and they were now turning into her street.

Laura lived in Cod's Head Row, Shoreditch. It was an area of London once synonymous with grinding poverty but now synonymous with grinding affluence. Quite literally, given the preponderance of artisan coffee roasters.

Despite being situated in the London of 2018, most of the Cod's Head Row businesses were more in tune with the mediaeval countryside. There was a shop selling hand-churned butter and another trading in obscure artisanal cheeses. 'Nigel Forage', the greengrocer, stocked only the produce of local allotments and leaves hand-gathered from the nearby park. Laura never bought those. The nearby park contained far too many dogs.

The fact that these establishments served a thriving local community of drystone-wallers, glassblowers, weavers, blacksmiths and spoon-carvers only exacerbated Laura's feeling of being stuck in the rural fourteenth century. Since when had the inner city got like this?

Laura lived in a scruffy first-floor walk-up above Gorblimey

Trousers, a self-conscious pie-and-mash caff run by husband-and-husband team of ex-Google executives. On either side was Reaping the Whirlwind, a scything workshop, and Bodgers, which made chopping boards from reclaimed wood and stamped them with expletives. Opposite was Barberella, which sold beard oil made from reclaimed fatbergs. Laura's flat, which was the second in the building she had occupied – the lease having expired on her former top-floor apartment – reflected none of the local trends. There was no shred of dawn-gathered indigo in it, not a single artisanal ceramic and no upcycling of any description. If anything it was downcycled, the last building on the street not to be carefully restored in a manner suggesting it had never been altered.

Laura got out her keys and unlocked the battered front door. As it rattled shut behind them, she felt her heart beat faster in anticipation of the night ahead. Perhaps, this time, Harry might stay longer. The whole of tomorrow, even. It was Saturday, they could go for a walk, have lunch, go to the park. She crossed her fingers that her upstairs neighbour Edgar was out at one of his raves. Edgar was a manic depressive trust-funder with wild, unbrushed hair, oversized geek glasses and a passion for fisherman's jumpers and psychobabble. While he could occasionally be amusing, he was more often relentlessly boring in a very loud, droning voice. The music that he played at all hours was loud and boring as well.

Fortunately, the flat, as she let herself in, seemed quiet. No thumping was coming from the floor above.

Harry followed her in, looking about him in amusement. 'No one could accuse you of overdecorating.'

Laura shot him a look. 'Ever heard of minimalism?'

But like most of Laura's style statements, the bareness of

the flat was less to do with aesthetics than lack of money. It consisted of a bedroom, a sitting room with a kitchen at one end, and a tiny bathroom. It was completely bare apart from a mattress on the floor in the bedroom and a rail for clothes, a scratched leather sofa in the sitting room and mismatched table and chairs in the kitchen. And yet the building's elegant bones were still visible; the high ceilings, original panelling and long windows with thin old glass and shutters you could close at night. The broad, unvarnished oak floorboards were dented with what Laura liked to think were the seventeenth-century heels of Huguenot silk-weavers. Many had fled France for Britain to escape religious persecution and settled in Shoreditch because it was cheap. Refugees from Paris, not unlike her. They would, Laura felt, be bemused by the number of Parisians who now flocked to the area because it was expensive and blew fortunes on punky cushions and statement wallcoverings.

'Thanks,' said Harry, as she handed him a can of lager from the fridge and took out a box of eggs. 'You're not having curry?'

Laura shook her head as she broke the eggs into a bowl and then opened the window to snip off herbs from the pots outside. They were from cuttings that Mimi, her Parisian grandmother, had given her. She grew herbs in a window box that overlooked the whole city. Something of the view, Laura felt, had gone into the herbs. They tasted like Paris to her.

Mimi stayed on Laura's mind as she whipped up the eggs. She adored spending time with the indomitable elderly Frenchwoman who had brought her up from infancy, shared with her the tiny Montmartre flat and lovingly supervised every aspect of her life.

Adding salt and pepper and tipping the fluffy mass into

the frying pan, Laura wondered what Mimi was eating now. Together with her three closest Parisian friends, her nonagenarian grandmother had recently thrown old age to the winds, unleashed her inner explorer and embarked on a series of what seemed non-stop tours of the globe. 'The Fat Four' as they called themselves, although none was even remotely plump, were currently on a cruise of the southern hemisphere, and quite out of WiFi's clutches. The knowledge that she would not be able to speak to her grandmother for months was dispiriting; Mimi was a fund of wisdom on everything from lipstick to love.

A few minutes later, as they sat at the wobbly table, Harry glanced from his congealing heap of curry to the fluffy yellow omelette Laura was cutting into with her fork. 'That looks good.'

'Want some?'

She took her plate and slid on to his knee, parting her legs to face him. 'Close your eyes and open your mouth.' He obliged and she kissed him slowly. She put the plate down and the food was forgotten as they stood up as one. Laura led him to her room and the mattress on the floor.

Afterwards they lay amid the creased blue sheets. Harry smiled at her lazily and raised himself on one elbow, revealing a lick of hair in his armpit that made her swallow. How was it that she knew every inch of him so intimately, and yet didn't know him at all?

Suddenly he was standing up, pulling his jeans back on. 'I've got to go.'

'*Why?*' wailed Laura. He was spending the whole weekend with her, wasn't he? The night, at least.

'Because.' He bent and kissed her, sending a great new bolt of desire through her. She imagined it passing through the floor and blowing the single, unshaded lightbulb on the ceiling of the entrance hall.

'Where are you going?'

'If I told you I'd have to kill you.' Harry grinned.

Laura eyed him from beneath her dark fringe. A double bluff? 'Ha ha.'

She watched as he shrugged on the ancient black biker jacket that, had she not known better, she might assume he even wore in bed. But Harry wore nothing in bed, Laura remembered longingly.

'I'll be in touch.' He smiled, but a preoccupied smile, as if his thoughts were elsewhere already. Then he left the bedroom. The front door latch snapped shut behind him. He was gone. With a sigh, Laura reached for her laptop, and started preparing for the big Savannah Bouche interview on Monday. She might as well put the night to good use.

CHAPTER FIVE

At the end of the wide red Mall, the iconic façade of Buckingham Palace shone white against a clear blue sky. Atop the flagpole, the red and gold Royal Standard rippled. The sovereign was home. Home to receive another sovereign. Savannah Bouche, Queen of Hollywood.

Walking slowly through a St James's Park frothing with white spring blossom, Laura rehearsed her questions. She had imagined that, thanks to Harry's precipitate departure, she would have all day to read yet more research material. But in Saturday's small hours Edgar had crashed back with a Russian transvestite trio called Sink the Pink and woken her up. It had taken ages to get back to sleep, only to be woken again a few hours later by Edgar banging on the door begging for Xanax.

'I don't have any,' Laura told him blearily.

'Oh God oh God oh God!' Edgar had responded hysterically.

'Can't you just have an aspirin?'

Edgar had eventually calmed down after a cup of tea with two sugars. 'I could get into this stuff,' he told her, brandishing the mug, which was from a fleamarket and commemorated the Queen's Silver Jubilee. 'My dad knows her,' Edgar added.

'What, the Queen?' Laura asked satirically, as her neighbour seemed to be glancing at the monarch.

'Mm. She gave him a K.'

'A K?'

'Knighthood.'

Laura stared. She knew little about Edgar's background apart from the fact that it was wealthy. 'What does your dad do, exactly?'

'He's head of MI6,' Edgar yawned.

Laura sat bolt upright. '*What?* But that's. . . amazing.' Her thoughts flew back to the just-seen film. M suave in his three-piece suit, turning wearily from the Whitehall view to address the maverick 007. Was Edgar's father like that?

Supine on the battered leather sofa, purple-socked feet up on one of the arms, Edgar rolled his eyes. 'He so isn't. Dad just sits at a desk all day.'

'What's he called?' Laura was now thinking about Harry. Would he know him?

'Sir Philip Peaseblossom.' Edgar yawned again. 'Anyway, about last night. . .' He launched into a description of a Brixton club called Audioslag. 'You couldn't tell the gender of seventy per cent of the people there!' Edgar wiggled his purple feet excitedly. There was a large hole in the bottom of one of the socks.

Unlike Lulu's sex-change butler Vlad, who was very discreet, Edgar shoved his bicurious status in everyone's face, often literally. You didn't have to be Freud to guess what lay behind all this. Having failed at his expensive public school and dropped out of RADA, a life of transgender hedonism in Shoreditch was Edgar's obvious direction of travel.

What his father made of it was anyone's guess. And it was his father Laura wanted to talk about. 'What's his job like?' she asked, eagerly. 'Your dad's,' she prompted, as the eyes through the smeared lenses looked confused.

'Oh God, beyond boring. Then we went to this after-party at this thrash dungeon in a really rough pub in the Barbican. Then I fell asleep on the Circle Line. . .'

Laura would not be put off, however. She wondered if Edgar was visiting the family seat in Holland Park later. If so, she might try and tag along. Penetrating the inner sanctum of the head of the security services would certainly be something to tell Harry. Perhaps even impress him.

'Are you going to see your parents for lunch?'

'They're away this weekend, thank God.'

Laura battled disappointment. Perhaps Sir Philip was doing something very M-ish somewhere. 'Where?' she asked, nosily, she knew. But she *was* a journalist.

'At the country pile.' Edgar rolled his eyes again in what seemed an attempt at distancing irony.

Laura was interested. M had a country pile! 'Where is it?'

Through the smeared lenses of his geek glasses, Edgar flashed her a glance. 'God, it's so boring. Place called Great Hording.'

Great Hording. Wasn't that the place she had overheard being discussed in Umbra? The richest village in the UK? Laura's interested sharpened. 'What's it like?'

'A shitbox,' declared Edgar, but the subject was clearly making him uncomfortable. Soon after, he got up and went. As he left behind him a certain unwashed mustiness, Laura opened all the windows. Then, finally, she got down to her research.

Now, as she crossed the road by the white and gold Victoria Memorial, Laura felt she knew more than any human being needed to about Savannah Bouche. She even knew what the famous 'wet newspaper' tattoos meant. The one on Savannah's back was the genetic code of her favourite dog and down her right shoulder blade was a portrait of one of the others.

Savannah had famously rescued her pets from refugee camps whilst pursuing her humanitarian causes. The dogs travelled with her all round the world; images of the actress traversing the shining entrance halls of international airports with the pack of hounds at her heels appeared almost weekly. Each dog was named after a celebrated feminist or freedom fighter.

The new film, of course, was the reason for the interview. But Laura's real target was the star's current relationship. She was rumoured to be involved with a music star, although no one had yet uncovered his identity. Or hers. Savannah, who liked to keep the world guessing, had previously hinted at bicuriosity and her occasional attempts to appear highbrow further muddied the waters. Her latest lover could therefore be anyone from Cara Delevingne to Daniel Barenboim.

Brad Plant had told Laura to be on time, at ten exactly, to meet a Dr Edward Summer, expert in nineteenth-century architecture. He was to be their private guide around the palace.

As Laura got out her now-ringing smartphone, she saw that it was 9.50.

Brad Plant was on the other end. 'Savannah could be a little delayed.'

Laura was not especially surprised. Her experience of celebrities, especially Hollywood ones, was that their lateness was in direct proportion to how important they were, or thought they were. With someone of Savannah Bouche's wattage, the wait could be a long one. She bit back her frustration. There was nothing that she could do and any interview was better than no interview.

Dr Edward Summer was waiting in the Buckingham Palace ticket hall. He had little round glasses, a pink face which matched his bow tie, and a three-piece herringbone suit. All this, and his smiling benevolence, reminded Laura of Ratty from *The Wind in the Willows*. It was impossible not to feel cheered up.

'It's simply marvellous that Miss Bouche wishes to view the palace,' beamed Dr Summer. 'It's a wonderfully interesting building. Are you a fan of nineteenth-century architecture, Miss, er, Waters?'

'Lake. I don't know much about it, I'm afraid,' Laura confessed. Dr Summer, still beaming, rubbed his hands.

'Marvellous! It will be my pleasure to introduce you, in that case. Will Miss Bouche be much later, do you think?'

Yes, was the short answer.

'Oh dear,' sighed Dr Summer. 'Well, perhaps we could look through this while we are waiting.' He handed her the official palace brochure and Laura began leafing through pages of ornate rooms with red carpets and golden doors.

'As you're writing an article, perhaps I can give you some background,' the academic suggested helpfully. 'It was George IV who commissioned the architect John Nash to transform what had been previously known as Buckingham House into a grand palace.'

'Right,' said Laura, dutifully getting out her phone and typing this in.

'The sculptures include a superb likeness of Prince Arthur, son of Queen Victoria, by Carlo Marochetti. . .' the academic went on.

Laura did her best to type assiduously whilst simultaneously looking out for Savannah. It was difficult in such a crowded place. All around, hordes of excited tourists queued in roped-off sections for tickets. The area was ablaze with red carpet and gold cardboard swags and crowns. Even the people behind the tills had red, gold-buttoned jackets on, and two soldiers in bearskins added to the ceremonial effect.

'. . . today the State Rooms contain many of the greatest treasures from the Royal Collection. Paintings by van Dyck and some absolutely marvellous Sèvres porcelain. . .'

Laura typed dutifully on. Her heart, however, was sinking. It was now nearly eleven; how much later would Savannah be? Perhaps she had changed her mind. Perhaps she had realised she had picked a spot where she would be unable to bring her four dogs.

'. . . magnificent pair of chairs whose design was based on ancient Roman models. . .' Dr Summer continued. He clearly lived for this sort of thing. But the gasps of excitement Laura now heard from all around seemed occasioned by something other than antique furniture.

'Savannah Bouche!'

'OMG. It's really her!'

Laura looked around to see a tiny woman in vast black sunglasses approaching rapidly across the red carpet. Her frail build was emphasised by a trailing black poncho, a huge black status bag and bulky Ugg boots. But most of all by her companions, two fat, bald men with goatee beards in black combat gear.

'Savannah Bouche,' the people in the queues whispered. '*Savannah Bouche!*'

Skinny on screen, Savannah looked even thinner in real life. Behind the colossal sunglasses, her head seemed too big for her tiny body. Savannah had always denied having plastic surgery of any kind – 'in solidarity with the women of the world who have no access to cosmetic enhancement.' But up close and in the flesh, or what there was of it, Laura wasn't so sure.

The famous pout seemed to take up half her entire face. The famous cheekbones jutted out like plane wings. The famous dark hair was pulled into a ponytail of such artful carelessness only a top hairdresser could have done it. Admittedly, Savannah was only twenty-nine. But, Laura calculated, she had been twenty-nine for the past five years at least.

She stepped forward, hand extended. 'Miss Bouche. Laura Lake from *Society*.'

There was a blinding flash. As she blinked away the pain Laura saw, in negative on the inside of her eyelids, a huge Hollywood smile. The flash had been Savannah's teeth.

The guide was hovering expectantly. Laura gathered herself. 'May I introduce Dr Edward Summer, expert in nineteenth-century architecture?'

'My dear lady!' With courtly flourish, Dr Summer took Savannah's tiny hand and kissed it.

The actress gave an almost imperceptible shudder as she withdrew her child-sized fingers. Laura could just about hear her whisper agitatedly to her bodyguards, 'Where's my Purell?'

One of the enormous men produced a discreet bottle of disinfecting gel which Savannah spritzed quickly over her palms. Behind his little round glasses, Dr Summer looked hurt.

All around, hysteria was building. The gawpers in the ticket hall were shoving the rope barriers aside to take selfies.

'Let's get out of here?' Savannah said decisively from behind her shades. 'It's full of civilians.'

'On the contrary, the Household Regiment are present.' Dr Summer gestured at the bearskin-hatted soldiers. 'May I take your bag to the cloakroom?' he added helpfully. 'It looks rather heavy.'

The large black crocodile tote on Savannah's narrow shoulder did indeed look enormous. But she shook her head and tripped off on her doll-sized legs towards the 'Way In' sign. 'Come on, boys,' she sang over her shoulder to her outsize male companions.

Dr Summer hurried after her. 'I'm terribly sorry, Miss Bouche, but I have security clearance only for the three of us. Your, er, friends will have to remain here, I'm afraid.'

One of the friends now extended a tattooed arm as thick as a tree and grabbed the mild academic by his bow-tied throat. 'Nowyoulissanameesucker. . .'

The slotting, metallic sound of machine guns being primed heralded the approach of the bearskin-hatted soldiers. They weren't just for decoration after all. The selfie-takers fell back and there were gasps of shock as the British Army detached the Bouche security detail from the throat of the Buckingham Palace guide.

Dr Summer rubbed his neck and managed a nervous smile. 'My goodness me.'

'A misunderstanding,' said Savannah smoothly, turning her blinding dental beam on the soldiers. Evidently trained for extreme conditions, they stared back impassively. 'You'd better stay here, like the nice gentleman says,' she simpered at her bodyguards, who shuffled hurriedly back towards the entrance.

Laura rejoiced inwardly. She felt sorry for Dr Summer, but this all made great copy.

A rope was being lifted and barriers pushed aside. Dr Summer was leading them out of the ticket hall into the Palace proper.

Stretching before them was a wide, red-carpeted corridor. Carved gold sofas upholstered with red damask stood at regular intervals against white and gold walls. A line of enormous crystal chandeliers hung above. For a moment Laura forgot her famous companion and thought about the far more famous people who had lived and still lived here. Princess Diana had walked these very halls. The Queen still did. She was in the building. The flag had been flying outside.

'Do tell me about your latest film, Miss Bouche,' Dr Summer was asking pleasantly.

Savannah ignored him. She was taking a selfie with a portrait of Prince Andrew on the wall. This done, she studied the results thoughtfully.

'Or should I say movie?' Dr Summer beamed. 'We are, after all, famously two nations divided by a common language.'

'What?' Savannah sounded irritated at being interrupted.

'Your new film,' Laura prompted. Savannah was doing another Prince Andrew selfie now, from a different angle. Her phone case, Laura noticed, was the Union Jack in coloured crystals.

'O-kay.' The actress tossed her ponytail. 'So I did this film because of the importance of its message? My character's a strong female, it's a beautiful part and one I really empathised with.'

Laura scribbled all this down. It was obviously sales patter, but delivered with conviction. There was no doubt that Savannah could act.

'Goodness,' said Dr Summer, impressed. 'I must make sure I go and see it. What's the new film called?'

'*TaeKwondo Hippo*.' Savannah spoke with the same expectancy of recognition as might have accompanied the words 'Gone With the Wind'.

'It's an animation,' Laura put in, trying not to laugh.

'About a hippo who wants to drop a dress size? I play the hippo's glamorous younger sister? She's kind of a maneater and steals all her boyfriends?'

Some articles Laura had read had called this typecasting. They implied that, despite the rumoured involvement with the music star, Savannah was still looking around for a better offer. Probably wasting her time there though, Laura thought, watching the actress studying a portrait of the Queen and Prince Philip.

'The royal family are in this building, like, now?' Savannah asked, sounding urgent. 'Prince Andrew, he's here now, right?'

'I'm not familiar with His Royal Highness's diary,' Dr Summer told her.

Laura decided to steer the conversation back to the matter

in hand. 'So what's next?' she asked Savannah. 'What are your plans?'

This was the moment to ask about the latest celebrity lover. Might she get an exclusive? Laura felt her heart speed up, as always when she was on the verge of something big.

'Collaborations with other artists.' Savannah yawned. 'Musicians and stuff.'

'Musicians?' Laura pounced on the information. 'What sort of. . . *collaboration*, exactly?'

Savannah gave her a cool look in reply. 'For my charity, Spread the Love?'

'Any particular musician?' Laura persisted before Savannah could start banging on about valuing every global individual. But the actress had now walked off.

The tour continued. 'The ballroom,' announced the nineteenth-century architectural expert as they entered a vast chamber with an organ at one end and some thrones under a velvet drape at the other. 'This is where investitures and state banquets are held.'

Savannah's sunglasses swung in his direction. 'So this is where Angelina got her damehood?'

As Dr Summer was clearly confused, Laura stepped forward. 'Angelina Jolie the actress,' she murmured in his ear. 'She got an honorary DBE a few years ago. I think Miss Bouche feels a certain, um, rivalry.' So the cuts had said, anyway.

The next chamber had a vast bow window. 'The Music Room is where several of the Queen's children were christened.'

Laura's eyes roamed around, gathering up the details for her piece. There were blue pillars with gold capitals, red chairs, a shining wooden floor.

'Prince Andrew's still available, right?' The Bouche sunglasses were once again pointed questioningly at Dr Summer.

'Available?' the academic faltered.

'As in not married?'

'Oh. I see. Well he was married, of course, to Sarah Ferguson. But they divorced some time ago and—'

'He's not with anyone now, right?'

Now Laura got it. The reason they had come here was suddenly clear. Savannah wasn't with a mystery music star. Or if she was, she was thinking of upgrading. Into the Royal Family, no less.

An almighty row suddenly erupted. The air was full of the sound of barking dogs. Laura had not noticed them enter, but she now saw that half a dozen large and low-slung ginger-coloured hounds were swarming round Savannah's skinny black-Ugg-booted ankles.

They looked very familiar.

The noise was unbelievable. Tour groups in the room's other corners turned to stare and exclaim.

'The, whalstheirnames, the corgis!'

'哎呀'

'*Mon dieu!*'

'The Queen's corgis!'

'*Unglaublich!*'

'They're attacking that woman. . .Ohmigod, it's Savannah Bouche!'

'哎呀 Savannah Bouche!'

Laura had initially been unable to understand why the dogs had made a beeline for Savannah. They were seething round her feet, leaping up at her. But now she could see that the answer lay in the actress's bag. The enormous black tote over the celebrity shoulder was moving; bulging and shifting as though there was something alive inside it. Several things, even.

Faint yapping sounds could be heard. As Laura watched, a small doggy nose appeared. Then another.

'Dogs!' gasped Dr Summer. 'Good Lord, she's smuggled some dogs in!'

It was clear now why the actress had turned down his offer of the cloakroom.

'Pankhurst!' cried Savannah, as a tiny white scrap struggled out of its black-leather prison and dived fearlessly into the snarling pool of much larger dogs below.

'Mandela!' screamed the star as a furry yellow ball did the same. More barking and snarling ensued.

'How many more does she have in there?' Dr Summer gasped to Laura.

'Two,' Laura said, as, right on cue, a further pair of fluffballs somersaulted out to join the struggle. They disappeared into the squirming, yelping, snapping mass of bodies.

'Che! Mahatma!' A howling Savannah hurled herself towards the mêlée just as someone else entered the room.

'Holly! Willow!' exclaimed the small, elderly woman with iron-grey hair and glasses. She wore a dark dress, carried a large handbag and had unmistakable presence. 'Stop that at once!' she commanded, in a voice which seemed used to issuing them. Her tones were intensely patrician, slightly reedy and extremely familiar.

The effect was electric. The dogs stopped fighting instantly. The entire assembled company either sank into a curtsy, or bowed.

'Your Majesty!' breathed Dr Summer, reverently.

The Queen, having gathered her pets to her heels, folded her hands over her shining black handbag and shot a sharp look round the room. Laura watched the monarch's keen glance snag on the reigning, curtsying queen of Tinseltown. While nothing was said, and no criticism offered, the royal lips twisted slightly. The royal back turned and the presence was no longer present.

Laura sensed that Savannah's honorary DBE was no longer a possibility. Any designs the star might have on Prince Andrew were equally unlikely to come off.

She, on the other hand, had one hell of an article.

CHAPTER SIX

hree weeks later, Carinthia was still on compassionate spa leave. Laura remained in charge and, while initially nervous, had become gradually more confident in the role. She had finally succumbed to precedent, and had framed and mounted round the walls a collection of *Society* covers that had her stories as the main headlines. The awards Laura had won for them, and subsequent work, swelled the shelf of press awards previously won by Carinthia, which had not been removed.

Laura had, however, removed the pink fridge full of alcohol. She had also tackled the vexed question of the editor's chair. Carinthia suffered from a rare back condition called *vertebrae editrix*, or editor's spine, caused by lugging outsize designer totes about the place. To combat it she had taken up the succession of 'medical' seating solutions proposed by Bootcamp Billy her physiotherapist. These had ranged from birthing balls to exercise bicycles and had only made matters worse when Carinthia, in a fit of rage or excitement, or drunk, had fallen off them. The black swivel chair Laura had introduced, prosaic as it was, might have been a better as well as a safer idea.

Sitting in this chair, rocking gently backwards and occasionally swinging round just for the sheer fun of it, Laura felt more reluctant than ever to return to her former position as deputy editor. She hoped her boss would not come back.

Carinthia, however, had no intention of bowing out. She rang the office on a daily basis demanding to see issue plans and be conference-called into every ideas meeting. Laura could hear her now, breathing heavily down the phone, sniffing and emitting the occasional loud slurp, which seemed unlikely to be caused by water. She tried hard to concentrate on the editorial features meeting which had just begun.

From behind the big glass editorial desk, Laura smiled round at her staff. She did not intend them all to remain. She wanted new blood, fresh ideas, ambitious and talented people, not girls Carinthia had employed just for their social connections. She had always loved seeing the forest of hands when she asked which of them lived in houses open to the public.

Laura, on the other hand, was determined to introduce a more meritocratic regime. She had started by relaxing the hierarchy. The yellow sofa opposite her desk was no longer reserved for section editors. People could sit where they liked; first in was best seated. The days when Clemency Makepeace, Laura's bitter enemy and the former features editor, could sashay in last and ostentatiously take the best place, were over. As was Clemency herself. Laura had not seen her byline for some time and had heard a rumour she had left the country. Fingers crossed.

Laura picked up a glass of water. The first time she had sat at Carinthia's desk, the carafe had contained pure vodka. 'Ready?' she asked.

It would be interesting to see which staff members had taken on board the fact *Society* was now going in a different direction. Still glamorous, still witty, but more relevant to the young working women who were its readers.

The glass cubicle was packed solid. Unlike Carinthia, Laura invited everyone, including the newest intern – especially the newest intern – to the ideas meetings. Inspiration – inspo, as magazine people called it – could come from anywhere and anyone. When a discussion really got going, ideas flew like sparks. Laura loved it when that happened.

'Ready!' crackled the conference line. A crash followed, and a swishy liquid noise. It sounded as if, in her agitation, Carinthia had knocked her drink all over the phone. The line went dead.

'Okay,' said Laura. 'Let's start with fashion. Raisy and Daisy?'

The future of the two blonde fashion directors was one Laura was particularly doubtful about. She was fond of them, but they seemed incapable of understanding that things had changed. When she had asked them last week to produce the perfect job interview outfit their suggestions had included a £1000 jumper and a £695 document wallet.

The two blonde sisters rose to their feet, large printouts under their skinny white arms. 'I feel seriously pumped about this,' Daisy said brightly, fixing Laura with a dazzling smile made all the more impactful by neon green lipstick. '*Seriously* pumped.'

Daisy's *modus operandi* was to present her ideas as keenly as possible, in the evident hope sheer enthusiasm would get them through.

Laura looked at the images now being held up for her perusal, hoping she would understand them. Or, at least, like them.

A group of thin, sulky girls were standing by a rusting fence.

'What are they wearing?' she asked, having tried and failed to identify it.

'Sports bras reimagined in tablecloth plastics,' Raisy explained proudly. The sisters always spoke alternately. 'It's an out-of-kilter aesthetic that's having a moment.'

Laura reminded herself that a big part of the job as a glossy-magazine editor was to take the ludicrous seriously. Most of what came up was pretty silly, but distinguishing between good silly and bad silly was where the skill lay.

'It's a bit. . .' she began, searching for the word everyone in magazines used when they meant no. 'Niche,' she added, triumphantly.

Raisy looked as stern as anyone could while wearing black wellies, gold eyeshadow and an electric blue twinset. 'We need to reclaim PVC,' she asserted. 'Take it out of the ghetto of fetish fabric.'

Laura stared. 'I thought you said it was tablecloth plastic.'

'Fetish tablecloths,' Daisy smiled.

Demelza was holding the phone out and pulling an anguished face. 'Carinthia again. Shall I put her on speakerphone?'

The speakerphone was duly put on. There seemed to be a row at the other end. A nurse could be heard entering the room and removing what was evidently a banned bottle of vodka. 'Another? Who's *giving* you this stuff?' she was asking. Then, again, the line went dead.

'Right,' said Laura, relieved. 'Features.'

She had spiked Carinthia's planned articles – the fashion spread about shoes being worn on heads; the feature about bright young things playing ducks and drakes with their Smartphones, skimming them into the sea.

But what was she going to put in their place? The first proper Laura Lake issue had to be very, very special. Set out the tone and style of what was to come. Alert people that someone new was in charge.

The Savannah interview would have been perfect, except that it had run in the last issue edited by Carinthia, and a hopelessly emasculated version at that. Far from being, as Laura had assumed, thrilled at the revelation that the actress had her sights set on being a Windsor, Carinthia had insisted all unflattering references should be removed. The piece had been sent to Savannah before publication.

Laura had been aghast. 'You've given her copy approval?' Full veto, in other words! Licence to whitewash! Bland, unquestioning sycophancy, with no critical element whatsoever!

'Oh course I bloody have,' Carinthia had snapped back. 'How the hell else do you think I got her to agree to do it?'

'But you didn't! I set it up myself!' Laura felt sick with indignation and disappointment, as well as furious at Carinthia's appropriation of what had been her triumph. It didn't take a genius to work out what had happened. Nervous about what Laura might write after the

Buckingham Palace episode, Savannah had evidently instructed Brad Plant to lean heavily on Carinthia. The fact
that she had decided not to do the same with Laura was
some comfort. She suspected her, at least, of some integrity,
some journalistic values. But how were they to be expressed
now?

She needed another meaty story, Laura knew. One with
no copy approval. But there was no meat – literally – in
the piece Thomasella the food editor had just suggested
about wild hemlock fudge. Or the feature Selina the travel
editor was now outlining about holidays in decommissioned
coal mines being the latest in off-grid chic. The meeting
ended with the suggestion, from the beauty department, of
an interview with London's hottest new plastic surgeon who
speeded up recovery by hanging patients upside down with
their heads in a bucket of ice.

Laura imagined her grandmother's bemusement. Mimi
held that facelifts were too try-hard and that people should
enjoy the face they had today. 'Because it's the one you'll
wish you had in ten years' time, *chérie!*'

Later, as Laura picked at the moss salad ordered for
Carinthia's daily lunch which no one had got around to
cancelling, she rattled between her teeth the Montblanc
fountain pen her predecessor had left behind. A wave of
self-doubt broke over her. Perhaps being an editor wasn't
as easy as Carinthia had made it look. Perhaps she couldn't
do it after all.

As her confidence plunged earthwards, Laura firmly
reminded herself that Carinthia had made it look easy
precisely because all the work was being done by Laura.
She had effectively been editor for months. Of course she
could do it!

Especially now Clemency Makepeace was gone for good. Laura would never have to see those evil green eyes again. Nor that snake-like hair as red as Clemency's lipsticked smirk.

There was a knock on her door and Wyatt clumped in, in unflattering black combat trousers, nose stud gleaming in the overhead light.

'Sit down.' Laura gestured to the yellow sofa, which Wyatt looked at doubtfully. Since she had become editor, waves of gifts sent by advertisers and designers had crashed into Laura's office. Never before had she realised just how many freebies Carinthia routinely received. The smell of new leather was almost overpowering. 'Shove that stuff aside,' she told Wyatt.

Watching the intern move a turquoise fur jacket and pink alligator-skin rucksack, Laura reflected that, as a plus-size Goth, Wyatt was not in any sense a fit for a glossy magazine. But she felt she owed her something. Wyatt had been admirably discreet in the aftermath of the Nipples At Dawn incident. Several papers had wanted her to write her side of the story. She had refused them all. Now Laura had a suggestion to make.

'I'd like you to write a feature for me,' she said brightly, expecting Wyatt to exclaim in delight. No exclamation was forthcoming, however.

'It'll run in the magazine,' Laura added encouragingly.

Wyatt did not answer.

Laura suppressed her feeling of impatience. 'Don't you want to write?' she asked, knowing that this was a ridiculous question. Everyone on *Society* wanted to write. 'You want to be a journalist, don't you?'

'Not really,' Wyatt said bluntly.

Shock coursed through the acting editor. A journalist was

all Laura had ever wanted to be. She could not imagine the mindset of someone who didn't. 'Um, so at the risk of sounding obvious, what exactly are you doing here?'

Wyatt met Laura's gaze through resigned eyes ringed heavily with kohl. 'Because my mum made me and my dad bought it for me.'

Well, that was honest if nothing else. 'Oh,' said Laura, stumped. 'Right.'

'And it's really unfair.'

'*Unfair?*' Laura blinked. 'Internships here are very sought-after.'

'That's my point,' Wyatt said.

Laura passed a hand over her forehead. She was confused.

'Internships are unfair.' Wyatt raised her plump white chin defiantly. 'They're a closed shop for the well-connected. They stand in the way of social mobility and they skew the employment market so graduates can't get a paid entry-level job.'

Laura stared at her. She was right, of course. Wyatt had put her black-nail-varnished finger on something Laura had spotted too. The need to open up internship opportunities. Convert them into actual salaried posts, even.

'Tell me about your background,' she said, wondering if she had got it wrong and Wyatt came, not from a dynasty of City plutocrats, but a line of firebrand socialists.

'My dad's a banker.'

'Where does he work?' Perhaps he wasn't a very important one and Carinthia had exaggerated.

'He's deputy governor of the Bank of England.'

'And what does your mum do?' Perhaps she was a Marxist academic, a human rights lawyer or a shadow cabinet minister. They sometimes had wealthy husbands.

'Shops. Has Botox. Decorates the, um, houses.'

'Houses?' The slight, shamefaced pause had not been lost on Laura.

Wyatt shifted uncomfortably besides the pile of complimentary luxury leather goods. 'During the week we live in, um, Holland Park. But at weekends we live in the, um, country.'

Laura thought of Edgar, whose family followed the same pattern. She leaned forward slightly. 'Where in the country?'

'It's called Great Hording. You won't have heard of it.'

Laura tried not to look as if this was the third time she had in less than a month. First the women in Umbra. Then Edgar. Now this. She remembered the old journalists' adage: 'Once is interesting and twice a coincidence. But three's definitely a story.' Especially if it was the weekend retreat of both the head of MI6 and the Bank of England number two.

'What's Great. . . er. . . Hording like?' Laura tried not to sound too interested.

'Boring.'

Laura would not be brushed off so easily. 'Boring in what way?'

Wyatt sighed. 'Just boring.'

'Who else lives there?'

Laura stared at Wyatt until she gave in, dropped her eyes and gestured at Laura's desk. 'Well, *her*.'

Laura glanced down at the stern old trout pictured in the open newspaper. 'Dame Hermione Grantchester?' The interview she had just read had been breathless with excitement. *Short*, the much-anticipated next instalment of Dame Hermione's 'Saddle-Saw' series, written from the point of view of Napoleon's horse, was about to come out.

Nasty and *Brutish*, the first two, had both won the Booker prize.

Wyatt was looking at the wall now. 'Him too.'

She nodded at one of Laura's framed articles: 'YBAs: Twenty Years On.' The image above the title was of a famously notorious work; some underpants nailed to a chopping board.

'Zeb Spaw?' Laura examined the hammered-on Y-fronts yet again. They were made of a particularly hideous ribbed blue nylon. The chopping board, for its part, was covered in stains and food debris. The whole piece was disgusting and yet *Crucifiction* had launched the artist into the stratosphere. 'He lives in Great Hording?'

'Got a studio there,' Wyatt said flatly. 'And a ginormous mansion. He's horrible.'

Laura didn't need to be told this. Spaw had cancelled the interview last minute and left her scrabbling through previous articles to pull together her piece. But it was rather amazing that he lived there too. 'Anyone else?' she asked Wyatt. 'Politicians? Actors? Writers? Newspaper editors?'

She was half-joking, but Wyatt twisted her black-painted lips. 'All of those, actually – except no journalists.'

A great surge of excitement went through Laura. She only just prevented herself from slapping the desk in triumph. *Here* was her meaty story. Britain's Best Connected Village! The UK's Highest-Powered Hamlet!

Wyatt had slipped her a brilliant exclusive. Exactly the kind of social reportage piece she wanted to run. How could she ever have doubted that she was born to be an editor?

Wyatt was rising to her Dr Martened feet. 'Well anyway, sorry.'

'About what?'

'Not being cut out for magazine journalism. I'm pretty useless really.'

Laura beamed at her. 'I wouldn't say that. On the contrary, actually.'

Wyatt was barely out of the room before Laura was typing 'Great Hording' into Google Images. Strangely enough, nothing came up. Had she spelt it wrong? The mobile on her desk now rang and Lulu's name appeared on the screen. Another wedding emergency, no doubt. Last time they spoke the bride-to-be had been in meltdown over edible terrariums for the reception tables.

Laura's fears seemed realised when all that could be heard on the other end was heaving sobs. But she wasn't going to let Lulu bring down her upbeat mood. It would be something and nothing, it always was.

'What's up?' she asked cheerily. Perhaps it was the dress. Or dresses – Lulu had now settled on no fewer than three changes of couture gown for her simple country nuptials. South'n Fried, not to be outdone, had commissioned special diamond-studded wedding trainers from Tiffany.

'Is over!' Lulu wept.

'What's over?' Laura spoke slowly, aiming to understand. Perhaps the dress, or dresses were too long or too big. Over in that sense.

Lulu had dissolved into sobs again. But she was gasping something out; something that sounded like 'Marriage, he is off.' But couldn't be, obviously.

'Calm down, Lulu,' Laura counselled gently. 'Calm down and tell me what's wrong.'

'Oh, Laura! Am in dumpster!'

'What?'

'South'n Fried go with someone else!'

'But. . . what. . . I mean, when. . . I mean who?'

'Is big star. They spread love.'

'*What?*'

'Is charity,' Lulu managed, after a few incomprehensible efforts. 'Spread the Love.'

Spread the Love! Laura was sitting down but the world spun around her anyway. She gripped the edges of Carinthia's glass desk.

Savannah Bouche! 'Oh, Lulu, I'm so sorry!'

'Am devastating. You come round now, hmm?'

Laura hesitated. She longed to, but she was on the verge of a big story. She just needed to talk to Wyatt. 'I'll be there as soon as I can.'

CHAPTER SEVEN

Wyatt sat bent forward on the yellow sofa, picking black nail varnish off her plump white fingers. 'You wanted me?'

Laura nodded. All her online attempts to research Great Hording had come to nothing. 'Where is it?' she asked Wyatt.

'By the sea in Suffolk. Next to another village called Little Hording.'

Bingo, Laura thought. She could find that on a map. The thought of the sea was uplifting, she hadn't seen it for ages. Now all she needed was somewhere to stay.

'Goose,' said Wyatt.

'Excuse me?'

Wyatt smiled faintly. 'The Golden Goose. It's the pub in Great Hording.'

'Is it nice?'

'Not now. It's completely changed.'

'How changed?' Laura was interested.

'Well, it used to be just normal. It was called the Farmer's Arse – sorry, Farmer's Arms. We just used to call it the Farmer's Arse.' Wyatt looked down, a broad smile now playing about her black lips.

'So what's it like now?'

'Horrible. All designer rooms, celebrity chefs and kitchen gardens.'

'But that sounds quite nice.'

Wyatt's black eyes flashed in her plump white face. 'It is if you're stinking rich,' she said hotly. 'But not if you've been priced out of everything, like a lot of the local people.'

Laura was fascinated. Why was Wyatt so angry? Surely, as the daughter of the Bank of England's deputy governor, she was one of the stinking rich herself. Then there were the comments about the unfair internship. Wyatt seemed conflicted, to say the least. 'Go on,' she said, thinking this was all useful background material.

Wyatt seemed surprised to be encouraged. 'Well, it's just not fair, that's all,' she blustered. 'Why should some people have everything and others nothing? Why should some people make billions in bonuses and buy the houses other people's families used to own?'

It was, Laura thought, almost as if she was imitating a speech she had heard many times. But whose? And she was not finished yet.

'Why should former working farms become Marie Antoinette playgrounds with helipads and recording studios? Why should the village school shut down because the only children around go to private schools? Why should the village lanes, formerly bustling with life, now be empty apart from the lost Ocado van looking for the oligarch's mansion?'

This was too much for Laura, who burst out laughing. 'Sorry,' she said, seeing Wyatt looked hurt. 'It's just quite a funny image, that's all. But I'm sure it illustrates real social division,' she added hurriedly.

Wyatt's rhetorical zeal seemed to have left her. She sat on the sofa, radiating embarrassment. 'Is that all you wanted?' She was clearly desperate to leave.

Laura nodded. 'Thanks.'

Wyatt had barely left before she was typing 'The Golden Goose, Great Hording' into her phone's search engine. She waited, expecting the aforementioned gastropub to appear. But nothing appeared.

Laura tried again; again it brought nothing up. How very strange. She had entered it correctly, she had checked the spelling with Wyatt. It was almost as if Great Hording wasn't connected to the internet.

Was that actually possible?

Laura tipped back her chair and stared musingly at the striplights on the ceiling. It seemed to her unlikely. Wyatt's father was deputy governor of the Bank of England; Edgar's was the head of MI6. Both would need broadband of the most superfast variety. And Dame Hermione Grantchester presumably had publishers all over the world emailing her about rights, literary festivals, film deals. While Zeb Spaw would have an international network of gallerists and clients. There would certainly be internet in Great Hording. And if the Golden Goose was a business, a pub, it just had to be there. It would want to drum up business.

Unless – the thought now struck Laura – it didn't need

to. If it was very exclusive, it might actually want to keep people away. This idea gathered pace, and Laura's heart started to race. Was this the reason that Great Hording didn't appear online either? Because it was so smart, so full of the wealthy and influential, it didn't want outsiders to know about it?

Had it somehow taken all references to itself off the internet?

Laura hadn't realised that could be done.

But if you were rich enough, influential enough, powerful enough, presumably anything could be. The MI6 connection alone could remove whatever information it wanted.

Wow!

The hairs on the back of her slender neck stood on end. Headlines began to tumble through her excited editor's brain. 'Inside the Secret Village of the Super-rich!' This really was a scoop!

She twisted round on her chair, thrilled. She had to get to this place. As soon as possible, this very weekend. Now it didn't matter that Harry was away on a story. On the contrary. She would be away on one too, and a much better one. One that would make his curly hair stand on end, once he knew.

'The Rich List's Rural Retreat!' 'Britain's 'Most Powerful Private Parish!'

Laura took a deep, calming breath. She needed to plan. Finding Great Hording would be simple now she knew it was next to Little Hording. But staying at the Golden Goose was a different matter. How could she get in touch?

She twisted round on her chair again, seeking inspiration. On the third revolution, it came. If the former name of the pub was the Farmer's Arms, there was a good chance that the phone number would be the same. If she could find the old website online, she might have cracked it.

'Farmer's Arms, Great Hording', Laura keyed in, breathlessly. She waited, then groaned aloud as nothing came up. But hold on. Perhaps it was the Great Hording bit. She tried again, without the Great.

A link came up immediately. Laura opened it and found herself examining what could best be described as a straightforward establishment. The outside was grey pebbledash with a sagging Sky Sports banner; the large bar inside featured pine, swirly carpets and several fruit machines. The one picture of a bedroom featured a purple bedspread and brown, patterned curtains. While this would have been the height of retrochic in Cod's Head Row, no irony seemed intended here.

Holding her breath, Laura dialled the number. The other end picked up immediately. A disdainful voice spoke. 'The Golden Goose. Kiki Cavendish speaking.'

Bingo! Silently, Laura punched the air.

'Do you have any rooms for this weekend?' she asked, in the steadiest tones she could manage.

'Name?'

Laura considered. She would be there in an investigative capacity. 'Drake,' she said. 'Lorna Drake.'

'Sorry.' But Kiki sounded anything but apologetic. 'We're fully booked.'

Laura was instantly suspicious. Her name and the lack of a room were obviously connected. Why?

She thought quickly. 'I completely forgot to say. I'm a great friend of the. . .'

Oh God, what was Wyatt's surname? The family name of the Bank of England's deputy governor?

'The Threadneedles,' she finished in a rush, fingers crossed. It was not quite a lie, not quite the truth either. But she had a feeling it might just work.

'Oh, the Threadneedles.' Kiki's tone was now quite different. 'Um. Actually,' she added, slowly, and for all the world as if she were actually looking at a real bookings system, 'we've just had a cancellation. There is a room. With a rather lovely sea view.'

The room secured, Laura rushed out of Society House to get the Tube to Lulu's. All other British Magazine Company editors took cabs everywhere, partly because of their shoes and partly because they could. But Laura, in her flat Chelsea boots, preferred to get to places quickly. And never more so than now, with Lulu in distress.

As she ran out of the building, something glossy and red and a flash of green caught the corner of her eye. She screeched to a halt and looked back, but the glass of the revolving door distorted things and the figure she thought she recognised had disappeared into the lift. Red hair, pale legs in high heels, both Makepeace trademarks. But it could not be Clemency, she had been fired long ago and in circumstances making it impossible she could ever return. In any case, she, Laura, was editor now, and Clemency could not come back without her say-so.

She put the incident out of her mind as she dived into the Underground and, some ten minutes later, dashed up Lulu's broad, tree-lined street and, panting, rang the bell on the big security gate.

'Good evening.' As the grave voice issued from the intercom Laura smiled, recognising Lulu's imperturbable butler. Although, given what had just occurred with South'n Fried, even Vlad must be perturbed at the moment.

The door in the gate clicked open. Laura hurried in over the spotless flagstones concealing the vast underground stacking garage. Cone-shaped box trees in lead planters stood at regular intervals, a verdant hint of the lovely garden that spread beyond the house. You had to look closely at the planters to see the Vuitton logo, but it was there. Hardly anything Lulu possessed lacked an expensive label. The flowers in the garden maybe, but she was probably working on that.

Lulu's house rose before her, a wedding-cake white villa with a pillared portico and a glossy pink front door. One would never imagine, Laura thought, lifting the Chanel knocker and letting it crash back, that amid this splendour dwelt a broken heart.

Or did it? She had been expecting to be greeted by the butler and shown to Lulu's bedroom where the jilted bride lay sobbing in a heap. It was a surprise, therefore, to open the door and see Lulu's face beaming as if nothing untoward had happened.

'Are you. . . okay?' Laura ventured.

'Fine!'

Clad in tight white jeans and a long white cashmere cardigan, her golden hair tumbling glossily about her, Lulu indeed seemed quite at ease. The usual diamonds winked at her ears and neck and if there was one vast rock fewer on her engagement finger, it hardly showed. The gold trim on her massive sunglasses glinted cheerfully in the afternoon sun. But were they hiding eyes puffy with grief?

No, it turned out, as Lulu unexpectedly slipped them off to reveal a sparkling glance framed by false eyelashes two inches long, strongly marked eyebrows and her usual complex eye make-up involving smudges, sweeps and smokiness.

'Come in. We have champagne glass!'

There was scarcely time to be puzzled. Laura was now manhandled over the threshold into the heavily logoed hall. The familiar Stella McCarpet stared up at her and the little Hermès carriages raced happily over the walls. Above them, the separate gold letters of the Dior chandelier tinkled in the breeze as Lulu shut the door firmly.

Perhaps it was just natural resilience, Laura thought. Lulu was irrepressible and rarely miserable for long. But this was a quick recovery even by her standards. Only a few hours ago she had been screaming hysterically down the phone.

'You're feeling better?' she ventured, following Lulu's tightly clad white bottom as it bounced up the glass stairs to the sitting room. One of the sitting rooms. Lulu's colossal house had several. One of the upstairs rooms was devoted entirely to present wrapping.

'Big amount!' Lulu declared, flopping onto the Burberry sofa and inviting Laura to flop in the one opposite. She wiggled her bare brown toes in the blue Tiffany rug. 'Who care about South'n Fried? Savannah Bouche can welcome to him.'

'Has Vlad been talking to you?' That would figure. Lulu's factotum was also her confidante and her wisdom was legendary.

'Vlad say all man useless,' Lulu went on vehemently. The butler, Laura knew, spoke with authority. Vlad had been a man once; possibly one in the Estonian army. Glimpses into her past were as rare as they were astounding. 'Say I better off without.'

Laura nodded her approval, even though she didn't think she would be better off without Harry. But some men she had known had definitely been useless. She was, for example, definitely better out of any romantic entanglement with Caspar.

Her mind lingered on the two of them. What was Harry doing now, away on his mysterious investigation? And what was Caspar doing in Malibu? Borrowing a cup of sugar from Cher?

'We need drink!' Lulu was stabbing agitatedly at the big red button on her remote control, the one marked 'Champagne'. 'We are celebrating!' the heiress added.

'Celebrating!'

'Lulu's new life!'

Vlad, Laura reflected, had clearly done an amazing job talking Lulu out of her despondency and making her focus on the future.

'New life?'

'New life in country! In old willage.'

The smile froze on Laura's face. She wasn't sure how she felt about this. Lulu had been her friend in London since she had arrived, penniless and desperate. Without Lulu's help she would not be where she was now. And while she had flourished since then and could now stand on her own two feet, the thought of a London without Lulu was, well, unthinkable. Still more unimaginable was the idea of Lulu in a country setting. While she was keen on crafting, she tended to do it in a special crafting studio upstairs, next door to the present-wrapping suite.

'What willage. . . I mean village?' Laura asked.

Lulu beamed. 'Ambridge!'

'Ambridge?' Laura frowned. 'The place in *The Archers*?'

'Yes, yes!'

'But, Lulu, Ambridge isn't real.'

Lulu threw back her head and laughed. 'Of course is real.'

'No, Lulu, it isn't.'

The beringed hands mirthfully slapped the plump white-clad legs. 'But is on BBC two times in day! And on Sunday, whole hour!'

'Exactly. It's a radio soap. Not an actual real village.'

Lulu stopped laughing. 'Is not real willage?' Her tone was troubled. 'But is in Borsetshire.'

'Lulu, it's fiction. Borsetshire doesn't exist either.'

Lulu looked aghast. '*What?*'

'I'm sorry, Lulu.' Laura hated being the bearer of bad tidings.

The blonde mane was shaking sorrowfully about. 'Vlad will be devastating. What can I tell her?'

The butler now appeared, a brisk, morning-suited figure with a pale, impassive face and smooth, side-parted dark hair. She carried a tray bearing a gold-foil-topped bottle with a familiar label and two glasses.

'Hi, Vlad,' Laura said warmly. 'Good to see you.'

'Vlad!' Lulu wailed. 'Ambridge not exist, Laura say.'

Laura watched the butler put one arm behind her back and pour two precisely level three-quarter flutes of Moët. While her every move was professional, the bottle was definitely wobbling. 'Very good, madam.'

Laura felt horribly guilty. 'But there are plenty of other places in the country to move to,' she added brightly.

Lulu bounced up and down on the checked sofa. 'You hear that, Vlad? Plenty more places.'

'Very good, madam.' But the butler's previously brisk mien seemed now all gloom.

'Like where, Laura?' Lulu's sunglasses swung expectantly in her direction.

Laura took a nerve-stiffening swig from the flute she had just been handed. The wine danced deliciously on her tongue, but her mind was running on the fact that Lulu's emotional recovery and Vlad's happiness now seemed to be in her hands. It was useless to ask why or how. What could she suggest to Lulu?

She was going to Great Hording this weekend, of course. But only as a recce for her story on Britain's best-connected village. And the last person anyone wanted on a secret operation was Lulu. She was the very opposite of incognito. She was ultracognito.

On the other hand, this was becoming an emergency. Vlad had now exited the room in terrible silence and Lulu's gaze, still trained on Laura, had changed from expectant to agonised.

Laura gave in. 'I'm going to the country on Saturday,' she said. 'You can come with me if you like. See what you think.'

CHAPTER EIGHT

K iki Cavendish, manager of the Golden Goose, Great Hording, was out jogging early on Saturday. As always, this jerked her hair, streaked a subtle blonde, out of its signature pencil twist and sent the pencil itself flying. Her reading glasses kept shooting off her recently rebuilt nose and swinging from their chain. She had to stop frequently and replace both specs and pencil, which was annoying. But at least, outside, she felt less agitated.

The morning was fresh and clear, the fields glossy with dew, the very air shimmering with promise. As Kiki, resplendent in her favourite Muck Sweat designer leggings, crested the hill above the village, the sea tilted towards her like a polished silver plate. Her mind flew instantly to the engraved salver that was to be the prize at the coming evening's event.

Behind the toned muscles of her tummy churned a mixture

of excitement and dread. Would all go according to plan? It was absolutely crucial that nothing went wrong. At the Golden Goose, everything always had to be perfect, just as Jonny Welsh expected.

When Jonny had bought the Farmer's Arms two years ago, it had been, according to him, 'a grotty village pub full of grotty village people.' But he had spotted its potential and given it a multi-million pound makeover. Out had gone the swirly carpets, anaglypta and flashing fruit machines. In had come squashy sofas, open fires and retro one-armed-bandits. Floorboards were exposed and varnished and York stone flags laid down. Vintage croquet sets spilled artfully from long wooden boxes. A mini spa was installed, using milk-based artisan beauty products humorously called Smelly Cow. A Michelin-starred chef was recruited and a kitchen garden provided for him by a horticulturalist dripping in Chelsea gold medals.

But there was something else, too. Exclusivity of the most rigidly enforced type. Not only champagne bars and media rooms, but the assurance that local plutocrats would meet only others on their level as they downed Saturday lunchtime oysters or soaked up Sunday hangovers with braised shin of Suffolk beef. It was a daringly different take on the traditional all-welcoming pub model. But as drawbridges everywhere were being raised over the widening gulf between rich and poor, Jonny sensed, yet again, that he was ahead of the hospitality business curve.

Kiki had played her part in this success story. And not just by acting as the village's effective gatekeeper – checking the Approved Guest Names list every time a non-resident circumvented the internet blackout and rang up to book a room. It had also been her idea to provide hand-reared, small-producer bacon sandwiches to read with the Sunday papers, accompanied with ketchup bottles bearing silver lids from Tiffany. Her experience among the sophisticates of the metropolis had taught Kiki that there was nothing the truly rich prized like simplicity. Even vulgarity, if done in a sufficiently witty and tasteful way.

Now, hot on the heels of the bacon sandwich initiative, she hoped her latest scheme would please Jonny even more. When Kiki had agreed to leave a prestigious London nightclub to run the Golden Goose for him, she had secretly hoped that her relocation package might include becoming Mrs Welsh the Second. She and Jonny had once been lovers, after all, and surely he was bored of his wife by now. It hadn't happened – yet – but Kiki was sure that with everything she was doing to reinforce Jonny's position as the centre of village life, he couldn't fail to see what a good choice she would be.

Unfortunately, he was not convinced by her latest idea, not yet at least. 'A pub quiz?' he had repeated in scorn. For all his business brilliance he sometimes was, Kiki thought, as behind the times as his grey mullet hairstyle.

'Quizzes are massively popular right now,' she told him. 'And we could do a brilliant one here. Think about it. Great Hording's got some of the most competitive people in the country. There's nothing they'd like more than to show off.'

'You'd better be right,' Jonny warned.

'Oh I am,' Kiki assured him, fervently hoping that she was. If the quiz was a success, they might get back together. If it was a failure. . . but no, that did not bear thinking about. There was no room for failure in Jonny Welsh's world.

Something big and green now reared up very fast in front

of her and Kiki, heart thudding with fright and leaping aside just in time, recognised the Ocado van. Again. 'Moron!' she screamed, relieving some of her agitation and wondering why it was, whenever she attempted to exercise in the lanes around Great Hording, she was almost mown down by this vehicle, which was invariably lost. It was lost now, Kiki could see, as the passenger-side window slid down and the driver, a different one from usual but still grinning inanely, leant over towards her.

'I can haz house of Fred Needle?'

Kiki eyed him accusingly. 'You almost killed me.'

The driver evidently spoke no English. He continued to beam benignly. 'House of Fred Needle, madam, pliz.'

Kiki hesitated. Either she could jog off and leave him, or she could give him directions to Addings, the Grade II William and Mary mansion where Richard Threadneedle, deputy governor of the Bank of England, spent his weekends.

She felt disinclined to the latter course – why should she help this moron? On the other hand, taking the former would only mean the van would fruitlessly circle the village again and next time might hit her properly. Resignedly, Kiki pointed the way down the shaggy-hedge-lined lane to the Threadneedles' huge double gates, where a winding gravel drive led up to a wisteria-swathed frontage.

By the time Ocado's engine had faded into the distance and the sweet sound of birds once more filled the air, Kiki had turned off the lane and was running down a grassy route between two fields. They belonged to Tim Lacey, part of his Hollywood estate. The name served to remind the village – should it forget it for one second – that the vast Lacey fortune had come from a brilliant career directing movies. The films had all been soppy romcoms, most famously *Tufnell Park* and *I Think I Might Be Fond of You.* But success was success.

The elegant Georgian box Kiki could now see below in the valley was Tim's house, Hollywood Hall. Like most people in Great Hording she found him utterly objectionable, with his cropped white hair and bumptious blue-framed glasses. But he was undeniably a village kingpin and getting his support for the quiz had been crucial. 'Absolutely, I'm brilliant at quizzes,' had been Tim's typically immodest response. 'I used to beat Nicole and Russell on set at Trivial Pursuit every time. And Nicole's a member of Mensa, but then, so am I.'

Kiki, her Botoxed brow now sticky with sweat, was back out on the main road. The next mansion to slide into view was Brybings, the vast new-build Palladian spread where Sergei Goblemov, the village oligarch, lived with his nubile third wife Anna. Anna, who had worked nights in a Vladivostok tank factory before breaking into modelling, had taken to the high life with zeal. Styling herself patron of the arts, her first act in Great Hording had been to commission Zeb Spaw to make an enormous floating sculpture for the Brybings lake. It was thirty feet tall, shaped unmistakably like a willy, made of semi-transparent resin and emitted a neon purple glow from within. Solar-powered, it floated slowly round, banging gently into the banks. As she jogged past, Kiki could see its pulsating violet tip over the estate wall.

As Riffs, a collection of red-and-white striped brick Victorian Gothic towers, twisty-topped chimneys, gargoyles and finials now appeared, Kiki slowed to a brisk walk. She reflected with relief that she had not had to ask the denizen of this dwelling to take part. The recent departure of former owner Roger Slutt had been greeted with delight in Great Hording, into whose midst the wrinkled ex-rocker had fitted as badly as he did into his trademark tight black leather trousers.

Kiki now glanced at her watch and forced her reluctant limbs back into a jog. Time was getting on. The Golden Goose staff would have arrived at work and she needed to go through tonight's requirements again. The food, especially. In a nod to witty authenticity she had decided that pie and peas were to be served at half-time. But the suggestion had puzzled Hervé, the Michelin-starred chef, who had never seen mushy peas in his life, let alone made them. His confusion had turned to disgust once Kiki summoned up a picture on her phone. '*Mon Dieu!* I train with Joël Robuchon, for zees?'

Pavel, the new Polish barman, was an easier proposition. He turned up early, stayed late and worked like a dog, but it was difficult to tell, from his impassive Slav face, how much he had understood of what a pub quiz was. But as the impassive face was also a very handsome one, Kiki was happy to re-explain. There was, as a matter of fact, little she wouldn't be happy to do with Pavel, but sex was out of the question. She had vowed to herself at the beginning of her career that she would only ever sleep up, never down. Shagging the barstaff was not the route to riches. Unfortunately, neither was shagging the boss, not so far, anyway.

The next building Kiki passed was the village hall. Outwardly at least this was Great Hording's least remarkable building. Essentially a long shed with four windows down each side and a simple, wooden double-entrance door, it looked nothing out of the ordinary. But Kiki knew, as did everyone else who lived locally, that ordinary was the last thing it was.

The uncomplicated exterior of the place was deceptive. This one-storey shack of cream-painted corrugated iron was the focus of some of the most powerful ambition in Great Hording. Meaning, given the nature of the residents, that this simple-looking local amenity was the centre of some of the most ruthless plotting on the entire planet.

The event around which all this revolved was the annual pantomime, a show with such kudos that there was no one in the entire village who was not desperate to get a part.

And here, Kiki suddenly saw with a shock, coming towards her down the sun-dappled street bearing a basket, was the person in charge of it. Lady Mandy Chease, wife of West End impresario Sir Alistair and mother of actor Orlando. And, more importantly than any of that, pantomime director *assoluta*.

'Good morning,' intoned Lady Mandy in the rich, ripe tones that had coaxed many a local magnate through *Aladdin*, *Mother Goose* and, last year, *Jack and the Brexit Beanstalk* in which the giant counting his euros had brought the house down. In the sort of inspired casting for which Lady Mandy was justly famous, the giant had been played by the nation's deputy bean-counter, Richard Threadneedle.

Kiki plastered on her brightest, most unctuous smile. She had never yet been selected for the panto, but she lived in hope.

Lady Mandy inclined a large head set upon a thick neck. She had piercing eyes beneath dark and bristly brows, a porcine nose and a square and solid frame which the wide-legged trousers she favoured did nothing whatsoever to flatter. 'We're all looking forward very much to the quiz night,' she said in her fruity voice.

'You're bringing a team?' Kiki's voice was sharp with excitement. Lady Mandy, who even in Great Hording saw herself as *prima inter pares*, rarely appeared in the Golden Goose. She had answered none of Kiki's emails asking whether she would be interested in entering the quiz.

'Indeed I am,' Lady Mandy replied graciously. 'A small gathering of fellow thespians. We're calling our team "Merely Players".'

Kiki laughed rather too long and loud at this. Lady Mandy was staring at her from under her alarming brows. 'Er, very funny. Um, *Hamlet*, am I right?'

'*As You Like It.*' Lady Mandy closed her eyes. 'All the world's a stage,' she intoned. 'And all the men and women merely players. They have their exits and their entrances.' She stopped. 'Speaking of exits, I had better get on.' She shook the basket. 'I'm picking simple country nosegays for the bedrooms of my houseguests. Orlando is coming, of course.'

Orlando Chease, Kiki remembered, not without an agreeable touch of *schadenfreude*, had been all set to be the new James Bond. But then it had all gone pear-shaped. Lady Mandy always maintained, in public at least, that the Bond part had been beneath him. But the Golden Goose gossip – Tim Lacey, as always – was that she and Sir Alastair had been livid and Caspar Honeyman, who had got the 007 part, was now a dead man in London's West End. 'But I seriously doubt,' Tim had added gleefully, 'that he's exactly desperate to be in *Blood Brothers* anyway.'

'He's bringing his new girlfriend, Savannah. Lovely girl,' Lady Mandy added, complacently. 'I forget her surname. Mouche? Louche? Something French, anyway.'

Kiki gasped. 'Not Savannah Bouche? The film star?!' But hadn't Savannah just announced a relationship with South'n Fried, the rapper? 'Are you sure?' she asked Lady Mandy.

Pantomime's greatest dame was raising her finger roguishly to her lips. 'All very hush-hush, I understand.'

Gosh, so the South'n Fried romance was over, already! Kiki felt about to burst with triumph at this tip-off. The whole world followed the Bouche love-life with the most bated of collective breath. And she was in on its secrets! On the most inside of tracks! 'It's quite. . . sudden.'

'That's showbusiness, my dear,' declared Lady Mandy. 'People fall in love very quickly and intensely.' The great nostrils flared in dreamy reminiscence. 'I remember when I first met dear Alastair. I was SM at the time. . .'

'S&M?' Kiki blurted. Who would have thought it? Lady Mandy in rubber with a whip!

Lady Mandy looked annoyed. 'SM! Stage *Manager*! For a play dear Alastair was directing. He was married at the time, then our eyes met across a crowded set – though actually it was Beckett and quite minimal. Just a dustbin and a tree stump. Anyway, that was that. The rest,' she added grandly, 'is theatre history.'

'Absolutely,' agreed Kiki, anxious to make amends.

Lady Mandy raised her well-padded chin. 'And dear Savannah will certainly sprinkle some stardust on your little quiz. And on my little pantomime too if I can persuade her to take the starring role in. . .'

Kiki held her breath. Lady Mandy had not yet revealed

the title of this year's panto. She hoped it would be *Cinderella*. With her legs, she would make a magnificent Buttons. Dandini, at a pinch.

'. . . *Cinderella*!'

Kiki gasped. She had to get a part! By any means necessary. She was always left out, and more important people cast. But not this year! Her knees shook as she prepared her speech. The director was alone, there would never be a better time.

'Lady Mandy, I don't know whether you've thought about parts yet, but I—'

'*Good*ness me, *what* a marvellous patch of meadow cranesbill.' Lady Mandy swept off, brandishing her basket. 'I'll see you tonight, my dear.'

Kiki watched the portly rear retreat down the lane and turn off to Promptings, the Chease spread, as it were. Dash Lady Mandy! Or words to that effect. She'd been turned down yet again.

On the other hand, she knew some top gossip and Savannah Bouche would be at the quiz. What a coup! Even in Great Hording, where top spies, oligarchs, cabinet ministers and bank governors were two a penny. Many of whom had celebrity and aristocratic friends, whose details were all on Kiki's jealously guarded database.

But there was fame and there was FAME, and Savannah Bouche belonged to the LATTER category. And she was coming tonight! Jonny was going to blow a gasket. If this didn't reignite things between them, she didn't know what would. And then, when she was the second Mrs Welsh, or Lady Welsh by then – Jonny was always lobbying for honours – Lady Mandy could stick it where the sun didn't shine.

She was entering the village street now, the last part of her route before she reached home. Glowing with triumph and restored self-confidence, Kiki power-strode past the shops, admiring her lower limbs in their dazzling leggings.

For someone in her fifties, she looked pretty good. Much better than Nessa Welsh, who was short and ran to fat. Well, she would soon be regretting not taking more care, taking Jonny for granted, imagining he would never divorce her. Ha!

Kiki paused before the pale-blue-painted portals of the Great Hording Bookshop, and felt a flood of gratification. Dear Mr Delabole had done what she suggested and made a tie-in display. On the shelves in the window were Ben Fogle's *Britain's Best Pub Quiz Jumpers* and Stephen Fry's *Quiz Quester's Quinquereme* among others. Perfect!

'Good morning, Ms Cavendish.'

The soft, well-spoken male voice was addressing her from beneath the fanlight in the doorway. Kiki met the mild, intelligent gaze of Peter Delabole. She experienced a significant rise in her heart rate and a powerful rush of heat which defied the moisture-wicking properties of her Muck Sweat designer crop top.

Peter was tall, handsome and, like her, single and in his early fifties. His eyes were as azure as the paint of his bookshop and she loved the way they crinkled up, combining the suggestion of humour with the far-sightedness of an admiral assessing the horizon.

'Kiki, please!' she chided flirtatiously. 'And good morning to you too, Mr Delabole.'

'Peter, please,' he rejoined, giving her one of his rare smiles. Peter was so understated, Kiki thought, rather longingly. He was the quintessential bookshop owner, in his graph-paper shirt and Shetland v-neck pullovers in shades of sand. He wore cords, but not the violently new, violently red ones favoured by most other men in the village. Peter's cords were well-worn and usually brown or green. He wore brogues, but ones that looked to have been handed down from his grandfather fifty years ago, rather than hand-built by Lobb just last week.

'All ready for the pub quiz?' Peter's smile widened and Kiki's heart twisted. Perhaps Peter was attracted to her as well. His long blue eyes were certainly lingering on the toned, tanned arms revealed by the crop top with its witty neon piping.

Rather reluctantly she reminded herself of her rekindled hopes with Jonny. A liaison with a bookshop owner, however charming, was not part of the plan. Remember, she told herself. You only sleep up. Never down.

'Yes,' Kiki flashed Peter her own assisted-white smile, 'there's been an amazing take-up. Even Lady Mandy's coming.'

Peter nodded his head of wavy brown hair shot through fetchingly with grey. It was one of the few male heads in the village with its original colour. 'Lady Mandy was in here yesterday,' he said. 'And so was Tim Lacey. It took me most of the morning sweeping up after them.'

Kiki gasped. The two were famously rivals, but had there actually been a fight?

'All the names they'd dropped,' Peter explained dryly, crinkling his eyes again.

After Kiki had stopped laughing, they discussed the quiz. Peter, very sportingly, had offered to act as questionmaster and quiz compiler. Kiki, he insisted, would be doing him a favour. He could put any quiet moments in his shop to good use, and there were volumes all around to consult on the various categories. These would reflect the areas of expertise represented by the residents of Great Hording. Politics, Theatre, Film, Literature, History and Art.

Talk turned to the various teams. Neither of them could imagine who or what sort of a team Zeb Spaw the famous conceptual artist had assembled. 'My guess is a dog, a can of beans and a urinal,' said Peter.

Kiki's face fell. 'Do you think so? I was rather hoping for Tracey Emin.'

'I wonder who the Threadneedles will bring.' Peter nodded down the street to where the elegantly etiolated form of Kate Threadneedle had hovered into view. 'I know Mark Carney's stayed recently, and Warren Buffett's a good friend.'

Excitement filled Kiki at the prospect of such financial big beasts. Then she remembered the phone call from Lorna Drake several days ago. She had not yet checked out her claim to know the residents of Addings.

'Excuse me,' she said to Peter, and dashed off.

'Can I have a word?' Kiki bounced in her trainers over the spotless cobbles and came to a halt in front of her quarry.

Kate paused in her Heel de France ballet flats, tanned hands shoved into the pockets of her skinny jeans. She looked the other woman up and down. Along with many local wives, Kate suspected the pub manager was after her husband. Along with many local wives, Kate was not wrong.

Kiki, undaunted, fixed her with a wide white beam. 'Someone called Lorna Drake's coming to stay at the Goose this weekend. Says she knows you.'

The banker's wife wrinkled her forehead as best she could. 'Lorna Drake?'

'That's right.' Kiki watched the tight, tanned face expectantly.

'Never heard of her.'

Kiki paled. Had she been fooled by a nobody?

'Is it possible she is a friend of Wyatt's?'

Kate rolled her eyes. 'Are you joking? Wyatt doesn't have any friends. Not round here, anyway.'

Kiki was surprised at what almost amounted to a confidence. Perhaps the rumours about Kate's secret daytime drinking were true.

'Apart from that blasted boy in Little Hording,' Wyatt's mother went on, her plumped lips pressing together hard.

Kiki looked down to hide the interest dancing in her eyes. She had heard about this too. They made an unlikely Juliet and Romeo, the plump, blue-haired Wyatt and skinny Kearn from Little Hording. But what they shared with the teenagers from Verona was strong parental disapproval.

Kate had gone into the deli now, and Kiki's amusement was succeeded by fury. Damn Lorna Drake! That most dreaded of all Great Hording eventualities had almost happened. Their social Garden of Eden, their enchanted isle of the elite, had nearly been infiltrated by a civilian.

Kiki strode back towards the Golden Goose, sheer indignation powering her pace. There were a million and one things to do concerning the quiz but top of the list was a phone call to Lorna Drake. She would now not be coming to Great Hording after all.

Placing her smartphone to her ear, Kiki cursed as she

narrowly avoided a large Bentley coming rapidly up the village street. It was like that damn Ocado van all over again.

CHAPTER NINE

I t was Saturday morning and, after considerable delays in Lulu's wardrobe, they were finally on their way to Great Hording. The result of Lulu's sartorial deliberations was an outfit she felt suitable for the country. Which it may well be, Laura thought; which country was the question. And in what era.

Loosely speaking, the style was twenties aristocrat on acid; a pair of beige jodhpurs teamed with a yellow checked waistcoat and a neon green tweed jacket shot through with hot pink. They were combined with a Hermès scarf and a pair of riding boots so tight and shiny it made Laura wince to look at them. A small black bowler with a veil, under which her blonde locks were neatly tucked, completed the ensemble.

Lulu's excitement knew no bounds; ever since leaving

Kensington she had been sharing her plans for her new rural existence. 'I can be NFI!'

'NFI?' Laura was puzzled. People at *Society* were always talking about people who were Not Fucking Invited. 'NFI to what?'

'Hunt.'

Light dawned. 'You mean MFH? Master of Foxhounds?' Laura suppressed a groan. Lulu on horseback slashing at sabs with her whip? Galloping over hedges with her teeth bared?

Lulu's interest seemed mainly sartorial, however. 'Hunt clothes so pretty. Pink my favourite colour.'

'Hunting pink is actually red,' Laura pointed out.

'So why is called pink then?' The gilding on Lulu's black sunglasses flashed challengingly.

'Just fashion, I guess.' Laura remembered a row when Carinthia had exploded over a clothes shoot. 'It's too black! I hate black!'

Raisy had been impressively unfazed. 'But black's the new blue,' she had soothingly pointed out. 'So it's blue really.'

They had turned off the motorway and were now on a country road lined with green hedges and overhung with shaggy trees. The rounded flanks of hills rose at either side to a horizon of cloudless blue. It had been ages since she had been in the country, Laura thought. She had quite forgotten how beautiful it was.

'We at willage yet? Big Horing?'

'Great Hording. No, not yet.'

Lulu rapped on the glass dividing the chauffeur from the chauffeured. 'Drive faster, Vlad!'

Laura shared her impatience. She too was desperate to

check in at the Golden Goose and relax. The end of the working week had been dispiriting.

To be called up to the sixth floor on Friday afternoon had not alarmed her initially. As editor of the British Magazine Company's flagship title, Laura now reported directly to the all-powerful managing director, Christopher Stone. It was normal that he would want to see her occasionally.

Nonetheless, trepidation had seized her as she took the lift up.

The memory of the red-haired woman she had seen entering the building earlier this week had flashed in Laura's mind. Clemency? No, someone else. Had to be. Or a figment of the imagination, a drifting ghost from the ghastly past.

The silent sixth floor was decorated like a gentleman's club. Walls were dark-wood-panelled and hung with gold-framed portraits. The rich, thick blue carpet down which Laura hurried seemed to gobble up the soles of her Chelsea boots. Rounding the corner, she almost collided with someone coming the other way. 'Sorry!' she began, before gasping and recoiling with shock. The someone was her oldest enemy. A woman who, from school onwards, had contrived on every occasion to bring Laura down. 'You!'

'Nice to see you too,' said Clemency sweetly. Along with a leather biker jacket she was wearing a pair of tweed shorts, black tights and thigh boots with stiletto heels. A powerful scent of perfume swirled about her.

'Why are you here?' Laura did not beat about the bush. Clemency Makepeace had been sacked from *Society* and the British Magazine Company. She was supposed to have left the country.

Clemency laughed. She tossed a long ginger tress over her black leather shoulder and eyed Laura through layers of smoky shadow. 'Wouldn't you like to know, Miss Ace Reporter?' She swept off, trailing a musky slipstream behind her.

Laura's knees, annoyingly, were shaking and her mood, already nervous, now verged on hysteria. Had Clemency been to see Christopher?

Outside the CEO's office, his secretary Honor was studying the *Standard* over half-moon spectacles. The colour of her petrol-blue polo neck was echoed in her crisply pleated tartan skirt. In the light from her pleated silk desk lamp, her low-heeled black patent buckled shoes gleamed. There was nothing retro-geek about Honor though; she had been wearing all this first time round.

She was in her late sixties, sharp as a tack and a genius at etiquette, having, it was rumoured, been the mistress of two dukes along life's way. This was important to Christopher, who was a galloping snob, but what mattered to Christopher's wife was that Honor was old enough to be his mother. Christopher's wife had been his assistant herself, back in the day.

Laura tried to get a grip on herself. 'Hi, Honor,' she said warmly. The warmth was unforced. She loved Honor; everyone did. For all her racy past, she combined efficiency with kind concern and considered cheerfulness a moral obligation.

Honor glanced up over her specs and her elegant, high-boned face flooded with genuine delight. 'Hello, Laura dear. Go right in. He's expecting you.'

Inside his office, Christopher Stone, hands in pockets, stood facing a window which took up one entire wall and overlooked the roofs of Mayfair. As ever, he was shoeless. He thought better in his socks, he had told the *Financial*

Times in the recent interview of which all the staff had received bound copies.

'Laura, so nice to see you.' Christopher turned, beamed and stuck out a pressed white cuff with a tanned hand at the end of it. There was a house in the south of France, Laura remembered from the *FT*. Ménerbes.

Christopher's smartwatch sent her thoughts flying to Caspar. A posh kettle, he would say. Long ago, he had given her a lesson in rhyming slang. Kettle and hob, fob. Of course Caspar, now a fully fledged film star, would have any number of posh kettles.

Christopher Stone's posh kettle now flashed at her in a seigneurial wave. 'Come and sit down.'

Laura sat at the large, polished burr-walnut desk, the historic ship's bridge from behind which successive CEOs had steered the British Magazine Company. Fred Astaire had tap-danced on it. Elinor Glyn had sprawled on it. Mrs Simpson had mixed Manhattans on it; according to the *FT* interview her monogrammed cocktail shaker was still in the bottom drawer. Norman Parkinson had signed contracts on it (and served up some of his famous sausages). Twiggy had posed on it. And now Laura Lake sat at it.

'Thanks for coming up,' the managing director said, as if it had been a matter of choice. He had swung his feet up on the desk and was giving her an easy smile. Something about the easy smile made Laura even more uneasy.

Should she get a question about Clemency in first? But what if Christopher hadn't seen her after all? Laura's oldest and bitterest enemy might merely have been dropping a CV off to Personnel, which was also on this floor. She could be traipsing around every magazine house in London doing the same. Laura felt her spirits rise. Better not to mention her in that case. Let sleeping dogs – or cats in Clemency's case – lie.

Instead, she stared at the pink silk soles of the managing director's long, elegant feet. He had told the *FT* that he bought his distinctive hosiery in bulk from a small store in Rome that sold socks to Vatican cardinals.

'I've been thinking about you,' Christopher went on, addressing his well-kept fingernails. According to the article, his manicurist had waiting lists for his waiting list.

Laura waited. Christopher allowed a thick silence to gather before looking suddenly up through the big, round toffee-coloured spectacles from Manhattan's leading bespoke optometrist. 'I've just been talking to someone very interesting,' he said brightly.

Alarm charged through Laura. This had to be Clemency. She forced herself to smile, however, and sound bright right back. 'Really?'

'Yes. A writer with some great ideas and very good contacts. Excellent celebrity access.'

Laura was unable to keep up the pretence. 'You can't mean Clemency Makepeace?'

Christopher's steely beam continued unwavering. 'Indeed I do.'

'But she was sacked last year,' a dismayed Laura pointed out. 'In the wake of a criminal trial.'

'But she wasn't actually guilty of anything,' Christopher smoothly countered.

'Not *proved* guilty, no.'

A faint furrow rippled the smoothness of the managing directing brow. 'Here at the British Magazine Company we pride ourselves on attracting the best talent. And if occasionally that talent falls in with dubious company in the course of its investigations, perhaps that is only to be expected. Occupational hazard,' he added, his eyes behind the horn-rims still locked on Laura's.

'Dubious company' obviously meant the jewel gang ringleader with whom Clemency had been sleeping.

'Is that what Clemency told you?' Laura struggled to sound calm.

'Precisely,' said Christopher, showing his even white Harley Street teeth. 'And it seems she has been using her time well since leaving us. She has been in America making some very useful friends. She's in a position to offer us interviews with a number of major celebrities, all of whom she is close to, any one of whom would make an excellent front cover.'

Laura felt her mouth fall open. 'For *Society*, you mean?'

Christopher bestowed upon her his brightest beam. 'Of course. Why else would I be talking to you about it? You're the acting editor of *Society*, are you not?'

Laura agreed that she was.

'Quite.' Christopher leant eagerly forward, his eyes bright beneath neatly trimmed Jermyn Street brows. 'But you need support. Talented as you are, you lack the experience.'

'I've run the magazine for nearly two months,' Laura reasoned. The managing director ignored this.

'Carinthia has been in touch with me,' he went on, unpromisingly.

'She's been in touch with me too. Most days.'

Stone ignored this too. 'Carinthia thinks, and I tend to agree with her, that a co-editor would be just the thing until she comes back. At which point we can see what happens.'

Laura blinked. This was like a bad dream. 'Clemency, you mean?'

Christopher nodded. 'Carinthia recommended that I see her. She's been quite the frequent visitor at the, um, spa. Or so I understand.'

Laura's fingers clutched at the chair arms. She remembered the clank of vodka bottles down the phone line. The nurse asking where the contraband supplies had come from. So it was a conspiracy. Carinthia, jealous, was plotting with Clemency to oust her.

'You're proposing that Clemency comes and works as joint editor of *Society*?' It was so loathsome a prospect it was hard to get the words out.

'Exactly!'

Laura remained in her seat. The temptation to rise, tell Christopher to stuff his editorship down his boxer shorts (Charvet, like his shirts) and storm out never to return was almost overwhelming.

But it would be a rash thing to do. She was brilliant at her job, she loved it and she wanted to keep it.

As Christopher blithely allowed another of his ghastly silences to gather, Laura prayed silently to the ghost of her foreign correspondent father. He had faced many a challenging situation. How would he get out of this one?

The answer came immediately. Just go along with it. Fight it from the inside. Both Clemency and Carinthia fought dirty, but she would have no chance from the outside.

Laura smiled at Christopher. 'Fine.'

'Big Horing!' Lulu's excited voice broke into her thoughts. The Bentley had reached the outskirts of somewhere clearly very smart. There were gold flashes of weathervane and the tops of mature trees showing behind high garden walls.

Glossy horses grazed in fields of glossy grass edged by glossy hedges. A beautifully painted sign, 'Great Hording', beneath a colourful coat of arms announced that they were at their destination.

With an effort, Laura pushed aside the miserable events of the previous afternoon. The story she was going to write about this place would see off all her rivals and defeat all her enemies. The Secret Village of the Super-Rich! The Hidden Hamlet of the HNIs!

Lulu's sunglasses were twisting from left to right. 'Is great shopping!'

The small town centre was prettily Georgian, with higgledy-piggledy shops in sugar almond shades. The carefully preserved old façades were all bow windows, fanlights and bullseye glass. Hand-lettered signs protruded at right angles and hung like a row of flags. Stone steps led up to pillared doorways and occasional gaps between buildings gave sparkling glimpses of a cobalt sea fringed with lacy waves and edged by golden sands. White seagulls circled overhead in an azure sky. No wonder, Laura thought, that anyone who was anyone wanted to come here.

'Look! Is James Bond!' exclaimed Lulu, making Laura's heart jerk within her chest. Caspar was here?

She was both surprised and disturbed by the excitement she felt. But Lulu was not pointing at her former lover. She was indicating a shop called Taking the Biscuit. There was a grey-iced version of the iconic Aston Martin and biscuit villains of the past including Blofeld and Dr No and the spy himself in icing black tie. They were dotted about a biscuit landscape including biscuit explosions, biscuit helicopters and biscuit versions of Moneypenny and Prudence Handjob, the Bond girl played by Merlot D'Vyne.

Laura raised her phone to take a picture for Caspar. Then she lowered it again. What was the point? He wouldn't reply. She hadn't heard from him for ages. Perhaps she never would again.

'Fast! Fast!' Lulu urged. 'Want get to hotel!'

Vlad obediently put her foot down and the car shot past a well-preserved blonde in dazzling leggings, smartphone clamped to her ear.

The Golden Goose was at the end of the street. Laura stared at it, amazed.

The rough pub of the Farmer's Arms website had been utterly transformed. What stood before them was a graceful inn with an air of mellow, well-cared-for age. The pebbledash had been removed to expose the original brickwork, which had been painted white and superimposed with the establishment's name in swirling sage script. On the smart sage sign was a painted gold goose.

Laura could not remember the previous roof but it certainly hadn't been thatched. Also brand new were the ancient diamond pane windows snuggling under the straw and the venerable studded oak front door with the large pink roses round it. Outside the front, by the blackboard chalked with 'Champagne Bar' and 'Fresh Langoustines', were round wooden tables shaded by white parasols. To the side was a parking area with gravel so thick as to be halfway up the tyres of the row of gleaming performance cars.

Wow. Laura could hardly wait to get inside. Let alone get her hands on some langoustines, not to mention a glass of champagne.

The phone in her pocket now rang and Laura reached for it. 'Lorna Drake?'

Laura had no difficulty recognising the cutting tones of Kiki Cavendish. She sounded very angry as she explained in no uncertain terms that the room at the Golden Goose was cancelled.

Laura was aghast. 'But why?'

Kiki evidently had no intention of explaining her reasons. 'The room is no longer available,' she said crisply and cut off.

Laura, in the back of Lulu's Bentley, bit back her frustration and forced herself to think. There were two obvious possibilities. Either Kiki had checked with the senior Threadneedles and discovered Laura had never met them, or Kiki had checked with Wyatt and found Laura was a magazine journalist. Come to think of it, perhaps she had done both.

Lulu's arms were folded crossly in her neon tweeds. One polished boot swung in annoyance. . . 'So where we go now for glass of Moët, hmm?'

Laura looked out of the window. A signpost pointed the way to Little Hording, and her natural optimism kicked in. Perhaps it was a smaller, cuter version of its Great neighbour. They probably wouldn't have *grande marque* champagne, but there might be a glass of prosecco. They could do worse than try there.

CHAPTER TEN

'Is like 'orror movie.' From behind her sunglasses Lulu regarded the Fishing Boat Inn, Little Hording, in disgust. She had not even got out of the Bentley.

Laura, who had, could only agree. Before the entrance – or maybe the exit – a scabby patch of grass held a collection of faded plastic buoys, rotting rope and rusting, unnameable metalware. Within the blocky, uninspiring building itself, the once-white paint was peeling from the windowframes.

In the rear of the car, Lulu pouted. 'Is not nice in this willage.'

Nor was it. While Great Hording was all heritage buildings and lovely shops, Little Hording comprised a row of dreary cottages huddled gloomily above a brown and bouldersome beach. In the far distance was a sullen sea and a bent figure throwing a stick for a dog. The dog did not take up the invitation. The sun similarly eschewed any suggestion that it should shine and there was a dispiriting cold wind.

'We go back to Big Horing, hmm?'

'There's no point,' Laura said. 'I've told you. They made a mistake with the booking. There's no room at the inn.'

'Mistake, rubbish,' said Lulu.

Laura agreed with this assessment, but it didn't make any difference.

'We go back there.'

Laura shook her head. She had no intention of facing Kiki Cavendish in the flesh. If, as was almost certainly the case, the pub manager suspected her motives, it would not help if she knew what Laura looked like. Better to stay below the radar and conduct operations from a distance.

'I'm staying here,' she concluded. 'And so are you.'

Consulted en route, the Fishing Boat Inn's weary-sounding landlady had confirmed that two rooms were free. 'They're all free, to be honest.'

'Lulu will not stay here!' said Lulu now, vehemently.

From the driver's seat, Vlad cleared her throat in solidarity.

'In which case, you'll have to find somewhere else. Or,' Laura added, hopefully, 'go back to London.'

A rickety-looking pair of youths in tracksuit bottoms grey as the distant sea, the peaks of baseball caps protruding from beneath their hoodies, now approached. One was vaping copiously. They stared at the car and, catching sight of Lulu, did a double take. 'It's Miss Piggy,' exclaimed the vaper.

Laura glared at them, whilst privately acknowledging they had a point. Lulu's round face could look porcine in certain lights, and her neon-tinged aristocrat-at-the-races look was undeniably cartoonish.

'I see you later, hmm?' Magnificently ignoring her detractors, Lulu waved at Laura.

'Where are you going?' But the window had shot up and the car engine burst into life. Laura could only watch as the Bentley glided away.

Turning back towards the pub, she was relieved to see that the vaping youths had gone. She picked her way carefully over the broken ground to the back – or possibly the front – door.

While empty and not especially warm, the pub's interior looked slightly better than the outside. It was simply furnished, with pine tables and chairs, but seemed clean. There was a fruit machine, but only one. The muzak was on low.

'Can I help you?'

Someone had appeared behind the bar. Unexpectedly, it was one of the youths, although without his hoody, baseball cap or vaping friend. His close-cropped brown hair was revealed, and two sharp eyes either side of a long nose. He wore a red T-shirt with Lenin on it.

Laura decided that she couldn't face anything further without a drink. 'Glass of wine, please.'

'Red or white?'

The three most depressing words in the English language, someone had said. Laura had never understood why. 'No wine left' would have been far more depressing.

'Red, please. Have you got a wine list?'

'Only got one sort. *Chateau Lave Ecran*.'

Laura repeated the name to herself. She knew the phrase. *Lave écran*. Screenwash. '*Chateau Screenwash*?'

'Well, that's what I call it. It's not very good, but no one round here seems to mind. They're mostly lager drinkers anyway.'

Laura decided to chance it, and regretted it instantly as the bartender produced a screw-top bottle of red and blew the dust off it.

Very possibly this was the most depressing wine in the English language. Sipping, and trying not to wince, she explained that she had reserved a room on her drive here.

The boy reached for a book. He looked up, frowning. 'Mr Lack, it says here.'

Laura reddened. Admittedly it had been a pathetic effort at a *nom de plume*. 'It's du Lac, actually.' The French for Lake. 'Miss du Lac, I guess.'

'My mum must have written it down wrong.' The boy closed the book. 'But you're Laura Lake the journalist really. Aren't you?'

Laura was gobsmacked. 'How do you know?'

'Wyatt Threadneedle is my girlfriend.' His tone was matter-of-fact.

Laura just stopped her mouth dropping open in time. She turned it into a smile. 'Wow. That's quite a coincidence.'

He shrugged. 'She said you might be coming here, and to look out for you.'

Laura tried to maintain a calm expression. How had Wyatt known? Had she guessed why? And had Wyatt, Laura wondered, foreseen what would happen at the Golden Goose? Another thought struck her. 'Is Wyatt here – I mean, in Great Hording – this weekend?' If she was, perhaps she could stay at her family seat. Investigating the village of the rich was going to be tricky from this distance, especially without a car.

The boy shook his close-cropped head. 'Her parents have sent her on a course to make her own perfume.'

'How strange.' Wyatt had never seemed the perfume type to Laura.

The boy smiled. It was a smile of such warmth and width that it not only put his sizeable nose in perspective, but gave sparkle to his eyes and lit up his whole face. Laura, previously struggling to see what Wyatt saw in him, wondered no longer.

'Last weekend it was a cookery course in Cornwall. And why do you think she's doing the internship in London? Her parents are trying just about everything to split us up. I'm not their type, you see.'

Laura felt a kindling of sympathy for – given their location – the starfish-crossed lovers. This boy was intelligent and pleasant. And say what you like about Wyatt – plenty of people at *Society* did – she was definitely different. She saw below the surface. Just so long as she didn't see what had brought Laura to the area.

'Wyatt reckons you're planning some kind of exposé of Great Hording,' her host offered next, which made the horrified Laura fumble for the nearest bar stool and plonk herself down in shock. 'Are you?'

Laura hesitated. To admit her mission might well be to end it on the spot.

'She hoped you were,' the boy went on. 'That's why she risked breaking the rules and telling you about the village. We both think Great Hording's got it coming.'

A relieved Laura now remembered what Wyatt had said about internships and the unfair distribution of wealth. And that speech about the Ocado van. Her gaze rested on the Lenin T-shirt again. Had love persuaded the privileged daughter of ultra-capitalists to see a different point of view?

The boy gestured down at his T-shirt. 'Wyatt bought me this. She says most kids in Great Hording think Lenin was in the Beatles.' He smiled at her again, this time a tad apologetically. 'Look, I'm sorry Daz was rude to your friend. He was well out of order.'

Laura was grateful the subject had moved off her investigation. 'Well, he *was* rude. But it's true that Lulu is never knowingly underdressed.' She glanced out of the plain, uncurtained but nonetheless clean windows, half-expecting the Bentley to slide back into view. But it was probably on its way back to London.

'I'm Kearn, by the way.' A thin hand with biro scribbles on the back was extended across the bar to her. 'My mum and dad run this pub.'

'And you work here too?' Laura liked Kearn, but he seemed to have pretty dead-end prospects.

'When I'm not studying thermochemical algorithms.'

As she looked mystified, he added, 'It's a branch of computer science. Shall I show you your room? Or rooms. There's no one else staying, so pick whichever you like.'

Upstairs, Laura selected the middle of three identical possibilities. All were plain and clean with MDF furniture, functional bathrooms and views of the distant brown sea. If you had a very small cat, there might have just been room to swing it.

Kearn paused by the door. 'Let me know if you need any help.'

Laura, unzipping her overnight bag, looked up. 'Help?'

'With your piece. About Great Hording.'

Laura decided to continue with her policy of neither confirming nor denying. She pulled out her pyjamas.

'I can tell you all about the place if you are. Everyone who lives there, and what's happening tonight at the Golden Goose.'

Laura, while desperate to press him, was still not entirely sure he could be trusted. This whole left-wing act could merely be a front, to get her to show her hand.

Kearn went on. 'The pub is a complete closed-shop, socially speaking. A local pub for local people. Local rich and famous people. So the pub quiz they're having tonight's going to be quite something.'

'Pub quiz?' Laura was unpacking her sponge bag. But her heart was hammering. 'Tonight?'

Kearn turned away from the doorframe. 'Well, I'll leave you to it. If you're not writing a piece, you don't want to know.'

'I might want to know,' Laura said quickly. 'Just out of. . . interest. Pub quiz, you say?'

'Yeah, the locals have all formed teams – lawyers, artists, writers, politicians – Jolyon Jackson's heading up that one.'

'*He* lives in Great Hording?' The larger-than-life, even notorious Minister of Defence? It was getting more and more difficult to seem interested in her toothpaste.

'Yeah. But anyway, catch you later.' Kearn strode off down the corridor.

'Kearn!' Laura shouted. 'Come back here! Tell me everything you know!' As his grinning face reappeared in the doorway she added, 'Okay, I admit it. I'm writing a piece.'

★

An hour later, Kearn had finished his briefing and gone off to his delayed computer studies. Laura flopped back on the bed, hand aching from taking notes, head spinning with all the information she had been given.

At the very centre of her whirl of thoughts was the knowledge that her suspicions had been wrong. The Great Hording story was not a good one. It was a brilliant one.

The place was the weekend home of the rich and famous, yes – the Zeb Spaws, the Tim Laceys, the Jolyon Jacksons, the Alastair Cheases. But it was also the retreat of some genuinely powerful people, not just Wyatt and Edgar's fathers and a cabinet minister but several distinguished judges, two permanent secretaries heading up big government departments and some senior armed forces personnel.

That all these celebrities, oligarchs and Establishment figures were about to compete against each other in the world's ultimate, if completely unknown, pub quiz was too good to be true. But it was true and she could turn it to her advantage. Kearn had offered to lend her his bicycle, and had provided her with a map. And while Laura hated exercise, there were times when it could not be avoided. Just now, her career hung in the balance. She must go to the Golden Goose and bluff her way past Kiki Cavendish. An exposé of Great Hording in general and an account of the pub quiz in particular would knock Christopher Stone's salmon-pink socks off and make it impossible for Clemency to compete. Then the job share idea would be dropped and Clemency thrust back into the outer darkness where she belonged.

CHAPTER ELEVEN

As Laura pedalled up the bright high street of Great Hording in her tight dark jeans, the owner of the bookshop was just locking his azure-blue door. His smartphone was wedged between his shoulder and his chin and as Laura heaved herself past, a few words of his conversation floated towards her. The language was not English, but over her straining, heaving breath, it was difficult to make out what it was. Not French anyway, Laura's attuned bilingual ear told her. Rather, something rolling and Slavic-sounding. Perhaps he was taking an order from the oligarch.

But as her concern was less the polyglot denizens of Britain's poshest village than getting to the pub before the quiz began, Laura pedalled faster. Past Taking the Biscuit, where a staff member was dismantling the Bond display, past Chocolateers, whose window boasted a selection of nettle nougat and curry ganaches, and past Di's Deli, 'Home of the UK's First £100 Sourdough Loaf!'

At the Golden Goose, at the end of the street, all was peace and quiet. It was just past four o'clock; lunch was long since over, even for the most determined lingerers. And the evening's events were yet to begin. The only clue as to what would later be taking place was the casually scribbled notice on the blackboard outside. 'Pub Quiz Tonight. All Welcome.'

Of course, all were not welcome; anything but. So how would she get in? Laura dismounted and stood beside Kearn's bike, relieved to be off the uncomfortably narrow plastic seat and the grimy drop handlebars from which unravelled tape dangled.

Behind the pub was a big and well-kept garden. Pieces of contemporary sculpture were displayed in gravelled areas connected by twisting paths. Not all the pieces were entirely beautiful, Laura thought, regarding what looked like an enormous marble bum. At the bottom was a gate and beyond that, the sea. She would walk along the shore until inspiration struck.

Laura leant Kearn's bike against a Jeff Koons-style giant silver dog and walked down through the lush lawn dotted with lemon trees. They had actual lemons on them. There was clearly a balmy microclimate; the weather here was as perfect and favourable as everything else in Great Hording.

The gate at the bottom was set in a fence of unvarnished silvery wood. A Perspex anchor lounged against it. Laura pressed the latch to reveal, spreading before her, a pristine beach as yellow as vanilla ice cream. At each end, embracing it like arms stretched towards the sea was an outcrop of rock topped with grass and tumbling with flowers. What looked like the ruins of an ancient chapel stood on one of them, its old stones catching the afternoon sun.

The beauty of the place struck her forcibly. She noticed how the beach glittered with shells and iridescent clumps of foam. 'It's where the mermaids had their bath!' a woman in a striped Breton top was smiling to an impossibly cute boy with a blond basin cut. Then she lifted him up and hugged him.

This image of maternal perfection sent pure longing shooting through Laura. She turned away, a lump in her throat, and walked quickly to the ocean's edge. The water was blue and glassy and turning constantly with white ruffs of foam. The way it rippled up and down reminded her of fingers playing the piano.

A memory came shooting back. A beautiful, dark-haired soloist in a glittering green dress. Her long white fingers had danced over the keys in precisely this way.

Harry had not told her where they were going, insisting it was a surprise. As he had led her through Kensington Gardens, the air had been warm and heady with flowers. The grass had glowed intensely green beneath a sky of hot blue. The still-strong evening sun had blazed back off the golden figure of Prince Albert enthroned under his Gothic canopy. Everything had seemed more vivid than usual, especially the Albert Hall.

Despite passing the venerable red building on the bus countless times back and forth to Lulu's, Laura had never gone to a concert here before. The great neo-classical auditorium thrilled her. She loved the red velvet seats, the mighty organ pipes, the eccentric Promenaders with their collecting buckets and coloured shirts. Laura couldn't play a note herself but knew from Mimi the importance of live performance. Her grandmother believed it fed the soul, which showed in the face. 'Go to the theatre, to museums and concerts as often as possible. It gives you a healthy glow.'

That Harry was taking her to a Prom was more than unexpected. She had never imagined he was a classical music fan. His subsequent revelation that his parents had taken him here every summer when he was a child made her feel, suddenly, that she was being shown something very intimate and important. And more was to come.

'Were your parents musicians?' she had probed during the interval, to which he had nodded yes, adding that he had been a music prodigy himself but had had to give it up after both his parents died.

But about what had happened and when, Harry would not be drawn. 'I couldn't afford to keep up my studies so I went into journalism,' was all he would add over his Spitfire beer at the bar in the magnificent carved lobby, as the red buses trundled past on Kensington Gore. 'But I still go to concerts when I can, wherever I am in the world.'

'That's so sad!' Laura had exclaimed, the ice in her Pimm's freezing into her hand like the cruelty of Fate itself.

Harry had shrugged broad shoulders in the inevitable leather jacket despite the best seats in the house. Everyone else in their row had worn black tie. 'Not really. I'd never have made it. Didn't practise enough. I took all my grades but I can't play a thing now.'

Watching him over her brimming, fruit-filled tumbler, Laura wondered whether to believe him. There had, she felt, been a hunger to the way he had watched, and listened, to the soloist. It had been a contemporary piece, something plinky-plonky that she had not recognised. But it held Harry spellbound. She had felt him hold his breath when the fingers paused before playing one last plangent chord. Then, as the white arm on the stage floated up in the air, indicating the first half of the performance was over, Laura had sensed beside her a great releasing of tension. He had lived every note. Did he have a piano in his flat, wherever it was? She vowed, one day, to find out. In the meantime, it was just another piece of the jigsaw that was Harry, a jigsaw that had, then at least, seemed to be getting bigger, more intricate and more interesting.

The second half of the concert had featured music by Ravel whom, Harry whispered, was his favourite. 'I love a bit of French romanticism.' She had stared at him in surprise, but his attention had been on the conductor, an iconic, silver-haired figure in a black polo neck, not waving his arms about as expected but seemingly controlling everything with his eyes, and a twitch of his fingers. French romanticism! Did that mean her? The wonderful possibility that it was added to the excitement of the concert's finale, with the wild cheering and the foot-stamping and the conductor, evidently a Proms favourite, going off and coming back on again only to take a seat in the front row with the crowd, much to their delight.

Harry leant over to her. 'I love the black bra under your white shirt. Like notes on a sheet of music,' he whispered, under cover of the cheering audience. On the crammed bus back they had snuggled together, and back at her flat he had made love to her more passionately than ever before. The memory made her tingle even now. And there had been other musical outings, always last-minute and spontaneous; he had taken her to the opera too, but. . . Oh, what was the point of thinking about all this?

Laura took a deep breath and looked up. The sky above was huge and blue, full of billowing clouds that didn't seem to move at all. They were fantastically shaped; here was a whale, there a rabbit. Maybe one was a Jeff Koons dog. She sighed. What on earth was she doing here, on her own, plotting to break into a stupidly exclusive pub quiz? How was that ever going to work, let alone save her career?

She felt suddenly foolish, then cross, then melancholy. If only Harry was here to walk up and down this heavenly beach with her, hand in hand. To skim stones, to jump back from waves, to do all the ordinary stuff they never did because he was never around. Feeling practically suicidal now, Laura looked at the happy couples and jolly families bounding about the beach. It was all so bloody Boden catalogue. Fathers in board shorts stood at the water's edge as children attached by the ankle to surfboards plunged happily up and down. Watching on the beach, black Labradors at hand, were smiling mums whose rolled-up grey cotton trousers exposed slim brown calves, their shiny, tumbly hair flashing with blonde highlights. There were cricket-playing grannies in arty jackets, floaty scarves and silver jewellery. 'Owzat!' yelled a grandson, catching one of them out. The very sand was full of everyone else's happy, fulfilled lives.

Children's names were written in it; Ethan, Ella, Ariadne, Alfie. Had her own father ever written her name in the sand? Laura doubted it. He had worked in sandy places; the Middle East especially. He had died there too, in a helicopter crash, working on a story. He was buried somewhere in the desert. She had never seen his grave.

As for her mother, the very idea of sunshine sent Odette into hysterics. She would need at least two hats, lashings of Factor 100 and sunglasses as big as welding goggles before she would consider the afternoon sun, let alone the midday one. As for playing games, she believed running ruined your ankles. Which it probably would in her case, given the six-inch heels she routinely wore. Laura dug her hands deeper into the restrictive pockets of her tight jeans, almost relishing the pain. Thank goodness Odette was happily – if that was the word – installed in Monte Carlo (of all places, given her horror of sunshine) and she need see her only once a year. She had never been much of a parent.

Not like Mimi. But even she had never played cricket on a beach, not like the ones surrounding Laura here. The rules mystified her, as they did all French people, and exercise – the clothes involved especially – frankly horrified her. *No man should ever see you in sweatpants, chérie.*

What would Mimi do now, Laura wondered, fighting the impulse to phone for a cab and take the train to London and thence to France. There was nothing for her here in England. She was wasting her time, what was the point? And she was already twenty-three. . .

Feel your heart beat, chérie, take a deep breath, listen to yourself. Laura could hear her grandmother's voice as clearly as if she were next to her. *Do nothing. Absolutely nothing. Moments like this, they help you regroup. You alone are responsible for what happens to you.*

Laura stretched, and felt stronger, strangely enough. The feeling of hopelessness was fading. She was aware of other sensations now; sea breeze, her glowing face – no SPFs, Mother! With her back to the sea, she looked at the rear of the main street, the pale blue, pink and peach-painted buildings. Glancing at the pub, she spotted something she had not seen before, at the top of the garden. That current horticultural must-have, a shepherd's hut, and through one of its diamond-shaped window panes the keen-sighted Laura thought she could make out a familiar silhouette. A silhouette that bore a striking resemblance to Miss Piggy.

CHAPTER TWELVE

It was now an hour before pub quiz lift-off, and Kiki was ready; touch of mascara, sweep of bronzer, swoosh of lip gloss, hair twisted up in its signature pencil, reading glasses halfway down her nose. At the social level she dealt with, obvious sartorial effort was frowned on. The problem was, looking as if you weren't trying was twice as hard as actually doing so.

Kiki's clothes reflected the same unforgiving casual glam aesthetic. Her black Muck Sweat tracky bots flowed loosely yet revealingly round her thighs. Her lithe, Pilates-toned torso was revealed in a tight white T-shirt under a purple strappy top. On the tanned, laddered bones of her braless chest lay a single diamond on a silver chain. Pewter-painted toenails poked out of special edition designer Birkenstocks. Admiring herself earlier in the long driftwood-framed mirror propped up against the wall of her bedroom, Kiki had felt that she more than fitted in with the wives of the local masters of the universe.

But did the bar-room? Jonny Welsh had insisted on his signature witty touches, but getting the balance right had been tricky. Kiki had never been quite certain about the behind-the-bar wallpaper. It was white with black scribbles all over it, supposedly inspired by Einstein's doodles. And did the tables slashed with savage cuts really work?

The carpenter who had made them had apparently been inspired by the saw-marks in his workbench. His workbench had been in Walthamstow, just as the spoon carver behind the salad tossers had worked out of Bermondsey. The drystone waller Kiki had employed in the garden had been from Shoreditch and even the blue cushions in the window seats had been dyed in Beckton by a part-time urban climber who gathered indigo from Epping Forest. It seemed that no one in the country did country crafts any more. If you wanted authentic rustic, London was the place.

Kiki walked slowly round, humming softly to the bespoke pop curated by a top DJ in Brooklyn and sent by computer file every Tuesday. She would have preferred Radio Two, but Jonny had ruled it out. 'We're not a bloody supermarket aisle.'

The saw-marked wooden tables had been arranged in groups of six, the maximum size of each team. Jolyon Jackson, predictably, had tried to wriggle round the diktat and bring more. 'Got a super gang of fruity party workers. Great girls, jolly bright some of them, just down from Oxford. PPE.'

'I'm afraid you can't, Minister,' Kiki had told him.

Jackson's exophthalmic blue eyes had bulged even further beneath his trademark messy brown fringe. 'Seriously?'

'Honestly, no.'

Kiki knew, even so, that 'no' wasn't a word Jolyon Jackson had in his vocabulary, any more than 'honestly'.

On each team table a sign was attached by a tiny clip to a small stand. Kiki examined them. 'Development Hell' was the team of movie people got together by Tim Lacey and apparently included a hot young star whose identity had yet to be revealed. Kiki had everything crossed for Aidan Turner, with whom Tim claimed to be in talks for *Les Misérables 2: Electric Bugaloo*. 'After my massive success in romantic comedy, a musical's the next logical step,' he had told *Radio Times*.

Kiki flicked a speck of dust off the 'Politicos' table. This was Jolyon Jackson's team, situated nearest the bar as Jackson would certainly be its most enthusiastic patron. 'Legal Eagles', next door, was the predictable description of the village team of top barristers. 'Bean Counters' was Richard Threadneedle's collection of fellow bankers. 'Page Turners' was the literary team got up by Dame Hermione Grantchester. 'My Quiz Team' was Zeb Spaw and his cohort of concept artists.

'Can't you think of anything more exciting?' Kiki had asked the celebrated underpants-crucifier.

Spaw had stared at her scornfully from under his trademark Soviet-era Russian fur hat and through the yellow lenses of his wraparound sunglasses. 'It's an artistic statement. Ever heard of Tracey Emin's *My Bed*?'

'Does that mean Tracey will be here?' Kiki asked hopefully. She and Spaw were friends, as was well known.

Spaw's unnerving yellow gaze remained unblinking. 'Who of us is ever here?' he asked. 'What does here even mean?'

Oh well, Kiki thought. She had one bona fide star turning

up. Here was the 'Merely Players' table, with Savannah Bouche and Lady Mandy, plus Alastair and Orlando Chease too, presumably.

Pausing by a table which bore the team name 'The Dumb Blondes', Kiki bit her glossed lip. She had initially had no intention of hiring out the Golden Goose's newly delivered shepherd hut to the unintelligible, bizarrely dressed new arrival. For one thing, the decor was still in transition. Jonny had ordered a retro-hipster look, but kitsch vintage items tended to be on the big side and space inside shepherds' huts was limited, to say the least. At the moment it looked like an explosion in Shoreditch.

Kiki had stood in the doorway regarding the woman in vast sunglasses and hi-vis tweed in the back of the big black Bentley. She was obviously wealthy, but that was not the point. No one in Great Hording knew her, and she was not on Kiki's database. So that should have been that.

'We have no rooms left,' she had repeatedly told the blonde. 'No Room Left! *Pas des Chambres! Keine Zimmer!*'

'What about that one?' Lulu pointed at the garden's latest embellishment, white-painted, four-wheeled, Bluetooth-enabled and clearly unoccupied.

Kiki had thought fast. 'That shepherd's hut is reserved for. . .'

'Shepherd? Hmm?'

'For residents of the village,' Kiki finished.

Lulu had taken this calmly. 'OK, I buy house here.'

Kiki was astonished. People didn't just appear in Great Hording, demand a room at the Golden Goose and then, on being refused, announce their intention to become a resident. 'There are no houses for sale round here,' she said in her snootiest voice.

This wasn't, in point of fact, entirely true. Riffs, ex-residence of the undesirable ex-rock star Roger Slutt, was currently on the market, although an exclusive market inaccessible to the ordinary househunter. Details appeared with only one estate agent, viewable only on the dark web and through possession of certain passcodes.

'No property? But is big willage, hmm?' Lulu looked sceptical.

'No property,' repeated Kiki firmly. *Especially to nobodies like you*, was the unspoken coda.

Then Kiki's celeb-detector, honed over many years of high-level exposure to HNIs, kicked in. A familiar, infallible prickling at the back of her neck told her that, actually, this blonde wasn't a nobody. She was famous.

How had she not recognised her? She was the celebrated billionheiress Lulu, former fiancée of the rapper South'n Fried. He had left her for Savannah Bouche – who was now secretly dating Orlando Chease, son of Lady Mandy of this very parish.

It occurred to Kiki that here was a way of revenging herself on that ghastly, pompous old battleaxe. If Lulu and Savannah were to be in the same room, sparks would certainly fly. This would be vastly entertaining for the regulars and acutely embarrassing for Lady Mandy.

'Actually,' Kiki added, 'there could be a property. And if you really want to stay, the shepherd hut just might be available. Oh, and you really must enter our pub quiz this evening.'

Now though, Kiki was rather regretting revealing that Riffs was for sale, let alone inviting Lulu to the quiz. How could she have thought that trouble with Savannah, let alone Lady Mandy, was a good idea? She tried to calm herself down. Lulu was sure to hate the house – it was hideous. And with any luck she wouldn't come to the quiz either. Quizzes were obviously not her forte, as the team name she had chosen suggested.

Kiki finished checking the tables and turned towards the bar. Behind the fashionable scoured slate facade, engraved with early Clash lyrics, Pavel was polishing glasses. With his jutting cheekbones, full mouth and fair hair curling almost to his broad shoulders he looked, as he always did, wildly handsome. His tall, broad-shouldered figure was shown to best advantage in the pub's regulation black shirt and black trousers, the regulation chic little hessian pinny tied round his narrow waist. He was laughing at something with Rosie, the blonde barmaid with the rolling local accent and skin like strawberries and cream. Watching them, Kiki felt a stab of jealousy. Pavel was obviously keen on his voluptuous co-worker, who looked even better than he did in a clinging shirt and tight trousers.

Kiki now braced herself to go into the kitchen and taste Hervé's mushy peas. He had been working on them for days and no one had been allowed near. She went towards the kitchen with her fingers crossed.

Hervé's menu leaned towards the experimental; quail's entrail ice cream with ground oyster-shell mash was one of his signature dishes, along with mackerel bone salad with onion dust. The kitchen had so many Bunsen burners, Petri dishes and test tubes that it looked more like a chemistry lab than somewhere food was prepared.

At the back, where there were a few actual stoves and preparation counters, Hervé's red Paisley bandanna could be seen moving about. He spotted her and raised a tattooed arm. 'Over 'ere, Kinkee!'

This mispronunciation never failed to irritate her. She was 99 per cent certain it was deliberate. As she passed a cooking station, Kiki caught the eye of one of Hervé's sous chefs, a young boy she was not sure she had ever heard speak. He was working on something with a blowtorch, but it was not, for once, Hervé's celebrated emulsion of scorched holm oak – 'who knew that wood could taste so good!' one of the reviewers had raved – but something unusually normal-looking, a pie in a big square dish, its crust beautifully brown and decorated with the crest of Great Hording in pastry.

'Fantastic!' Kiki exclaimed, in relief. Only now did she realise just how much she had feared that Hervé might take the pie and mash brief and turn it into pie and mash-flavoured midget gems, or something similarly high concept and weird.

She beamed in welcome as she reached the stove he stood by, wearing the ancient lace-up shoes he always wore instead of chef's clogs. His footwear had once belonged to the great Escoffier, or so Hervé claimed.

From the side of a huge aluminium pan, the chef fixed Kiki with a baleful eye. 'Kinkee. Nevair in my life 'ave I been asked to produce sumzing like zees!'

'But it looks great, Hervé!' Kiki peered into the pan. It actually was mushy peas! What was more, Hervé had got the green just right. Among the many things she had feared was a violent chip-shop verdancy, but this was tastefully restrained. 'You judged the food colour perfectly.'

From beneath the piercings on his shaved eyebrows, Hervé's brown eyes flashed. 'Colour! There ees no colour!'

He must, Kiki thought, have sourced some very special peas, in that case. Perhaps those from the kitchen garden.

The thrice-gold-medalled horticulturalist had planted at Hervé's request, a rare semi-wild native strain called Duchess Blue. It was very tricky to raise and required a huge amount of expensive attention. Pound for pound, Kiki had once complained to Hervé, they cost as much as pearls. His response to this had been to serve them necklace-style, connected with edible, gold-covered saffron and served in a crab-biscuit jewel box.

'May I taste?'

'*Bien sur!*' Hervé plunged his tattooed forefinger into the mush and brought up a clump which he stuck in his mouth. 'Genius!' he declared, smacking his chops and reinserting the digit. Kiki watched, uncertain about the hygiene but eventually crooking a delicate finger and skimming off a spot.

She tasted, frowning. It was cold, which she had not expected. And very garlicky, which she had not expected either. And there was another taste, bland but slightly nutty, which most definitely was not that of peas, not even Duchess Blue, which had a slightly chickeny flavour. She slipped her finger back in and tasted again, eyes closed, concentrating hard.

The thing was, she knew this taste. This smooth, oily texture, too. Expectation fought recognition. Recognition, in its turn, fought disbelief, but ultimately recognition prevailed. She lowered her finger and raised her chin. Her eyes were cold, angry.

Beneath his red bandanna, the celebrity chef's stubbled face radiated expectation. 'Well? You like, Kinkee?'

'For fuck's sake, Hervé,' Kiki exploded. 'This isn't mushy peas! It's mushy avocados!'

'Is what you show me on smartphone!'

'No it wasn't! That was peas!'

Hervé's eyes were blazing. '*Piss?* Is impossible to make – *piss* – look like – *that!*'

'Hervé, the chip shops of Britain have been doing it for *a hundred years!*'

Hervé twisted his lips. 'Am not interested in shit shops of Britain! You eat mushy piss here? Thank God for Brexit!'

Kiki stormed out of the kitchen, stunned at the disaster that had so unexpectedly presented itself. Pie and mashed avocado! It would be disgusting. She would be a laughing stock.

The fact that Hervé had used every avocado in the place was yet another headache. People were wild about avocado on toast at the moment. It was a favourite on the breakfast menu, usually to fill up after Hervé's minimalist suppers.

Oh God, what was she going to do? She had promised mushy peas for the quiz menu and there had been an enthusiastic take-up.

'Takes me back to my old nan's back-to-back in the alley,' said Sir Jeremy Young, Great Hording's most senior barrister and leader of the 'Legal Eagles' team. He loved to remind everyone of his hard-scrabble background and make it clear that his rise to the top of the Bar was not the routine achievement of someone privately educated.

'We always have mushy peas at the English barbecue in LA,' Tim Lacey put in loudly. 'Kate gets them flown over from Harry Ramsden's.'

But there was no time now to get them flown from Harry Ramsden's. Or anywhere else. There was less than an hour to go. In Great Hording you could get anything from caviar to Kobi beef. The more recherché and expensive it was, the better. Italian village cheese rolled under the knees of octogenarian *nonnas*? *Si!* Sourdough from an Elizabethan bacillus? Verily. Butter churned in a vintage pastis barrel by a former Facebook CEO? You got it. But oven chips, microwave pizza, mushy peas? Forget it. Completely unobtainable.

Kiki thought and thought and thought. She cudgelled her brains into thinking some more. And then, suddenly, she hit on the answer. There *was* one place.

It was not somewhere she had ever imagined being of any use. But right now, it seemed the only hope.

Kiki stumbled out of the kitchen and into the garden. Leaning against the vast silver Koons dog was a filthy racing bike, the ragged tapes on its drop handlebars dangling off.

Staring at it, Kiki remembered Jonny mentioning a new sculpture. Here, presumably, it was. She needed to find a better place to display it than this. But first things first.

She dragged her smartphone from its purpose-built pocket in the flowing Muck Sweat trousers, made a swift search online, then dialled.

CHAPTER THIRTEEN

The shepherd hut looked adorable from the outside, its baby-blue-painted wooden wheels lifting it high off the ground. Laura climbed the short flight of white wooden steps and opened the pretty white wooden door.

'Whoa!'

The shepherd this hut was aimed at was obviously au fait with fashion, like the Shoreditch scythers and weavers she knew. The decor was kitsch irony in overkill. On narrow shelves and along the skirting Disney character lamps jostled with Catholic ephemera. There were photo cubes, bowling pins, snowdomes and Spanish dolls. There was a jukebox, a large plastic Oscar and a giant ice-cream sundae. The walls held framed retro cigarette adverts and images of Elvis.

'Lulu?' Laura called doubtfully. She had been certain it was Lulu she had seen at the window – but it was impossible to now see her among all this hysterically patterned detail.

'Low-ra!' What Laura had thought was a poster of Brigitte Bardot now came to life. A hand flashing with rings waved from some cushions printed with classic rock album covers. Lulu was lying on a bed covered in a crocheted blanket beneath rows of Kim Jong-un bunting. She was swiping away at her phone; approaching, Laura saw she was looking at pictures of houses.

'Is strange place, this pub,' she announced, looking up. 'I ask for croque monsieur,' she added, gesturing at a plate on the floor with a biscuit on it. 'But they send me gingerbread man.'

Laura, hungry as always, bent and broke off the man's leg. Cycling had given her even more of an appetite, as well as aching calves and blisters. The countryside round here looked deceptively flat. 'Croque monsieur?' She took another nibble. The terrain round here wasn't the only thing playing tricks. This biscuit looked like ginger but it tasted amazingly like toasted cheese and ham. 'I think it's a kind of haute cuisine version of it. It might be a joke, croque monsieur, shaped like a man?'

Lulu looked unimpressed at this culinary sally. 'Menu here rubbish,' she complained. 'All essence of beansmoke. I ask toast and avocado, but no avocados, Kiki say. So anyway. You join me in pub squeeze with willage, yes?'

'What?'

It sounded like some sort of gang bang and while Laura would do anything for a story, she drew the line at group sex.

But then the penny dropped. 'Oh, the pub *quiz*!'

The mass of blonde hair nodded up and down.

Laura loved quizzes, they had been one of the few things she had enjoyed at boarding school. Her general knowledge was considerable, largely thanks to her grandmother.

Mimi saw Paris as one big free history, literature and art lesson and as Laura grew up, had taken her to every museum, gallery, cultural site and celebrated garden the city offered.

And yet, for all her knowledge, Laura's team never won the Saturday night inter-house quiz competitions at school. Clemency Makepeace's always did. But only because it cheated.

'You come?' From among the Bowie and Rolling Stones cushions, Lulu's sunglasses were pointed questioningly at her. The gilt trim had a hopeful glint.

'Sure.' Laura suppressed her concerns about Lulu in a knowledge-based competition. Winning didn't matter, anyway. So what if they lost spectacularly, she and a scatty billionheiress alone against Great Hording's finest? She would have great notes for her article.

'Okay, is good.' Lulu broke off Croque Monsieur's arm. 'So now we talk tactics, humm? Special subjects, yes?'

Laura stared. 'You've got one?' Fashion, presumably. Lulu's grasp of that subject was phenomenal. Laura had seen her pick up a single sequin from the logo-carpeted floor of one of her wardrobe rooms and know instantly not only what garment it came from, but which part.

The sunglasses flashed chidingly. 'Am being good at geography.'

'Geography?!'

'Yes! Have visited many countries. And you?'

'Erm, well, I'm quite good on history, art and literature.'

She was expecting Lulu to look impressed, but the full, pink-glossed lips twisted doubtfully. 'Not science, math?'

'Not really,' Laura confessed. She had passed muster in these subjects but no more.

'Is no matter. If not have answer just look up on smartphone, hmm?'

'Lulu!' Laura was outraged. This was precisely the method Clemency Makepeace had used year after year with such success. 'That's cheating!'

Lulu shrugged. 'But we have hole in brain, hmm?'

'Gap in knowledge?' Laura guessed, reaching over and snapping off poor Monsieur Croque's other arm. It was delicious, a million times more so than the deep-fried sausage Kearn had rustled up for her what seemed like hours ago now. They deep-fried everything at the Fishing Boat Inn, he had explained. He had worked out, using thermochemical algorithms, that it was the most economical use of time and energy. He had also offered her mushy peas, which she had declined.

'The quiz might not be that hard,' Laura suggested, without any real conviction. Given Great Hording's leading lights in every imaginable field of expertise, it was likely to be set at a fiendish level.

'Will be impossible!' exclaimed Lulu. 'Kiki tell me set by man in bookshop with mind like mousetrap.'

'Brain like a steel trap,' translated Laura.

The giant sunglasses were flashing agitatedly. 'Will be werry hard and Lulu not like to lose!'

Well, you better prepare for it, Laura thought, looking out of the small shepherd hut window with its ironic net curtains pulled back on little ironic ruffles. Outside, bright green leaves rippled in the breeze and between them Laura could see a van drawing up alongside the rows of shining sports cars – a van so battered and rusting and so utterly out of place in the manicured purlieus of Great Hording that it could only be lost.

Two figures now emerged from the vehicle. They were skinny, hoodied and baseball-capped and one was vaping copiously.

'Kearn!' And what was the other one called? Daz?

Only now did she remember that she had not returned his bike. Was that why Kearn was here? In indignant pursuit? Laura scrambled for the door, sending a pile of eighties electropop singles scattering in her wake.

She emerged from the shepherd hut just in time to see Kearn and Daz loping off towards the pub entrance. They bore on their shoulders packs of green tin cans swathed in plastic. Unlikely as it seemed, they were delivering some kind of food.

But the question of what comestible Kearn, son of an establishment that deep-fried everything, could possibly be delivering to the exclusive Golden Goose, suddenly paled in comparison to what else struck Laura now.

They needed a maths and science specialist for their team. And here, right in front of her, was a man studying thermochemical algorithms.

The bar-room of the Golden Goose was filling up. Rich evening sun slanted through the diamond-pane windows over the York stone flags reclaimed from a brothel in Bahrain. There was the thump of expensive handbags meeting saw-mark-ravaged tables.

Air scented with Diptyque's 'La Plume De Ma Tante' rang with chatter, laughter and excited exclamation, plus the rapid fire of champagne corks. Behind the 'White Riot' lyrics engraved on the front of the bar, Pavel and Rosie struggled to keep up with demand.

Kiki, draped gracefully on a bar stool, watched the corks fly from the champagne bottles. They were selling a record amount, which would help with the deficit created by the eye-watering sum that Kearn from the Fishing Boat Inn had extorted for his cans of mushy peas. But profit had never been the point. The Golden Goose was all about influence. And influence there was here tonight, in spades.

Not that it was necessarily evident. Richard Threadneedle in jeans looked more like a holidaying vicar than the second most powerful man in British banking. At the Politicos table, portly Jolyon Jackson who had been crammed into pinstriped suits all week was now exploding out of jeans and a pink checked shirt. His long-suffering wife Annabel, MD of a children's clothing company called Nanny Knows Best, wore a shapeless shift and a tense expression. Hardly surprising, given that the Politicos team included a pair of the fruity graduates Jolyon had mentioned, lean in wrap dresses, tossing shining hair about and flashing insincere smiles.

On the next table Wonky de Launay, the society florist famous for inventing the jam-jar posy, and Willow St George, the celebrated clean-eating chef credited with making the spiraliser sexy, sat with their hedgefunder husbands. More people who would need to put their phones away, Kiki thought, watching the husbands, with their blue shirts and slightly mullety hair, frowning into their screens. Wonky and Willow were shrieking with Anna Goblemova, the young, blonde and very gorgeous third wife of the thickset village oligarch, Sergei. He too was squinting into his screen with mean little eyes. She would, Kiki nervously decided, leave it to Pavel to tackle him about his phone.

Jeremy Young's barristers all looked suitably terrifying,

lean-faced with hawk eyes and thick pepper-and-salt hair. Evidently eager for battle to commence, they were sipping water in an impatient sort of way.

Zeb Spaw's table, by contrast, were all drunk. According to Pavel, who had ears like a lynx, My Quiz Team had front-loaded on My Absinthe at Etchings, Spaw's mansion just outside the village. Zeb's Vietnamese wife Dung wore a pink fright wig while his Brazilian mistress Carla – the ménage was a perfectly peaceable one, apparently – sported a child's silver plastic tiara. The artist himself wore his usual fur hat, wraparound shades and pleased-with-himself expression.

Something huge and purple caught Kiki's eye: Dame Hermione processing to her seat in one of her regulation pleated tent dresses. She was followed by the rest of Page Turners; of the three middle-aged women, Kiki had heard, the thin and haunted-looking one was Dame Hermione's publicist while the one with badly dyed hair was her long-suffering editor. Of the two egg-bald men with round glasses, the more cheerful-looking one was Dame Hermione's husband Derek. He ran a novelty publishing company producing feline-themed cartoon versions of classic titles. *The Great Catsby* and *Bleak Mouse* made far more money than his wife's Booker winners. Or so rumour had it.

Right at the back, to Kiki's relief, was the empty Dumb Blondes table. So Lulu had seen sense and decided not to turn up. She was less relieved about the so-far-empty Merely Players table – had that pompous old boot Lady Mandy decided to chuck the quiz after all? And where was Development Hell – that overbearing midget Tim Lacey, his train of Hollywood producers and his hot young star? Kiki groaned inwardly. She should have known better than give those teams such a prominent position. Now everyone could see her failure.

However, Lady Mandy or no, Tim Lacey or no, the show must begin. The crowd were getting restive and, in the kitchen, God only knew what was happening to the mushy peas. The sooner they were out on plates the better.

Peter Delabole was trying to catch her eye. She felt grateful for the comforting smile he now flashed her. His quiz questions were filed neatly in a plastic folder next to the discreet half of bitter before him. No witty craft beers or hipster gins for him, Kiki thought admiringly, giving him the thumbs up.

Peter descended from his stool, cleared his throat and immediately the crowd fell quiet. He had such authority, Kiki thought, watching the lean figure in the cords and graph-paper shirt with longing. But then she reminded herself she never slept down, only up. Although after tonight, if the teams didn't get here, she might not be sleeping anywhere.

Peter Delabole looked about him with a cryptic smile. 'My lords, ladies and gentlemen. The moment you have all been waiting for. Tonight's inaugural Golden Goose Quiz can now begin.'

CHAPTER FOURTEEN

Few men could resist Laura in full persuasive throttle. Kearn was certainly not one of them. Within seconds he was putty in her hands and signed up to the Dumb Blondes quiz team. 'But I'm not blonde,' he bleated, as, now, he crossed the car park between the two of them.

'Me neither,' Laura reassured him. 'Don't worry, it's only a tactic. Lulu wants everyone to underestimate us.'

Another group was arriving, shuffling in the bumptious wake of someone short with thick white hair, a red face and modish blue glasses. He looked, Laura thought, like the Union Jack.

'Come on!' he shouted over his shoulder. 'Don't you just love quizzes? Reminds me of *University Challenge*.'

'I used to watch that on telly,' said a young man slouching at the back of the group with what might have been reluctance. He was resplendent in baggy orange trousers, a shirt of hysterical pattern and a jaunty pork pie hat.

That voice! Slightly croaky, drawling, satirical. Recognition ricocheted through Laura, jangling every nerve-ending. But how could it be?

The red-faced man stopped and turned to the hat. 'I didn't *watch* it, lovey, I was *in* it. *Won* it, in fact! Me, Richard Curtis, Eddie Redmayne and Tom Hiddleston!'

The hat slowed down further and allowed the gap to widen before hissing, to nobody in particular, 'Pompous twat!'

That was it for Laura. Before she could stop herself, she sprang forward.

'Caspar!'

The hat stopped and straightened up, shocked. A confused hand pushed the straw brim yet further back. A pair of round brown eyes met hers, then rolled slowly up and down the length of her. 'Laura Lake,' said Caspar. 'You look fantastic.'

'You look. . .' Laura paused, taking in the silly hat, the open Hawaiian shirt, the sequinned flip-flops and the orange trousers with their tight legs and huge baggy bottom, 'like a film star, I guess.'

'Like a wanker you mean?' Caspar looked himself wryly up and down. 'If you think this is bad, you should see the rest of Tinseltown. At least I haven't got guybrows and a man-bun. Not yet, anyway.'

Lulu and Kearn, the latter with a disbelieving look at Caspar, had gone on ahead into the Golden Goose. 'What are you doing here?' Laura demanded.

'My agent made me. Tim Lacey might direct the next

Bond, apparently. If I want to keep my job I need to keep him onside.'

So that was who the short guy was. Laura wrinkled her brow. 'But – Bond films? Doesn't Tim Lacey make cheesy romcoms?'

Caspar altered the angle of his hat despairingly. 'Precisely. I'll be starring in films called *Thunderball, Actually* and *The Man with the Golden Wedding Invitation*.'

Laura snorted. She had forgotten how funny Caspar was. The memory of his flakiness was still strong, however. Their last phone conversation came back to her. The magazine interview he had promised and failed to deliver.

'I've got a bone to pick with you.'

'I know, I know. The interview.' Caspar took off his hat and ruffled his hair, an appealing gesture which, despite Laura's efforts not to let it, appealed. 'My agent again. He made me go with *Vogue*. 'If it had been up to me. . .'

He had hold of her hands now, his touch shooting bolts of excitement up her arms and straight into her heart. He was staring into her eyes with that melting gaze that had charmed Bond girls, Moneypenny, Laura herself in the past. Even Mimi, sternest of judges, had found Caspar irresistible.

'Bugger off, Caspar!' Laura shoved him away. 'Stop acting. You're not in front of the cameras now.'

'No, much more importantly, I'm in front of you!'

Caspar took a step forward and before Laura could say or do anything, she was in his arms and his tongue was in her mouth. She struggled to resist, but soon found herself submitting and then kissing him back with equal ardour.

Feeling her pelvis start to melt, Laura realised this was leading in one direction only. A direction she had vowed never to go again, especially as she now had a boyfriend. Sort of.

She pulled her mouth away. 'For fuck's sake, Caspar!'

'I couldn't have put it better myself.' His large eyes were narrow with lust and his breath was coming fast and short. 'Oh God, Laura. Can't we go somewhere. Like, now?'

He took her hand and placed it deep in the baggy folds of his trousers. What was within was as stiff as a baseball bat and more or less the same size. 'I've got a room upstairs, not that I've been in it.'

Laura's fingers closed around the baseball bat. She swallowed, seriously tempted.

Caspar's sweating palms skimmed the breasts below her shirt. 'Christ, Laura. Still not wearing a bra. Talk about chapel hat pegs. . .'

That broke the spell. 'Sod off, Caspar. We're entered in a quiz, or have you forgotten?'

'I'd much rather enter something else,' Caspar lamented, as she dragged him to the Golden Goose's entrance. 'Might you relent and see me later?' he begged, as they approached the bar, from which whoops and shouts of a football-stadium level were issuing.

Things were clearly already going with a swing.

Laura eyed him. Harry shot across her mind, then out the other side. She hadn't heard from him for weeks. And Caspar had form as a red-hot lover. And it had been a long time.

'Maybe,' she said, then led him into the fray.

★

Kiki, sitting at the end of the bar with a glass of champagne, was watching events unfold with the satisfied air of one who had done her utmost and was now reaping the reward.

There were a few flies in the ointment, even so. Lulu's turning up to take part had been a nasty shock, especially given that her teammate was big-nosed Kearn from the Fishing Boat Inn who had so royally ripped her off over the mushy peas. Normally she would have thrown him out, not least because the sight of him might upset Kate Threadneedle. But he was with the unbudgeable Lulu, who would certainly not go without a fight. A scene was the last thing Kiki wanted.

Given that Lulu was there, it was just as well Lady Mandy and Savannah Bouche weren't, but neither was the promised Hollywood superstar on Tim Lacey's Development Hell team. Kiki didn't recognise any of them.

Still, Peter had been an inspired choice as questionmaster. Apparently unruffled by the size and excitability of the crowd, he had explained clearly, calmly and with great care the rules of the quiz. There were to be two halves with ten rounds, each on a different subject. There would be five questions in each round. Answers were to be written on the sheets provided on the tables. At the end of each round, sheets were to be handed to the next table for marking. The sheets with the final scores on were to be given to Peter, who would maintain a running total. There was to be no, repeat no, use of smartphones.

Wackademicals, the Oxbridge dons and historians' team, was already on a roll. The first round, Hit and Myth, had contained a lot of questions about gods and they had celebrity TV classicist Margaret Tache on their team. Her trademark long auburn plait swished excitedly about as she bent over the table in one of her trademark togas, whispering the right answer. No one would have understood if she had spoken aloud, as she was communicating in Latin.

The teams swapped sheets at the end of the round, as per Peter's instructions. The answers to round one were read out, amid much groaning, apart from among the Wackademicals, where Margaret Tache was punching the air and shouting, 'Victrix!'

Two latecomers now entered the bar. Kiki's heart soared with the mixed hope and dread that it might be Savannah. But this lean girl with long dark hair cut in a fringe, dark jeans and a tight, dark-blue shirt, was much too tall. Savannah, as was well known, was a midget.

The man, who wore orange baggy trousers, looked much more familiar. Really, really familiar. Kiki gave a strangled yelp, and her glass wobbled dangerously in her hand.

'Miss Cavendish?' Pavel was leaning enquiringly over the bar. Kiki felt a wet sensation on her tummy. She had spilled her champagne. But she could not have cared less.

She had been quite wrong about the lack of Hollywood superstars. Making his way across the reclaimed Bahraini Yorkshire flagstones was one of the most recognisable actors in the world. Caspar Honeyman, the reigning Bond. The reason she had been made to buy all the 007 biscuits was now clear.

Slimey's People, the security service team put together by MI6 boss Sir Philip Peaseblossom, might have been expected to greet the arrival of their fictional counterpart with derision. But they were staring more than anyone, Kiki saw.

'Caspar! Dear boy, we were wondering where you'd got to!' Feeling the eyes of the room upon his star guest, Tim

Lacey rose to divert them to himself. 'You're just in time for the history round!'

'How's it going?' whispered Laura, slipping in next to Kearn.

'Not bad. Lulu turns out to be quite good at mythology. We didn't get as many right as they did.' Kearn nodded towards the Wackademicals, who included, Laura saw, the well-known TV historians Mary Horsley with her trademark side-parting and Guy Winter with his trademark smoulder. 'But we're keeping our head above water.'

Laura eyed the equipment on the table. Besides the sheets to be used for the answers, scrap paper had been provided to work out the various clues. Laura slid a couple of sheets towards herself. Between questions she would take notes for her article.

Questionmaster, dishy in a low-key way, she wrote. *Could do with haircut though.*

Peter smiled benignly around. 'First question. A tricky one, this. What links Louis XV with the colour purple and Britain's national dish?'

'I know that!' Laura was filled with excitement. She leant forward. 'It's pompadour! The Marquise de Pompadour's real name was Jeanne Poisson – fish – fish and chips is the British national dish. Pompadour's also the name of a purple flag.' Mimi had been especially hot on the mistresses of the French kings.

Lulu's eyes were round with amazement. Kearn wrote the answer down.

At the Wackademicals table, all was not well. 'Actually, I don't know absolutely *everything* about history,' Guy Winter muttered defensively.

Mary Horsley was looking equally blank. She was famous

for fronting her programmes wearing the clothes of the period under scrutiny, and to judge from her leg o'mutton sleeves and flower-heaped straw boater, the current project was Edwardian.

'Our national dish is chicken tikka masala, surely!' Jolyon Jackson was stage-whispering at the Politicos table. 'And Louis XV was well known to be a massive fan of curries. Purple ones especially.'

Typical Jackson bullshit, thought Laura, rapidly taking notes. She knew from her monitoring of the papers that the minister routinely waffled about subjects of which he knew nothing. With an election looming, he had been waffling even more than usual.

'Next history question.' Peter smiled round. 'Who was the little gentleman in black velvet?'

The Wackademicals continued to look at each other blankly. 'Dudley Moore?' ventured Mary Horsley. 'Ronnie Corbett? Jamie Cullum?'

They don't actually know anything, wrote Laura gleefully.

'Look, the researchers do most of the work on the programmes, okay?' Guy Winter huffed.

'Don't ask me how I know this,' Laura hissed *sotto voce* to her teammates. 'But it's the mole that made the molehill that William III's horse stumbled over.'

'Amazingballs!' exclaimed Lulu, while Kearn scribbled it down.

The next round was art, or You've Been Framed.

'Yay!' cheered the artists, most of whom were now so drunk they could hardly sit up.

Peter smiled at them serenely. 'Question one. What was Giotto's O?'

The artists stared back at him indignantly. 'Who's what?'

'The O of Giotto. The famous Renaissance artist?' Peter prompted, his eyebrow raised.

The famous contemporary artist looked at his colleagues. 'What's he fuckin' talkin' about?'

'I know!' whispered Laura. 'The Pope in the thirteenth century wanted to find the best artist in Italy. Giotto would only draw an O on a piece of paper but it was a really perfect one and the Pope gave him the gig on the back of it.'

As her teammates stared at her, impressed, Peter cleared his throat.

'Next art question. What was Picasso's middle name?'

Zeb Spaw leant over his table. 'Bert,' he hissed. 'Definitely.'

'Is Ruiz!' whispered Lulu. 'My father have Picasso on second biggest yacht.'

The next round, Let's Get Physical, was about science, although Jolyon Jackson, cuddling up to his fruity cuties, seemed to have another interpretation in mind. Kearn knew all the answers to this round, and to the subsequent Your Number's Up maths one. Lulu was as good as her word in the geography round. She really had shopped all over the world.

'Paramaribo, is in Surinam!' she whispered to Laura, who was manning the pen. 'Know well, have nice Chanel saleslady.'

The next round, News and Views, was current affairs.

The Politicos, eager to demonstrate their credentials, greeted each question with knowing laughter followed by much conspiratorial huddling.

Something caught Kiki's eye towards the end of the round. Something rectangular and very bright, glowing in the darkness below Jolyon Jackson's table. Recognising the landing page of a well-known search engine, Kiki realised that the Defence Minister of the government seeking re-election was using the internet to answer a question about his very own Prime Minister.

She gripped the base of the fresh champagne glass that Pavel had recently passed her. Should she say anything? But Jackson would be sure to deny it, shameless liar and perjurer as he was. He would bluster and face her down. It would be her word against his hundreds of words. And this was only a pub quiz anyway, not a matter of national importance. She would say nothing. No one else had noticed, anyway.

At the end of the quiz Peter brought the papers to Kiki. 'We have a problem,' he whispered.

Her heart sank. Had Peter seen Jolyon too?

'The Dumb Blondes.' Peter shook a piece of paper. Kiki frowned. They couldn't possibly have won, could they? An airhead party girl, the boy from the Fishing Boat Inn and some anonymous brunette surely could not triumph over the cream of Great Hording.

Kiki took the paper and looked at it. But instead of the totals she was expecting, she saw scribbled notes. Snatches of conversation and incidents from the evening. *Buffoonish minister. . . historians know bugger all. . . Kiki Cavendish, mutton dressed as lamb. . .*

Kiki looked up angrily. 'Who wrote this?' Was it Kearn? But the handwriting looked feminine, loopy, almost French.

Peter met her gaze gravely. 'We have a spy in the ranks,' he said.

CHAPTER FIFTEEN

Laura's head was spinning with the victory champagne Lulu had insisted on buying. Theoretically, the Politicos had taken the trophy. But Kearn had incontrovertible evidence that the Dumb Blondes had won. His mathematical brain had kept tabs on every table simultaneously and recalculated the relative scores after every round.

Laura, long used to losing quizzes she had actually won, was philosophical, especially with Caspar dragging impatiently at her hand.

Lulu had been indignant at first about the victory of the Jackson team. 'Cannot believe arse.'

'Ears, Lulu.'

But her sorrows were soon drowned in Dom Perignon and a long chat with Anna Goblemova about Dolce & Gabbana.

Kearn's view was that such beastliness was to be expected

of Britain's corrupt political overlords. He was looking forward to updating Wyatt when she came back from her enforced perfume course. 'I've spoken to her just now, she's making one called Money,' he told Laura.

'Money?'

'Yes, so people can literally stink of the stuff. She's expecting it to go like hot cakes in Great Hording.' With that, Kearn went off to find his bike and cycle back to the Fishing Boat Inn.

'By the big silver dog in the garden,' Laura told him, aware of an impatient Caspar at her elbow. He had just been nobbled by Wonky de Launay. 'I hope you don't think I'm being critical,' gushed the proprietor of Spirit of the Hedgerow, Chelsea's most fashionable and expensive florist, 'but I've noticed the flowers in Bond films are looking a bit tired. Those big eighties displays. I could come on set and update them. A few trailing field blossoms here and there. . .'

As Caspar looked bewildered, Laura hid a smile. Willow St George had joined in now, perfectly toned arms pushing back dark hair as long and straight as a waterfall. 'And I could update some of the food refs. Bond needs to ditch the martinis, for a start. Right now it's all about chilli and swamp moss shots, packed with toxin-blasting pond vitamins.'

Elsewhere, the bar-room was heaving with the great and the good and their post-mortem quiz chat.

'You bastard, Jackson!' Sir Jeremy Young punched the minister good-humouredly on the shoulder. 'Might have known you'd get the one about the PM's favourite crisp flavour. Pipped us at the bloody post.'

Kearn came up to Laura. 'My bike's on a plinth in the garden.'

Laura frowned. 'Leaning against a plinth, you mean?'

'No, on one. Like it's a statue or something.'

Laura advised him to wrench the bike off and strode after Caspar, who had finally escaped Wonky and Willow.

'Remember, buttercups and wild garlic!' the former called after him.

'Double-distilled orange-pip alcohol!' yelled the latter.

Caspar's room at the Golden Goose was every bit as luxurious as Laura had imagined. Walls painted a soothing sage were pierced with deep mullioned windows set with black-leaded diamond-pane glass. The polished wooden floor was scattered with toe-sinking sheepskin rugs. Deep armchairs in green tweed check had contrasting throws tossed over the back. The bed was big, four-postered and piled with white linen. There were lamps everywhere, silk-pleated shades on vintage bases, and the occasional rustic antique.

'Ooh, biscuits!' A Taking the Biscuit presentation box sat on the bed. Laura pounced. The half-time pie and mushy peas had been far from substantial. Three dots of green sauce – the peas, presumably – had been presented alongside an inch-square cube of pie. White plates the size of a hub cap had made it all look minuscule.

Laura carefully peeled off the Union flag sticker sealing the pink tissue paper and held up a man-shaped confection wearing an icing black tuxedo. 'It's you!'

Caspar looked indignant. 'The legs are far too short!'

Laura suppressed a snort. The fact was, Caspar, while extremely handsome, was slightly lacking on the height front. Particularly compared to tall men like Harry.

But she could not think about Harry now. Especially as

Caspar was pulling her down on the bed. Laura unbuttoned her shirt and prepared to relinquish all inhibition. Caspar was a daring, imaginative lover who liked novel positions. He was sure to have put the time since they last had sex to good use. This would be lovemaking Tinseltown style.

Her expectations were more than met. Caspar was eager to demonstrate a new range of moves called the Hollywood Kama Sutra.

'This one's called the Casting Couch,' he was explaining, when something caught Laura's ear. She twisted the right way round and disentangled herself. 'What's that noise?'

Something loud was approaching, *thubba thubba thubba*. It sounded like a helicopter.

Caspar took no notice. He closed in on her again. 'And this one's called Basic Instinct. You sit there with your legs crossed. . .'

Laura pushed him aside. The sound of blades whipping the air was as unmistakable as it was deafening. 'It sounds as if it's landing in this room!'

'Oh, the chopper.' Caspar yawned. 'Hear them so often these days I hardly notice.'

Laura was at the window. What looked like a vast, gleaming black insect was lowering itself into the sculpture garden, right on top of the giant silver Jeff Koons dog. Except that, as Laura watched, the dog was sinking into the earth, leaving behind it a large rubberised circle painted with a huge white 'H'.

'What's going on?' Caspar demanded from behind. As Laura explained, he yawned elaborately. 'Integral helipad sculptures are so ten minutes ago in Malibu. Now it's all about pools converting to parking for private jets.'

The helicopter landed and the whirring blades slowed,

then stopped. The black-tinted door of the cockpit now opened and loud, yappy barks could be heard. Laura's eyes widened. Was flying your pets about by helicopter a thing in Great Hording? But before she could identify the dog owner, or check whether the animals were in their own chopper with dedicated pilot, Caspar's hand closed round her wrist and she found herself pulled back towards the bed. All desire for journalistic detail now left her, to be replaced by desire of another kind entirely.

Afterwards, they lay smoking amid the huge white pillows, tricking the smoke alarm by exhaling towards the open windows. 'Wow,' said Laura, not entirely satirically. 'I've just been screwed by James Bond.'

Caspar groaned. 'Must you?'

'What?'

'Mention Bond. I was just trying to forget him for five seconds.'

Laura propped herself on her elbow to face him. 'The burden of fame?'

'It's bloody tough, let me tell you,' Caspar whined. 'The workouts are a nightmare.' He raised a vast tanned bicep. 'And I've got to go jogging every morning. I hate jogging! Loathe it!'

'Oh, come on, Caspar. It's better than when you were a struggling actor.'

A theatrical sigh. 'You know, I kind of miss that?'

Laura was astounded. 'Miss dressing as a Grenadier Guard on stilts outside the Royal London Experience?'

'At least it was. . .' Caspar paused. 'What's the word?'

'Crap?'

'No.'

'Embarrassing?'

'Authentic.'

Laura changed tack. 'Well, what about that flat in Brixton?' It had been the most disgusting thing she had ever seen.

Caspar shook his thick, dark hair regretfully. 'You know, I kind of miss that too? It had character.'

'Well, it didn't have a loo seat,' Laura reminded him. 'Or any cutlery. You all used the same spatula to eat cold baked beans from the tin.'

'Happy days!'

Laura was sitting up on the bed now, slender arms folded over her naked breasts. 'The French call this *nostalgie de la boue*,' she told him. 'Nostalgia for the mud. Looking back fondly on a ghastly way of life you couldn't wait to escape at the time.'

Caspar let his head fall back among the pillows. 'You're right, of course.' He shot out a contemplative smoke ring. 'I am supremely fortunate to be the current face of a half-century-old five-billion-dollar franchise whose plots have spanned the globe, the sexual revolution. . .'

'But the Bond girl's called Prudence Handjob!'

'You should have heard what they wanted to call her. It wasn't Hand, I can tell you that. Anyway, as I was saying, 007's survived the Cold War, 9/11, the title *Octopussy* and George Lazenby. So why,' Caspar wailed, rolling his head to face hers and looking tragic, 'aren't I *happy*?'

Laura was speechless. Fame was all Caspar had ever wanted. 'You poor, poor thing,' she eventually managed, ironically.

Caspar took this at face value. 'I know! It's unbelievable.' His manicured hand met his moisturised forehead. 'Why does no one take me seriously?'

Laura stared. 'But you're playing James Bond. No one takes him seriously.'

Caspar reared up in the bed, eyes blazing. 'But why not? Our production values are sky high! And I'm a brilliant actor!'

Laura eyed him cautiously. Caspar had always been self-deluded, but this was on a whole new level.

'I've looked at the algorithms,' he went on excitedly. 'Adultery and murder have never been out of style. Nudity peaked in the seventies though.'

'What are you talking about?'

'Oscar nominations, of course. Haddock's been looking at the stats.'

'Haddock?'

'My English butler in Malibu. Didn't I mention him?'

Laura suppressed a smile. 'So what has, um, Haddock come up with?'

Caspar took a deep breath, closed his eyes and let rip. 'One in every seven Oscar-winning movies has been about World War Two. Husbands and wives are the most common relationship in Oscar-nominated films. The commonist occupation is a doctor. Nearly one in five scenes are set in restaurants.'

Laura considered. 'So if you have a war film with a married doctor in a restaurant, you'll sweep the board?'

Caspar ignored her. 'Plenty of British spies in World War Two,' he stated confidently. 'And Bond spends a lot of time in restaurants. He also knows lots of doctors – Dr No, for instance.'

'So what are you saying?'

Caspar looked at her indignantly. 'Isn't it obvious? That we should start thinking of Bond as an award-winner. Oscars might be some way off, admittedly. . .'

He stopped and glared at Laura again, as if daring her to agree.

'But there are others. The International Film Awards, for one. Known as the Ivys. They're new, it's the first ceremony this year, but people think they'll be very prestigious. Be good if Bond could win one. Something's got to make it all worth it,' Caspar groaned.

Laura had heard enough.

'Check your privilege!' she scolded. 'Remember how desperately jealous you used to be of Orlando Chease!'

Caspar snorted at the reminder of his former great rival, who had – albeit briefly – previously been in the frame for the Bond part. 'God, where is *he* now?'

'About half a mile away.'

'You're joking.'

'No, really. He lives here, well, his parents do.' She had picked this up from Kearn. 'They were all supposed to be at the quiz, I think.'

Caspar's attention had wandered. He was rummaging in the biscuit tin and picking out an iced Moneypenny. Then he dropped it with a groan.

Laura eyed him ironically. 'What's the matter? Her legs too short as well?'

'No, it's the bloody diet. Practically all I am allowed to eat is egg whites.' Caspar rubbed his smooth, well-tended face. 'Honestly, Laura, I used to think that line about money not bringing you happiness was a lie made up by rich people to stop the rest of us murdering them.'

'You mean it isn't?'

'No!' Caspar clutched his hair theatrically, although not hard enough, Laura noticed, to actually risk pulling any of it out. 'Money *can't* buy you love, Laura.'

Laura's thoughts flew to Savannah Bouche. It could certainly buy her. Was she still with South'n Fried? Things seemed to have gone rather quiet on that front.

Caspar's large, brown, long-lashed eyes were trained on her meaningfully, Laura noticed. He now flashed her his most sincere smile. 'Which is why it's just so great to be back with you, babe.'

'Back?' She raised an eyebrow. They had never exactly been a couple in the first place. Just where was this leading?

'I've missed you,' Caspar murmured, edging his body on to hers again. 'You're the only woman I've ever really loved.'

'Oh yeah?'

His brown eyes were wide with sincerity. 'It's true. I'll never forget how we met.'

'On Amy Bender's bed!' They had been part of a contemporary art installation in Paris. Laura giggled at the memory.

He was gazing at her beseechingly. 'We'll always have Paris, won't we, Laura?'

'What exactly do you want, Caspar? We've had the sex, you don't have to smarm up to me any more.'

Caspar looked hurt. 'It's not just sex, Laura. I think you and I could have a meaningful relationship.'

Laura was so surprised that her mind entirely emptied for a moment. When everything reloaded, there was Harry. She felt suddenly terribly guilty. But why? He obviously wasn't worrying about her.

'But what about Merlot?'

'Who?'

'Merlot D'Vyne? Who played Prudence?'

'That's over.' Caspar was playing with her hair. 'She really wasn't very deep.'

'You mean you are?'

Caspar sighed. 'Stop getting at me. I want to be with someone I can trust. You can't imagine the flaky women out there.'

Like Savannah Bouche, for instance. 'I think I can,' Laura assured him.

Caspar was turning his warmest and most sincere gaze up to melting point. 'Now I've found you again, I don't want to let you go.'

'Well, it wouldn't have taken Sherlock Holmes to find me. I've been sitting in the *Society* office five days a week for over a year.'

'Laura, I'm serious. You're the woman for me.'

But are you the man for me? Caspar was notoriously unreliable. He had let her down before. Because of him, she had been alone and vulnerable in London. But she had found her own way in the end, spectacularly well too, which was why, try as she might to summon up those old feelings of anger, Laura couldn't.

He put his face close to hers. His breath held only the faintest suggestion of mushy peas, with an after-tang of champagne. 'Laura. Listen to what I'm saying. I love you.'

Difficult words to resist, of course. And when delivered by a devastatingly handsome man she was, despite herself, extremely fond of and helplessly drawn to, all the more irresistible. For all her efforts not to let it, a flash of excited hope went through Laura. She believed in love – she had grown up in Paris, after all. Like all French women she loved the idea of love as much, if not more, than love itself.

He was nuzzling her neck now. 'Actually, I adore you.'

She arched her back and angled her chin so she was

staring at the room's beamed ceiling. How many lovers, over the centuries, had looked up at these same beams?

He had hold of both her hands and was wrapping her arms round himself. She felt herself ricochet wildly between steady self-belief – of course he should love her, Caspar was a flaky worm and she was a wonderful person – to absolute disbelief because one of the most famous film stars on the planet was begging for her affections.

'Say you'll be with me!' he implored.

She felt her grip of the situation slipping. Time had passed, after all, since their last encounter. Perhaps he had changed, and not just in the sense that his formerly hairy chest was now waxed smooth and the colour of butterscotch and his formerly soft tummy was a rigid six-pack. Should she let herself trust him? Or would he – yet again – turn out to be a huge and hurtful waste of time?

One of Mimi's maxims floated to the front of her mind. 'Just because you have only one life doesn't mean you should be afraid of wasting it.'

'But you're in LA, with Haddock,' she pointed out. 'Next door to Cher.'

'Great woman!' put in Caspar quickly. 'You're gonna love her! She's so funny. Know what she said to me the other day? "Gee, Caspar, I can't believe I'm still dancing about on a stage. I thought I'd be dead by now."' He shook his head. 'Awesome.'

Laura cut off further celebrity reminiscences. 'And I'm based in London.'

To where she would return tomorrow, in fact. She felt a powerful, terrible longing to stay here, in this soothing sage-white room, and make love to Caspar for ever.

'London! But that's great!'

'Why great? It's about three thousand miles from Malibu.'

'The Ivys!' There were lightbulb signs in his eyes. 'They're being held in London! You can come with me! It'll be your first official outing as the new woman in my life!'

Laura stared. 'Is that what this is all about? You just want me as arm candy at an awards ceremony?'

Caspar laughed long and hard at this. When he recovered he said, 'Are you joking? There's no way I'd take you if I didn't love you. When was the last time that hair saw a salon?'

'How dare you? And, anyway, you haven't even been nominated yet.'

'No, but I will be. Come here.' He closed her objections with his lips. 'We hardly started the Hollywood Kama Sutra. Let me show you the Executive Producer.'

CHAPTER SIXTEEN

Laura awoke to find sun streaming across the Golden Goose's crisp white duvet. Through the fishnet effect of the diamond-pane windows the sky showed a sparkling blue. It was going to be a beautiful day. A beautiful day with Caspar. They could go down to the beach, walk hand in hand at the edge of the sand, paddle in the frothing waves, show the glamorous families that she too knew how to enjoy herself.

Laura stretched luxuriously, extending her arm to touch Caspar's warm, still-sleeping body. It touched only rumpled cotton, however. She sat up. Caspar had gone. A note lay on the sheet in his familiar uncertain handwriting and yet more uncertain spelling. 'Soz, babes, had to go jogging. Then being picked up by limo. You looked too beautiful to wake up. See you at the Ivys. Be in touch soon. Cxxxx'.

He had added for good measure a particularly crude drawing of one of their more adventurous positions.

Laura sighed, rolled over on to her stomach and stared at the window. The sky outside seemed less blue now. Why hadn't he woken her and taken her with him? He would be going back to London to get his plane, after all.

Why were men always leaving her in bed? She was an independent woman with a brilliant career – well, it would be, once she had written her article about Great Hording. She was beholden to no one and she made her own way.

Laura threw back the duvet and sprang out of bed. She had work to do, an investigation to begin. No time like the present, Laura thought, diving under the power-shower and gasping at the Niagara force of it. And really, it was just as well Caspar had gone. Her cover would have been, not just blown, but blasted to smithereens. She would see him soon anyway, at the Ivys.

She finished in the bathroom and put the clothes abandoned last night on the floor back on. Fortunately they were so tight the creases did not show. Then she closed the door and slipped downstairs. She was hungry, as always in the mornings, and the smell of coffee, for a half-Frenchwoman especially, was almost too much to bear. Breakfast was one of the few subjects over which she and Mimi disagreed; the latter always skipped it, with an eye to her *ligne*. But the Englishwoman in Laura was partial to her morning toast and marmalade. To bacon sandwiches even more, and she could smell those too. According to a brochure she had half-read in Caspar's loo, the pub did legendary ones, with meat from rare-breed pigs fed on ambrosia and served in golden sourdough with ketchup in diamond-encrusted bottles. Or something like that.

But they were not for her this morning. She had to get out of the pub without Kiki Cavendish seeing her. The manager definitely now had suspicions. Last night she had cast many a dark look over at the Dumb Blondes table and there had been an obvious confab with the question-setter about whether they could be allowed to win (the answer, obviously, had been no). But it was more than that; her notes had gone missing. Laura had a horrible feeling that she had handed them in by mistake, thinking that they were answer sheets. That Kiki was now on to her was all her own fault.

Loud voices were coming from the bar as Laura tiptoed down the stairs. She recognised the booming tones of Jolyon Jackson the Defence Minister, but not bantering, as last night when he had been the life and soul of the party. He sounded incandescent with rage and was yelling about press intrusion, a bloody cheek, a gross breach of trust, a private event and what the hell fuck shit did Kiki think she was doing?

Laura reached the bottom of the stairs. The pub's rose-fringed front door stood open before her. Bright morning light, spilling over the stone floor, lit a shining path to the outside, to freedom. No one would see her leave. But if a government minister was shouting at the manager about press intrusion, it was Laura's job as a reporter to know why. Especially if, as seemed likely, her lost notes had something to do with it. Damn the moment of triumphal madness that had distracted her attention and made her hand in her papers with the rest!

She turned back towards the entrance to the bar, revising as she did her previously critical view of the pub's excess of hipster decoration. The retro one-armed bandit and the old-fashioned twist-handle bubble-gum machine had a useful space between them. One in which she could listen without being seen, whilst hearing and seeing everything. Laura slid in and crouched down. What exactly was going on?

'How dare you let an arsing journalist in the bar?' the Defence Minister was yelling. 'We don't do journalists in Great Hording! That's the whole arsing point of it!'

Within the bar, amid the strange slash-top tables and bizarre scribbly wallpaper, Jolyon Jackson was still going at Kiki hammer and tongs. His broad back, made broader still by a vast rugby shirt in belligerent red and black stripes, was turned to Laura. In front of him she could just see Kiki, resplendent in several vest tops at once and the trademark flowing black trousers. She was twisting her hair up frantically into its pencil and her eyes, bereft of the glasses which had slid off her nose and were swinging from their chains, were wide and scared, as well they might be.

Jackson picked up a broadsheet newspaper from the neat pile in which the Sunday press was customarily arranged at the Golden Goose and shook it hard. The property, money and homes sections slithered from the bundle and crashed on to the polished stone floor.

'Look at this!' Jackson's huge, hairy hand, its signet ring flashing in agitation, shook the paper's front page. 'It's a disaster!'

Kiki took a deep breath and positioned her reading glasses carefully back on her nose as if she was seeing the headline for the first time and had not set eyes on it at five that morning when Pavel, having been to get the papers from the newsagent in Lowestoft, knocked on her door and tactfully left an edition on the threshold before slipping away. Just as well, as Kiki, plucked from deep sleep to grab a towel about her before opening the door, had let it go in sheer horror after looking down to see these words leap up at her from the front page.

JACKSON CHEAT SENSATION!
New Profumo Affair erupts at posh village pub quiz

Beneath the headline was a huge photograph of the Defence Minister checking his smartphone under the table with obvious furtive intent. This in itself was no surprise to Kiki; she herself had seen him flout the rules. The question was, who had taken the picture?

'They're comparing me to Profumo!' Jackson wailed. 'A man who had to resign after it emerged that he was sleeping with the same woman as an arsing Russian diplomat!'

Kiki furrowed her tanned brow. She was well informed on many subjects; reigning celebrities, in-vogue decorative styles, what suited the fashionable over-fifty. But she had little knowledge of history. 'I'm not sure I follow, Mr Jackson. You're not sleeping with the same woman as an arsing. . . I mean a Russian diplomat.'

Jackson's huge hairy hands clutched despairingly at his face. 'Can't you arsing see? They're drawing a parallel, making the point that I'm a defence minister who's done something untrustworthy. They're saying if I can't even obey the rules of a pub quiz, how can I be trusted with keeping the country safe?'

Kiki didn't disagree. The thought of Jolyon Jackson with his finger on the nuclear button had never been especially reassuring. But the interests of Jonny Welsh and the Golden Goose took priority. Her erstwhile lover had already been on the phone several times this morning demanding an explanation.

In her hiding place beside the one-armed bandit, Laura was staring though the plastic top of the sixties bubblegum machine. Had Jonny Welsh been there he would have explained that the gumballs inside were absolutely of the period, tracked down at great effort and expense on an obscure East European website specialising in vintage British sweets.

Laura was not looking at them, however. Focused on the events in the bar-room, she was rigid with excitement. A wide reader, interested in politics, she knew all about the Profumo affair. The gravity of Jackson's situation was immediately obvious to her. It may have been just a pub quiz, but this could well be a resignation issue.

The penny finally dropped with Kiki too. 'You mean you'll have to resign?' she said to Jackson, trying to keep the hope out of her voice. The village only tolerated him because of his political influence. Without it he would be run out of town, as Roger Slutt had been.

'Of course I arsing won't!' The red face was now very close to hers. 'Who took the photos?'

Wedged in between the bubblegum machine and the one-armed bandit, Laura was asking herself the same question. It seemed to her that it could have been practically anyone. Everyone in the bar last night had smartphones. But why would they betray the village and compromise everyone's privacy? A Pyrrhic victory of this nature simply didn't make sense.

Kiki folded her arms. A light gleamed in her eye as she faced down the furious minister. 'I do have a suspect,' she told him.

Laura leaned forward in her gap, the better to hear.

One of Jackson's mighty red fists made contact with a roughly sawn table top. 'Ow!' he yelled, shaking out the sausage-like digits. 'Tell me who they are! I'll kill them. I don't care if they're Lady Mandy arsing Chease!'

Between the retro machines, Laura held her breath. Great Hording was turning out to be a far better story than she could ever have hoped for.

'It's not Lady Mandy,' Kiki said, regretfully. She paused before delivering, with a drama even Lady Mandy might have appreciated, 'It's that ghastly little oik from the Fishing Boat Inn!'

Laura clapped a hand to her mouth to stop herself shouting in protest. She had been with Kearn all evening and knew for a fact that he had not brought his phone out once.

Jackson's indignant fist again hovered over a bar table, but then appeared to think better of it. The eyes now boring into Kiki's looked slightly puzzled. 'Not the one who resisted Welsh's planning application? I had the arse of a job to talk the Mayor round. Bloody oik had convinced him that the loss of the Farmer's Arms as a local pub for local people would make Great Hording a weekend dormitory for rich Londoners.'

'Which it would,' Kiki agreed. 'And did.'

'Exactly! That was the whole point. Bloody Mayor got all uptight about it though. Had to get his wife off a fraud rap and his cleaner a passport before he'd wave Jonny's application through.'

Laura gasped in surprise, but also frustration. Damn her dim-wittedness for not switching her phone on to capture this evidence of corruption in high places. She was wedged in very tightly, but even so might be able to pull it out if she took care. Her fingers inched towards her back pocket. The minister continued to reminisce. 'Bloody oik. Or oiks. There were plenty of them, as I remember. What did they call themselves? The Little Hording Popular Front?'

Kiki nodded, pleased with how easily her theory had caught fire. She couldn't say she had actually *seen* Kearn take the photo, but the sheet of notes that Peter Delabole had shown her proved that someone in the room was recording events with malicious intent. There was, as Peter said, a fifth columnist in the ranks. A serpent had entered the Great Hording Eden. And who else could that serpent be but Kearn? The resentment Little Hording felt about Great Hording was well known. And Kiki's fury about the inflated mushy peas price was still raw.

'But what was he doing here?' Jackson asked suddenly.

Under his bulging gaze, Kiki shrank with fear. She had not anticipated this question and had no answer. It now occurred to her that her theory had a flaw in it. She herself had opened the citadel gates to admit Kearn's Trojan pea-laden horse.

'Because the whole point of this place is that we don't let outsiders in,' Jackson continued.

Kiki's mind skittered about, wondering who to curse most. Kearn? Or Hervé? It was his fault just as much. If he'd made proper mushy peas in the first place, none of this would have happened.

She swallowed. 'Er. . .'

Laura, on the verge of pulling out her phone, now lost her balance and knocked the handle of the bubblegum machine. The process set in motion could not be reversed. A handful of small, hard balls released themselves and rained down on to the reclaimed stone floor. The noise was like machine-gun fire.

In the bar, the Defence Minister jumped. 'What the bollocks was that?' He had visited only one army base, but it had been more than enough. His wife, however, remained unsympathetic to his claims of PTSD.

Knowing discovery was imminent, Laura leapt out of her hiding place. Too late, however. With a speed born of much jogging around the village environs, Kiki was in the passage in a flash and bearing down on her, eyes flaming with outrage above her reading glasses. A skinny brown arm shot out and grabbed Laura by the wrist.

'What the hell do you think you're doing?' rasped the pub manager. It was the girl from last night, she recognised angrily, the slim, dark-haired one who went off with Caspar Honeyman.

'Getting a bubble gum,' replied Laura, attempting an insouciant smile. It was the obvious reply.

'As if!' snarled Kiki. But while she was acting angry, inside she was hugely relieved. This girl had saved her from having to answer Jackson's question, and provided a decoy into the bargain.

The Defence Minister had by now lumbered out into the passage. 'Who's this?' He looked Laura up and down, not unappreciatively.

'She was in Kearn's team last night,' Kiki accused. 'She must be another member of the Little Hording Popular Front. All that's being stirred back up again. It's a full-blown conspiracy! They're spying on us!'

The better part of valour is discretion. The phrase flew back to Laura from some long-ago English lesson. Meaning that it was better to run away in some situations than hang around and argue the toss.

This was all too obviously the case here. But Jackson was blocking the door and Kiki defended the bar entrance. There was no way out.

CHAPTER SEVENTEEN

Help came from an unexpected quarter. All three parties now became aware of a tremendous noise outside. It sounded like two women screaming, but how could it be, in peaceful Great Hording?

Kiki abandoned her interrogation of Laura and rushed to the pub's rose-framed front windows. It was difficult to see what was going on; a crowd of women in high-end leisurewear stood between her and the action. As usual at this time on a Sunday morning, Great Hording was alive with the lean, toned wives of captains of industry out on their jogs. Something, however, had made them all stop and gawp.

Kiki dashed outside, only to find her view blocked by Dung Spaw, whose large, pink, fluffy jogging costume, 'Gym Bunny 1', had been runner-up for the previous year's Turner Prize. She wiggled through the crowd, past Anna Goblemova, resplendent in gold Lycra leggings and a gold sequinned vest, and Margaret Tache and Dame Hermione, the former in a T-shirt printed with the floor-plan of the Parthenon, the latter in enormous tracksuit bottoms.

'Anna looks like the wife of some particularly spendthrift emperor,' Dame Hermione murmured loftily. Margaret Tache need not think she was the only person who knew about classical culture.

'But, my dear, isn't that just what she is?' returned the leading Latinist. 'Oligarchs are contemporary Roman emperors, are they not? Goodness me, what are these ladies shouting about?'

It was the question that Kiki, too, was asking herself. But it was impossible to tell. She couldn't even make out who they were, as both were wearing sunglasses and seemed to be made mostly of hair. Some big blonde hair was struggling with some long, dark hair, although the dark hair seemed to have the advantage, performing a number of martial-looking chops and kicks. 'Get away from me, you maniac!' screamed an American accent. A chorus of yaps seconded this remark.

There was a collective gasp of recognition. 'My God, it's Savannah Bouche!' cried the childrenswear entrepreneur Annabel Jackson, who seemed more excited about this than the disaster currently engulfing her husband. Given the routine humiliations of being married to him it was possible, Kiki knew, that she thought he deserved it. 'And her dogs! Mandela, Pankhurst, Mahatma and Che! Aren't they just adorable?'

'Not sure that's the word I'd use,' pronounced Margaret Tache, as the four scraps of fur viciously nipped the ankles of their mistress's assailant. 'Rather, they put one in mind of Cerberus, who famously guarded the entrance to Hades.'

"Or Henry VIII's faithful lapdog Tickle," put in Dame Hermione swiftly.

The great classicist stared at her suspiciously.

The rest of the group were watching competition of a more physical nature. The Hollywood actress and her opponent were going hammer and tongs.

'She certainly learned a thing or two on *TaeKwondo Hippo!*' winced Dung Spaw.

'Savannah!' shouted Sabrina Lacey, rushing over to the flying legs and arms. 'What in hell's name are you doing here? Tim's going to be just so thrilled. . . Why didn't you tell us— *oof!*'

She was shoved out of the way by the resurgent blonde, whose new tactics were to grab and punch.

Margaret Tache tossed her trademark plait over her shoulder. 'This reminds me of the celebrated episode in *Livy* when the emperor's concubines resolve to settle their differences physically!'

'And I am reminded of the famously deleted scene in Shakespeare's unfinished *Edward VI*, where the village women fight over who was first in line at the well,' added Dame Hermione, not to be outdone. 'Look at all the hair she's pulling out!'

Clumps of the brunette's hair were scattered all over the neatly raked gravel.

'Was all extensions,' Anna Goblemova said triumphantly.

The air resounded with a slap and a howl. A pair of mirrored aviator shades wheeled through the air. The dogs, evidently believing this was a game, rushed after them and brought them back, depositing them at Lulu's feet.

'Will teach you steal my man!' shouted the blonde in a throaty accent that seemed of every nation and none. She picked up the glasses and hurled them away as far as possible. Off went the dogs once more.

'It's Lulu!' cried Anna Goblemova, who was addicted to *Hello!*. 'Huh, she got quite a left hook.'

Under the impact of this very hook, and the knuckleduster effect provided by Lulu's jewellery, Savannah now staggered sideways, tripped up on her own hi-tech trainers and fell over. Something square, solid-trousered and set-faced now entered the fray. Mindful of the fact that the pantomime cast was still to be announced, the crowd parted respectfully at the approach of Great Hording's most influential resident.

'Savannah!' boomed Lady Mandy, wielding her basket of simple country nosegays like a weapon. 'My dear, what on earth is going on? You've been out jogging for simply *hours*. We all began to wonder what on earth had happened to you.'

Flat on her back, apparently winded, the actress did not reply.

'Why's she staying with Lady Mandy?' Willow St George hissed to Wonky de Launay.

Wonky was checking her jogging make-up in her FitBit's integral mirror. 'Guess she wants a part in the panto as well.' Her tone was entirely without irony.

Lady Mandy continued seizing the situation by the scruff of the neck. She stormed up to Lulu. 'Kindly explain yourself!'

Lulu, absolutely unfazed by theatreland's most-feared battleaxe, placed tanned hands dazzling with diamonds on her generously curved hips. She made an unlikely pugilist in her flowing Céline trousers and Victoria Beckham shirt, but that she was an effective one was indisputable. Savannah Bouche, devoid of most of her famous hair, her famously pneumatic mouth given an extra boost by Lulu's upper cut, lay unconscious at her feet. 'She steal my fiancé!' Lulu announced, meeting Lady Mandy's furious glare with the indignant glint of her impenetrably black sunglasses.

'Nonsense!' returned Lady Mandy. 'Savannah is in a relationship with my son Orlando. That is why she is here in Great Hording.'

There was a collective gasp from the listening crowd. 'So it's all over with South'n Fried!' exclaimed Margaret Tache, putting what everyone was feeling into words.

Lulu was staring at Lady Mandy. 'Is over?' she demanded disbelievingly. 'My fiancé and slag-tart husband-stealer?'

Lady Mandy brandished her basket. 'I object to that description of my future daughter-in-law.'

Laura, who had escaped through the back of the Golden Goose and was now edging her way round, saw a small, noisy pack of dogs dart past. She immediately connected them, not only with a certain incident at Buckingham Palace, but with the yapping from the helicopter last night. She had, she realised, witnessed, or at least heard, the arrival of Savannah Bouche.

Thank God Caspar hadn't. Fame whore as he was – for all his complaints – the sheer celebrity wattage of the superstar would have knocked him sideways. Laura would have spent the night with Lulu and the Kim Jong-un bunting.

Why was Savannah in Great Hording though? But perhaps it wasn't so surprising. Everyone else seemed to be, except for South'n Fried, of course, currently Busting global Ass. But hold on, what had Lady Mandy just said?

Future daughter-in-law?

So Savannah had chucked South'n Fried already? And for Orlando Chease? Laura paused, apprehension now mixing with her amazement. How was Lulu going to take this?

A loud ring of laughter broke the ominous silence. 'Ha! Savannah Bouche is your outlaw daughter!' cackled Lulu. 'Well, good luck with that, you know? Will minutes last five, hmm?'

The figure on the floor now stirred unexpectedly. In a swift athletic movement, Savannah leapt to her feet like someone from an action movie, which indeed she was. She turned to face the staring crowd. 'As a matter of fact,' she yelled, 'I am no longer engaged to Orlando!'

That was over too! Laura had heard of love lives like revolving doors, but Savannah's was more like the spin cycle on a washing machine.

'Ha!' shouted Lulu again, even more triumphantly this time. 'You see? My sharp end exactly! My, how you say, point!'

Among the crowd there was a dead silence. Everyone who had been staring at Savannah now turned to stare at Lady Mandy, whose face had been host to an amazing variety of expressions ranging from shocked to furious. Now realising herself the cynosure of all eyes, she took a deep breath, straightened her mighty shoulders and prepared to deliver the speech of her life.

'I cannot,' she intoned in the crisp diction famous for reaching the very furthest seats at the back of the Royal Shakespeare Theatre (albeit only in the soundcheck in her job as junior stage manager), 'imagine what on earth you mean, my dear. Last night, when you finally arrived by helicopter – several hours late, I might point out, and with a large number of dogs. . .'

'I had a meeting with my agent,' Savannah interjected

crisply. 'About a new role in a really big film.' Her eyes glittered venomously as she looked at Lulu. 'And you can have your fiancé back, girlfriend. Talk about useless. Turns out he's more into papier-mâché than private jets.'

The heads of the crowd turned to Lulu to see how this last remark went down. The billionheiress tossed her hair back. 'Is too good man for you,' she stated, with dignity.

'And for you, it seems,' Savannah returned with a curl of her famously pillowy lips. 'He left you, after all.'

'Like your horrible dogs leave you!' retorted Lulu. 'Where they gone, huh?'

Savannah looked around. Lulu was quite right, since the final mighty hurl of the mirrored Bouche sunshades, there had been neither trace nor bark of Pankhurst and co.

'My babies!' shrieked the actress, rushing off in her hi-tech trainers.

'Just where do you think you are going?' Lady Mandy yelled after her.

Savannah did not stop. 'Once I get my babies,' she shouted over her shoulder, 'I'm outta this dump.'

There was a stir of outrage among the crowd, all of whom had sunk millions into this dump. Kiki was aghast. A Hollywood superstar describing Great Hording in those terms might well be the beginning of the end. Lady Mandy, her face red with fury, drew herself up to deliver the ultimate riposte. 'If you think,' she shouted after the tiny, sticklike figure, 'that you will be allotted a role in the forthcoming Great Hording pantomime, you have another think coming!'

Somewhat unexpectedly, Savannah did react to this. She had got as far as Peter Delabole's bookshop when she turned and shoved her middle finger in the air.

'Well, *really*!' gasped Lady Mandy. 'Talk about gratitude!

We Cheases were about to raise that girl from mere fame to the level of thespian royalty!'

'Oh my God, I'm about to miss *The Archers* omnibus!' cried Kate Threadneedle in a panic.

Lulu was not slow to grasp the huge significance of this. 'And is big showdown between Eddie Grundy and Lynda Snell!' she gasped, rushing into the car park.

Exclamations of horror echoed hers and within seconds the entire crowd had dispersed. All that remained to hint at the recent dramatic events were Savannah Bouche's hair extensions scattered on the gravel.

With a final, despairing glance round, Kiki went back into the pub to face Jolyon Jackson. He had taken full advantage of the facilities and was downing his fourth pint and fifth gourmet bacon sandwich as he flicked through the parts of the Sunday papers that didn't directly allude to him.

Lulu, recovering her dignity, called from the car park to Laura. 'Vlad has come. We all go back to Kensington. Listen to *Archers* on way, hmm?'

'I've just got to get my bag,' Laura said, remembering it was somewhere among the snowglobes in the shepherd hut.

In the driver's seat, Vlad politely cleared her throat. 'I took the liberty of retrieving it and placing it in the car boot, madam.'

'You think of everything, Vlad.' Laura scrambled into the back gratefully.

'Ssshh, is Lynda Snell!' Lulu admonished.

Laura smiled to herself as the great car glided away. What a weekend it had been. She had discovered a great story and rekindled her relationship with a particularly favourite old boyfriend. Who had asked her to the Ivys, a prospect which seemed both terrifying and fabulous.

If, at the back of her mind, there was a Harry-shaped guilty shadow, Laura determinedly pushed it away. What did he expect?

The car purred down the village lanes. Past Addings, past Promptings, past Etchings, past the village hall that was the focus of so much hope and fear. Past the Ocado van that, even on a Sunday, seemed to be continuing its hopeless efforts to deliver to the local oligarchs.

It was on the final bend, as they passed the Goblemovas' glowing neon lake sculpture, that a movement in the hedgerow caught Laura's eye. The shape of a tall, broad-shouldered dark-haired man flashed across her vision. She wrenched herself round to stare out of the back window, unable to believe what she had just seen.

But had she just seen it? He could not possibly have been there really. He was a figment of her imagination, given shape by her guilt at having slept with Caspar.

Laura settled herself in the back seat and closed her eyes. She was overexcited. She had had too little sleep. Or maybe she was just mistaken. Because it was obviously absolutely, completely out of the question that she had just seen Harry Scott in Great Hording.

As Lulu revelled in *The Archers* omnibus, Laura called Harry repeatedly. But the phone line rang unanswered with a fuzzy, distant, foreign tone. She felt sure now that the figure in the hedge had been someone else. Or simply imagined. And that Harry was far away, engaged on his new investigation.

She racked her brains to recall what, if anything, he had said about it. Her efforts yielded nothing beyond the memory of him shrugging on his leather jacket and leaving the flat in Cod's Head Row. That seemed like a million years ago, though was in reality only a few weeks.

As *The Archers* ended and *Desert Island Discs* began, Laura expected Lulu to turn off the radio and discuss the latest sensations in Ambridge. She seemed absorbed in her smartphone, however, tapping concentratedly away.

Kirsty Young's interviewee was Roger Slutt, the famous rock star. He seemed to have chosen records mainly by himself. In between he related a series of expletive-studded rock rites of passage. These ranged from the obscure start in the backstreets of Stepney to the moment of total burn-out during an eighties tour of Japan.

'It was BEEPing meltdown, man. Shoved my BEEPing gold suit down the BEEPing toilet,' Roger informed Kirsty in his rasping Liverpudlian accent. 'Took a lot of BEEPing flushing, I can tell ya.' His distinctive tobacco cackle ended in a series of rheumy coughs and a dull beating sound that could have been the much-admired presenter banging him on the back.

Laura thought of Carinthia, who had yearned to be sent away to Radio Four's desert island. She had kept an ever-changing list of tracks on her iPod just in case. The *DID* call had not come, however. And when Carinthia had eventually been sent away, it was to rehab. Compassionate spa leave, rather.

From where, it seemed, she had been doing a serious amount of meddling. With Carinthia's help, Clemency Makepeace had been drafted in to co-edit *Society* and would no doubt arrive when Laura returned tomorrow. Large as life and ten times as ghastly.

Well, Laura resolved, she would show her who was boss.

As the person on the ground, the woman on the spot, she had the advantage. It was her feet under the editor's desk. Clemency could just go and sit outside with everyone else.

'Yeah, BEEPing snobbish BEEPing BEEPS.' Roger was continuing to turn the airwaves blue. Laura turned her full attention back to *Desert Island Discs*. She had half-heard something interesting, but what?

'You're saying country life wasn't entirely successful, then?' Kirsty was prompting in her pleasant but penetrating manner.

'You could BEEPing say that. BEEPing nightmare from start to BEEPing finish,' Roger rasped. 'Wasn't BEEPing posh enough for the villagers, was I? Was I BEEP. Thought I was nasty and common, they did. Always BEEPing complaining about my BEEPing parties. Didn't like that I'd altered the BEEPing name of me 'ouse to Riffs.'

'Riffs?' repeated Kirsty, obviously amused.

'Yeah, like guitar riffs, you know? 'Lectric guitar, tool of me trade, yeah? I put in a guitar-shaped swimming pool as well. They went BEEPing postal over that. . .'

Laura frowned. Riffs rang a bell. Wasn't there a house of that name in Great Hording?

'And Ekaterina, that's my wife—'

'I've read that you met her when she delivered some packages to, er, Riffs?'

'S'right. Me statins. Dead romantic it was. Anyway, she don't like living in the middle of BEEPing nowhere either so we've sold up and gone back to London. She takes me clubbin' every night now. Anyone'd think she wants me to kick the bucket and leave her all me money, ha ha. . .' The sentence dissolved into another coughing fit.

'Your next record, please, Roger,' Kirsty hastily cut in.

Words spoken in a strange accent now drowned out the radio. A pair of intensely black sunglasses were turned questioningly in her direction from over the rear of the front seat. Lulu was talking to her, Laura realised.

'Is done! I buy house!' she announced triumphantly.

'What? Just like that? Without even viewing it?'

'Like that, just. Have instructed lawyers. Boring legal stuff happen this week and I move in next Saturday.'

Laura wondered whether she would ever get used to Lulu's extravagance. She bought houses like other people bought shoes and she bought shoes like – well – like no one else. Laura thought she knew the answer to her next question, but she asked it anyway. 'Lulu, the house wouldn't happen to be in Great Hording, would it?'

The diamonds in Lulu's ears winked triumphantly. 'Owner very happy to sell to me. Say willage need someone like me in it. Say is just what they deserve.'

'And the house is called. . .'

The sunglasses flashed happily. 'Riffs.'

CHAPTER EIGHTEEN

S unday night in Cod's Head Row was the worst ever. Edgar returned at four in the morning with some Mexican dancers picked up in a club called Rear Entry. 'Come in and have a caipirinha!' he invited when Laura, unable to bear any more carousing directly above her bedroom, went upstairs and banged on his door.

'No thanks,' she snapped, tempted to threaten to tell his father of Edgar's doings, now she knew where he lived. The money tap might then be turned off and her troublesome neighbour made to move away. She desisted, however; this was Shoreditch and who might take Edgar's place did not bear thinking about. His predecessor had been a TV survival consultant who hoarded piles of twigs and crossbows and whose supplies of live mealworms had made their way down into Laura's flat.

She set off for work next morning with heavy eyes. She

had drunk so much coffee she was shaking. She could have done with an extra hour – an extra six hours – in bed, but was determined to reach the office early and stake her territorial claim. It was only just past eight o'clock when she tiredly slipped through Society House's revolving door and nodded at the security men behind the desk.

One looked up from the *Sun*. 'Cheer up, love. Might never 'appen.'

Laura stopped herself from snapping that it already had. But perhaps she was being over-pessimistic. People were always changing their mind in Magazineland. Maybe Clemency wouldn't join the staff after all. Or maybe the scene last week on the sixth floor, in Stone's office, had just been a bad dream.

Her own office, as she pushed open the familiar white door, looked normal enough. Perhaps a little tidier, but that would have been Roberta, the cleaner. As she walked towards the glass-walled editorial box she realised that something definitely had changed, even so. Someone she did not recognise sat at Demelza's desk.

The woman was young and extremely attractive. She wore glasses, but in the way a model for a line of spectacles did, to draw attention to a beautiful face rather than because she needed any optical assistance. She had huge lips and high cheekbones. Long, glossy hair swirled with gold was caught in a full, high ponytail. Her sleeveless fitted red dress revealed the slim, straight shoulders and long arms of a supermodel, and the legs folded beneath the desk were correspondingly colt-like and endless, although end they did, in elegant high-heeled beige pumps.

She turned a long-lashed hazel stare on the gaping Laura. 'I'm Karlie, how can I help you?'

Laura, tired and confused, gripped the edge of a nearby desk. This happened to be Thomasella's the food editor's and she felt her fingers push through a soft cardboard lid and into something soft and mushy.

'Clumsy!' said Karlie. 'That's the new pink hummus you've just shoved your hand into.'

Laura stared at the rose-coloured slop on her second and third fingers. She rather liked hummus but was reluctant to lick it off in front of this absurdly assured creature. Clumsy? How dare she? And why was it pink?

'Made with Himalayan raspberry salt,' Karlie supplied, displaying a disturbing knack for mind-reading. Laura blinked. She was sure she hadn't spoken aloud.

'How. . . I mean. . . why?'

'The man who just delivered it told me all about it.'

Laura pulled herself together. 'Not the salt,' she snapped. 'You! Who are you? Where's Demelza?'

'I've just told you,' Karlie said calmly in a strangely accentless voice. 'I'm Karlie. And Demelza's having a break.'

A break? Laura's secretary had only just returned from her latest holibobs, as she called them. On whose authority was she taking yet another? She, Laura, was the boss round here.

'You don't make the decisions any more,' said Karlie, again as if Laura had spoken aloud. With a swing of her ponytail, she nodded towards the editor's office.

Laura looked, and her heart briefly stopped in her chest. Someone was inside. Sitting at the desk. Someone with long, curly red hair. Clemency Makepeace!

'How dare she?' Laura muttered under her breath. 'How *very* dare she?'

'Because she's the editor,' said Karlie.

Laura glared at her. 'Actually, she's the *co-editor*.' She had to force the words out, they stuck in her throat. '*I'm* the other editor. And that's my office! I was in it first!' She stormed towards the glass door of her former sanctum and wrenched the handle. It did not open. Was it stuck? Laura rattled it. Not stuck, she realised. Locked.

Locked out of her own office! How horribly undermining and humiliating.

Ignoring Karlie's cool surveillance, Laura banged on the glass. But Clemency neither looked up or gave the smallest indication she was aware of Laura's presence.

She was calmly reading a set of page proofs. *What* page proofs? the enraged Laura wondered. What right did she have to sign off any section of the magazine?

'Hey!' she shouted, banging the glass again.

Inside, Clemency picked up the telephone and spoke into it. She still didn't look at Laura but turned her face sufficiently towards her for her pitying, slightly smiling expression to clearly be seen. What could also be seen was that Clemency had had a considerable amount of work done since their last meeting. The slanting green eyes looked even more catlike, her nose looked slimmer and her cheekbones looked higher. Surgery, wondered Laura. Or just filler?

Clemency spoke too softly for her words to be heard. She put the phone down and returned composedly to the page proofs.

They were, Laura saw with a rush of fury, some she herself had rejected weeks ago, Raisy and Daisy's fetish tablecloth sports bra shoot. 'Hey!' she yelled, striking the windows with her fists once again.

It was now that she noticed her framed front covers had

been taken down from the editor's office walls. They had been replaced with photographs of her arch-enemy. One was a studio shot in which Clemency was posed with pensive hand under her chin, the light streaming through her red hair so it appeared like flames round her head. Hell flames, Laura thought. The others were of Clemency with celebrities, hugely blown up from the smartphone selfies they looked originally to have been. Posing with Cara Delevingne, posing with Savannah Bouche. Posing with Caspar, even. This one sent a knife-thrust of white-hot fury through Laura. When she finally got in the office – *her* office – that would be the first one off the walls.

But that was not all, Laura now saw. The shelves were empty; all her journalism awards, plus Carinthia's various trophies for Services to Dry Cleaning, Champagne Drinker of the Year and so on had been removed. Seeing the distinctive top of one of her predecessor's awards – shaped like a gold hairbrush and awarded for Lifetime Achievement by the blow-drying industry – poking out of the waste-paper bin, Laura felt an angry tightening in her chest. Red mist floated before her eyes. Perhaps, after all, it was just as well the office door was locked.

A phone shrilled somewhere and made her jump. Karlie, behind her, was holding out a receiver. 'Call for you.'

Laura remained where she was, reluctant to cooperate. Karlie covered the receiver with a slim manicured hand. 'You'd better take it,' she said in her accentless voice. 'It's Christopher Stone.'

Doubtfully, reluctantly, Laura took the phone. 'Christopher?'

'Laura.' The MD's tone was terse. 'I've just had a most concerning call from Clemency.'

So that was who she had been ringing. The cheek! Laura hurled a burning look towards the glass office walls. This time Clemency met her molten gaze with one that combined triumph with amusement. She followed this with a yawn, then returned to the fetish tablecloths.

'As you know,' Stone went on, 'the idea was for you two to work together in harmony. . .'

Harmony!

'. . . but it seems there's been an unfortunate scene already this morning. Poor Clemency's temporarily locked in the editor's office. Something went wrong with the handle, apparently.'

Oh yeah? The disbelieving words wobbled on the edge of Laura's tongue. With a mighty effort, she choked them back.

'The poor thing suffers from acute claustrophobia and she's desperately trying to stave off a panic attack,' Stone went on. 'But she tells me you're trying to break the door down and it's really not helping. She feels she might lose control at any minute.'

Laura felt that she might do the same, and in seconds, not minutes. The inside of her head was a white fuzz of static fury. She could see Clemency smirking from the desk and knew she was being provoked. To give in to the urge would be to let Clemency win. 'I see,' she said, in the steadiest voice she could manage.

'I have to say I'm disappointed, Laura,' the managing director continued. 'For you to act in this dramatic fashion is very unlike you and doesn't, I have to say, bode well for a productive working relationship.'

'But—'

'Clemency assures me, however, that she would be happy

to accept an apology and we can take it from there.'

This was too much. 'An apology! But Christopher, she's taken down all my pictures! She's thrown all my trophies in the bin!'

'Clemency mentioned that there had been some disturbance in the office. She says the cleaning staff have broken items over the weekend. I've instructed HR to disengage the current hygiene operative and find a new one.'

Laura thought of Roberta, the smiling Filipina who counted herself blessed to work in a magazine office. She took great care with everything – polishing Laura's awards with especial reverence – and was thrilled whenever Laura gave her a brand-new issue to send home to her mother. She showed her appreciation with occasional gifts of wonderful home-cooked food which Laura would find on her desk, warm and fragrant beneath the tinfoil. And now Roberta would be laid off because of Clemency's casual lie, a lie designed to get Laura into trouble. Tears of fury and frustration stung Laura's eyes.

She could not let Clemency win. Her eye caught the page proofs of the fetish tablecloth sports bras. She took a deep breath and forced herself to sound calm.

'Of course I want to work well with Clemency,' she pushed out between gritted teeth. 'However, we need to practise a little more collaboration. She seems to be passing pages that I'd put on hold.'

There!

'Ah yes, I'm glad you've brought that up. Clemency informs me that there are quite a few features commissioned by Carinthia that you've seen fit to spike since taking over as,' Stone paused before adding, 'ahem, *acting* editor.'

The pause and the ahem were not lost on Laura. A

familiar fear slithered coldly through her belly. Clemency Makepeace had only just got in the building and already her job was in danger. Again.

She thought of the Great Hording article. If she kept her job long enough to write it, surely it would save her.

Christopher continued, ominously. 'A piece about the new hemlock fudge was mentioned, and the current craze for off-grid holidays in decommissioned coal mines. Clemency thought they made perfect *Society* features.'

'But—'

'She also mentioned a piece about bright young things playing ducks and drakes with their smartphones. A delightful idea.'

'A slightly old-style *Society* one though,' Laura managed to force out. 'It had its ridiculous aspects.'

'Why ridiculous? Just fun, I thought, and so did Clemency. She couldn't imagine why you'd spiked an article about the fashion for wearing shoes as hats, either. I told her to revive it anyway. Really, Laura, I must say I agree with Clemency that your instinct as an editor seems to be open to question.'

'Clemency said that?' Laura wanted to roll on the floor in a foetal position and scream.

'Indeed she did. And I have to say, Laura, that I agree with her when she ventured to suggest that you're not, after all, quite ready to be an editor yet. So what we've decided is that Clemency takes the helm and you back her up as deputy editor. How does that sound?'

Like a nightmare, Laura thought, biting so hard on her biro that it snapped. But it would obviously be madness to let that show. She raised her chin and beamed at her

adversary through gritted teeth as she dropped the
mangled plastic pieces in the bin. It might be round one
to Clemency, but she would win in the end. The question,
as ever, was how?

CHAPTER NINETEEN

'I'm fresh out,' Edgar said when Laura knocked on his door a few days later. She had decided she could use a caipirinha after all. 'Been drinking them all afternoon.'

Laura would normally have considered this a waste of time and pathetically typical of Edgar. But now, after the best part of a week filled setting up the demeaning articles Clemency had burdened her with, she had a different view. A day spent guzzling industrial-strength cocktails would have been a sight more fun than trying to locate famous people and their pets. Even Carinthia hadn't descended to this level.

She and Edgar went to Gorblimey Trousers, the downstairs pie-and-mash joint run by Bill and his husband Ben. They were ex-Google executives who, in the spirit of Silicon Valley innovation, had supplemented the pie and mash with a large, slick bar. The place, as usual, was crammed with gangs of nerds from nearby Silicon Roundabout. They were knocking back tequila slammers and accidentally setting fire to their facial hair with flaming sambucas.

'You look all-in, dearie!' cried Bill, pumping his cocktail shaker. Both he and Ben were the type of Americans who imagined they had no American accent at all. They had taken this delusion a stage further by affecting the cockneyisms they felt fitted their new calling.

'What's with the long boat-race?' Ben demanded. 'You're all down in the north and south.'

'Those sad mince pies!' Bill added. 'Fed up of being all on our Jack Jones, are we, dearie?'

The two of them were obsessed with Laura's romantic fortunes. They both considered Harry wildly dishy. 'Lovely bottle and glass,' they said to Laura; a reference to his bottom, she gathered. They had been dismayed to hear the relationship was over.

'As a matter of fact, I'm not on my Jack Jones,' Laura told them. Caspar was the one bright spot in her life at the moment.

'Oooh! Who's the lucky man?' trilled Bill.

'Not him, we hope,' Ben whispered, nodding his modish-tousled head after Edgar. He had spotted someone he knew and was now shoving towards them through the forest of beards, laptops and cups of craft coffee, knocking everything over with his satchel as he went.

'Clumsy fucker!' shouted a man in a tweed cap.

'Dyspraxic fucker, actually,' Edgar replied with dignity.

The someone Edgar was going towards was Esme, the frowny blonde who lived in the top flat in Laura's building. She was a life coach whose own life was currently in meltdown. Her boyfriend, a samphire-gatherer who ran a website called Dreadful Trade, had just dumped her after a row that the entire street had heard.

'Come on, dearie!' Bill slid a glass of champagne across the zinc counter-top towards her. 'Tell us everything! Who is he and when can we meet him?'

Laura looked from Bill to Ben. She was dying to tell them she was going out with a hugely famous film star. They adored celebrity and would be thrilled for her. They would get on like a sambuca on fire with Caspar, who also liked to talk in rhyming slang. But could she trust them?

'She's cracking, I can tell!' Bill nudged Ben. 'Look at that smile.'

'She *so* is! Come on, Laurypops. Tell your Uncle Ben!'

A sudden flood of reckless happiness possessed Laurypops. Oh what the hell. Why not?

'Back in a sec!' Bill trilled as he and Ben were now pulled away to take part in a selfie with some architects wearing white Nehru jackets to which CCCP badges were pinned. The Soviet nostalgia made Laura think of Kearn and the fact that Wyatt had today been given her marching orders by Clemency. 'Wrong hair, wrong weight, wrong shoes, wrong attitude, wrong wrong,' she had been heard saying to Karlie afterwards. 'What editor in their right mind wants someone like *that* about the office?' They had both then looked accusingly at Laura.

Sod them all, Laura thought now, taking a triumphant sip of her champagne. Why was she even worrying, when she had an international film star up her sleeve? No magazine managing director in his right mind would get rid of someone with such contacts. Or demote her, for that matter. Why on earth hadn't she mentioned it today? Laura shook her head. Sometimes she just didn't think.

'Come on, smile!' Bill and Ben were urging the architects. 'Flash us your Hampsteads!'

Hampstead Heath, teeth, Laura recalled.

An edition of the London *Evening Standard* lay on the end of the bar She pulled it towards her.

The front page headlines were hard to take in. She was tired and a little tipsy, but even so, what she was reading could not be possible.

CASPAR BONDS WITH BOUCHE
007 is Latest Love of Sizzling Star

She closed her eyes and opened them again. But the words were still there. Laura seized her glass of champagne and downed it in one, then looked back at the newspaper. The letters had not melted away or rearranged themselves. They had not moved at all.

'Apparently they met out jogging!' Bill called from across the bar.

'Jogging?' Laura looked up, bewildered.

'Savannah says in the article that their eyes met through the morning mists of some ancient Suffolk village!'

'What?' Heart hammering, Laura read the paragraphs again. Caspar *had* gone jogging. He had left a note to say so. And what had Lady Mandy yelled at Savannah? 'You've been out jogging for simply *hours.*'

What had made no sense before was now hideously, obviously clear. Early one morning, just as the sun was rising, deep in the English countryside in one of the tree-shaded lanes of Great Hording, two Hollywood superstars had, quite literally, run into one another.

'We collided round a corner,' Caspar was quoted as

saying. 'I fell over. When I looked up there was Savannah in her tight Lycra. And her dogs in theirs. They all have specially designed sportswear.'

Laura's teeth were chattering with the sheer shock of it all. Caspar was making a dreadful mistake. Savannah Bouche would only be using him.

Caspar, it had to be said, did not seem to see it that way. 'Savannah completes me,' he told the paper. 'She's the yin to my yang, the words to my music, the custard to my pudding. Actually, scrub that. She doesn't eat a lot of pudding.'

To be fair to the journalist, they hadn't been quite convinced. Wasn't Caspar, they asked, apprehensive about the future of the relationship given the revolving door of Savannah's love life?

'The revolving door closes here,' the actor answered, happily mixing his metaphors. *His tone was rapturous*, the writer noted.

Laura was appalled, almost more for Caspar than herself. He had let her down yet again, but seeing him fall into the undersized, shellacked Bouche claws was horrible. He had no idea what he was getting into.

'We've committed to each other by both having tattoos done of the Pacific fault lines, in solidarity with earthquake victims,' was Caspar's final word.

Laura shoved the paper back down the bar. She doubted Caspar knew where the Pacific even was, despite having flown over it countless times. As for love, this was nothing of the sort. It was lust. Or, given Savannah was involved, maybe just an evil spell.

She gazed gloomily into her empty champagne glass. Laura had never been the self-indulgent type and her natural resilience was now asserting itself. She was disappointed, but her encounter with Caspar had only been a one-night stand. She had been right to take his avowals with a pinch of salt and she felt glad, in retrospect, that she had teased him so much. While she had hoped for more, what had happened was hardly a tragedy; she'd had a lot of fun. It would be quite some time before the Hollywood Karma Sutra faded from her memory.

Thursday afternoon. Laura had just returned from interviewing, under Clemency's instructions, the owner of a Chelsea children's boutique who had cornered the market in aspirational dress-up wear. Costumes available included consultant paediatrician, barrister and newspaper editor. 'My customers see their children as the leaders of tomorrow,' said the supermodel-like shop owner. It was, Laura thought, all very Great Hording.

She was looking forward fervently to the next opportunity to escape both *Society* and London and go to the countryside with Lulu. Even if, now, Great Hording looked unlikely to save her career. The 'Elite Enclave' article was obviously on hold, possibly permanently. There had been no point even mentioning it in features meetings that revolved around the UK's top five aristocratic nudist beaches and the best stately home lakes for wild jet-skiing. Anything remotely critical of the moneyed classes would obviously be thrown out.

The boutique interview had been doubly boring because Laura had had to note the shop owner's every remark down by hand. She had been unable to find her smartphone before leaving the office. She had looked everywhere and asked everyone, even Clemency, who had been especially unhelpful. 'So that was actually a phone?' she said sneeringly. 'I thought it was borrowed from a museum for a shoot.'

Laura had ignored her. So what if her mobile was old? She didn't have the money to update it whenever a new one came out. It still worked, didn't it?

Her desk, as Laura now returned to it, looked depressingly tidy. Clemency had lost no time in reintroducing, in an even more extreme form, the draconian diktats about orderliness that Carinthia had previously imposed. It wasn't just about desks and jackets draped over chairs now, it was about pens lined up at right angles to keyboards and drawers subject to random inspections. One junior assistant had had her belongings cast over the carpet tiles and Clemency walking through the mess, crunching a bottle of nail varnish beneath her high heels. The bright pink stain could still be seen in the centre of the office, flashing a warning to all.

Laura hated having to toe – as it were – the tidy line but there seemed no sense in deliberately courting danger. While it increasingly seemed pointless even trying to remain in the job, her pride and natural sense of justice resisted giving in and handing the advantage to Clemency. Why should she?

She started up her computer and began to rummage around her desk again for the missing phone. No sign. It was strange, especially given the instrument's age and decrepitude. No one was likely to have stolen it, after all.

Instinct now made her glance over to Clemency's secretary. It seemed to Laura there was something distinctly familiar about the phone Karlie was peering intently into.

'That's *mine*!' Laura muttered, leaping to her feet and sprinting across the office. In doing so she narrowly avoided a collision with a rail of clothes being pushed by the new intern who had replaced Wyatt. Anais was a dozy Sloane with a scar on her forehead caused by the impact of her diamond necklace while headbanging. In the *Society* of Clemency Makepeace, this kind of thing got you a job, albeit an unpaid one.

But anyone who wore family jewels to the mosh pit probably didn't need a salary, anyway.

'Give me that!' Laura snatched her phone out of Karlie's elegant hand.

Karlie, as usual, was utterly unapologetic. 'Excuse *me*,' she said sarcastically. 'I just found it in the bin and was trying to find out whose it was. Clemency wants you, by the way. She's in her office.' There was an emphasis on the 'her'.

Laura turned and went reluctantly in to what, for a brief time, had been her own domain.

Wearing her trademark red dress and matching lipstick, her fiery hair adding to the general diabolical effect, Clemency sat behind the glass desk on her own individual take on the editor's chair. This was a specially commissioned David Linley throne made of rare English fruitwoods and featuring built-in shoe storage. 'This celebrity hen thing,' she said, waving a printout at Laura.

Laura's heart sank. Given her superior research skills, finding a famous person who kept poultry hadn't been all that difficult. But writing something interesting about a celebrity chicken-fan had been impossible. Just what was there to say?

'It's all wrong!' Clemency stormed, driving her point home by tearing the printout in half. It seemed to Laura rather extreme. She had done her best, after all.

'Could you explain why?' she asked, keeping her tone steadily neutral so Clemency could not accuse her of insolence and complain to Christopher about her.

'You were supposed to write *as* the chicken, not about it.'

'As the chicken? You mean – impersonate it?' Was impersonate even the word, given that it was a bird?

'That's right. So get out there and start again.'

Laura took a deep breath and returned to her preternaturally tidy desk. Having humiliatingly lost her position as *Society*'s editor she was now hanging on by her fingertips by assuming the identity of a celebrity chicken. Would she even make it to the end of the week?

CHAPTER TWENTY

It was a stunningly beautiful morning and Kiki was jogging down a valley at whose end the sea rose like a glowing blue wall. The air vibrated with the heat to come and the sun was bright though the hour was early. Sticky light like sugar syrup slicked over the leaves of the trees. The birds were singing so loudly she could hardly hear herself think and the colours of the hedgerow flowers were dazzling. Kiki had no idea what any of them were, but she knew what they could be worth. She had seen some in arrangements by Wonky. Despite all this loveliness, Kiki's heart was sore. And not just because her new leopardskin Lycra sports top was a size too small. All was not well. Trouble had come to Paradise. Distrust was in the air. Suspicion stalked the land.

Something big and green now roared round the corner and almost knocked her over. Pressed into the hedge, gasping, Kiki glared at the driver of the Ocado van. The passenger-side window slid down and the driver leant over towards her.

'I can haz house of Sir Gay Gobblemoff?'

'Fuck off,' yelled Kiki.

'I apologise. Sir Gay Fuckoff, then?'

'Don't you have satnav?' Kiki snapped before remembering that Great Hording was a satnav-free zone. Another thing Sir Philip Peaseblossom had arranged in the interests of village privacy. For what *that* was worth now.

The van roared off, leaving Kiki alone with her troubles. Great Hording, she knew, was not the happy place it had once been. It looked as lovely as ever and was going about its business much as usual. But things had changed since the dread night of the pub quiz. Villager had turned against villager, each suspecting the other of leaking the image of the cheating politician to the press. Jolyon Jackson himself had disappeared to London while the fuss died down. Whether he would be forced to resign remained uncertain, but, as befitted a defence minister, he was fighting an intense rearguard action. Images of him striding cheerily round children's wards had appeared daily ever since. There was probably not a sick infant in his entire constituency who had not been kissed or given a playful punch on the shoulder, injuries notwithstanding.

She could learn from his tactics, Kiki thought. Distraction was the way to repair a reputation. The Golden Goose's role in the Great Pub Quiz disaster might be forgotten if she could make it the centre of some other successful diversion. The question was – what?

Perhaps a party for the village, to bring everyone together and smooth things out after the recent disturbing events?

Kiki saw that she was jogging past Addings, weekend home of the Threadneedles, and remembered that she had seen Wyatt in Fore Street only yesterday. With her blue hair, black lipstick and Gothic clothes she had cut a very different – and much plumper – figure to her social peers, blonde girls with endless legs and hardly started shorts. Rumour had it that Wyatt was back for the summer, having been sacked from *Society* magazine. Well, Kiki thought, lips tightening, if she thought she was inviting Kearn to Great Hording to see her, she had another think coming. Suspected – thanks to Kiki – of photographing the cheating Jolyon Jackson, the troublemaking runt was *persona non grata.*

The crazy collection of red and white striped towers, steep fish-scale-tiled roofs and pennants, spires and gargoyles that was Riffs was coming into view and Kiki was reminded of another Great Hording outcast: Roger Slutt. She had heard him on the radio a day or two before; his remarks about Great Hording had been far from complimentary, although he hadn't mentioned the village by name, thank God.

Riffs was now on the market, guitar-shaped pool and all. But the rumour currently doing the village rounds – apart from the ones about Jolyon – was that someone had bought it and would be arriving this weekend. Who this someone was, not even the massed powers of Great Hording could establish; Roger Slutt's legal representatives refused to release the name.

Flitting across Kiki's mind came the uncomfortable memory of her conversation with Lulu. But nothing seemed to have come of that, thank God. She had certainly not viewed it; someone would have seen her, if so.

George Clooney had been mentioned. Now he and Amal

had twins they were reportedly looking for somewhere more private than Berkshire. The urbane actor would be the perfect choice, Kiki thought, to fill the last gap in the village's range of top people from every sphere. She wondered if the new tenant would nab a part in the Great Hording pantomime. Lady Mandy would be announcing the lucky *Cinderella* line-up any minute. Her cast list for the annual entertainment was subject to change right up until the last minute, depending on who was in or out of favour. It had the status of a state secret, except much more important, as Sir Philip Peaseblossom was the first to admit. No one was party to what it contained until the mistress of ceremonies was ready to release it.

Lady Mandy had let it be known – in ringing, fruity tones at every possible opportunity – that she was putting the finishing touches to the line-up. Which was why everyone at the moment was treating her with more than usual reverence. Everyone wanted one of the special yellow envelopes in which Lady Mandy would disseminate details of their part and scheduled rehearsal times. Those who had failed to land a role would get the news in black envelopes.

On the day the envelopes were expected, everyone hovered by their letter boxes and watched eagerly for the postman. Some had even been known to waylay him and bribe him to open his sack, allowing them to remove the black envelope that would otherwise publicly announce their failure. Yellow envelopes, by contrast, were opened at the most public places possible, in Fore Street usually, or in the bar of the Golden Goose.

Kiki, who had received her share of black envelopes over the years, was desperate for a yellow one. It wasn't simply that she longed to stride the stage with tights and satin breeches showing off her best features. She also longed to mingle on equal terms with a village which, by and large, tended to treat her as a servant.

It now occurred to her that her agenda and that of the Golden Goose could be combined. She could hold a party for the successful cast of *Cinderella*! She would offer a free champagne reception, to get things off with a bang. Lady Mandy, whose parsimony was as well-known as her penchant for champagne – 'one develops such a taste for it in the world of first-rate theatre' – would be unable to resist such an offer. The suggestion that Kiki be cast as Dandini would surely be viewed favourably.

She would, Kiki decided, go to Promptings straightaway and make Lady Mandy the offer on the spot. Speed was of the essence; the dread pantomime director might be even now stuffing the all-important envelopes.

Kiki felt quite cheered up. Perhaps her chances of replacing Nessa Welsh and marrying Jonny had not gone up in smoke after all. The possibility that they had, and Jonny's fury about the headlines, was by far the worst aspect of the entire quiz night meltdown. He had made it clear that a further breach of village security, and with it a lowering of village confidence, was out of the question. The Jackson headlines could not be repeated. But her new idea, Kiki reasoned, was foolproof.

The gate of Promptings gave on to a garden studded with memorabilia from Lady Mandy's own thespian days and the still-booming career of her impresario husband. The entire proscenium arch from *The Phantom of the Opera* might have overwhelmed most lawns, but the Cheases' was a large one and could take it.

The Chease doorbell played the tear-jerking theme tune to *Ginger's Bought It*, the fighter-pilot musical on which Sir Alastair's fortune was founded. Somewhat unexpectedly, Orlando Chease opened the door. He looked, Kiki thought, rather the worse for wear. His hair was wild and unbrushed, his feet were bare and while he wore a black T-shirt bearing an image of a huge gold cheeseburger (was it some sort of play on his name, Kiki wondered), its bravado was not borne out by his expression. This was best described as hangdog. Grief, Kiki assumed. He was obviously suffering following the loss of his fiancée. She arranged her features into an expression of commiseration.

'How are you, Orlando?' she asked sympathetically. His eyes were red and bloodshot, and his shoulders slumped in the doorway so she could see the hall behind him. It was filled with framed photographs of various Cheases with leading lights of the acting business. There were sepia ones with Charlie Chaplin, and fifties black and white ones with Laurence Olivier and Vivien Leigh. Coloured ones included Lady Mandy with Judi Dench and Sir Alastair with Ralph Fiennes.

Kiki's roving eyes now returned to Orlando. He was looking at her with a new expression, one she couldn't quite read. Apprehension, possibly. Or maybe just misery. Better get it out of the way, she decided. Deal with the elephant in the room or, in her case, on the doorstep.

'I was really sorry to hear about it,' she said.

Orlando's scarlet-tinged eyes widened. 'How the hell do you know?'

'I'm afraid,' Kiki said gently, 'everyone knows.'

Someone appeared behind him. 'My son!' Lady Mandy boomed theatrically. 'Who is here?'

Orlando was bent over, as if in pain. 'Everyone knows, Mother!'

'What?!'

Lady Mandy now appeared in the doorway, shoving aside her offspring with one well-aimed thrust. The grande dame of am-dram looked considerably less pleased with herself than usual. Her fearsome brows had disappeared into the roots of her wire-like grey curls, her mouth gaped and her eyes bulged. 'It's got out already?' she demanded. 'Everyone's seen it?'

Kiki stared at her, puzzled. Lady Mandy had been there when Savannah had announced the news in person to the whole village.

'Betrayal of the most heinous nature!' Lady Mandy raised her hands, palm upward. 'Deceit beyond measure!'

Kiki sympathised. That Bouche had met Honeyman while jogging in Great Hording was frustrating in the extreme. Had she been a few minutes faster, or perhaps slower, she might have ended up with him herself. 'Savannah has a lot to answer for,' she agreed.

There was a gasp. Perhaps two. Both Orlando and his mother were now staring at her. 'You mean it's her?' Lady Mandy cried. 'She's responsible?'

Kiki nodded. She may as well go along with this pantomime, she decided. It might get her a better part in the other one.

Orlando was shoving his hands convulsively through his hair. 'I can't believe it. She never seemed the type.'

Kiki suppressed a snort. Where had he been? Mars? Savannah Bouche's romantic track record was a car crash.

'I mean,' he went on, 'she could certainly use a smartphone. But she hardly had the skill set for hacking.'

'Hacking?' Kiki frowned.

The two Cheases stared at her again. 'What else do you think we're talking about?' asked Orlando.

'You and Savannah. Breaking up.'

He gave a hollow laugh. 'I had a lucky escape, by the sound of it. But she couldn't have swapped me for a more deserving man. I wish her and Caspar all the luck in the world. He's going to need it.' Orlando's eyes gleamed with malice.

'So what *are* you talking about?' Kiki was now thoroughly confused.

'The cast list! For the pantomime!' Lady Mandy shook her phone. 'I've just been Google alerted about it! Someone's hacked into it and released it on the internet!'

CHAPTER TWENTY-ONE

I t had been a wretched week for Laura. After her initial breezy acceptance of it, Caspar's betrayal had hit her hard. She felt vulnerable about everything at the moment. Friendship, work, love.

What had been occasional thoughts about Harry now became obsessive brooding. Things they had done in the past came back to her. It all seemed so wonderful. Compared to Caspar he appeared resolute, noble and dependable.

Well, up to a point. He was still absent and incommunicado, of course. But wasn't that, Laura asked herself, the very reason he seemed so perfect? Because he was the unattainable ideal?

The memories could be set off by anything. A snatch of opera blaring from a passing bicycle taxi brought back the evening Harry bundled her in his scruffy car and hurtled – as much as one could hurtle – through south London. 'Where are we going?' she had kept asking, and he had refused to answer, talked about other things, until the hard, grey motorway had given way to soft, green, shaggy country lanes not unlike those round Great Hording. The land had become rounded and dippy, like the swell of green waves, and she could sense the sea wasn't far off. Then they had turned into an imposing entrance and people in evening dress were suddenly scattered everywhere, carrying picnic baskets, drifting with flutes of champagne.

'Welcome to Glyndebourne,' said Harry.

She had turned to him, eyes sparkling, but he was already out of the car and heading to the men's, whence he emerged what seemed a split second later, dazzlingly glamorous in black tie. He calmed her own fears about not being smart enough. 'You look wonderful!' (Luckily, she'd been in the white shirt and black bra combo again.) Then he had led her to the middle of a glossy lawn bordered with scented white flowers and scattered with champagne picnickers in ballgowns. He had opened his own hamper, beautifully packed, brimming with delicious and exotic things.

'You made this?' Laura was amazed.

He shook his head of dark curls; he had picked it up in Mayfair at a deli near the US Embassy.

She seized on this. 'You were at the US Embassy?'

But Harry, pouring champagne, would not be drawn. 'What do you know about *La Traviata*?' he asked, handing the glass over.

By the end of the evening Laura felt she knew all there was to know about it. The heart-tugging music, the passionate performances, the desperate tragedy, the glamorous surroundings, the champagne, and most of all Harry, made a mixture of amazing intensity. She felt taken apart and put together again. No one had ever had this effect on her.

'Did you find it sad?' he asked her, about the opera.

Laura thought. 'The saddest bits are the happy bits, because you know what is coming and they don't.'

She had been surprised to see his eyes shine a little bit brighter at this. Had he known then what was coming for the two of them? That soon, he would be gone, possibly for ever.

She reminded herself how he had warned her many times that radio silence was something she would occasionally have to deal with. Their first date, at the secret NDY Club – Not Dead Yet, the haunt of foreign correspondents just back from the field and their diplomatic and media associates – had made it clear that he moved in a secret world. His work meant that he was away without contact for long periods of time and while he would never say why, she could guess. His phone was being tapped. People were hacking his emails.

He had never asked her to wait for him. Still less had he insisted she keep chaste like a wartime bride. He probably wouldn't mind about Caspar, but it was this very thought that made Laura regret that now all the more bitterly.

She longed to feel Harry's strong, leather-sleeved arms around her and hear his low, amused voice making light of her worries. Every night, in the flat in Cod's Head Row, she found herself half-listening for his foot on the stair. But the only feet on the stairs were those of Edgar and his nightclub companions, most recently some Lithuanian sailors moored up against HMS *Belfast*. 'How *On the Town* can you get?' Edgar had enthused when, inevitably, Laura arrived at his door to remonstrate. He and the sailors had been doing a Gene Kelly routine and one mariner was still tap-dancing in the sink.

Harry would also have helped her bear the humiliations daily heaped on her by Clemency. If it had been bad under Carinthia it was now ten times worse. The ghastliest moment of the past week had been when Laura received a call from Honor, Christopher Stone's secretary, asking her why she had failed to present herself for lunch with him at Two Shepherd Street, his exclusive club.

Laura was horrified. 'I didn't know I was supposed to!'

'It was in your diary,' Honor said, sounding unusually steely.

'It wasn't! I swear to you, Honor. I wouldn't miss lunch with Christopher!' Or Two Shepherd Street, which served delicious shepherd's pie and cauliflower cheese and supersized Smarties as nibbles with the coffee.

'I asked Karlie to put it in your diary,' Honor insisted, unintentionally providing the breakthrough.

'She never said anything to me about it!' Laura was on the point of exclaiming before realising this sounded like an excuse at best, incompetent at worst. She fudged it with Honor, and stormed over to Karlie.

'I gave you a note about it,' Karlie claimed, coolly. 'It must have got lost on that horrendously messy desk of yours.'

There had been – quite literally – stony silence from Christopher since the incident. Laura expected any day to be given the sack. She had had to think fast to bolster up her position and it was during a features meeting over which Clemency was presiding with flashing eyes and thumping fist that the ideal position-bolsterer suggested itself. Clemency was haranguing the assembled about the need for a suitable female interviewee for a forthcoming issue. Someone widely admired and glamorous yet mysterious and inaccessible. Someone who no one else had interviewed.

'Well *obviously* Her Majesty would be perfect!' she stormed at the hapless Anais. 'Except she doesn't normally do press. Any other bright ideas?'

Laura, thinkingly longingly about Harry, now had a very bright one. 'How about Ellen O'Hara?'

From the other side of the glass desk, bolt-upright against the David Linley throne, Clemency narrowed her green cat-eyes. 'Ellen O'Hara of the *Sunday Times*? The foreign correspondent?'

She looked surprised, as Laura was herself. The suggestion had come from left field and had seemed almost to make itself, born, she supposed, from her recent reflections about the NDY Club. It was here, with Harry, that she had first met Ellen. The veteran correspondent had presented an impressive and glamorous figure, her swept-back glossy blonde hair, white shirt and fawn trousers giving her a Grace Kelly air.

'That might work,' Clemency admitted reluctantly. 'Her father's a marquess. She's very *Society*.'

Laura blinked. No one had mentioned the marquess at the NDY Club. It had not been relevant. What very much had been – so far as Laura was concerned – was that Ellen had known her own father, Peter Lake. They had been fellow reporters at the time his helicopter crashed in the desert.

'Think you can get her?' Clemency challenge-sneered.

Laura nodded confidently. Ellen would agree, for her father's sake. Plus, she was devoted to Harry. She might even know something about where he was; they pooled resources on stories from time to time.

Clemency's narrowed green eyes glittered. 'Do you know her? How?'

Laura had no intention of revealing anything about this. Harry had sworn her to silence about the NDY Club, which switched locations regularly and whose existence was secret to all but its members. And sometimes even to those who had been there. Once or twice since he had left Laura had returned to the backstreet where Harry had taken her. She had knocked on the worn door of the battered building where celebrities and battle-scarred hacks alike had pressed the admission button. But the building now was empty; the club had moved on.

She met Clemency's eyes, and those of Karlie. Both women were staring at her hard, suspiciously. Laura shrugged and smiled. 'Oh, you know. Met along life's way. As you do.'

But perhaps their meeting had meant nothing to Ellen after all. Laura had emailed her at her paper, but so far there had been no answer.

Now it was Saturday morning and she was driving up to Great Hording with Lulu and Vlad to spend the weekend at the former's new country estate. Despite not having ever laid eyes on the actual place Lulu was full of plans for Riffs. Excitement had made her more than usually incoherent. The back of the car was heaped with fabric swatches, colour charts, wood samples and magazines about interior design and gardening. They slid all over the footwells whenever Vlad turned a corner which, as they had now reached the twisting country lanes, was often.

Laura, burdened as she was with her own troubles, was nonetheless pleased that all Lulu's distress about South'n Fried seemed to have evaporated. She was now thinking of nothing but redecorating. Would she continue the theme of designer logos that characterised the Kensington mansion? Laura wondered. Would Riffs, too, have a BalenciAga in the kitchen? As they rolled along Lulu handed her a copy of a weekend newspaper, pointing excitedly to a stern-looking man with a black quiff and a blue goatee.

'Is famous designer Bingo Borgen. Minuscule ideas, hmm?'

'Minimalist,' corrected Laura, reading the accompanying article in which Bingo declared himself sceptical about the need for conventional flat floors. 'We need to challenge our preconceptions.' He appeared to have the same questioning approach to windows. 'Are they truly necessary? Darkness is underestimated as a decorative force.'

'He sounds awful,' Laura said firmly.

The billionheiress had moved on, however. 'And here is famous gardener.'

Laura took the magazine now being offered to her and examined its cover. A bearded youth wielding a hoe and wearing a T-shirt declaring 'A Weed is Just a Plant in the Wrong Place' smiled out from above the headline 'ZAK ATTACK. Horticulture's Hot New Face'.

He was certainly very red in the face. Perhaps it was sunshine. Flicking to the corresponding interview, Laura learnt that Zak viewed grass as a destructive monoculture which he preferred to concrete over wherever possible. 'People underestimate the simple beauty of cement.'

'You're not seriously thinking of doing that,' Laura said to Lulu. 'Concreting over your garden.'

Lulu shrugged. 'Am keeping brain open, hmm?'

Laura left her to it and turned her own attention to the newspapers. The general election campaign was about to begin and some of the government's leading lights featured heavily in the first few pages. Here was yet another photograph of Jolyon Jackson terrifying some poor child in hospital. Laura read the accompanying copy carefully. There was no mention of his caddish conduct at the pub quiz. People were forgetting already. Great Hording's reputation as a haven for the rich and privileged appeared to have survived.

Or had it? The headline on the next page read, 'CLEAN-EATING GODDESS EMPLOYED SLAVES IN RESTAURANT.'

The goddess being referred to was a certain Willow St George, whose Spiraliza chain of eateries were well established in the capital. The article accused her of employing illegal immigrants on wages of a pound an hour. Looking at the photograph of the red-lipsticked woman with the dark, glossy hair, Laura was certain she recognised her from the Golden Goose pub quiz. Hadn't she been the person telling Caspar that Bond needed to update his food refs?

But Willow was going to have to do some updating of her own. Someone, it seemed, had leaked her accounts which showed that the food queen of clean was not only a brutal taskmaster – quite literally a slavedriver – but someone who regularly expensed McDonald's takeaways. The report ended, 'Has the reputation of the duchess of detox taken a toxic turn?'

'We're here!' shouted Lulu, bouncing up and down and clapping her hands as Vlad drew the Bentley's shining bumper up to a pair of huge, black, iron gates into which wrought-iron gold guitars were set below the scrolled iron letters 'RIFFS'. As the gates opened, the right-hand side peeled away bearing just the well-known abbreviation FFS, which made Laura smile. On the evidence of *Desert Island Discs*, this could well be deliberate.

As they proceeded up the tarmac drive, the smile on Laura's face became awe. The house was incredible. Fantastical, with its spread of red-brick towers and turrets. It looked more like an Oxbridge college, or a very fancy boarding school, than anywhere someone actually lived. Perhaps this was because it had both a clock tower – its diamond-shaped clock-face winking gold in the sun – and a chapel. Both of them reminded Laura unpleasantly of her own school, and from here it was impossible to stop her thoughts bounding to Clemency Makepeace. She looked at her phone, but there was still no message from Ellen. A cold feeling went through her insides as she imagined the glamorous veteran reporter glancing at her messages under a hail of bullets somewhere very hot and violent, then rolling her eyes in scorn at the pathetic professional depths to which Peter Lake's daughter had sunk.

'Is good, no?' Lulu asked, her sunglasses flashing excitedly as she opened the car door and sprang out to examine her domain. Vlad put the brakes sharply on; the car was still moving. Lulu's clothes glinted in the sunshine almost as brightly as the clock tower. To help blend seamlessly into the rural scene she had bought herself a quilted gold husky and a pair of silver Wellingtons.

Laura clambered out behind her and went to stand with Lulu at the edge of a strangely shaped swimming pool. The voice of Roger Slutt on *Desert Island Discs* came back to her. 'I put in a guitar-shaped swimming pool as well. They went BEEPing postal over that. . .'

The pool's still, blue surface, on which a number of brown

leaves floated, reflected a biplane circling round and round in the sky above. Though neither Lulu nor Laura realised it, this was Tim Lacey, a keen amateur pilot who habitually used his licence to snoop on his neighbours. Like everyone else in Great Hording, he was desperate to know the identity of the new arrival. 'The only thing I can say for sure,' he reported to his listening wife in the vast Hollywood House kitchen, 'is that it's not George and Amal. It's two women, one fair and one dark. Over.'

Sabrina was only half-listening, as she was eagerly scanning the leaked pantomime list, which all village residents had received in a group email from Lady Mandy's hacked account. 'Anna Goblemova's playing Cinderella' she reported to her husband. 'Which everyone knows is only because Sergei's invested bazillions in Alastair's company.'

'Who's Prince Charming?' It had better be him, Tim thought.

'Haven't got there yet. Philip Peaseblossom's the front end of the donkey. And you're the back.'

'*What*?' Tim was exclaiming. But it came out as 'Wha— FUCK!' because he noticed only just in time that he was flying straight at the chapel windows of Riffs. He yanked violently on the joystick and the aeroplane soared upwards with mere inches to spare.

'Is welcome flypast, you think?' Lulu asked as she and Laura watched this dramatic display from the ground.

Laura doubted it, but had no alternative theory to offer.

'Or is local fly club, hmm? I join maybe.'

'*No*,' Laura said decisively.

A hurt-looking pair of sunglasses was turned on her. 'So why not? Want join in local clubs, yes?'

'How about golf? Or vegetable-growing?'

This suggestion found favour. 'Wegetables, yes.' Lulu nodded her mass of long, blonde hair. 'Grown own truffles, hmm?'

Laura and Lulu had now reached the mansion's vast front door. With its huge iron door-knocker and Gothic carvings, it looked like something from a Hammer Horror. As Lulu pushed it open, Laura expected Max von Sydow, a candelabra in each hand, to greet them. And Norma Desmond waiting beyond, ready for her close-up.

What actually waited beyond were Roger Slutt's decorations. Cupids frolicked on the painted ceiling of the entrance hall. Gilt frames were carved with goddesses. There were four colossal chandeliers and a carpet swirling with woven ribbons, billowing and blue, over a woven sea of pink flowers. The curtains at the massive windows comprised five layers of pink, blue and gold brocade roped back with an enormously thick silk rope whose tassels were weighed with chunks of crystal. In one corner stood a shiny white baby grand, in another a gold harp.

'I like.' Lulu was looking assessingly round, hands on hips. 'Is simple English country style, yes?'

By way of Louis XIV multiplied by an oligarch with blingtastic bad taste, Laura thought. Was there an undecorated inch in the entire place?

Lulu's silver wellies squeaked on the parquet as they walked on into the dining room. Below a gold stucco ceiling was a vast black shiny dining table whose legs were short, thick, fluted gold pillars. Surrounding this monstrosity were twelve black velvet chairs with carved gold legs and gold skulls atop the seat backs. It looked like the meeting room of a particularly flamboyant satanic cult.

'Mirror is black, why?' pondered Lulu, trying to see her

reflection in the huge dark looking glass set in a gold frame writhing with snakes.

'It's a telly,' Laura guessed.

Adjoining the dining room, accessed by double doors lined with padded silver leather, was a hideous bar whose backlit mahogany shelves were crammed with crystal decanters. In an adjoining room Laura caught a glimpse of some red flock wallpaper and a gleaming gold urinal.

Lulu had by now moved on to the bar top which was made of glass and embedded with bullets. Instead of beer, the pull-handle pumps served pints of a range of champagnes. 'Is genius!' Lulu exclaimed in delight as she yanked a foaming stream of Moët on to the floor.

For all its Versailles style, the whole place was computerised. There was a central control room with wall-to-wall banks of screens, buttons and flashing red and green lights.

'Is called SmartButler,' Lulu enthused, consulting her tablet. 'You press button on tablet, bath run, yes?'

Laura's eyes slid to Vlad, standing politely by the door ready to do her mistress's bidding. As befitted the smartest butler Laura knew, her expression, as inscrutable as ever, gave no clue to what she was thinking.

Lulu, on the other hand, clearly just wasn't thinking. Tact had never been her strong point. 'SmartButler in kitchen too,' she said, consulting her tablet. 'You switch on from yacht, robot take food out of freezer and put in stove, hmm?'

The Frenchwoman in Laura could not think of anything more ghastly. Cooking by robot? Missing out all the wonderful, soothing, sensual stages of selecting, peeling, chopping, stirring?

From the door came what might have been a sigh.

'Is there a wine cellar?' Laura asked quickly, not just with a Frenchwoman's interest in vintages but because the wine in the Kensington house was Vlad's special responsibility. She prided herself on selecting exactly the right bottle for whatever food was being served.

Lulu looked up from the screen, her sunglasses glinting excitedly. 'SmartButler choose wine! You type in what eat, is all.' Laura gathered that you knocked in a few numbers and an appropriate bottle of exactly the right temperature would rise up a chute from the capacious cellar. The design, apparently, was based on the hydraulic shell-loading system in a battleship.

She did not dare meet Vlad's eye after this. Given the circumstances, a knock – or rather a slap – on the silver padded leather double doors came as a rather merciful interruption.

'Yoo hoo!' Kiki meant to trill merrily as she came into the room. But the degree of unpleasant shock and recognition meant she just blurted, starkly, 'You!'

'You yourself,' replied Lulu.

Kiki's reflexes were less fast. She had suffered one tremendous shock already that day in the shape of the revelations about Willow's criminal Spiraliza chain. Thankfully, Great Hording had not been named. But the story had come hard on the heels of the leaking of Lady Mandy's cast list and, before that, the Jolyon Jackson horror.

It was beginning to look as if someone was targeting the village and picking off its distinguished denizens one by one. Certainly, this was what it was looking like to Jonny, who was having kittens and demanding Kiki put a stop to the scandals. But while Kiki had now firmly convinced herself that Kearn from the Fishing Boat Inn was behind them, she could prove nothing. It had been a disappointment to find that Sir Philip Peaseblossom, to whom she had turned in her hour of need, was quite unable to arrest and imprison her number one suspect with no evidence. So what was the point of *him*? Kiki asked herself angrily.

Once again she was relying on distraction to head off her incandescent boss. The identity of the new owner, or owners, of Riffs, should, she had calculated, do just that.

Her horror at realising it was Lulu, the street-fighting It girl, and her friend the dark-haired slut who had slept with Caspar Honeyman and eavesdropped on her conversation with Jolyon Jackson, was absolute. That the room stank like a pub bar the morning after – a scent with which Kiki was more than familiar – supported what she already knew. These women were no good for Great Hording.

'What do you want?' Laura was looking at Kiki with her arms folded. She suspected that the woman was here out of sheer curiosity, and her suspicions were confirmed when Kiki went red.

'I wanted to make sure you were happily settling in,' she said in a strained voice.

'We're settling in fine, thank you.' Laura continued to give Kiki a hard stare.

'Well, I must be off to my pantomime rehearsal.' Kiki backed out of the room in her best special-edition designer Birkenstocks, worn in honour of the occasion.

The one bright spot in all the current ghastliness was the fact that Lady Mandy had, finally, given her a small part. It was not on the leaked list; Kiki's name, crushingly, had not featured at all. Dung Spaw had been given the coveted part of Buttons, and Kate Threadneedle was playing Dandini.

But the lure of a free champagne party had, after all, been enough for the great producer to graciously cast Kiki as 'Mine Hostess' of the Village Idiot, the pantomime's pub. It hadn't seemed an especially brilliant role, given that it was non-speaking. 'But, my dear, landladies have a great theatrical history. Take Mistress Quickly, in *Henry IV, Part One*,' Lady Mandy had boomed. Only once Kiki returned to the Golden Goose and consulted BardOnline did she discover that Mistress Quickly had run a brothel.

'Pantsomime?' Beneath her thick tumble of blonde hair, Lulu's diamond-dangling ears pricked up. 'There is pantsomime here?'

Too late Kiki realised her mistake. But there was no hope of this unacceptable stranger crashing the hallowed circle of village thespians. 'Great Hording puts on its own performance every summer,' she said haughtily, stalking towards the door with her chin in the air.

'But is Christmas, pantsomime, yes?' Lulu sounded puzzled.

'Not in Great Hording,' Kiki informed her snootily. 'The entire village decamps in December to Klosters or the Caribbean. So the pantomime's in summer instead.'

'Is great!' Lulu's glossy pink lips spread in the brightest of smiles. 'I have part, yes?'

Kiki turned on her Birkenstocks. 'I'm afraid it's all been cast.'

There was a stubborn glint in the sunglasses that now turned on the pub manager. 'Is who in charge of pantsomime?'

Kiki had had no intention of revealing it. But now it struck her that Lady Mandy in full pompous sail was the least that Lulu deserved. Accordingly, she gave full details of the hallowed producer, and of the location of Promptings.

'Is your behind!' Lulu declared suddenly.

Kiki clamped both hands on her rear. 'What?'

'Is your behind!' roared the billionheiress, again.

'What's wrong with my behind?'

'Is what they say in pantsomime,' Lulu chortled triumphantly. 'Is your behind! I practise, hmm?'

Laura and Lulu watched as Kiki stalked out through the silver-padded doors with as much dignity as she could muster. 'I go down there, yes?' Lulu said. 'To the cheeselady. You come too?'

Laura shook her head violently. Her horror of amateur dramatics dated back to school productions where she would be third spear carrier watching her hated enemy take the lead part. Clemency, unsurprisingly, was a talented dissembler whose scheming Lady Macbeth had been especially admired.

CHAPTER TWENTY-TWO

L ulu and Vlad drove off to beard Lady Mandy in a sudden burst of rain, but this had eased off by the time Laura walked up the Riffs driveway to wander round the village. The birds were powerfully singing. Seeing them hopping about the dripping trees she wondered how anything so tiny could make so much noise. Or why, come to that. Was it a matter of territory, or just for fun? Laura, a city girl, had never considered such questions before. She wondered if the country might be growing on her, even Roger Slutt's maximalist version of it.

In pretty Georgian Fore Street, the song of blackbirds gave way to the cries of seagulls. They circled around, yellow-beaked and white-winged, in air blue and bright with the reflected light of the ocean just behind the row of shopfronts. The wet cobbles were steaming under the strength and warmth of the sun. It felt as if the place had been washed and was now drying like clothes on a line.

Laura lingered, looking in the shops. Here was the Post Office Stores with its jars of traditional sweets in the windows. Caribbean Limes. Uncle Joe's Mint Balls. Coconut Mushrooms. She grinned, imagining Mimi's reaction. Her grandmother thought the English made the strangest sweets in the world. Liquorice bootlaces? *Sérieusement?*

Centre of the window display at Neverland, a high-end toyshop, was a doll's house featuring its own media room, home gym and garage with tiny sports car and Land Rover. Each bedroom had a flat-screen TV and en suite bathroom. Great Hording in miniature.

Here was a boutique, The Dreamy Englishwoman, which sold floaty clothes in muted shades – not Laura's sort of thing at all – and here was the bookshop, painted the sort of clear, bright pale blue that lifted the spirits just to look at it. The window was filled with the latest releases, all obviously hand-picked to suit the locale. Front and centre were Dame Hermione's Saddle-Saw novels. 'We've all read *Nasty* and *Brutish*,' affirmed an elegantly handwritten placard. 'And we simply can't wait for *Short*!'

Laura remembered the understated, slightly shabby but definitely handsome quizmaster; this was his lair. She stood aside as the door opened and a tall, fair, lean man came out. The barman from the Golden Goose, Laura remembered. He had struck her as a civilised sort, quite the type to go in bookshops. He was Russian, or perhaps Polish; both big book-reading nations, of course.

If Great Hording was the quintessential English seaside village, this had to be the quintessential bookshop. Shelves painted the same jolly blue as the shop's exterior filled every inch of wall, rising from sisal floor to stucco ceiling, stuffed with volumes on subjects whose categories were advertised with neatly lettered signs. Here and there along the shelves small recommendations had been attached below particular volumes. Some were quite funny: 'The ultimate coming of aga story,' it said beneath a new novel about moving to the country. Rather to her disappointment, the bookshop-keeper with his worn cords and world-weary charm had not yet materialised. No one sat at the small desk at the shop's shady rear, equipped with a till and a small computer.

Laura continued to peruse the shelves.

The 'Local Author' section would have filled a smaller bookshop just by itself. The variety, reach and sheer size of Great Hording's collective influence was amazing.

Here was *Superspook: A Life of Philip Peaseblossom*; *Blue Moon: The Riotously Unofficial Biography of Jolyon Jackson*; *Banking On It* by Sir Richard Threadneedle and *Towards A Fundamental Interpretation of The New Legal Corporate Alternative* by Lord Jeremy Young, QC. The shelf devoted to Dame Hermione was enormous and contained, in addition to the expected canon, a good many steamy Mills & Boons she had penned early in her career when trying to get off the ground as an author. Margaret Tache was also well represented, with *Catullus's Underpants: A Life of Rome's Raunchiest Poet* being the latest release.

Laura browsed on. Here was *The Future Is Breezeblock* by Bingo Borgen; the same blue-bearded architectural maestro Lulu had been so excited about on the way up. Laura hadn't realised he lived in Great Hording and wondered what his house was like. Breezeblock, presumably. And wonky-floored with no windows.

Speaking of Wonky, here was the celebrated florist's book

Through A Hedge Forwards. Laura flicked through the lavishly illustrated 'About Wonky' section. Here she was in tight, faded jeans outside a smart white-painted shop in an expensive Chelsea street. Behind rows of parked Bentleys and shining Aston Martins were ranged wooden buckets of dock leaves and rosebay willowherb. Beneath this were testimonials from simple country-flower lovers ranging from the Duchess of Porthminster to the chairman of Goldman Sachs by way of South'n Fried, 'multi-Grammy-winning recording artist and owner of MotherF****r Records.' Where was Lulu's erstwhile fiancé now? Laura wondered. Still roaming the globe on his 'Bust Yo Ass' tour, presumably. Having had his ass – or at least his heart – conclusively busted by Savannah Bouche.

'Former Ralph Lauren model Wonky trained as a wild florist at the Académie des Fleurs Sauvages, Paris,' the introductory article went on. 'Wonky has four children, Wolf, Echo, Norman and Lucky Blue, and homes in Italy, America and France as well as London and the English countryside. Famous for inventing the jam-jar posy, Wonky believes that simple is always best.'

Laura closed the book and moved on down the shelf. Here were *UberDirector* by the ever-modest Tim Lacey and *F*** Art* by Zeb Spaw, an exhibition catalogue to go with the sell-out Serpentine show of the same name.

And here, oh dear, was *Good To Goji* by Willow St George, a compilation of favourites from her successful chain of clean-eating Spiraliza restaurants. Presumably in view of recent developments, it was marked at half price, but even that seemed steep to Laura leafing through recipes for crisped carrot peelings on shredded cardoon root sprinkled with carbonised toast dust. Willow beamed blissfully out from the back cover, blissfully unaware of the fate that awaited. And here she was being clean, green and queenly, beaming at a grizzled old cheesemaker at a farmer's market and holding a dripping mozzarella. There was not a Happy Meal in sight. Laura slid the volume back and passed on.

She felt she would like to buy a novel. For all its decoration there were no books at Riffs, nor bookcases, come to that. Her bedroom, which had belonged to one of Roger Slutt's granddaughters, was a loud pink festooned with drapes and crowns. The odd volume might tone down this effect.

Did this bookshop, Laura wondered, have a second-hand section? She liked books that were worn, that showed evidence of having been read and enjoyed. Pre-loved paperbacks would also be cheap.

She walked around, looking carefully at the shelves for creased black or orange spines denoting Penguin Classics. As she neared the back of the shop she heard the low murmur of a voice. The bookseller must have an office there.

At the same time she spotted a slender section of shelving whose contents looked more worn than all the whizzy new productions around it. She went over to look.

Here were the classics, many she knew, some she didn't. Here too was a collection of hardbacks with worn leather spines. One caught her eye immediately. *Indigenous Fats and Waxes of Norway*. Who even knew that this was a subject?

Harry would love it, she felt immediately. He adored obscure facts about unusual things. Perhaps she could buy it for him. She pulled it out; a damp, musty smell rose to her nostrils as she opened it. No price was visible on the thick, cream pages, their edges brown with age. She began to read, and smiled. This book was so Harry. He would adore that Norwegian fishermen used whale fat to weatherproof their houses, and that there was a type of crisp made from dried blubber.

'Excuse me. I must seem very rude. I didn't hear you come in.'

The bookshop proprietor was suddenly at her elbow. His blue eyes twinkled with welcome and his long, rather sensual mouth stretched in a measured smile. Noticing that he didn't reveal his teeth, Laura thought of how her grandmother would approve. '*Never* show your gums, not in smiling, not in talking.' Great dazzling Hollywood beams *à la* Savannah Bouche filled Mimi with horror.

'It doesn't matter. I've been looking round.' Laura was watching him carefully for any sign that he remembered her from the pub quiz. He had been in charge of it and had ultimately had to deny them the prize. He would have obviously taken on board Kiki's opinion that she was a troublemaker.

And yet there seemed no spark of recognition in the bookseller's frank blue gaze. His name now suddenly came back to her. Peter. Peter Delabole.

'Can I be of any assistance? Is there a particular book you're looking for?'

Laura waved *Indigenous Fats and Waxes of Norway*. 'I'd like this one.'

The bookseller looked apologetic. 'I'm terribly sorry. But that book's actually not for sale.'

'So why's it in the bookshelf?' Laura challenged.

'Yes, quite. A perfectly valid question. The answer is that

it seems to have got there from a box of books I just bought at auction and haven't catalogued yet. I'm so sorry. Not very efficient of me.' He pulled a rueful face.

'Can't you catalogue it now?' Laura felt that she really wanted the book for Harry, even at the risk of seeming stubborn.

'That's not really possible, I'm afraid. I really am sorry. You are absolutely right, of course. I need to overhaul my system. But just for now I'm stuck with it.'

It was impossible not to be charmed by him, nor respond to his obvious embarrassment. It would be churlish, Laura felt, to insist.

'May I?' Peter Delabole deftly removed the volume from Laura's hand, closed it and placed it securely under his tweed-jacketed arm. 'If I might make some alternative recommendations,' he added, steering Laura back towards the front of the shop, 'we are fortunate in having a number of well-known local authors. Dame Hermione Grantchester's probably our biggest name. *Nasty* and *Brutish* are very popular. Have you read the Saddle-Saw series?'

Under his warm blue gaze Laura felt herself unravelling. 'Er. . . no.'

The measured smile reappeared, slightly broadened. 'Goodness me, you've missed a treat. They're about Napoleon's horse Marengo, they're absolutely fascinating. It's all written from his point of view, you see, and the bits about the Retreat from Moscow, when Napoleon was suffering from haemorrhoids, are especially well-imagined. One might almost imagine Dame Hermione was writing from personal experience.'

Laura left Great Hording Books with a copy of *Nasty* in a smart blue bag that echoed the shop's azure livery. She regretted not getting *Indigenous Fats and Waxes of Norway*, but it had mainly been intended for Harry, so what was the point? Now Laura was out of London and away from all the places which reminded her of him, her obsession seemed to be fading. She felt more able to take stock and face the fact that she might not be seeing him again. But so what? Laura squared her shoulders and tilted her chin upwards. She could cope without a man.

But she could not cope without food. She was hungry, and here was Di's Deli, with its old-fashioned delivery bicycle propped outside it. The shop looked wonderful, if rather expensive, its windows featuring bottles of champagne, pots of caviar and tins of foie gras arranged in wicker hampers fitted with leather straps and padded with muted checks. Picnics in Great Hording were clearly smart affairs.

The doorbell pinged as Laura entered. There were more baskets inside, as well as colourful tins of Italian biscuits and gleaming bottles of oil, wine and vinegar with elaborate scrolled labels. Loaves of all shapes and sizes were arranged like something by Arcimboldo. A large glass chiller cabinet displayed what were presumably fashionable salads in painted china bowls. What, Laura wondered, was dukkah? Ancient Grains sounded like something from the British Museum. A blackboard above the cabinet announced that the soup of the day was edamame. Had someone really popped out all the tiny green beans, only to make them into soup?

'Can I help you?' A young woman had appeared from a back room, large and truculent in a ribboned straw boater. It made an odd contrast with the blue hair and black lipstick beneath it.

'Wyatt!'

'Laura!' The belligerent expression in the thickly made-up eyes changed to amazement.

'Love the hat. What are you doing here?'

'I could ask you the same thing. You're not here to spy on me as well, are you?'

Laura admitted that her spying days were over. The piece was on hold.

Resplendent in a Di's Deli apron, her erstwhile intern rolled her eyes. 'I don't mean that. It's me that's being spied on now. It's like living under the Stasi. My parents watch me all the time. And Di.'

'She owns the deli?'

Wyatt nodded. 'She's out at the moment, thank God. Gone to the helipad with a delivery.'

Laura recalled the Jeff Koons dog statue.

'Our friendly local oligarch wants some sausages,' Wyatt added.

'Can't she just take the bike?'

'This is Great Hording, remember. Sergei's in St Petersburg right now. The bangers are being choppered to his private jet.'

Laura whistled. 'So why is everyone spying on you?'

'Because of Kearn. He's Public Enemy Number One. Since the quiz.'

He was pretty amazing.' Laura smiled at the memory; the three of them wiping the floor with the massed ranks of Great Hording. Cheating MPs and all.

'He is amazing.' Below her dead white make-up, Wyatt flushed with pleasure. 'Not that anyone round here thinks so. They all think he's behind the stories that are getting out. About Jolyon Jackson, Willow and Lady Mandy's list.'

'Which one is Lady Mandy?'

Wyatt grinned. 'She's this ghastly pompous hag who holds the village over a barrel about her pantomime. The list is of who's got what part.'

The terrifying old bat who had shouted at Savannah, Laura remembered.

'Everyone's desperate to be in it, even my parents. It's a sort of collective madness. But Lady Mandy's so picky even Kenneth Branagh wouldn't stand a chance. I think he's been turned down in the past, actually.'

With a stab of concern, Laura thought of Lulu. If competition was this tough, she wouldn't have a hope of a role. 'But why are they blaming Kearn? He's done nothing.'

Wyatt's smile died away. 'But he does computer studies. And . . . well. . . he has form. The Little Hording Popular Front. He led a group which resisted the planning application for the Golden Goose. And he very nearly succeeded, except the council changed their mind at the last minute. The Mayor had the casting vote.'

Laura remembered the conversation she overheard between Kiki and Jolyon Jackson in the Golden Goose. And, further back, the remarks Wyatt had made in her own office. About the Farmer's Arms once being a local pub for local people and Great Hording's great sense of entitlement. She had been behind Kearn all the way, all the time. But what had he been behind? Perhaps he wasn't blameless after all.

'It isn't him!' Wyatt said fiercely, shoving a lock of blue hair back up into her boater. 'And the Popular Front never hacked into people's private lists and released them on the internet. Kearn is innocent.'

'Of course he is,' said Laura, staunchly.

Wyatt gave her a grateful glance. 'It's really hard,' she confessed, looking suddenly vulnerable. 'People are being so horrible about him. He's trying to study for exams and doesn't need this hassle. And the pub's being boycotted; anyone in Little Hording with links to Great Hording's being told not to drink there. Kearn's parents are worried sick.'

'What an awful situation. Has he no idea who's actually behind all the leaks?'

Wyatt's boater twisted from side to side. 'None. Everyone assumes he's guilty, though. My parents won't let me see him or even talk to him. I'm not allowed on the internet or anything. They've taken my phone, even.' Her eyes flickered hopefully about Laura's pocket.

'Here,' Laura said, taking the hint and fishing out her smartphone.

Wyatt seized it gratefully and rushed into the rear. 'Won't be a sec. Cough hard if anyone comes.'

'Okay,' said Laura, hoping she was aiding star-crossed lovers and not abetting a treacherous plot. She needed to find out with all speed; in other words, go to Little Hording and see Kearn. Wyatt was clearly convinced of his innocence but Laura was not so sure. He had the skills, motive and also the opportunity to have made Jackson's cheating public at least.

Later, she would get Vlad to drive her over. See him face to face. Get to the bottom of things.

CHAPTER TWENTY-THREE

Walking back to Riffs, carrying her book bag in one hand and the self-consciously retro wax paper and string parcel from the deli in the other, Laura wondered how Lulu had fared with Lady Mandy. She feared the worst, in which case the small piece of gold-leaf ewe's cheese and the truffle sourdough baguette, which had been all she was able to afford, wouldn't help much. Wyatt had slipped in a free seaweed and pomegranate aril salad, but mainly as something in which to bury the borrowed smartphone so Di, the returned proprietor, wouldn't see her handing it back. Getting it out on the way home, Laura had had to wipe off clinging vegetation and plenty of oil.

She entered the huge, carved front door of Riffs to find Lulu dancing excitedly round the entrance hall. 'Am in pantsomime!'

'Lady Mandy gave you a part? That's unbelievable.'

Lulu's sunglasses flashed reprovingly. 'Lady Mandy love me!' she declared, clasping both hands in ecstasy to her quilted bodice. She had, Laura saw, dressed for the visit in John Galliano at his most exuberant; the difference between herself and an actual pantomime heroine was so slight as to be non-existent. Perhaps it was this that had influenced the queen of the village's amateur thespians.

'Did you audition?'

'No. She say she love me because I fight Savannah. Cheeselady hate Savannah because she dump cheese son.'

Laura grinned admiringly. 'Wow, Lulu. You always find a way, don't you? What's the part?'

'I am sleeper.'

Laura frowned. Wasn't *Snow White* the one about sleeping? Or *Sleeping Beauty*, come to that?

'Grass sleeper,' Lulu added, making Laura think again. Wasn't there one called *Babes in the Wood*?

Then she realised. 'Glass slipper? You mean, you're the actual shoe?'

'Yes, yes! Is special harchitectural one. Kind of boot-shaped. Made of brizzblock. Is by Bingo Borgen, you know?'

'You're playing a breezeblock boot?'

Lulu was too excited to listen. 'Is panto, all famous people in willage do stuff? Zeb Spaw do scene, hmm?'

'Zeb Spaw paints the scenery?' God, what was that going to look like?

'Mmm-hmm.' Lulu was dancing about again. She was like a child when excited. Her joy was infectious and lit up the room. Even this room, blazing with mirrors and gilt, which was quite well lit up already.

'And Wonky do garden, hmm?'

'Cinderella's garden?'

'My garden! Wonky lovely sister.'

'What?' Laura pressed her hands to her temples. 'Whose lovely sister?'

'In panto.'

'You mean Ugly Sisters?'

It took some time to decode the facts. Wonky de Launay had arrived at Promptings shortly after Lulu. She had no intention of playing an Ugly Sister, and once Lady Mandy had agreed to rename the part more flatteringly, Wonky and Lulu had got into conversation. Wonky, who obviously didn't let the grass grow under her feet – especially if she could stick it in a jam jar and sell it – had offered to help Lulu overhaul the garden at Riffs.

'She give me good price!' Lulu enthused. 'Want to do rustic planting. Buttertubs. Daisies.'

'But they're weeds,' Laura pointed out. 'They're free.'

Lulu was not listening. She was full of Wonky's vision. Central to this vision, it turned out, was transforming the guitar-shaped swimming pool into a guitar-shaped herb garden.

'Is good idea,' Lulu stated firmly. 'Who can swim in outside pool in England anyway?'

Laura looked out through the multi-curtained windows of Riffs. The earlier rain had given way to a fine calm afternoon, with the droplets on the grass glittering under a strengthening sun. You could probably just about swim in such weather. And why had Lulu bothered to move to the seaside if she held such views about alfresco bathing?

There was little time to dwell on this because Vlad now

entered the room. Laura was relieved to see her. After the humiliations of SmartButler, for her to consider her position would have been understandable. Vlad raised her chin. 'I regret to report something of a hitch with the computer system, madam.'

Laura stared at her, hard. The butler met her gaze unflinchingly.

'Is what happen?' Lulu exclaimed.

Vlad explained in her usual restrained and respectful tones but Laura was sure she could hear triumph in the butler's account of how the robot in the wine cellar had started shoving antique vintages into the recycling. And how, while Vlad had been unpacking upstairs, the revolving six-foot shoe tree had lost control and spun like a roundabout in a children's playground, firing spike-heeled footwear in all directions. 'I fear that the system may be something of a danger, madam,' was Vlad's sober conclusion.

Laura looked down to hide a smile. How much of what had happened was really an accident? Lulu, meanwhile, looked at Vlad in dismay. 'We call someone to fix, hmm?'

'I know someone,' Laura said, thinking quickly. Kearn. She needed to see him and this would kill two birds with one stone. She could talk to him face to face and he would have the system under control in seconds – in the sense that he would be able to shut it down completely. Maintaining SmartButler was going to do nothing for employee relationships.

She turned to Vlad. 'I'll contact him. Perhaps you could go and get him.'

Vlad met her gaze steadily. Possibly slightly truculently.

'He's very good, and he'll obviously do his best,' Laura went on. 'But I'm not saying he'll be able to fix it altogether.'

The butler's stiff features relaxed. 'Very good, madam. I'll get the car ready.'

Kearn arrived an hour or so later. Being picked up by a chauffeured Bentley had caused a sensation in Little Hording, he said. 'Attracted quite a crowd, it did. My mum was straight out there with the free pork pies. One or two stayed for a drink, so that came out of it, at least. Where's this malfunctioning system then?'

Vlad escorted him to Riff's central control room from which he emerged some twenty minutes later. 'It's terminal,' he said.

'Is terminal, yes,' Lulu agreed with a toss of her hair. 'But can you fix terminal?'

Kearn shook his head. His close-cropped hair and ungainly features contrasted dramatically with the flowing locks and noble cheekbones of Che Guevara on his T-shirt. But Wyatt, Laura knew, considered him quite perfect.

'It's quite an old-fashioned system,' Kearn explained, 'and some of the parts are obsolete. My recommendation is that you simply disconnect it and carry on with the normal circuits.' He exchanged the slightest of slight glances with Vlad.

Lulu submitted with little more than a shrug. Laura sensed she had lost interest in SmartButler anyway. Wonky was due any moment and she needed to prepare for this great meeting of horticultural minds. 'Go to put my ho dress on,' she said, which seemed inappropriate, to say the least. Laura had long learnt, however, not to come between Lulu and her wardrobe.

Her own interview with Kearn took place over tea. It

was served by Vlad with all the trimmings; a Versace tea set from the London house and a matching cakestand with tiny smoked salmon sandwiches, cakes and biscuits.

'Wow,' said Kearn, tucking in with gusto. 'Crusts off and everything. I've never had tea this posh.'

'You deserve it,' Laura said warmly. The more at ease he felt, the more likely he would be to confide in her.

They were sitting on Riffs' terrace, a paved stone patio leading out from the windows of the satanic dining room. The furniture here was just as overdecorated; great padded thrones in bright Indian print glittering with sequins and heavy with tassels. Above them loomed large, intensely decorated, fringed Oriental parasols. All you needed was a few elephants.

The sun was now fully, strongly out and bounced brightly off the surface of the swimming pool where Wonky, in her usual uniform of tight jeans and tight white T-shirt, was standing with Lulu sporting a gardening vibe. Her gold handbag was shaped like a trowel and the advertised ho dress turned out to be just that – printed with hoes.

'I think dandelions over here, in this corner,' Wonky was saying. 'And perhaps speedwell here, and birdsfoot trefoil. I can get the plants at cost from my supplier in Nicaragua.'

Laura turned her attention back to Kearn. Now was the moment. She decided not to beat about the bush.

'All these leaks,' she said. 'Who's behind them, do you think?'

He was sipping from one of the Versace teacups. The gold on it flashed in the sun. 'No idea. Everybody thinks it's me, of course.'

'They do,' Laura agreed. 'And of course you've got form.'

He didn't bluster, as she had expected. Rather, he reached

for another sandwich and nodded. 'The Little Hording Popular Front.'

'And you had the opportunity,' Laura added.

'At the quiz, yes,' Kearn agreed. 'I could have taken that picture, easily.'

'And you probably know a bit about hacking.' Laura kept her voice matter-of-fact, but her insides were tightening as they always did when on the verge of a big discovery. Was Kearn about to confess to her? Decide the game was up?

'I do,' he concurred, selecting a cake with a swirl of pink frosting on the top, scattered with silver balls.

'You could have got Lady Mandy's list and found out about Willow as well.'

'I could,' Kearn shifted in his seat.

A few seconds elapsed.

'So,' Laura said, toying with the tassel trim on her chair. 'Did you?'

A few seconds more of silence, during which Kearn looked at the paving stones. She waited, hardly daring to draw breath in case it should distract him from whatever confessional path he seemed to be considering. Excitement flashed through her as he raised his head and looked her straight in the eye.

'No.'

She wasn't sure if she was dismayed or relieved. 'No?'

'Please believe me, Laura.' Kearn leant forward. 'I'm the obvious suspect, and that's impacted on Wyatt. I would never have done it, precisely for that reason. I'm no fan of Great Hording and most people who live there, and I don't mind admitting it. But Wyatt is more important to me than any of them. So it wasn't me, no. I didn't take the picture and I didn't leak the information. But I'm as keen as you to find out who did. Because the sooner they're discovered, the sooner the heat's off me and the sooner I can see Wyatt again.'

CHAPTER TWENTY-FOUR

As the Sunday night train gathered speed, Laura fought to raise her spirits. It was a warm, close evening and staying in Great Hording seemed infinitely preferable to returning to the city. London, for the time being at least, had lost its allure. Formerly the focus of all her ambitions, it seemed to have much less to offer these days. Clemency Makepeace was in the job that was rightfully hers and forcing her to do demeaning articles. Her attempt to raise herself above them and interview Ellen O'Hara had come to nothing. There had been no reply.

In which case, Laura told herself sternly, she needed to find someone else to interview instead. So she'd better start looking.

Resolutely, Laura unpacked from her bag the great mass of Sunday papers she had bought in the station newsagent and began to study them. Predictably, they were full of the forthcoming general election. The Prime Minister, looking even more exhausted than usual, glared out from the front pages, promising a strong and stable government.

Whether Jolyon Jackson would be part of it was a moot point. He had entirely fallen from the news agenda; no pictures of him preying on children in hospital this weekend. The Great Hording-related story that all the papers were covering was Willow St George's junk-food-and-slavery fall from grace. 'QUEEN OF CLEAN'S DIRTY LITTLE SECRETS,' the *Sunday Times* headline, was typical.

There was good news for Caspar though. His dream had come true; his prediction had been correct. The nominations for the Ivys, the newly established International Film Awards, had just been made public and Caspar actually was up for Best Actor in *The Caucus Imperative*, the first Bond ever to be nominated for an acting award.

Exactly why, Laura could not guess. Caspar had only acted himself, but perhaps the judges felt Bond's display of macho vanity to be a thespian *tour de force*. Some of the arts correspondents covering the list thought so, while others less charitable sniped that it was a stunt to launch the fledgling ceremony. If so, it had been successful. The coverage was considerable.

Should she send him a congratulatory text? Laura wondered. No, he had been an utter shit to her – taking up with Savannah Bouche just hours after leaving her in bed. On the other hand, petty wasn't her style. She would be magnanimous.

The text had just gone when the phone vibrated in reply, provoking, despite herself, a leap of pure excitement.

It was not Caspar, however, but someone even better. Ellen O'Hara, who Laura had given up hope of hearing from, had finally replied. *Don't normally do interviews – I'm the reporter, not the story – but will make exception for you, for Pete's sake.*

The Pete's sake was not an expression of impatience, but a reference to her father, Peter Lake. Laura's spirits soared. Saved! She glanced up to the striplights on the carriage's ceiling. 'Thanks, Dad!'

Can you come to my flat Monday lunchtime? Ellen had finished. There followed an address in Shad Thames, on the river's south bank.

The text, Laura realised, must be several days old. Perhaps the weird scrambled atmosphere of Great Hording had delayed it. Because Monday was tomorrow!

She needed to prepare this interview carefully. Laura flicked hastily through the *Sunday Times*, looking for Ellen's latest report. That would give her something to start the conversation off, at least. There was nothing, however. Whatever story Ellen was now working on, it was either not finished, or not started.

Taking up her trusty smartphone, Laura started some online research. There was plenty about Ellen, and lots of photographs. Here in a refugee camp, there in a war-zone sandstorm, here with some villagers, there with a reigning monarch. Always groomed and glamorous with her characteristic loose chignon, red lipstick, white shirt and fawn trousers, like a latter-day Lee Miller.

'Her work has earned her the respect of her peers, the admiration of a global readership and the fear of dictators, despots, bigots and war criminals worldwide,' read one summary of her achievements. Laura felt suddenly apprehensive. What would such a bold and principled woman make of her job on the glitziest of glossies? Ellen

O'Hara was sure to think her a lightweight. An idiot, even.

Well, Laura told herself determinedly, I am not an idiot. I am Peter Lake's daughter and Harry Stone's sort-of girlfriend. Possibly. Or possibly not. But Ellen is in a position to give me some answers about both of them.

The Sunday train was hot and slow and it was well after nine when Laura turned the corner into Cod's Head Row. As ever, the place was alive with hipsters determined to make the weekend last as long as possible. As Laura passed Gorblimey Trousers, Bill waved from behind the counter. 'You look like you need a bubble bath!' he yelled.

'Thanks,' Laura shot back, offended. She could certainly use a shower, but it was none of his business.

'It means laugh, dear.' Ben had popped up inside the doorway, bearing a tray of cocktails. He nodded towards them. 'Come in and have a Vera. Take the weight off your plates.'

Vera Lynn – gin; plates of meat – feet, Laura remembered. She decided to take the two of them on at their own game. 'I'd love to,' she explained apologetically, 'but I've got to get upstairs. My Chalfonts are murder at the moment.'

She walked off, but not so fast as to miss Bill and Ben stretch their eyes and mouth, 'Chalfont St Giles – piles,' at each other.

Grinning, Laura opened the battered door to her building and started the weary climb up the dusty, uncarpeted wooden stairs. She was surprised to see, on reaching her landing, that her door was open.

Her first thought was Edgar. But how? She hadn't given him a spare key; who in their right mind would? Had he broken in looking for Xanax?

'Edgar?' Laura strode in, the heels of her Chelsea boots echoing on the thin old floorboards. The only sound was her own gasp; the flat had been ransacked. Admittedly, it was always messy, but this disarray was on another level. In the sitting room, cushions were strewn across the floor. In the bedroom, drawers had been pulled from the chest and Laura's small wardrobe cast across the bed, whose sheets had all been yanked from it and the pillows hurled in a corner. In the bathroom, the small mirrored cabinet was open, its contents in the basin. Even the loo roll had been dragged off its holder.

Whoever it was had been searching for something. But what? Nothing seemed to be missing; she had nothing, after all, to miss. Not in a material sense, anyway. The unkindest cut – in every sense – was the little herb garden Laura grew in pots outside the window. It had been completely, wantonly destroyed. Her unwelcome visitor had dug around in the soil with something sharp, cruelly levering up earth and uprooting plants. They lay spattered and dirty in the kitchen sink.

Looking around, hands pressed hard against her narrow hips, Laura felt a hot flame of fury roar up within. The mess was scary but the plants really hurt. They had come from Paris, grown from clippings from Mimi's Montmartre herb garden. It was Laura's belief that they tasted better than anything you could buy in London.

Having repotted them as best she could, Laura watered them tenderly and rinsed her hands. Then, fuming, she stomped up the next flight of stairs and banged violently on Edgar's door. After a few seconds it opened and a pair of wary eyes looked at her through oversized geek glasses topped by a mop of unbrushed, dark hair.

'Laura!' He sounded relieved. 'Thought you might be Diego from last night.'

'What's going on?' Laura stormed.

'I'm getting ready to go out,' Edgar returned mildly, opening the door to reveal a pale torso in a black string vest. 'New club tonight. It's called the Dog Track and—'

Laura cut him short. 'Spare me the details. What's happened to my flat?'

The eyes behind the thick glasses widened. 'Your flat?'

'Don't give me that, Edgar! You've obviously trashed it. Were you looking for pills?'

Edgar's mouth dropped open. 'Laura, I swear I haven't. I haven't been here all day. I've just got back myself.'

'Not been here all day?'

The shaggy head twisted in a no. 'I've been home, as a matter of fact. To see my parents.'

'To Great Hording?'

Her neighbour looked surprised. 'You know about Great Hording?'

Laura gave a noncommittal shrug.

'When Dad said they had a mole I thought he was talking about the garden,' Edgar went on. 'But it turns out some cat's putting all their secrets on the internet. It's the landlord's son from the Fishing Boat Inn, apparently.'

Laura, about to correct him, desisted. She didn't wish to hint at her own interest in the story, and anyway, they were going off the subject. If Edgar hadn't trashed her apartment, who had? And why?

'And good for him, frankly,' Edgar went on.

'Good for him?'

'I mean, bad news for the village, but good news for me.

Compared to him and his evil doings, I suddenly look quite harmless. Dad's even increased my allowance!'

Laura glared at him. 'Didn't you notice my door was open when you got back?'

The shaggy head shook guiltily.

Laura, exasperated, was about to vent her frustrations on his uselessness as a neighbour, but Edgar spoke first. 'Actually, Laura, I think it was shut.'

'My door was shut?'

'I'm sure it was. In fact I know it was. I knocked on it to see if you had any vodka.'

Laura stomped back downstairs, ruminating. If the door was closed when Edgar returned, it meant one of two things. Either the intruder had been in there, intruding, or he had not yet arrived. Meaning that the invasion of her property had only just occurred. She could have passed the ransacker in the street. The thought sent a chill down her spine.

Laura spent an uneasy night dropping off and then waking up suddenly with a jolt. She tried hard to convince herself that her visitor was some mere opportunist, who'd maybe slipped in behind Esme the life coach when she let herself in. So self-absorbed was Esme that a tank could follow her unnoticed. Either that or she would try to give it life advice.

So, an opportunist then. The lock on her door was only a latch; the sort easily opened with a credit card. She had been casual with her security, Laura realised. But what did she have to steal? Nothing that she knew of.

Although. . .

A chilling thought now struck her. Were her unwelcome visitors looking for something else? A laptop, maybe?

Computer files? Could they have found out about the exposure she was planning? Were the burglars working on behalf of Great Hording, whose all-powerful denizens would naturally wish to suppress any more bad news?

Or was she just being paranoid?

Laura was up with the larks – or the Cod's Head Row equivalent (early morning foragers passing beneath her window). She arrived in the office even earlier than usual. Even so, Karlie was earlier, wafting around in high heels and a white shift dress placing a sheet of paper on everyone's desk. Laura seized hers, expecting the worst. Was Clemency sacking everyone?

She read the notice and felt relieved. Clemency was merely demanding that no one brought phones to the daily meetings. If attention was to be paid, it was to be paid to her.

Laura spent the time before the rest of the office arrived researching her Ellen questions. She had had a remarkable career and had met practically every powerful person on the planet. 'She's like the sixteenth member of the UN Security Council,' one former US Secretary of State enthused. 'If she pays attention to an issue, so does everyone else.' Ellen sounded, Laura thought, more daunting all the time. Harry had said nothing about any of this when introducing the two of them at the NDY Club.

'What is it?' she demanded, twisting round irritably as, for the third time in the last ten minutes, Karlie came sashaying past her desk. She seemed to be looking at what Laura had up on screen, no doubt to report back to Clemency. But so what? Clemency had, albeit unwillingly, approved Ellen as a subject.

The Monday morning features meeting adhered to what had, under the new editor, become the accustomed formula.

The more trivial and posh the subject matter the better, which had been the rule with Carinthia too. The difference was that Carinthia had had a glimmer of humour, and could even be slightly subversive, while Clemency had absolutely none. Carinthia had stopped calling into the features meetings, although whether by choice or instruction was not clear.

Once everyone was sitting down (senior staff) or standing up (if you were a junior), the meeting began.

Venetia the interiors editor produced a small bottle. It was filled with something powdery and grey. 'Stardust!'

A disbelieving Laura listened as it was explained that this was actual dust from celebrities' houses, as gathered by their cleaners. 'You can get a mixture, or particular slebs' particular dust, but that's more expensive.' Venetia shook the vial. 'Sprinkle a little Stardust everywhere!'

'Genius!' said Clemency.

Selina the travel editor had been to a resort with a bison-only restaurant.'

Anais looked puzzled. 'I didn't realise bison went to restaurants.

'It only *served* bison,' explained an exasperated Selina. 'And you could buy a Lichtenstein off the walls.'

'But isn't Lichtenstein a country—' Anais was beginning, when Clemency cut in.

'Put it in the next issue!'

Raisy and Daisy were referencing game-changing re-invention, or perhaps game-changing reinvented referencing. Laura was too busy thinking about her Ellen interview to follow all that they were saying. Her experience anyway was that the more closely you listened, the more confused you got. Whatever they were doing, they were doing it in a turquoise velour pointy hat (Raisy) and a transparent military fieldjacket (Daisy).

Laura had thought the meeting over when Clemency's dangerous, sharp green eyes suddenly swung on her. 'Bouncy Castle's wolfoodle,' she snapped.

'Bouncy. . .?'

Clemency glared. 'Castle. Her real name's Lady Rose but everyone calls her Bouncy.'

'What's a wolfoodle?'

'A cross between a wolf and a poodle. Bouncy's is called Attila. Do it next for the pet series. After the chicken.'

Laura had no choice but to nod and hope the meeting would not drag on much longer. She was meeting Ellen for lunch at her flat and would have to set off in ten minutes.

After protracted consideration of whether bondage toe-rings were the new must-have accessory, Clemency wound things up. 'Back to your desks.' Not saying thank you seemed to be part of her style.

Laura returned to her workstation to find her phone, once again, had disappeared. She had no doubt who the culprit was.

Karlie smiled a pearly white smile up at her. 'I don't have it. Security came for it while you were in the meeting.'

'*Security?*'

'Apparently you've been contacting persons in touch with terrorist groups.'

There was a collective gasp. Everyone in the office was listening. '*Terrorist* groups?' repeated Laura.

Clemency's secretary tossed her glossy blonde ponytail. 'Security monitor all calls going to and from the building. According to them a text had been sent this morning from you to a person well known to the security services.'

Laura, now understanding, slapped her hand on Karlie's desk with frustration. 'That was Ellen O'Hara. She's a war reporter, she deals with these people. I'm interviewing her today. I was texting her to confirm the rendezvous.'

Karlie maintained a glassy smile.

'I need the phone back!' Fear had gripped Laura's insides. It had Ellen's address in it. As well as all her notes and questions. Without it she would not know where she was going. Or what she was asking.

'I'm afraid security are examining the phone. They could be some time.'

Laura's mouth fell open. 'But I need it *now*! I'm going to the interview in a minute.'

'Can't help. Sorry.' Karlie picked up the phone. 'Is that you, Honor? Just to say that Clemency's on her way. She'll meet Christopher in the lobby in a few minutes.'

Laura stood rooted to the spot. She felt suddenly certain that this was part of a plan, a plan Clemency was behind. But why did Clemency want her phone removed from her? She was writing a feature that would benefit *Society*, after all.

Then, suddenly, Laura got it. Clemency had set her up to knock her down. Allowed her to arrange the interview and get Christopher interested only to make sure she failed to deliver it.

Well, she bloody well would deliver it!

Laura grabbed a notebook and pen and headed out of the door. She'd just have to rely on old tech, and her wits. It would hardly be the first time.

It was Monday lunchtime in the Golden Goose, and quiet. Kiki Cavendish was eating at her desk; avocado on toast

– supplies were back to normal now – washed down with lemon in hot water. Hervé still hadn't quite got the hang of this, serving the entire fruit at a rolling boil rather than just a slice. Sometimes it was hard to believe he was a top-flight chef.

From where she sat she could see the bar and the disarmingly boyish, side-parted head of Sir Philip Peaseblossom enjoying steak and ale pie with one of his spooks.

As with mushy peas, Hervé had not been keen to produce this traditional British dish and mixed vodka instead of beer with the meat and offal. As this was the version Sergei Goblemov preferred when he dined at the Golden Goose, Kiki had kept it on the menu.

The spook seemed to be enjoying the revised recipe too. But then, he was an old Moscow hand. Kiki was trying hard not to stare at him or betray in any way that she recognised him as the focus of a recent tabloid manhunt after details were revealed of a plot to impeach the American president. Journalists had pursued him all over the country to a number of so-called safe houses. But there was nowhere safer than Great Hording, of course, where a figure such as this could hide in plain sight and drink a pint of beer in her pub. Kiki felt it was a sign that, following recent upheavals, Britain's most fortunate village was slowly returning to normal.

Looking away over the sculpture garden, Kiki took a deep, relieved breath. She had been especially comforted by Sir Philip's assurance that his best and finest tech people were investigating the source of the recent leaks. Kearn from the Fishing Boat Inn was on borrowed time.

She took another bite of avocado toast, tried to sip the

water without the lemon hitting her nose and continued her morning's task; updating her confidential list of Great Hording's inhabitants and their associates.

There were a number of alterations to make. One of Tim Lacey's daughters had a new boyfriend. His name was Damright Jones and he was seventeen, a former young offender and modelling's new 'It' boy. Kiki took her time studying the adverts in which Damright appeared in boxer shorts, or with his jeans unzipped. Perhaps it wasn't out of the question, Kiki thought, that Ottoline Lacey's 'hot felon' was connected with the leaks. But surely not. Damright was clearly as dim as a tree and Tim Lacey, whose Hollywood estate stood to depreciate in value, would never allow any such thing.

The next piece of updating concerned Lulu, now a bona fide villager thanks to the purchase of Riffs. That house, Kiki thought angrily, was a menace, allowing in all manner of undesirables. Lulu's associates – the mole Kearn most obviously, and the dark-haired girl Kiki was now sure was the Lorna Drake who had tried to book a room – were still more dangerous.

She had mentioned as much to Sir Philip Peaseblossom who had promised to act on it. 'Don't worry, my dear Kiki,' he had grandly assured her. 'We've got it covered. Walls have ears in Great Hording. Every window has a camera.' Kiki did not say that this was exactly what she was afraid of and what had caused all the problems in the first place.

She saved her updates, took another bite of toast and turned to the next item on her agenda; a refresh of the Golden Goose's decor. A place with such a sophisticated clientele needed to stay one jump ahead of developments on the interior design front. The question was what jump, and in what direction?

The Mad Goose Group's consultant interior designer, the internationally famous Buzzie Omelet, had advised 'a more lively aesthetic.' Plans had been drawn up accordingly and here they were now in Kiki's inbox. Opening the file, Kiki read that every redecorated room would have its own beehouse, dumb-bells, NutriBullet and trimphone in RAF blue.

Kiki didn't like the sound of this at all. Nor did she especially like Buzzie, who she suspected of being her rival for Jonny's affections. She planned to thwart her redesign plans with a daring new aesthetic of her own.

Kiki was wondering about a bondage effect with black leather walls, enlarged photographs of nipples and standard lamps with basques instead of lampshades. It was a strong look, which she planned to showcase in the shepherd hut to start with. But would that work? There was a real possibility that shepherd's huts themselves were over. Maybe the wheels could be taken off. Yes! That was it! The Golden Goose would start the trend for – sex huts!

Kiki triumphantly finished her toast and sent the idea off to Jonny. He would love it, she was sure. And now what? The afternoon stretched gloriously ahead, perhaps beginning with a spot of abdominal kneading followed by a massage with essential oils and a Himalayan salting session. She might end up feeling like a focaccia but it was important to put the facilities she presided over through their paces and make sure that standards were being maintained.

After that, maybe a spot of ear candling. She needed to make sure her aural facilities were in tip-top condition. There was a pantomime rehearsal this evening in the village hall, just a skeleton run-through for those villagers still be in Great Hording on a Monday. Most, of course, had returned to the capital to run the country, if not the world.

Tonight, Kiki exulted, her interpretation of the role as landlady of the Village Idiot – a role created especially for her! – would, under the expert tutelage of Lady Mandy, take its first tentative but ultimately triumphant steps in public.

Yes, things were definitely looking up. So much so that Kiki decided to permit herself one of her favourite indulgences, a sneak peek at Mail Online. It had been at least half an hour since she last looked.

Three minutes, no more, Kiki told herself sternly as she pressed the icon on her desktop. Not including the time it took to load the page. She watched the paper's Gothic title appear, expecting to see the same Sidebar of Shame she had recently read, packed with improbably named, skimpily clad blondes whose short-lived, fly-on-the-wall fame couldn't be more different from the masters and mistresses of the universe, the truly powerful, amongst whom she spent her days.

The headline had changed, Kiki noticed idly. Previously it had been something about Kate Middleton's dress causing the Poundworld website to crash, but this new one looked more interesting. She read it again, more carefully.

TINSELTOWN MELTDOWN AS TOP DIRECTOR'S
PRIVATE EMAILS LEAKED TO STARS AND
STUDIOS

Hollywood was today in uproar as private emails from the
account of Tim Lacey, celebrated director of *Tufnell Park*,
were distributed widely among. . .

In the Golden Goose's shady bar, Sir Philip Peaseblossom's highly trained eye caught a sudden movement. 'Didn't happen to notice what that was, did you?' he murmured to his companion.

The hunted spy, spearing the last piece of kidney, looked round. 'Oh, that manager woman's just fallen off her chair. Looks like she's fainted.'

CHAPTER TWENTY-FIVE

In normal circumstances Laura loved the London riverside. Especially the South Bank with its view of St Paul's and, at night, the illuminated buildings of the Square Mile. Now, however, as she hurried along the Thames Path, her insides tugged with panic.

She could remember only that Ellen lived in Shad Thames, some converted Victorian waterside warehouses adjoining a shopping centre. But there were probably hundreds of flats there; however would she find her?

It was not only frustrating but humiliating. Ellen, an experienced journalist, would think it pathetic she had lost her phone through such an obvious trick.

Laura hurried past the London Dungeon and the bars and restaurants lining the narrow cobbled streets. There was cloak-and-dagger atmosphere here for those who paused to detect it; shadows of footpads and Elizabethan playwrights. But Laura rushed on towards the brick warehouse buildings; storage for goods from the river in bygone days but now, fitted with glass balconies and zooming lifts, the home of wealthy metropolitans. Scanning the rows of windows, Laura wondered which one belonged to Ellen, and in which block. She glanced at her watch; three minutes to spare, and felt clammy with panic.

'Laura, isn't it?' The voice came from behind. A woman's; low-pitched and authoritative. Laura wrenched herself round. Blonde hair, red lipstick, a white blouse. And, for some reason, a pint of milk.

'Ellen!'

'I'm so glad we found each other! I was running late and my phone's dead.' She was in front now, cutting through the drifting shoppers, leading the way into one of the buildings.

Hurrying after her, Laura shot a look up at the blue London sky. Saved again. Thanks, Dad! Peter Lake must be in despair by now, even so, at such an incompetent daughter. She needed to make a success of this interview, for all their sakes.

In the small, shiny lift, Ellen eyed her apologetically. 'I'm just back from Heathrow. I got your message on the red-eye.' She waved the pint of milk. 'This is all the shopping I've managed to do. Lunch might be a bit scratchy.' She flashed a red-lipsticked smile.

Laura smiled back. She was about to say that she wasn't hungry anyway, but realised that wasn't the case. Not only was Laura, like all Frenchwomen, always hungry at mealtimes, she was especially hungry today as following last night's drama at Cod's Head Row she had completely forgotten to eat. Mid-morning, she'd pinched a handful of Haribos from the fashion desk – Raisy and Daisy lived on them, along with cigarettes – but that hardly constituted breakfast. Especially after a weekend of Vlad's eggs, bacon, sausages and toast. There was nothing quite so full nor quite so English as breakfast prepared by a formerly male Latvian.

They emerged on the top floor and Laura followed Ellen into an apartment laid with blond wood. Light flooded in from floor-to-ceiling glass doors that took up the entire wall and led to a balcony overlooking the river.

Ellen twisted the key and pulled back the heavy panels, which glided easily down their rubber-lined grooves. The smell – fresh, briny – and the sound of the river floated up; seagulls, the honk of boats, the general roar of London, borne on the moving tide. The view was stupendous; the City's glass towers, Tower Bridge, the Tower itself. *London, thou art the flower of cities all*, Laura thought to herself, looking down the wide highway of glittering water.

'What a place,' she breathed, thinking if she lived in this apartment she would just sit out all day on this neat little balcony and watch the world go by. Even a stellar international career wouldn't be enough to tear her away.

'You look just like him, you know.' Ellen was appraising her coolly, slim, tanned arms folded in the white shirt which even an overnight flight didn't seem to have creased. 'Tall, dark and handsome. That was Peter.'

Laura felt something twist within her. This woman had known her father. Worked with him.

'He was a great journalist,' Ellen added. 'The very best. I learnt most of what I know from him.'

'I learnt nothing from him,' Laura said enviously. 'I never

knew him at all. Not really. There are a few memories, very faint ones, but that's all.'

Leaves rustling in the bright sun. The cool stone floor of a white-walled house. The scent of cigarettes. The sound of a man laughing. A staccato noise that might have been gunfire, might have been typewriter keys.

Ellen was smiling at her. 'You didn't need to learn, you inherited it. You're a very good writer, you know.'

'You've seen my stuff?' Laura was surprised.

The red lips spread in a wry grin. 'I love *Society*. You couldn't make it up.'

'You're teasing me,' Laura accused, dismayed.

'No, no. Your work is the best thing about it. You've done some great reports. Your Three Weddings one.' Ellen shook her blonde head. 'Amazing. What are you working on at the moment?'

Laura opened her mouth, preparing to tell her about Britain's Best-Connected Village. Then she hesitated. It was a great story, and Ellen was a great journalist. A much more experienced one too; she might do a much better job. Could she trust her?

'Celebrity pets,' Laura hedged. 'Bouncy Castle's wolfoodle. What my father would have made of it I can't imagine.'

'He would have been proud,' Ellen said staunchly. 'How's your mother, by the way? Shallow as ever? Sorry, that's a bit rude.'

'Not at all,' Laura assured her. 'Probably more so, if anything. Lives with her third husband in Monaco.'

'Yes, that would figure. God knows what she was ever doing with a brain like Peter. Who's the husband? A semi-celebrity hairdresser, I'm guessing. Gets flown out to yachts to give oligarchs' wives the full Mrs Khrushchev.'

Laura was giggling. 'Spot on. He's called Leon.'

'With a tan deeper, crisper and more even than the Feast of Stephen?'

'Exactly.'

Ellen clapped her hands. 'Priceless. I'd expect nothing less of Odette. Quite a woman, I always thought.'

'Definitely,' Laura spoke ruefully.

'She taught me a lot about war reporting,' Ellen said, unexpectedly.

'*What?*' This was a whole new angle on her mother.

'Absolutely. After I heard she used to claim designer underwear on Pete's exes, I decided to do the same myself. I don't know where I'd be without it now.' Ellen's blue eyes sparkled in a manner Laura wasn't entirely sure was serious. 'Victoria's Secret came in very handy in East Timor, I can tell you.'

They talked about clothes for a while. Her unvarying white shirt, tan trousers and loose chignon were, Ellen explained, less about an iconic style than about being practical. 'One less decision to make.'

Laura nodded. Her navy jeans and shirt were worn for the same reason.

'I love your French girl look,' Ellen said, generously. 'That fringe! Who does your hair?'

Laura remembered Carinthia asking the same thing when they had met in Paris. Laura's answer, '*ciseaux de cuisine*' – kitchen scissors – had made Carinthia assume Caesar de Cuisine was a top hairdresser. 'I do it myself. Cut it out of my eyes when it gets too long.'

'Me too!'

Ellen lit a cigarette. 'Want one?'

Laura slid one out of the proffered packet and inhaled

gratefully as the light was offered. The smoke slid into her lungs, sweet and head-spinning. 'Do you know what happened to my father?' she asked suddenly, seizing the moment.

The answer was a sequence of perfect smoke rings. 'Last I heard was what you've probably heard,' Ellen said. 'He was in a helicopter over the desert. With a guy from *Newsweek* and another from AP. Seems they were shot down.'

'But nothing was ever found.' Laura took another long drag of cigarette.

Ellen shot Laura a sympathetic glance, finished her cigarette and shoved its butt in a plant pot in the balcony's corner. She pressed a hand on her shoulder, and went back inside.

Laura stared at the river briefly, then followed. This meeting was about Ellen, not her.

Her subject, however, had disappeared. Tracking her down, Laura passed a couple of open doorways and glimpsed a bare but functional bedroom and a plain white bathroom. No decoration was visible here any more than in the apartment's plain sitting room. But with a view like that, perhaps you didn't need it.

Ellen was in the apartment's small, shiny aluminium kitchen, opening and shutting cupboards and fridge doors. She turned to Laura apologetically. 'Shit. I've literally got nothing.'

'You must have *something*.'

'A couple of cloves of garlic. Some ancient spaghetti. That's it. No wine, dammit.'

'I can make something from that.' Laura crouched to

rummage in the cupboards. 'And look, you've got oil, and salt and pepper. And a tin of anchovies! This is a feast! Stand aside!'

The intrepid Ellen, veteran of war-torn cities the globe over, meekly obeyed and watched as Laura filled up a pan for the pasta and began to chop the anchovies. It would have been better with some spinach and pine nuts, as in Mimi's recipe, but there was definitely a sauce here.

'Just talk,' Laura said, when Ellen asked if she could do anything. Chatting over cooking was the best sort of chat. Absorbed, yet relaxed. She and Mimi had done it most nights. 'Tell me about your career.'

Ellen pulled a face. 'Do we have to? Can't we talk about food instead?'

'What about memorable meals of your career?' Laura suggested.

'Brilliant idea!' Ellen was immediately off, relating anecdote after anecdote that Laura, peeling and energetically pounding, carefully committed to memory.

'In Iran they have this wonderful dish with almonds. I ate it with the Ayatollah. . .'

Chop, stir, sizzle. Laura shook the pan and listened.

'There's a particular chicken stew they make in Syria with saffron, served with sweet rice. I ate it with a family there, as bombs dropped in the background. . .' The expression in Ellen's eyes was distant, reminiscing.

'In Baghdad I ate quails stuffed with rose petals. . .'

Laura's stomach rumbled as she drained the spaghetti and stirred in the warm sauce, making sure to coat every strand. This was going to make a great feature. Perhaps it could actually be a series over several issues; Ellen's derring-do stories woven between delicious recipes. Thomasella, the food editor, was one of the few remaining staff members possessed of a brain. She would immediately see the point and such an unexpected combination of elements was very much the *Society* Laura had hoped to create as editor.

Ah well. No point crying over spilt milk, or spilt rose water; a central ingredient of Middle Eastern cuisine, as Ellen was explaining.

'Got any bowls?' She hated to interrupt her subject in full flow, but they'd be eating out of the pan with forks otherwise, which was a bit too close to Caspar in his Brixton days. How far he had come, with his Ivys nomination. She pushed him from her mind. Best actor, worst friend.

'Sure.' Ellen rummaged in another cupboard. 'Oh wow. Look what I've found!' She waved a gold-foil bottle with a distinctive red seal on the label. 'Someone gave me this Moët ages ago. I'd forgotten all about it.'

'Let's drink it!' urged Laura, adding for the benefit of journalist Ellen that her French grandmother always had a glass with the morning papers.

'Why?' asked Ellen, easing off the cage around the cork.

'She says the news looks better that way.'

Ellen hooted. 'She's right!'

The bottle wasn't cold, but Laura had the answer.

'Got any ice cubes? We could drink it French style, *à la glace*.'

'Gosh, yes. I drank it like that with the Macrons.' The veteran war correspondent pressed a button on the fridge front. A stream of ice cubes rattled out.

Laura beamed. 'Perfect.

Reminiscing again, she followed Laura back and forth

between the balcony and the kitchen, carrying plates, setting the table. Laura was beginning to feel very at home in the apartment; very at home with Ellen too. How much nicer it would be to live here than Cod's Head Row. She swallowed at the memory of last night's intruder. What if they came back again?

'. . . and so President Trump had to shut up after that. Oh wow, is that lunch? You're a magician!'

It looked pretty good, Laura had to admit, especially sprinkled with a handful of bright green shreds; the next-door balcony had a parsley pot which she had just been able to reach.

Ellen brought the champagne in a couple of whisky tumblers, ice cubes clinking. 'If you drink it like this,' Laura explained, 'it doesn't make your breath smell.'

Ellen grinned. 'The things you know, girl. Harry was right about you.'

Laura, who had been raising her first forkful of pasta to her mouth, now put it down. Shock rippled through her. Her appetite, she found, had completely drained away.

'You okay?' Ellen was spreading the square of kitchen roll Laura had found for napkins over her narrow knees.

Laura was far from okay. Harry's name, flung so unexpectedly into the air, echoed like an explosion. 'It's just that,' she managed eventually, 'I haven't heard from him in a while.' *Although I thought I saw him the other day.* She stopped before she could say this. Ellen might think she was a fantasist.

'Radio silence?' Ellen was twisting pasta round her fork.

'Kind of.'

'Goes with the territory.'

'What is the territory though?' The million-dollar question. Would Ellen tell her?

'You can't seriously expect me to answer that.'

But having broached the subject, Laura had no intention of retreating. 'Is he doing something dangerous?'

'Can't tell you that either.' Ellen forked in more spaghetti. 'Believe me, I would if I could.'

Laura was frustrated. 'Can't you tell me *anything?*'

'Just one thing.' Ellen lay down her fork and took a contemplative swig of Moët.

'What?'

'He's pretty keen on you.'

Laura was too surprised to speak for a second. Then she said, 'He's got a funny way of showing it.'

Ellen forked up more pasta. 'This is amazing.'

Laura eyed her. 'You were saying?'

'Oh yes.' The blue eyes twinkled. 'He's keen, take it from me. I've known him with girls before. Plenty of them.'

An icy-cold wave broke over Laura. Was this the moment she found out that Harry had a wife in every port?

'Don't worry. He wasn't in love with them.'

This begged a question Laura couldn't bring herself to ask.

Perhaps Ellen sensed this, because she said no more on the subject. They returned to the topic of war-reporting until the pasta was finished, the bottle was drained and the sun went behind the clouds. A breeze began to blow down the river. 'I have to go,' Ellen said, frowning as she stubbed out another cigarette.

At the door, Laura turned to her. 'Say hi to Harry if you see him?'

'If I see him.'

'And. . . give him my love.'

Ellen nodded. Her sudden smile made the sun come out again, even though it hadn't. She pressed Laura's hand. 'Don't give up on him,' she said. 'He needs you.'

CHAPTER TWENTY-SIX

Laura barely noticed the journey back to the office. She felt full of joy and hope. Harry needed her. He might even love her.

It filled her with with longing. She was more desperate to see him than ever before.

On the Tube, she stared down at her hands and felt tears gathering in her eyes.

Exiting at Oxford Circus, Laura forcibly pulled herself together, squaring her shoulders, raising her chin and tucking her hair behind her ears. She must put Harry out of her mind now and spend the next few hours dealing with whatever Clemency chose to throw at her. But she had her Ellen interview now, despite all attempts to thwart it.

Back in the office, her phone had reappeared. She looked over to Karlie. 'No controlled explosion then?' Laura asked sarcastically.

But Karlie and the rest of her colleagues were staring hard at their computer screens. Another Clemency edict, Laura assumed as she went over to discuss the food interview idea with Thomasella.

Among wedges of caviar-infused Parmesan and jars of pearl soup, Thomasella, too, was glued to her screen, open-mouthed.

'I've got this great idea—' Laura began, before the food editor interrupted.

'Oh my God! Have you seen what he says about Angelina!' Thomasella clamped a skeletal hand to her mouth.

'What are you talking about?'

Thomasella stared up at Laura. Like most women who wrote about food and wine, she looked as if she never indulged in either. She was pale and stick-thin in a black crochet minidress, dark hair in an elfin crop. 'The emails story, of course!'

'Emails?' Whatever this story was she had missed it, along with her phone.

'The leaked Hollywood ones!' You can't believe what this guy's been saying.'

Leaked! Laura's stomach rolled over. 'Which guy?'

'Tim Lacey. The director. You know, he did *Tufnell Park* and *I Think I Might Be Fond of You.*'

Even as Laura dashed back to her desk and pulled the story up on her own screen, her thoughts were flying to Wyatt and Kearn. This really was not going to help.

Tim Lacey certainly hadn't held back. Studio heads, top publicity people, celebrity chefs, TV anchorpersons and leading screenwriters had been insulted just as thoroughly as Oscar-winning actors. A famous action star reportedly had chronic flatulence, a gorgeous actress had huge hairy feet and a smoothie heart-throb was gay with a beard for a wife. 'And she's gay herself,' Lacey had added, for good measure.

Lacey had also freely passed on what Tinseltown's best and brightest had said about each other. A bumptious British TV host had galloping halitosis, a famously philanthropic director was in reality 'as mean as mouse shit', a teen actor's BO made your eyes water and Savannah Bouche was 'a gold-digging vampire'. This was hardly news to Laura, but that her peers shared this view certainly was.

The biggest headlines, however, concerned Savannah's secret unflattering view of Caspar, ostensibly her paramour. 'Bond's a Brainless Blowhard with a Dick You Need a Telescope to See' was the quote most papers had used in their headlines. Savannah had evidently passed this treacherous view on to her agent, who had told Tim Lacey, who had, albeit inadvertently, now told the world.

Unfair, Laura thought. Her view was that Caspar's equipment was more than adequate. But it probably depended on what you were used to. A brainless blowhard, though, was hard to dispute.

Given Caspar's recent treatment of her, a little *schadenfreude* on her part would not have been unjustified. But a tiny corner of her felt sorry for him, knowing he would be hurt. Caspar, ever heedless of the impact of his own behaviour, was anything but resilient when others upset him.

Laura's main concern was for Kearn, however. Of all the Great Hording-related leaks, this was the worst. Wyatt's boyfriend was going to get lynched at this rate. He should leave the area, but Laura was pretty sure he wouldn't. Not when doing so would look like an admission of guilt. And mean leaving Wyatt behind.

Laura scrolled through her contacts, bringing up Lulu's number.

'Is what?' Lulu's voice was a heavy whisper. 'Am rehearsing, yes? Lady Mandy explaining me my motivation.'

'But you're a glass slipper! Sorry, a breezeblock boot!'

Lulu was affronted. 'Is still needing tell me what is thinking, hmm?'

'Look,' said Laura, cutting straight to the chase. 'You need to help Kearn.'

'Is about Tim Lacey story?'

'You know about it?' But of course she did. Lulu was in Great Hording. The eye of the storm. The epicentre of the earthquake.

'Everyone talk about it. Kiki faint. Lady Mandy punch air.'

'Give Kearn sanctuary at Riffs. Otherwise there are going to be riots.'

'Is riots already. Tim run out of town. Of willage. You see what he say about Sergei?'

'I haven't got to that bit yet,' said Laura, scrolling down until she found Tim's scorchingly ill-advised remarks on some of his films' financial backers. 'Goodness.'

'Would have been badness,' Lulu remarked, adding some of the threats Sergei had made. Kneecapping had been the least of it.

Laura felt panic rise. 'We've got to help Kearn. We need to look after him.'

'Because he is escape goat, hmm?'

'But hopefully not, if you get to him in time.'

Lulu promised to send Vlad to Little Hording, and returned to her rehearsal.

Laura put her phone down on her desk. As she did so, something moved behind her. She turned to see Karlie walking softly off, delicate nose high in the air.

She opened a new file and began to write up her interview with Ellen. She typed rapidly, committing to the keyboard the details of the light-filled riverfront flat, and Ellen talking about war and pomegranates, gunfire and rose water against a background of hooting Thames barges. But of the conversation that made most impact, she did not type a word. 'He's pretty keen on you. . . he wasn't in love with them. . . he needs you.'

Her phone was ringing. She stared at it, momentarily disoriented. She had been somewhere else altogether.

'Can you believe it?' The voice was young, male, and powerfully indignant. 'Can you *believe* what she said about me?'

'Caspar!' The second she had uttered his name, Laura could have kicked herself. Karlie was hanging around again. Taking her phone, she went out of the office. There was a little atrium area by the lifts, with plants and sofas. She could talk there without being overheard.

'She told me she loved me,' Caspar complained.

Pointing out that he had said exactly that to her would not help, Laura sensed.

'I put up with her. And her damned dogs. They bite everyone – even Steven Spielberg. Completely undisciplined. Aggressive. Spoilt. Loud. Horrible.'

'The dogs?'

'No, Savannah. How dare she say that about my crown

jewels? She's had more surgery on her twinkle than most women have on their face.'

Before Laura could say anything – and what, indeed, could she say? – he had launched into a monologue about atomic lip therapy, nose hair epilation, gluteal freezing and other edge-of-reason beauty rites. 'She wears caffeine thongs, Laura. Can you believe that?'

'Is caffeine a colour?'

'No, it's an impregnation.'

'Excuse me?'

'The thongs have caffeine in them. For a youthful yoni.'

The lift opposite Laura now opened to reveal Clemency in a tight red skirt and Christopher in his usual suit and pink socks. Laura straightened up hurriedly, but too late. Clemency smiled maliciously. 'Working hard as usual, Laura? Overseeing the office in my absence?' She then made a big show of saying goodbye. Christopher gave Laura the faintest of nods.

Caspar, on the other end, was howling in anguish. 'I thought Savannah and I would be together for ever!'

As the editor stalked triumphantly past, Laura leapt to her feet to follow. She was furious with herself, and with Caspar. She had just handed Clemency a copper-bottomed reason to complain about her. 'Look,' she muttered through gritted teeth, 'I've got to go.'

'You can't! I want you to help me! I want you to be my girlfriend, Laura.'

She stopped in absolute amazement. 'I can't believe what I'm hearing. After all the times you've slept with me and dumped me, the latest being only last week, what do you take me for? Be your girlfriend? That ship has sailed.'

'Not my real girlfriend. Just a pretend one.'

'You have,' Laura said, after taking a deep, steadying breath, 'completely lost me. And now I have to go. Sorry. Thank you for the kind offer, but it's a no.'

'Your phone keeps going,' Karlie observed, some ten minutes later. 'Aren't you going to answer it?'

Laura ignored her and cursed the malfunction – caused by the aril salad – that meant she couldn't turn off the ringtone. This was an especially embarrassing jingly pop tune that made everyone laugh when they heard it.

'I don't want to be your girlfriend,' she hissed, a few minutes later. She had shut herself in the loos to conduct this second part of the conversation.

'But I need you!'

'You said that before.'

'No, I really need you now. To come to the Ivys with me.'

'You're up for Best Actor.' And not without reason, Laura thought crossly. But why did he think this loverman charade would convince her yet again?

'You have to come with me. Savannah's telling everyone I'm obsessed with getting an award as Bond and that my personal ambition knows no bounds.'

Laura had never before thought it possible to agree with Savannah Bouche. But there was clearly a first time for everything.

'That kind of thing plays badly with the judges,' Caspar went on. 'They don't like feeling manipulated.'

'Is that right?' But Laura's sarcasm went straight over Caspar's head.

'I'm begging you! Come with me to the Ivys. Please!'

'But there must be millions of women in Hollywood who'd bite your hand off.'

'There are,' Caspar agreed complacently. 'Billions, in fact. Some of them pretty famous.'

'So take one of them!'

'It has to be you.'

Laura had had enough. She just wanted to get him off the phone. 'Why me? I'm just an old friend. A complete nobody.'

'Exactly!' said Caspar, gleefully. 'If I take you, a complete nobody, as opposed to someone everyone's heard of, it makes me look sincere. Like I'm loyal. Not too proud to be seen with a person a little rough at the edges.'

Words had temporarily deserted Laura. Rough at the edges!

'They love that in Hollywood,' Caspar went on blithely. 'Sincerity. Authenticity. Loyalty. That'll go down a storm with the judges, especially if I can get a press release out before the ceremony, saying I'm coming with you and you're from the absolute worst part of my past, complete rock bottom, when I was at my lowest.'

Laura had finally recovered the power of speech. 'What I know, Caspar,' she said in the calmest voice she could manage, 'is that you can doubly, trebly, absolutely sod off. And *never* call me again.'

Having delivered this ultimatum she flushed the loo with violence and wrenched the cubicle door open.

When she was sufficiently composed to return to the office, Laura found Karlie sashaying towards her. 'Clemency wants to see you. Now.'

The way to the editorial office was through a garden of bouquets stuffed in vases. There was nothing Clemency liked more than tribute, as designers and suppliers had not been slow to discover.

'Come in. Sit down.' Clemency's mouth was spread in a feline smile bright with slick red lipstick. 'On the yellow sofa, yes. Make yourself at home.'

Laura sat down apprehensively.

'I wanted to ask you about a story.' Clemency twisted a long, white finger through her long, red hair.

'The Ellen O'Hara one?'

The green eyes sparked with annoyance. 'Not that one. That one's boring.'

'Boring?' Laura gasped. 'But—'

The white editorial hand waved regally. 'I'm wondering about a completely different story. . .' The red editorial head dipped to one side, smiling winsomely. 'We've been wondering how to cover the Ivys.'

Laura's hands gripped the edge of the sofa cushions.

'People are saying they'll rival the Oscars one day.'

Laura waited. Just what was being suggested here?

'What we'd really like,' Clemency beamed, 'is an insider story. About the Ivys. And we all know how good you are at insider stories, Laura. Don't we?' The red lips were still smiling, but the eyes were hard as emeralds.

'You want me to do an insider story about the Ivys?' Laura was determined to bluff this out. There was no way Clemency could know. She had never mentioned her connections to Caspar in the office.

'A story about a night at the Ivys with one of the world's biggest film stars, one of the award winners too, with any luck, is just the kind of thing we are looking for.' Clemency raised her eyebrows enquiringly.

Laura's mouth dropped open. So Clemency did know. And there was only one way she could have found out. She stared, outraged, at her oldest and bitterest enemy. 'You just heard my conversation!'

Is this what had happened to her phone? It hadn't gone to security at all – she had only ever had Karlie's word for that anyway – it had been fitted with a tapping device?

'How dare you?!' she gasped. Was there no depth to which Clemency would not sink? 'That's outrageous!'

Clemency's hard, red fingernails, enamelled to match her lips, tapped on the glass surface of the desk. 'What would really be outrageous,' she said sweetly, 'would be for someone with such excellent connections not to use them, and for them to be, um, *let go* for refusing to.' She tipped her head on the other side now. 'Well, Laura Lake? Are you going to the Ivys with Caspar Honeyman? Or aren't you?'

That evening, Laura looked through her wardrobe. It was pitifully limited. Dark jeans, navy shirts, a trench and a skinny jacket weren't going to cut it at a film party. She'd have to borrow something from Lulu. Somewhere in Lulu's twenty-seven wardrobes of evening dresses there was a particular flowing, long-jacketed trouser suit that looked like liquid gold and, for all her general lack of interest in labels, made her heart race every time she saw it. She'd ask Lulu this weekend, when she went to Great Hording.

Caspar had been delighted at her apparent change of heart. 'You've come to the aid of your BFF!'

'Best Friend Forever?' Laura was slightly mollified.

'Big Famous Friend. Look, I'll get my people to send you

the details. Sorry, gotta go. Films to star in, interviews to give, contracts to sign. . .'

'Ha ha.' Good that he could still laugh at himself.

'I'm not joking. I really have got all that stuff to do. Blame *Kiev Chicken*.'

'Kiev chicken?' The breaded poultry dish which sent molten garlic butter spurting up at the unwary? Laura had heard it described as the Dry Cleaner's Friend. But weren't fried and fatty food off the menu for Caspar now?

'It's the working title for the new Bond film.'

CHAPTER TWENTY-SEVEN

R iffs had changed, Laura saw when she arrived in her
taxi on Friday night. Wonky de Launay and her vision
had certainly been busy. The guitar-shaped swimming
pool was now filled in and planted with what looked
suspiciously like nettles. The formerly colourful herbaceous
borders abounded with dock leaves and dandelions. The
flowerbeds under the house windows were full of rosebay
willowherb and wild garlic. In the strong, evening sun the
smell was powerful, and not entirely pleasant.

Lulu came skipping out to greet her, clad in the silver
wellies and gold quilted Barbour that were evidently her
Great Hording uniform. In the bright light the outfit blazed.
'Come see,' she trilled, dragging Laura round the improve-
ments and describing the industrial earthworks required to
achieve these effects. The docks, for instance, had arrived
in a ready-planted bed that had been lowered in by crane.

Laura listened, marvelling at the expense and effort resulting in making Riffs look as if it had been abandoned for twenty years.

Wonky had clearly seen Lulu coming. Laura told herself that surely it was better for her heiress friend to be swindled by a grabby gardener than a guy with bad intentions. Perhaps Lulu had been thinking the same thing, because she suddenly sighed and said, 'You know, Laura, am missing South'n Fried, hmm?'

'But he left you for Savannah,' Laura stoutly pointed out.

The mass of long, golden hair nodded in the sun. The densely black sunglasses flashed in agreement. 'Think has seen herrings of waist now, hmm?'

'Error of ways?'

'He skype me from Altamont.'

So South'n Fried was still circumnavigating the world on his 'Bust Yo Ass' tour, like a rapping Sir Francis Drake in jewelled trainers. Laura was about to advise against the contact, but didn't. There was something very endearing about Lulu's capacity to forgive.

They had reached the back of the house now, where there had been a formal rose garden was, well, what?

'Is my foraging patch!' But the clump looked just like dense weeds to Laura. Lulu was complaining that Vlad had not yet used any of it in the Riffs kitchen which, Laura gathered, had been behaving itself perfectly well since Kearn arrived on site. He had apparently been settled in the old stable block, where Roger Slutt had stored his collection of vintage submarines.

Wandering in under the block's ornate Victorian Gothic arch, the two women were greeted with the sight of Lulu's guest, close-cropped brown hair glinting in the sun, tinkering away with bits of engine. 'Roger left lots of different parts behind,' Kearn explained. 'I'm putting them together to make a U-boat. Something to do now I'm the Julian Assange of Great Hording.'

He grinned at Lulu, to whom he was quite obviously already devoted. It seemed she had provided him with a safe house, or, as Kearn called it, safe mansion, not a second too soon. Feeling against him in the village had now reached fever pitch, Laura learnt. But now Kearn was safe, he could turn his attention to clearing his name. Which meant exposing those whose crimes he was accused of – if he could find them.

'I can tell that they got in by hacking weak passwords,' he told Laura. 'But who "they" are is impossible to establish. GCHQ don't seem to know either.'

'You've been in touch with GCHQ?' That he had such connections was a surprise.

Kearn did not reply, just raised a fine ginger eyebrow.

'You've *hacked* into GCHQ?' Laura breathed. 'Couldn't you be prosecuted for that?'

Kearn grinned and picked up a spanner. 'I don't hack in as myself, obviously. I'm usually North Korea. Or Russia. Sometimes even the FBI, which is true, actually.'

'You work for the Federal Bureau of Investigation?'

'No, the Fishing Boat Inn.'

Given such distractions, it was not until much later, over dinner, that Laura remembered the gold suit for the Ivys. 'Is saving children,' Lulu said, chewing on a piece of tournedos Rossini. The fillet of beef topped with foie gras was her favourite, and they had had fresh oysters to start. 'Simple country food, hmm?' Lulu had said, without irony.

'You've donated it to a charity shop?' Laura was

dismayed. Lulu's generosity was laudable, but what was she going to wear now? Vast as it was, her friend's 'occasion' wardrobe tended towards the short, tight and spangled.

Could she, Laura wondered, borrow something from the *Society* fashion cupboard? It was the least Clemency could do to help. She ran mentally through what she had last seen in there. Shoots currently planned by Raisy and Daisy included the new trend for wearing two pairs of trousers at once. And the reverse bikini, where the top was worn as the bottom. 'Dry-humping the zeitgeist,' as the fashion editors put it.

There was also the designer who made exquisite, full-skirted dresses which he then set on fire. The burnt and charred remains were what went in the shops and on the models.

Possibly not the fashion cupboard then. Laura put the clothes problem to the back of her mind. After a week with Clemency she craved the peace and quiet of the countryside.

On Saturday morning, after one of Vlad's full Englishes, Lulu announced that she had a panto rehearsal. 'You come!' she urged. 'Lady Mandy might give you part. People drop out all time because licks.'

'Licks? Oh *leaks*.'

'Jolyon, Willow, Mandy, Tim. What next, hmm?'

The village hall, as they entered it, was dark. All the curtains were closed, focusing the attention on the brightly lit stage. At the back was something strange that looked like. . . well. . . but couldn't possibly be, especially as stomping in front of it was Lady Mandy, clutching a script and crammed into jeans that made her broad beam look all the broader. The other onstage figure wore tight PVC trousers and a tiny white top. She was holding a broom upside down and sweeping with the handle end.

'Cinders difficult part for Anna,' Lulu whispered. 'Never use brush before. In Sergei houses, many servants.'

A bear-like figure with heavy eyebrows now barrelled on stage. 'Sergei Cinderella father,' Lulu explained. 'Lord No Money.'

'Baron Hardup, you mean?' Laura snorted. She hadn't credited Lady Mandy with a sense of humour. 'Great characterisation,' she remarked appreciatively.

Witty direction too. Gloriously sending up the popular image of an oligarch, Sergei, emanating menace, was pacing about and growling Russian into two phones at once.

Lady Mandy threw him an irritated look. 'You're not in this scene, Sergei. Please go and make your phone calls somewhere else.'

The Russian stomped angrily off.

'He doesn't seem to be enjoying it much,' Laura remarked.

'Only do so can keep eyeball on Anna,' Lulu hissed back. 'She make sex with Zeb. Sergei go to mad.'

'*What?*'

'Oh yes.' Lulu nodded sagely. 'Make sex together. On stage.'

'In front of everyone?'

'Mmm-hmm.' Lulu's sunglasses flashed emphatically.

Was something being lost in translation here? The oligarch's wife and the local celebrity artist could not possibly have staged an erotic show in Great Hording's village hall, could they? On the other hand, she had commissioned him to make the giant glowing purple willy sculpture for Brybings. . .

Lulu waved a hand. Her diamonds glittered in the footlights. 'Sex there at back of stage, hmm?'

'You mean the set!' Laura steeled herself to look at it again.

Her initial impression was correct. It really was a vast, protruding bottom made of pale pink plaster. Huge plaster hands clamped either side pulled the cheeks apart. Laura had imagined it an unfortunate optical illusion, but Zeb Spaw's involvement put a whole new cast on things, as it were. 'It looks like a bum,' she said.

'Bum, yes.'

'Why's there a huge bum at the back of the stage? This is *Cinderella*.'

'Is post-modernist spatialist Willage Idiot, Zeb say.'

Laura rubbed her face. It had been a long week. 'So it's a visual metaphor? The pub's called the Village Idiot and a village idiot is like a tramp, and this is a bum, and. . .'

Lulu's hair flew about in a nod. 'Is concept art, yes!'

'Who's that standing next to it?' Only now did Laura notice a large man in black wearing a headset, arms folded, expression forbidding.

'Is security guard from Zeb gallery in London. Taking bum when pantomime finish. Sell for millions.'

They were interrupted by a shout from Lady Mandy. Cinderella was receiving some acting training, and not looking very happy about it.

'No, no! *Declaim!* Like this!' Lady Mandy's vast chest reared skywards with a deep intake of breath. 'A man from the royal palace has come/Bearing an in-vi-ta-e-cee-on. . .'

Anna struggled to imitate her, whilst simultaneously grappling with the broom. She clearly could not sweep and talk at the same time.

'Ever heard of scansion, dear?' called a sarcastic female voice from the stalls. It sounded to Laura vaguely familiar.

'Script by Dame Hermione,' Lulu explained in an undertone. 'Sell translation rights in sixteen languages, hmm?'

'It's about counting the beats.' An urbane male voice floated out of the shadows somewhere near the great author.

'Thank you so much for explaining that, Peter!' A positively smitten-sounding Lady Mandy beamed towards the darkness of the stalls. 'I simply don't know what I'd do without your help as a prompter. You're an absolute marvel. You keep this village going, you really do.'

'I do my best, Lady Mandy,' came the chivalrous reply. 'But I am a factotum, merely. The credit for everything goes to you. You are, if I may say so, the presiding genius.'

'You may say so,' Lady Mandy graciously allowed.

Laura settled on one of the wooden chairs and watched Lulu play a scene in which the Slipper and Cinderella argue about Cinderella's address.

'Is Three, Pantoland High Street!'

Lady Mandy heaved on stage, palms aloft. 'No, no, *no*, Lulu! Three, the High Street, Pantoland! Now, Sergei, are you ready? It's time for Baron Hardup's big number with the landlady of the Village Idiot.' She looked around. 'But where's Kiki?'

Kiki was hurrying through Great Hording. Her heart was racing, not just with the effort – she was used to jogging, after all – but with terror. Jonny had called about the sex huts just as she was leaving and while she was pleased about his support, and additional suggestions for manacles and chains, the conversation had put her departure back by some ten minutes. Now she was late for rehearsal and the fear that Lady Mandy might give her part to someone else added a spring to her step.

She could not lose her big chance! Not now she had been finally accepted among the village elite. And certainly not now she was about to show Lady Mandy just what she was made of, acting-wise. Thanks to YouTube, she was now fully briefed on the Method. The non-speaking part of the Village Idiot's landlady might be silent, but it would be full of power.

The village hall door loomed at last before her sight and Kiki burst in, panting, to find the rehearsal well under way on the stage. It wasn't a part of the panto she recognised. Several figures, including Lulu, Lady Mandy, Dame Hermione and Peter Delabole were crowded round a bulky figure on the floor. The back of the stage looked unusual; the scenery had gone. Zeb's enormous bottom with its parted cheeks was missing. Oh no, wait, it was on the stage floor. It seemed to have collapsed.

Kiki approached, alarm pulsing through her. And now alarm turned to horror. Lying beneath the vast buttocks, apparently stunned, lay Sergei. His eyes were closed and a red line of blood trickled out from his mutilated ear.

Anna was nowhere to be seen.

CHAPTER TWENTY-EIGHT

Sergei was not popular, but the violence of the accident shocked everyone. The only positive aspect was that Kearn could not possibly be at the bottom, as it were, of this one.

Rather, the finger of guilt seemed to point firmly in the direction of Anna and Zeb.

Anna's going outside for a cigarette at the exact moment her husband was crushed by a pair of colossal bum cheeks struck many as coincidental. Had she arranged it with her lover?

Zeb's alibi was also anything but sound. He had been due to conduct an interview with *Einzurstendeneuebaten*, a German art magazine. He had failed to turn up. While this was par for the course, Zeb's well-known excuse on such occasions, that absence is actually presence, seemed suspicious in the context. Had he been behind the scenes of the village hall, waiting for his moment?

Sergei, meanwhile, was recovering in a private hospital surrounded by bodyguards. According to his doctors, the blow from the bum would have killed someone with a normal cranium.

'Goblemov's skull is like solid concrete, and an inch thick all the way round,' Kearn reported. He had been following the emails of the various doctors. The ease with which he hacked into the hospital was amazing. 'Simple when you know how,' he said.

And yet, brilliant as he was, he had got no further with the Great Hording information leaks – frustratingly for Laura, who was intending to weave the exposé into her article. She was working on it nightly, although the new developments meant it changed all the time and got longer. At this rate it was going to be the size of *Anna Karenina*, or *Anna Goblemova*, which might be a good title, come to think of it.

On Sunday evening, Vlad drove Laura back to the station. It was a beautiful evening; warm, scented and full of the thick light of summer. Hedgerows dancing with flowers edged fields brilliant with grass; the glossy flanks of cattle wound slowly over the lea. As the road climbed the smooth curve of the hill, Great Hording was suddenly revealed, its cluster of sloped grey roofs giving way to pale yellow sand and white-lace-edged blue sea. A turn in the road and it was gone; she would not now see it for a week, a week in which she would be stuck in the city under the merciless cosh of Clemency and her acolyte Karlie. Laura groaned. Then, suddenly, she was bolt upright.

Something – someone – had just flashed past. Laura stared

out of the rear window. A girl on a bicycle. Nothing unusual about that, of course. It was just – was there something familiar? Mid-twenties, long arms, supermodel legs, large spectacles. Long straight blonde hair that rippled behind her in the breeze, like a flag. Karlie!

There was no doubt about it. Laura knew it with all her senses. She definitely hadn't imagined this figure. There it was, a dot in the distance, even now.

She had only just recovered from this shock when another swept through her. They were passing someone else she recognised. A tall man with broad shoulders. Young, with dark hair. Standing just back from the road, in the lee of a gatepost, as if he were waiting for someone.

She had seen him for a second only, but there was no doubt. Harry Scott. Definitely him this time.

Confused, shocked but most of all excited, Laura breathed deeply to calm her rioting heart. There could be an explanation; she had texted Harry about her previous sighting of him in the village. Had that brought him here to surprise her? She got out her phone and checked it. No message.

Or was there another, more obvious reason? Laura stared at the car's white padded ceiling. Karlie and Harry. In the same place at the same time. That was why he was here! He had a tryst with Clemency's horrible secretary!

A rush of heat spread through her, for all the car's powerful air-conditioning. This was why he had not been in touch! And what lay behind Karlie's superiority, the impression she always gave of knowing something Laura did not! It explained everything!

Had they met in London? Did it matter? The point was, Ellen had been wrong. Way off the mark. Harry didn't love her after all. And he certainly didn't need her!

'Is everything all right, madam?' came the solicitous enquiry from the chauffeur's seat. 'You look, if I may say so, rather pale.'

Laura stumbled onto the train. All the way back to London she stared at the newspapers without reading a word. Harry and Karlie.

The train wheels, rattling down the track, repeated it endlessly. Karlie and Harry. . . Harry and Karlie. . . Karlie and Harry. . . Harry and Karlie. . .

Back in Cod's Head Row, Laura hurried past Gorblimey Trousers. She was in no mood for the good-humoured cockney barracking of transplanted Californian tech executives. Still less the possibility that her flat might, once again, have been broken into. Please God it hadn't. She could not, Laura felt, endure another shock that day. Her heart thudded in her chest as she opened the front door of her building, crashing it loudly behind her before going up the stairs as noisily as possible.

The flat was as she left it, however. Perhaps, after all, the initial break-in had been speculative, unconnected with the Great Hording investigation.

Another positive was that Edgar seemed to be out, so Laura took advantage of the undisturbed quiet to polish her report. Writing always soothed her, the choosing of words, honing of sentences, the shaping of ideas into paragraphs. It took her jittery, unsettled mind to another place, somewhere she was in control. Even if she had no real idea what was going on in Great Hording. Probably less now than she did at the start.

After a while she stopped and reread what she had

written. Confusing as it was, it seemed significant. The feeling that she was on the verge of something important was growing. The explosive series of leaks, Sergei's near-fatal accident, the burgling of her flat, the disappearance of her phone, the appearance of Karlie in Great Hording, followed by that of Harry. How was it all connected?

She tried his phone again. Unsurprisingly, he did not answer. Had it really been him? She had been certain before, but everything suddenly seemed in flux again. Perhaps she had imagined it. Perhaps she was going mad. Perhaps the strain of the last few weeks was taking its toll.

Laura put her head in her hands, summoning the spirit of her indomitable grandmother, currently with the Fat Four on the high seas somewhere south of Australia. What would Mimi do? The answer came immediately.

Eat, of course. No one could make sense of anything on an empty stomach.

And she was starving, she realised. The fridge in her apartment held only a limp head of iceberg lettuce and a half-eaten packet of bacon. *Mais voilà!*, she seemed to hear Mimi say. What was she looking at if not a *salade aux lardons*?

As the chopped-up bacon sizzled fragrantly in the pan, Laura whipped up Mimi's vinaigrette. *Salt, one part vinegar, one part water, two parts olive oil, pepper. Mix all of the ingredients in a bowl. The trick is salt first, then vinegar, then water, then oil, and pepper last of all. In that order, without fail! Then add what you like: old-fashioned grainy mustard, shallots, chives. . . There are as many vinaigrette recipes as there are women.*

As she ate, sitting at her open window overlooking the sparkling, night-lit city, Laura felt stronger. Now, finally, her thoughts could turn to the other magazine story she was supposed to be writing, the one Clemency actually wanted. The Ivy Awards were taking place at the end of the week, on Friday evening.

And yet neither Caspar nor his people had been in touch. Like Harry, he had not returned her calls. As with Harry, there had been radio silence.

She reached for her laptop. According to the Sidebar of Shame on Mail Online, Caspar was currently filming in Morocco. There were images of him in a desert tent surrounded by writhing belly dancers. Any one of whom looked like a better red-carpet companion than her.

Laura took another sip of red wine. Two glasses had brought on a philosophical mood. Oh well. As Caspar had so generously pointed out, she lacked the grooming and gloss for a full-wattage celebrity evening. But there was no doubt this would mean trouble at work.

And while she'd hung on to the *Society* job for as long as was humanly possible. Perhaps it was time to accept that the odds were stacked against her at the British Magazine Company. Clemency would definitely fire her now. She'd never get her editorship back. Time to let that dream go too.

CHAPTER TWENTY-NINE

I t was just as well, it turned out, that she had been stood down at the Ivys. Lady Mandy now suddenly brought the first night of the Great Hording summer pantomime forward. 'She want performance before anyone else drop out,' Lulu said gravely. 'She on edge of knife. She start all rehearsal saying "overture and beginners" but there is no overture and not many beginners now everyone go Tuscany until scandal blow over.'

Laura said nothing about any of this to Clemency. For her to continue in her job, the editor must continue to believe that the insider film awards story was still on track. But Laura had never been an especially effective liar, no means as accomplished as her office superior. Clemency might well have guessed the truth had it not been for one thing.

Karlie had left. Suddenly, and with no explanation.

Laura had dreaded encountering the self-satisfied secretary the Monday after spotting her in Great Hording. Overnight she had tried to convince herself that there was no evidence, only coincidence, to link Karlie to Harry. If Harry it had really been, anyway.

But there was still Karlie's snooping and phone-tapping to account for, which made sense if the secretary had been spying on her love life. And the fact she had disappeared rather seemed to confirm suspicions. Perhaps she had seen Laura drive by in Great Hording? And, as a result, wanted to avoid her.

Laura had tried to consult Ellen about the mystery. But Ellen's phone went unanswered and Laura's calls to the foreign desk of *The Sunday Times* elicited only the information, from a harassed-sounding editor, that she was away. The window through which she had managed to slip in and see her was a rare one, Laura realised.

At least Karlie's absence infuriated Clemency, who reserved the right to disappoint people at a second's notice but bitterly resented being let down herself. Her efforts to recruit a replacement were not going well. In just one morning, Human Resources sent three candidates, all of whom were crying in the loos by lunchtime. Clemency, engaged in an orgy of assistant-bullying, had no time to bully Laura as well.

Laura felt far from cheerful, even so. Her Caspar piece was clearly not going to happen, her interview with Ellen was on the spike, and her only 'live' commission, the in-depth investigation of upmarket West London children's shops, was both shallow and dull. She could barely bring herself to think of what her derring-do father would have made of them.

This morning's daring assignment had been Wibble Wobble, an emporium owned by a pair of former supermodels. It sold wind-up vintage televisions, children's-wear with a Scandi vibe and calfskin docking ports for baby's iPad. Their bespoke euro-pop remix of the *Sesame Street* theme tune echoed in Laura's ears as she walked back towards the Tube. Midway along a row of shops was a branch of Save the Children – and something gold and glittering was in the window.

Laura paused and gasped. The suit! Lulu's liquid gold two-piece was in the window, rising like a glittering tree from a ground cover of second-hand Hermès bags. But of course there was no need to buy it any more.

All the same, looking at the shining outfit in all its flashy exuberance, Laura felt a stir of regret. It would have been fun to wear it.

She was walking away when her phone went.

Harry? With a rational explanation as to what he had been up to?

'Hey!' drawled the other end, un-Harryishly.

'Caspar? Where are you?'

'At Claridge'sh!'

'Are you drunk?'

'I've jusht flown in! Come on down!'

Crossing the gleaming marble chequerboard lobby of Claridge's, Laura cursed the ease with which she had been persuaded to come. The grandeur made her feel self-conscious. Everything was so shiny and smart. Perhaps Caspar was right – she was rough around the edges. The memory of what he had said angered her afresh. Where was he, anyway? She looked about, but none of the smooth types in the silky chairs in the pillared and chandeliered lounge fitted the handsome, excitable, bulge-eyed template of her most infuriating friend. Perhaps he had forgotten already that she was coming. Or had gone somewhere else, with someone more interesting.

'Madam?' A young woman in a smart, dark suit was at her elbow. Her voice was low with suppressed excitement. 'Mr Honeyman is in his suite. He asks if you would go up.'

The lift was like a small, ornate room, manned by a smiling attendant. She could get used to this, Laura thought. No wonder people lived in this hotel for weeks.

Caspar's suite had shining double doors and its own small gold doorbell. Seconds after she pressed it, the door was opened by a morning-suited butler. 'Haddock!' Laura exclaimed, assuming this was Caspar's legendary gentleman's gentleman.

The smoothly combed dark head inclined. 'Certainly, madam. We serve it in several ways: kedgeree, omelette Arnold Bennett. . .'

'Haddock'sh at home in Big Shur!' burst in an excitable voice from behind. 'Thish one comesh free with the shweet!'

Caspar sprawled on a chaise-longue in a sitting room with Marie Antoinette furniture. The coffee table before him was crowded with empty glasses. His arms were so dark with tattoos he looked as if he had lace sleeves on. He had thick gold hoops in his ear and a T-shirt that said 'HOAX' in Scrabble letters.

And what had happened to his hair?

'You've got a man-bun.' Laura tried to keep the horror out of her voice.

'Like it?' He touched it self-consciously.

Laura hesitated. She hated man-buns. They were greasy, slobby and suited no one. And with shaved sideburns, as Caspar had, they looked especially dim.

She decided to sidestep the issue of personal preference. 'Did James Bond have a man-bun? Tattoos?'

'I'm trying to drag him into the twenty-firsht shentury,' Caspar responded.

Laura's mouth dropped open. 'He's going to have them in the film?'

The man-bun nodded. 'I'm trying to convinsh the producersh.'

'Are they taking much convincing?'

'It'sh shafe to shay that our vishionsh aren't aligned at thish time,' Caspar slurred, before emitting a resounding belch.

Laura escaped to the bathroom – one of the bathrooms, as it turned out. It was vast, marbled and heaped with white towels, none of which seemed to have been used yet. There were two basins, one labelled 'FACE' and the other 'TEETH'. The shelf above the 'FACE' one contained a line of jars, presumably arranged by the butler, including caviar skin luxe cream and protein glaze. The 'TEETH' shelf hosted an extensive 'whitening system'. Laura thought of the one small bottle of baby oil which, in the Mimi tradition, served her as moisturiser, body lotion and conditioner. Caspar must have needed another entire plane just for his beauty products.

She emerged to find Caspar busy with the butler. 'Five shotsh of white tequila,' he was instructing.

'In the same glass, sir?'

'Yessh!'

Would the man-bun-sporting, tattooed, tequila-drinking Bond catch on? Laura wondered. She doubted it.

She lowered herself into an overstuffed armchair and looked about the ornate sitting room. There were so many patterns she felt a migraine coming on and the carpet was so thick her boots sank up to the ankles.

Caspar took the five-shot tequila off the silver tray now being offered him. 'Another!'

At least Caspar had remembered his duties as a host. Laura was desperate for a drink now. But when the second tequila arrived Caspar tossed it back as he had the first.

She felt disgusted and indignant. Why had she bothered to come? What was she doing, sitting watching a drunk, self-indulgent actor drink and self-indulge? What had happened to Caspar? Alcohol and fame had turned him into a monster; even more of a monster.

'I'm the biggesht shtar alive!' Caspar toasted himself delightedly with his twentieth shot of tequila. 'You know, it'sh great to shee you. Laura. The more famoush I get the more important it ish to me that I hang out with old friendsh. Normalshy, you know?'

Laura's eyes dropped to the 'HOAX' T-shirt. Irony? Double bluff?

'I went to Taylor Shwift'sh birthday party on Rhode Island. Shtayed with Rushell Crowe. He hash hish own pub, did you know?'

Laura nodded. Carinthia had run a feature in *Society* on the back of it; 'Personal Gin Palaces of the Rich and Famous'.

'*Another!*' Caspar roared at the butler.

'You're drinking an awful lot,' Laura remarked.

'It'sh the method,' Caspar replied. His eyelids were drooping now and his chin sinking into his chest.

'What method?'

'You know, acting. You inhabit the shoul of the charactersh you play.'

Laura hesitated. 'You mean. . . you're drinking a lot so you can get inside the soul of James Bond? Does he even have one?'

'It's a profound shike. . . shike. . . pshychological dishlocation,' Caspar managed, after huge effort. 'I'm shagging loadsh of girlsh as well. I'm a martyr to my craft. That's why they've gotta give me the Ivy for Besht Actor.'

And here was the cue she needed. She got up hurriedly. 'Well, good luck with that.'

A drunken nod. 'Thanksh.'

'Who are you taking with you, just out of interest?' It would be useful to know, as Clemency was sure to ask.

Caspar heaved himself up on an elbow and gave her a puzzled, unfocused stare. 'Whaddyamean? I'm taking you, of coursh.'

CHAPTER THIRTY

'Lulu, it's going to be fine,' Laura distractedly assured her friend. So many phones were ringing in the *Society* office it sounded like the aviary at London Zoo. There was no one to answer them. Almost all the staff members had resigned, unable to bear the despotic Clemency another second. Laura was one of the few left. It had been an unexpected lifeline; she was needed now and unlikely to be sacked. Unless Clemency herself got sacked, but that might also be an opportunity.

'Is not fine!' wailed the other end. 'You miss show!'

Clemency's own phone now joined the shrilling fray. It had been some days since the last temp had slammed out of the office and Laura had added editor's secretary to the list of jobs she now tried single-handedly to fill.

'Look,' she promised hastily. 'I'll come to Great Hording the minute the Ivys are finished. I've worked out the timings.'

She had, and to the split second, desperate to fulfil her obligations to both the friends who needed her. Lulu was obviously more deserving than Caspar, but as ever the actor had talked her round. On condition that she could go the moment the award had been handed over. No after-party, no nothing. 'I should be there in time for the grand finale,' she assured Lulu. 'Break a leg,' she added, as the office phones, which had temporarily stopped, now started up again.

'Wha. . .?!'

'A figure of speech. Actors say it to each other for good luck.'

'Is all bad luck though,' Lulu said gloomily.

Laura replaced the phone just as Clemency looked up from her desk and gave her an especially venomous glare.

Defensive, Laura knew. She now had quite a different take on her old enemy. The mass exodus of her staff, for all Clemency brazened it out, had made her vulnerable. There hadn't been a features meeting for days, and Laura knew, from the calls she was answering from Honor, that Christopher was fretting about the next *Society* cover. At the moment it was Lady Toots Winchester, who loved champagne-showers, had double-jointed thumbs and designed her own range of tweed bikinis. No wonder Christopher was worried.

'He thinks the magazine's out of step with the times,' Honor confided to Laura. 'What with the election and everything. He's worried *Society*'s going to become irrelevant.'

He had a point, Laura felt. The nation went to the polls the next week and the Conservative government seemed in disarray. Jolyon Jackson had only been the first; many leading MPs connected to him – some fellow cabinet ministers – had suffered setbacks after private information about them had emerged.

Not just politicians, either. During the last few days the internet had been awash with unflattering stories about people eminent in every imaginable profession. It was all very puzzling and, for once, didn't seem to have come from Great Hording. In Kearn's opinion at least. 'It's too general,' he had said last time they spoke. 'The leaks from here have been specific to village residents. But this new stuff is about, well, everyone.'

'Except journalists,' Laura pointed out. 'And that is very Great Hording, because no journalists live there. They're not allowed.'

'It's more probably because journalists don't print stories that hurt each other.'

Laura raised her eyebrows, but didn't argue. There were more important things at stake. 'Might it be WikiLeaks?' she asked.

'Julian says he's as confused as the rest of us.'

'You *know* him?' Laura was never quite sure if Kearn was joking or not.

The general confusion meant that Labour, the Liberal Democrats and the Greens were gaining ground. None were likely to champion a society in which the likes of Lady Toots would flourish. Her bikinis even less.

Perhaps this was what lay behind the sudden cold shoulder Clemency was receiving from people formerly desperate to ingratiate themselves. Laura had answered several calls in which a top designer's assistant's assistant explained they had run out of sample sizes, or the PA to a leading party-giver said they couldn't possibly squeeze in one more person. Further indignities included a hot new restaurant cancelling Clemency's lunch slot, a celebrity hairdresser 'losing' her booking and an airline refusing to upgrade her on a flight to an international fashion week in which she would now sit in the second row.

Laura had started to feel, to her surprise, rather sorry for Clemency. So much of her self-worth was invested in her position, a position she seemed increasingly ill-equipped to occupy. Laura was no longer privy to *Society*'s sales figures, but to judge from Clemency's face after meetings with Christopher, they clearly weren't going northwards.

She snatched up what had been Karlie's phone. The heavy breather, again. Two or three times a day she would answer to hear a strange buzzing and beeping followed by a rasping and gasping, then a guttural mutter in some foreign tongue. It was all very disconcerting.

On Friday afternoon, Clemency stalked across to her in her trademark red spike heels. She had been up in Christopher's office again. 'I'm not sure the meeting went so well dear,' Honor had confided. 'There was an awful lot of shouting.'

Clemency's face, framed by her roiling red mass of curls, looked shaken. Her eyes were glistening with what Laura, to her surprise, recognised as tears. 'You'd better make a good job of it tonight,' Clemency hissed. As threats went, it sounded more like a plea.

Laura nodded. 'I'll do my best.' To know that she might hold Clemency's future in her hands was rather dizzying. The tables truly had turned.

Clemency, spinning on her heel, paused. 'You might need to leave early. To get ready.'

Laura recognised this as being less an olive branch, more a whole tree. She was careful, even so, not to show it.

Clemency, even the new, humbled version, was still volatile, unpredictable and deceptive. 'Okay,' she said, guardedly. 'Thanks.'

She did need time to get ready, and buy her outfit into the bargain. Short-staffing – or no-staffing – at *Society* had meant no chance all week to go back to the Notting Hill charity shop.

As she thundered down the road from the Tube station, Laura prayed that the gold suit would still be there.

It was. Along with the perfect pair of high-heeled gold strappy sandals.

'Worn only once, on the school run,' the assistant confided. Caspar, of course, had not given a thought to how Laura would get from Cod's Head Row to the Royal Opera House, Covent Garden, where the Ivys ceremony was to be held. Fortunately, he had an efficient assistant, who sounded strangely familiar.

'Brad Plant!' Laura exclaimed, finally placing the voice explaining about the limo being sent to pick her up.

'Have we met?' the other end asked stiffly.

Laura reminded him about Savannah and Buckingham Palace. An agonised groan followed. 'OMFG. Seriously, that was a *nightmare*. I thought we'd be sent to the Tower to be executed. Dogs included.'

'You're not working for Savannah any more then?'

I got Caspar in the divorce, thank God. Okay, so the car's due in thirty minutes. Can I check the address? God's Head Road, right?'

Brad had barely got off the phone before it rang again. Lulu, with last-minute nerves about her performance.

'Am terrifying!'

'Lulu, you're playing a *shoe*. You've got *one* line.'

'Yes, but must convict audience. Make people disbelieve suspenders, hmm?'

'You'll be fine,' Laura assured her. 'Why are you worrying?'

The reply was unexpected. 'Is because I see girl who steal my money today.'

'What? Someone's burgled you?' Laura remembered her own break-in. Were the two linked?

'No, no. Saw bad girl used to work for me. In willage.'

Lulu had employed several personal assistants over the years, all of whom had gone by the time Laura arrived. All, by the sound of it, had sought to take advantage of her generous nature and relaxed attitude to security. 'You saw her in Great Hording?' Laura repeated. 'Are you sure?'

'She see me, she run away. Is bad person. Why she in willage, hmm? Rob more people?'

'You need to tell the police.' Laura's eye was on her watch. She had to go.

Lulu snorted. 'Police rubbish. She slimed through their toes last time. Escape.'

'Slipped through their fingers,' Laura guessed.

'I will get to buttocks of this off own racquet.'

Own bat? 'Well, good luck. Good luck with *Cinderella* too. I'll see you later.'

As, finally, Laura got in the car, it struck her how closely the pantomime story followed her own. She was going to the ball, or at least the Ivys. And while Caspar, to her, was hardly Prince Charming, plenty of others saw him that way.

The traffic around Covent Garden was gridlocked thanks to the award ceremony. Laura sat in her car while people stared in through the windows, pointing phone cameras at her. 'Who the hell even is that?' she heard them saying.

While interesting at first, this soon felt invasive and eventually so unpleasant that she lay down and pulled the rug over her. It was hot, scratchy and smelt of air freshener, but at least it was private.

The car inched forward. Beneath her rug Laura heard the noise levels increase. People were shouting.

'It's the red carpet, madam,' said the driver. 'Here's where you get out.'

Laura emerged, hot-faced and with ruffled hair, into a roar of noise and explosions of light. She closed her eyes against the painful onslaught and stumbled towards what seemed like the event entrance, waving the plastic pass Brad Plant had sent with the car.

'Over here! Over here!' People were yelling from all directions. Flashes were going off everywhere. It felt like torture, not the celebration of what humanity regarded as its highest achievement – celebrity.

Laura's senses were in complete disarray but she could see, above the blaze, the white glow of the front of the Opera House and, beneath her feet, an expanse of blood-red carpet.

People were processing gradually along it, pausing coquettishly with hand on hip for the cameras. And that was just the men. Tiny women with big hair brandishing chunky microphones were commenting on their outfits.

'Kate Beckinsale showcases a fetish tablecloth plastic sports bra. . .'

'Helena Bonham Carter in furry lederhosen, rocking her trademark boho style. . .'

'. . . Poppy Delevingne in a directional charred ballgown. . .'

'. . . Helen Mirren in a show-stopping platform-heel hat. . .'

Laura, getting used to it all now, gasped with excitement as a hugely famous couple started their slow parade down the carpet. It was like seeing *Hello* magazine come to life.

'Pair of fucking waxworks,' hissed a familiar voice from behind.

'Caspar!'

He looked almost respectable in black tie because the sleeves covered the tattoos. His shoes were polished – no doubt by the suite's free butler – to a mirror finish. But the Jack Sparrow earrings were still there, as was the ghastly man-bun.

'Isn't this great!' His teeth gleamed in the light of a thousand paparazzi flashbulbs. 'It's taken me ten years to be an overnight success!'

She clutched his arm. The sandals were much higher than they had looked. How had anyone done the school run in these? She doubted she could make it to the entrance without falling over.

She had taken a step forward, but Caspar had not moved.

'We wait till the end. That's when the really big stars do the carpet. When all the most important photos are taken. Right now it's all Schindler's B-list.'

An actress was being interviewed about her barely there bright orange dress.

'Wakes you up, doesn't it?' she beamed. 'It's my favourite colour and it's also the colour of hunger awareness across the globe.'

Laura felt Caspar suddenly stiffen. Presumably this was the cue to move off.

'Ready for your close-up?' she teased.

He looked at her narrowly. 'BFCU.'

'Is that a university?' Or an insult?

'Stands for Big Fucking Close-Up. Frames an actor above the eyebrows and below the mouth. An even tighter close-up focusing only on the eyes is known as a Sergio Leone because he filled entire screens with Clint Eastwood's squint.'

He was jabbering, Laura saw. She squeezed his arm, touched by this unexpected evidence of his vulnerability. 'Don't worry,' she said soothingly.

'Don't worry!' Caspar's eyes bulged almost into hers. His whitening-systemed teeth showed in a nervous snarl. 'Of course I'm fucking worrying. Savannah's here!'

'Savannah?' She had been nominated for an Ivy, Laura knew. Her latest film, *Watery Grave*, was a harrowing tale about Mediterranean people-smuggling. Savannah, playing a principled UN adviser who goes out on a limb to help, had been widely praised. 'People think she's a cross between Mother Teresa and bloody Princess Di now,' Caspar had complained. 'Bet she made it on purpose to get an award.'

'I thought she was filming in Africa,' Laura said. She had read a gossip-column story to that effect. The latest film was about genocide apparently; Savannah reprising her role as a principled UN adviser who goes out on a limb to help. Was it the same adviser, Laura wondered. The same limb?

'That was a decoy!' Caspar wailed. 'So she could surprise everyone! Look!'

Laura hardly needed to look. She could feel how the atmosphere suddenly crackled with excitement. Not to mention the barking of a great many little dogs. The paparazzi were going bananas and the crowd was screaming. And in the middle of it all, sailing down the red carpet was Savannah, her hair piled high and secured with a tiara, her tiny, thin body rising from the huge pink tulle skirt like a stick from a cloud of pink candyfloss. From her tiny thin hand extended four glittering silver chains, each one attached to a tiny, yapping creature decorated with a pink tulle bow.

The commentators were in overdrive;

'. . . era-defining gown made from recycled bottles and worn with diamonds from happy mines. . .'

Caspar was chewing his nails in anguish. 'We'll be head to head for Best Actor!'

'Why?' asked Laura.

The USP of the Ivys, Caspar now hysterically explained, was that they were gender neutral. There was one award for Best Actor; one for Best Supporting Actor too. This meant the Ivys was half the length of the usual film ceremony; another USP.

Nor was this all. Savannah's appearance in the flesh, Caspar explained, drastically reduced his Best Actor chances. The way the Ivys worked, was that, in each category, the biggest star who showed up got the award. That had been him, until his ex-girlfriend's advent. 'She's only doing it to get at me!' Caspar howled. In which case, Laura thought, she had certainly succeeded.

Laura touched his arm, mid-rant. 'Um, if Savannah's gone in, doesn't that mean the A-list are all in the building?'

The blood drained from Caspar's face. 'Oh God. You're right! It's just the techies now. Best Original Song. Best Use of Lighting. Aaagh!' Grabbing her hand, he yanked her on to the red carpet just as the last of the paparazzi strolled away. Which was just as well, as it was all Laura could do to keep her balance.

'Oh my God,' Caspar was moaning. 'What if she *wins?*'

CHAPTER THIRTY-ONE

In the great red and white foyer, below the vast and glittering chandeliers, Laura stared around at the cream of the acting profession. Everyone was there. From edgy Brit actors in parkas to Hollywood royalty in Prada, accessorised by billionaire husbands.

Something hit Laura on the head.

'Awesome!' A nearby starlet picked a bag of Krug-flavour Haribos out of her hair. A small balloon was attached to it. 'They're sending sweets down from the roof. How cool is that?'

Laura didn't think it was cool at all. Being in the Opera House wasn't either. She had underestimated the effect it would have. Harry had brought her several times, most recently to see the tragic *La bohème*. Fuelled by double-distilled orange-pip alcohol being circulated on trays, the celebrity clamour around her swelled. The drinking and chatting reminded Laura not only of Covent Garden's glamorous champagne bar, where Harry always splashed out on a whole bottle, but also the desperate end of *La bohème*'s poor heroine, ill-treated by the man she loved, reunited with him only when it was too late. Come to think of it, the plotline recurred in most of the operas they had seen together. Had Harry, Laura thought bleakly, been trying to tell her something? Hint at what to expect?

Caspar, next to her, was talking to a woman in a quilted jacket with watchful eyes. The editor, Laura had gathered, of an influential gossip column. Caspar's voice came floating over, all wistful regret. 'Savannah and I? Well, never say never. We're giving each other some respectful loving space at the moment. . .'

As the woman moved off towards George Clooney, Caspar grabbed a cocktail and downed it in one. He whirled round on a young man in a bootlace tie tapping him on the shoulder. 'I was wondering,' the youth said timidly, 'if you had any advice for budding actors?'

Caspar fixed him with an unhinged glare. 'Have you got a skin like a fucking rhinoceros?'

The young man backed away, alarmed. 'Steady on,' whispered Laura. Caspar was obviously near-hysterical.

As he plunged away again through the crowd, Laura shuffled alone through polished doors with bevelled glass panes and found herself in the auditorium. It was as crowded with celebrities as the foyer; you could barely move for famousness, like the Tube during rush hour, Laura thought. Yet what was this but celebrity rush hour? Over there was Nicole Kidman, statuesque in a column dress and towering over her tanned country-singer husband. Nearby was a glazed-looking Leonardo di Caprio, a blonde hanging on to his arm for dear life. Laura grinned to herself. Caspar had told her it was an actual physical fact that di Caprio couldn't see brunettes.

It was impossible, despite these distractions, to stop the memories of Harry from crowding back. In this auditorium he was everywhere. 'It's the most beautiful room in London,' he had said, pointing out the Classical detail on the plastered ceiling and how the dying house lights glowed pink just before the performance started. No detail had escaped him; the shine of the conductor's shoes, the way the trombones left for the backstage bar and skidded back in just before they were due to play. It had all been so romantic and she had loved it all so much. That he might now be showing the same things to Karlie felt like a hot knife in her insides.

An orchestra was playing 'There's No Business Like Show Business'. Was it, Laura wondered, the one she had last seen here, that had twisted her up inside with their playing? As they switched to 'Tomorrow', she hoped not. After the passion of Puccini, it seemed a comedown.

It was a small relief to see that the stall seats in which she and Harry had sat had been taken out of the auditorium. They had been replaced by round dinner tables decorated on a theme of the nominated films. This simplified things. She just needed to go to the *Caucus Imperative* one. Presumably that was the table with Union flags flying from the middle of the flowers, which were themselves arranged in the shape of guns.

Reaching it, Laura saw that the *Watery Grave* table had been positioned, either provocatively or from sheer bad luck, next to theirs. The four silver engraved dog bowls were a giveaway, as were the table decoration; a central glass tank of water in which a toy boat and various figures were bobbing.

The place mats were themed too. *Watery Grave*'s were broken pieces of wood, as if from a smashed boat, while those on the Bond table were of the celebrated scene in *The Caucus Imperative* when the spy, wearing Union flag swimming shorts of Tom Daleyesque skimpiness, escaped from his pursuer by joining – and winning – the Olympic 100 metres final.

The menu was propped up in the table centre, and Laura examined it with interest. Loin of venison, chocolate ganache with caramel ice cream. Delicious. Her stomach rumbled and her spirits rose. But dinner was clearly some time off. If people drifted towards the tables, it was only to move place cards around. How rude, Laura thought. Not to mention frustrating. How was she ever going to get away to Great Hording? The bulk of the gathering was still fraternising at the far end, by the doors. She could see Colin Firth and his wife talking to Eddie Redmayne and his. Fame looked smaller in real life.

'It's okay!' Caspar flung himself into the chair beside her. His spirits seemed greatly restored. The orange-pip alcohol or something he'd been doing in the loos? Neither, it turned out. 'I've won, apparently,' he whispered, ripping off his black tie and opening his collar to reveal the top of a new tattoo on his chest.

Laura peered at it. She could see letters and numbers. 'What does it say?'

'"Best Actor. The Ivys. 2018". I got a bit overconfident, I guess.'

No wonder Caspar had been so worried.

Ages passed and people continued to mill about. Caspar

got up again and went off with his talent agent. An increasingly impatient Laura went to the loo which was full of famous people taking selfies of each other. Seeing an international celebrity everywhere she looked was beginning to feel strangely normal. Back at the Bond table, people were finally starting to sit down. Someone asked her, 'Did you know that Cubby Broccoli actually began his career selling broccoli?'

Laura tucked gratefully into the loin of venison but all around people ignored the food whilst downing an endless and increasingly bizarre sequence of drinks. She watched Caspar worked his way steadily through espresso snakebites, moonshine daiquiris and something called a double-whammy absinthe blaster.

As the minor trophies were handed out, the recipients attempted to outdo each other in the humble background stakes.

'I think that everyone should wait tables at some point in their life.'

'I had croup as a kid. I was always in the vaporiser tent.'

Or they thanked an endless list of colleagues.

'She is by far the most committed and dedicated third grip I have ever worked with.'

'The director was awesome. A lighthouse of searching calm in a sea of crazy.'

Laura was aware, at the next table, of the searching lighthouse of Savannah Bouche's stare. She was watching Caspar with what looked like malevolent delight. Whether she recognised Laura from the interview – how long ago that seemed now – and the more recent Great Hording incidents was not clear.

A short and animated man won, appropriately enough, Best Animated Short.

'I'm gonna hug the hell out of you when the feeling re-enters my body,' he told his colleagues, who looked alarmed.

The Ivy for best TV programme was taken by the writer of a stately home series who said it was 'like winning the Nobel Prize'. Laura was aghast at his immodesty. And this on the stage where Fonteyn and Nureyev had danced!

The Best Supporting Actor category was won by a woman who had played Mrs Goebbels. 'What was it about acting like a Nazi's wife that appealed to you?' asked the provocative comedian, to laughter from the audience. The actress had a tough reputation.

Finally, the moment arrived. As everyone in the room stared at Caspar and Savannah, Laura felt under the table and squeezed Caspar's fingers. She was alarmed to see, a second later, Caspar raise both hands to check his man-bun. His agent, meanwhile, grinned at her meaningfully.

Up on the stage, his broad proportions haloed in the spotlight, the sardonic comedian fondled his goatee. The pop of champagne corks could be heard discreetly at the back. 'Not yet!' he warned, cueing a dutiful ripple of laughter.

He cleared his throat and opened the envelope. 'And the nominees are. . .'

The room was so still you could have heard a diamond-mounted Tiffany pin drop.

'Alex McGrimm, for *Skaghead*. . .'

That was a Glasgow-set drugs drama, Laura had gathered. The table concerned had a tartan cloth and flowers arranged in the shape of hypodermic needles.

'. . . Savannah Bouche, for *Watery Grave*. . .'

Thunderous applause greeted this. Savannah half rose, then sank again, expression sorrowful, head bowed, hand over her heart.

'. . . and last, Caspar Honeybun. . . sorry, Man-bun. . .'

He paused for uproarious laughter. Caspar beamed up at him, the best of sports. Only Laura was close enough to hear him chanting, in an ominous monotone, out of the corner of his mouth, 'And afterwards, I'm going to fucking *kill* you. . .'

'. . . for *The Caucus Imperative*.'

This was greeted with loud cheers from the Bond table, and frozen silence from the *Watery Grave* one, canine contingent included. The dogs were, in any case, making short work of the leftover venison. Polite applause from the rest of those present implied the audience was treading a cautious line between the two megastars.

'And the winner is. . .'

He ripped open the red envelope with plump white hands.

'Savannah Bouche for *Watery Grave*!'

'Waaaahhhhh!' shrieked a triumphant Savannah, at the exact same time Caspar shouted, 'Fuckinghellno!' He slammed his head into the Bond place mat as Savannah, amid applause and the film music played on a soulful single cello, leapt up with practised grace and bounded up on stage where, deftly avoiding the fat comedian's attempted embrace, she snatched his microphone with one hand, her Ivy award with the other and launched into her acceptance speech.

'Oh my goodness, dreams *do* come true. I wanna thank all of you who believed in me and this amazing project. In particular I wanna thank everyone who drowned trying to get to Europe—'

The fat comedian, who seemed to have been listening to something on an earpiece, now lunged forward and grabbed the microphone back off her.

'There's been a mistake,' he said bluntly, going to the edge of the stage and staring down at where Caspar still sat, slumped forward, forehead to the place mat. 'They gave me the wrong envelope. Bond, you've won best actor. *Watery Grave* gets the Ivy. . . for Best Costumes. . .'

The roars, cheers and shouts of amazement drowned Savannah's screams of fury, but had no effect whatsoever on Caspar, who seemed to have knocked himself out.

'Caspar! You've won!' Laura cried, shaking the tuxedoed arm, to no avail.

A tense official announcement, in cut-glass Covent Garden tones, was coming over the tannoy. 'The presenter was mistakenly given the wrong category envelope which, when discovered, was immediately corrected. We deeply regret that this occurred. . .'

All around where Laura sat beside Caspar people were hugging each other. Some gleefully, some wiping away tears as if overcome with the sheer emotion of it all. The air was full of exclamation.

'Omigod! Wasn't that the craziest Ivys of all time?'

How could it be? Laura wondered. It was only the first one.

'We just made history, hashtag most insane moment ever, it all felt like it was on another *planet*. . .'

Amid the excitement and the panic, Laura felt a tap on her shoulder. She turned round and looked up to see row upon row of faces; agitated, excited, alarmed. One stood out. She didn't just recognise it. She knew it.

'Harry!' she gasped, leaping to her feet. 'What the hell. . .?'

He put a finger to his lips, pulled her towards him with the strong hand she had so often dreamt about. 'Not now. We have to leave.'

She stared at him, confused. She had certainly meant to leave, but it was complicated now, with Caspar in a coma.

'You've got to come with me to Great Hording.'

'Well, I am. . . I mean, I was. . .' She looked down doubtfully at the Best Actor. Was life returning? Was that a fluttering around his eyelids?

'You've got to come now. Lulu's disappeared.'

CHAPTER THIRTY-TWO

Earlier That Day

How much longer, Kiki wondered, could she keep up the façade? Pretend that nothing had happened?

It had been two days since the dread moment she had opened her computer to find that her worst fears were realised and the Golden Goose's file of all the villagers and their contacts, the priceless Great Hording List, had been hacked.

The shock had been such that she had knocked her foxglove tea right into her flaxseed breakfast mix. But there was no doubt about it. That she could actually open and read the list was proof. For well over a week it had been inaccessible thanks to the complex system of passwords imposed by Sir Philip Peaseblossom. So much, Kiki thought angrily, for the best of MI6.

And now everyone's personal information was in the public domain. As well as details of where all their friends and acquaintances lived. Mobile phone numbers, email addresses, credit card numbers, online passwords were all there, along with much that was infinitely more incriminating. The tsunami of unflattering stories that had immediately appeared in the media was no surprise to her, even if the rest of the village found it a mystery.

'Everyone knows my husband consults an astrologer now!' Kate Threadneedle stormed. 'It's made a nonsense of his financial forecasts.'

The fact that Zeb Spaw had recently ordered *How To Paint* and *Drawing For Beginners* from his Amazon Prime account was also out in the open. No one was buying his claim that it was post-modern irony. Or, increasingly, his artworks.

The acrimonious correspondence which Dame Hermione had been conducting with a reader accusing her of lifting large chunks of *Black Beauty* was also online for all to see. Would Great Hording's artistic pre-eminence ever recover?

Would Kiki? If the leak became public, it would spell curtains for her career. Let alone her hopes of becoming a rich man's wife. Jonny would cut her off without a second thought and, as he had contacts everywhere, she'd be lucky to run a whelk stand in Blackpool.

It was with a tight, tense feeling in her insides that she had been going about her business ever since; planning menus, briefing bar staff, checking rooms that – for the moment at any rate – no one was staying in. That was another unexploded bomb, of course. While Jonny liked to say the Golden Goose wasn't about profit, it certainly wasn't about loss. Jonny's world was all about winning; if not money, then power and influence. All of which, as Kiki saw it, were leaking fast.

And then, early this evening, the phone had rung with Lulu on the end of it. Kiki had immediately assumed that she too was complaining about the leaks and it took some time to unpick both the cross purposes and Lulu's impenetrable idiom.

'You're saying that someone who used to work for you, a thief to put it bluntly, is in the village?' the pub manageress decoded, eventually.

'Is dangerous woman. Bad person.'

'What does she look like?'

'Blonde ponytail. Tall, like supermodel.'

Kiki didn't like the sound of this at all. There were more than enough supermodel-like women in the village as it was.

'Where did you see her?'

'Riding the bike down willage street. Is why she is here?'

You tell me, Kiki wanted to say. Everything she knew about the village was known by everyone else now, after all.

'I'll look into it,' she promised Lulu, through gritted teeth. It rankled to have to account for herself to the ghastly blonde whose advent in the village had been the start of the string of disasters.

She had returned to the bar to find Peter Delabole taking his usual seat at the beamed and polished bar. He courteously raised his modest half of ale and said, in his modest tones, 'Forgive me for asking, Miss Cavendish, but you seem a little distracted this evening.'

It was all Kiki could do not to fall on his neck and tell him everything. While she prided herself on being self-sufficient, some burdens were just too big for one person to bear.

She stopped herself, however. 'It's nothing,' she said, switching on her most dazzling beam and feeling her heart twist as Peter smiled his slow smile and crinkled his eyes. He really was so handsome, albeit in an understated way. And a not-at-all rich way, more was the pity. The laddered bones of Kiki's chest rose and fell in a sigh.

Peter nodded. 'Well, I won't pry. But if you ever wanted to talk, I'm always here.' The gold rim round his vintage watch – his father's, he'd once told her – glinted reassuringly as he extended his long, sensitive hand and sympathetically touched hers. The caress was only fleeting, but the effect was electric. Underslept and overwrought as she was, Kiki was pushed over the edge.

'Oh God, Peter. . .' One hand flew to her mouth, while the other grabbed his wrist.

He was off the stool in a second. 'My dear Miss Cavendish!' Feeling his strong arm about her, cheek pressed to the scratchy warmth of his ice-blue Shetland V-neck, Kiki was lost. 'I've been so worried. . .' she began.

She could trust him, she knew. He had, at her instigation, already fixed the pub quiz. He harboured secrets about the Golden Goose as it was. She began slowly, checking his expression for any sign that he was judging her, or disapproving. But the blue eyes held nothing but sympathy as she described the hacking of her sacred List.

'And then I got a call from Lulu. She says she's seen a thief in the village.'

A smile flickered about the ends of Peter's long mouth.

'A thief? With arrows up his suit and dragging a ball and chain? That would seem to match the cartoonish perceptions of our dear local billionheiress.'

Kiki shook her head. The pencil slid out and clattered on the floor. 'No, someone she says used to work for her. A woman. Blonde, with a ponytail, on a bicycle.'

'How very alarming. Well, we must do something about that, mustn't we?' This sent a warm wash of relief through Kiki. It was almost as if her problems were his problems too.

Kiki beamed at him. 'Do you think I should ring the police? she asked him. According to Lulu, this woman's a criminal. She's here to cause trouble.'

She was surprised to see Peter's benign features become suddenly flinty and hard. 'I think we should take care of her within the community,' he said. 'Isn't that the Great Hording way?'

'But how will we recognise her?' Kiki wondered. 'Lulu's the only one who knows her.'

'Well, we shall have to find Lulu,' said Peter. 'By any means necessary.' He stood up and cast a quick look round. The bar was empty apart from Pavel, who was polishing glasses quietly behind the bar. Meanwhile, in the kitchen, the distant crash of Hervé's pans could be heard.

Looking adoringly up at her champion, Kiki watched him nod his head at the handsome barman. As if at a prearranged signal, Pavel nodded back and placed his teatowel carefully on the side. He then went into the kitchen, where a conversation ensued in a foreign language that was definitely not French.

'Goodness,' said Kiki with nervous brightness. 'I didn't realise Hervé spoke Polish.'

Peter's eyes were cold and his expression set. 'It's not Polish. Everyone thinks it is but that's because they're stupid. Pavel is Russian. Hervé too.'

Kiki gasped. 'That explains everything!'

'Everything?' There was shock in Peter's tone.

'About the steak and kidney pie. Hervé puts vodka in it.'

Pavel and Hervé now appeared in the bar. They did not look at Kiki.

'Now,' said Peter. 'There's no time to lose.'

It was not clear to Kiki exactly who he was talking to. 'Now what?' she asked.

Peter looked at her. The look was not a pleasant one. He was feeling in his pocket. Pavel and Hervé were at either side of her. They took her arms. Kiki was about to scream when Peter pulled a cotton bookbag over her head with 'I Like To Party and by Party I Mean Read' printed on it. With that, he bundled her out of the room.

'You're joking!' Laura exclaimed, even though it was quite obvious that Harry wasn't. His face was set as he piloted his battered and elderly Golf through the Covent Garden traffic. The car smelt even more horrible than she remembered, as if it had spent a long time shut up in a garage. The footwell was, as ever, a sea of rubbish. That he hadn't bothered to clean it out for Karlie either was some comfort. There hadn't been time to ask him about that yet though. Something else was occupying all available bandwidth.

That Harry had been all round the world on his latest mission she could believe. That it had been so secret and dangerous he had not dared to contact her she could accept. That Ellen had helped with the story she could readily imagine. But what Harry had just said was frankly ridiculous.

'Great Hording has been targeted by the Russians? It makes no sense.'

'It makes perfect sense,' Harry growled, jerking to a halt to allow a group of international schoolchildren in baseball caps follow an exasperated-looking teacher over a crossing.

'But why? It's a country village. A small town by the sea. Why target that? I thought Russian hackers targeted Westminster, the NHS, the British establishment, that sort of thing.'

Harry was swerving round a hen party now. The bride-to-be was wearing flashing devil horns and shaking a pulsating trident.

'They did exactly that.'

Laura, in the passenger seat in her bright gold suit, felt that the already surreal evening was taking an even crazier twist. In a minute she would wake up and be in her bed in Shoreditch. Or on a sunny riverbank, like Alice.

But hopefully not. Because her quick journalist's brain had now seized the story. 'Of course!' she exclaimed. 'Great Hording is a microcosm of power in Britain. You've got cabinet ministers, the heads of banks and the security services there, top judges, army generals, literary lions, famous artists. . .'

Harry seemed more occupied with the gearstick than in Laura's discoveries. He had clearly worked it all out already.

'And by attacking Great Hording, they attacked the Establishment!'

Night-time London was speeding by. Progress was faster

now, the roads wider and emptier. 'But what did they hope to gain?' Laura mused, before a further flash of enlightenment illuminated what was left of the mystery. 'Oh God, why am I even asking that? There's a general election next week! Obviously the Russians want to disrupt as much as possible. Destabilise the nation.'

'Looks like it,' Harry concurred, his calmness and control in stark contrast to her excitement.

Laura frowned. 'There's one odd thing though. They must have known the village quite well. To know who to target.'

'It would seem so.'

'But I never met any Russians.'

'Not that you knew of.' Harry changed gear. 'But you certainly worked with one of them.'

'Kearn?' Laura guessed, spirits sinking.

Harry gave a bark of laughter. 'Hardly. He's been a very useful contact, in fact. Bright boy, that one. No, I'm talking about someone at *Society*.'

Laura turned her head so sharply towards him her hair slapped her round the face. 'Not Clemency!' Was it possible? She was an inveterate plotter, with proven spying abilities. And she wore a lot of red.

'Karlie. Real name Karla Cormicova. Works for the Russian security services. Petty criminal, confidence tricksters. Well-versed in the latest Kremlin mind-reading techniques.'

Laura clutched the door handle. It shifted in her hand; the passenger door never quite shut properly and could swing open without warning. 'Petty criminal? Confidence trickster?' Was this the person Lulu had seen in the village? And mind-reader? She remembered how Karlie always seemed to know what she was thinking.

'We've had our eye on her for a while. And once she was spotted in Great Hording, it was the proof that knitted everything else together.'

Laura stared at Harry in horror. 'I told Lulu to go to the police. But she said she'd get to the buttocks of it herself.'

He looked startled. 'What?'

Laura felt sick with guilt. She should have insisted that Lulu went to the authorities. By going maverick, her friend had walked straight into some dreadful net. 'She must have told someone else. Someone who didn't want Karlie's – I mean Karla's – identity revealed. So they grabbed Lulu.' She clutched Harry's hand. 'She's in danger.'

Somewhere in the back of her mind the realisation dawned that Harry had never been interested in Karlie, except professionally. It should have been a triumphant moment. But all Laura could think about now was Lulu. She shook Harry's hand. 'We've got to find her!'

'Steady on! We will!'

As the car swerved over the lanes of the motorway and Harry fought to straighten it up, amid admonishing honks from surrounding vehicles, another thought struck Laura.

'Why was Karlie there? At *Society*?'

'Isn't it obvious?' he returned, somewhat crushingly. '*Society*'s got a lot of upper-crust contacts. Very useful, given the Russians were attacking the Establishment. And, of course, you were there. She thought you might have information on your phone.'

Laura gasped. 'That's why she had it tapped! I knew there was something weird about it!'

'And why she burgled your flat.'

'But what was she looking for? *Society*'s deepest secrets? The Top Single Totty List for 2018? The only world domination plans she knew were those of West London's most superior children's stores. What would Russian intelligence, however aspirational, want with that?

Harry cast her another glance from the steering wheel. Longer, this time, and more intense. 'Can't you guess? Information about me, of course.'

'You?' Her heart was hammering so hard she could hardly hear herself speak. 'But there isn't anything about you in my flat. Or on my phone. You've never left anything and you haven't been in touch for ages.'

He looked at her for a long time. His expression was unreadable. 'I couldn't,' he said simply. 'If I had, you would have been in danger. They would have taken you to get at me.'

Laura supposed these words should strike terror into her heart. But their effect was to send her thoughts flying back to where the conversation had begun. 'Has Karlie got Lulu then?'

'We believe her associates have,' Harry replied. 'We're not sure who they all are, but we know one of them's posing as a bookseller.'

'Peter Delabole!' gasped Laura.

'That's one of his names. He started out as Andrew Redgrave. Cambridge, MI5, Moscow bureau. Double agent, the full Kim Philby.'

Laura was still shaking her head. She remembered the afternoon in his shop, his refusal to sell her *Indigenous Fats and Waxes of Norway*. When she told Harry she'd tried to buy it for him, he snorted.

'Would have been quite a present. Would have saved me a lot of time as well. They were probably leaving messages for each other in it.'

'Isn't that a bit. . . basic?' But Laura had no doubt he was right. Why else would Delabole have acted as he did?

'Given that everyone's hacking everyone else, it's one of the safest methods out there. An oldie but a goodie.'

He flashed her a wide smile and she suddenly felt ridiculously happy. Which of course she shouldn't, given that Lulu had disappeared. This was such a strange journey, full of dramatic revelation, some good, many bad.

'I wonder how they even came across Great Hording in the first place,' she mused. 'There's an internet blackout, after all.' She blushed, realising how silly this must sound. Hackers of the level evidently operating could no doubt find anything, anyone and anywhere.

In the intermittent glow from the overhead lights of the motorway, one straight eyebrow was quizzically raised. 'It's a good question, with an unexpected answer.'

'So?' Laura felt a flood of gratification. *A good question.* 'What is that answer?'

'Your friend Edgar.'

Laura's mouth dropped open. 'You're not seriously saying he's a fifth columnist?' Camp, chaotic, clubbing, string-vest-wearing Edgar? A more unexpected spy was hard to imagine.

'He might as well have been,' Harry said. 'As it was, the Russians knew he goes clubbing a lot, and that his father is Sir Philip Peaseblossom. All it took was a group of gender-fluid Baltic dancers to go with him back to his flat and slip something in his tea.'

Both of Laura's hands flew to her mouth. 'I met them! Sink the Pink!' Only now did the name seem significant. 'As in sink the left-wing?'

Harry nodded. 'They're coming from the Conservative

side of the Russian political establishment. That's why Sergei Goblemov was targeted. He fell out with the regime, which was why he came to England in the first place.'

Laura sat back in the passenger seat, her brain whirling. It all seemed too much to take in, and one matter alone was paramount. Lulu was missing. Her dear, potty, warm-hearted, theatrical billionheiress best friend. Would she ever see her again?

CHAPTER THIRTY-THREE

Lady Mandy was at her wits' end. Never, *ever* again would she volunteer to direct the Great Hording summer pantomime. The production couldn't have been more cursed if the cast had shouted 'Macbeth' twenty times each before starting rehearsal.

Scandal had dogged her crew from the start. A series of exposés had seen cast member after cast member drop out. Then the scenery had fallen on Baron Hardup. Now the glass slipper had failed to show for the first – and probably last – performance.

Really, thought the great director. What was the point? No one believed more than her that the show must go on. As ASM at the RSC, she'd helped many a beleaguered production limp to Act Five. Quite literally with *Titus Andronicus*, where the staging had been so bloody the Kensington Gore had arrived by petrol tanker.

But the show could only go on if there actually was a show. And now that Lulu too seemed to have bailed out, that left only the pantomime horse. The contents of that had changed so often Mandy couldn't even remember who was in it now. They hadn't turned up either, not so far anyway.

Nor had the audience. Word had evidently got around – as all words concerning Great Hording did these days, and at the speed of fibre-optic light.

In the empty village hall, Lady Mandy prepared herself for the final, ritual act. She went into the loo, unhooked the cloth from the back of the door – none of those nasty roaring Dyson things here – and hurled it on to the stage.

'What are you doing?' asked Wyatt Threadneedle, who, since packing it in at the delicatessen, had been assisting Lady Mandy when there were things to assist with. Increasingly, there weren't.

The look now turned on her was grim and weary. 'Throwing in the towel, dear. It's an old theatrical tradition when a production's got absolutely no chance of succeeding.' Lady Mandy sighed heavily. 'Never have I been so let down.'

'You can't blame Lulu for that,' Wyatt said loyally. 'She loved being the glass slipper. She's sure to have a good reason for not coming.'

Lady Mandy doubted it. The heiress, with her eternal sunglasses, piles of blonde hair, tiny skirts and tottery shoes, looked like a reason-free zone to her.

Wyatt was not fond of Lady Mandy. But so bleak did the older woman's face suddenly look, she felt sorry for her. Love – and sudden constant, easy access (not that her parents had any idea) to the object of that love – had transformed Wyatt's outlook from gloomy and got-at to joyful and generous. Nor was it just the outlook that was transformed. The blue hair was gradually giving way to a natural light brown, the black lipstick was now clear gloss and Wyatt's waistline was emerging from beneath the tummy rolls.

'Let's go to the pub,' she suggested, impulsively.

Lady Mandy, heavy brows drawn, looked about to refuse. Then her face suddenly cleared. 'Oh, what the hell. Why not? We always did in Stratford. The times we had at the Dirty Duck!'

Outside, in the warm darkness of the midsummer evening, Wyatt walked alongside the great director as she reminisced. 'Trevor – Nunn, of course – was so naughty! He liked to blow up crisp bags and bang them really loud! How Larry – Olivier – used to jump!'

'Stop a minute,' said Wyatt, holding up her hand. She had heard something.

'Whatever's the matter?' Lady Mandy resented being interrupted. Her moustache bristled indignantly.

'There it is again! Sounds like a gunshot.'

'Can't be,' Lady Mandy said sensibly. 'The Glorious Twelfth's months away.'

The phone in Wyatt's pocket buzzed. It had been restored to her by her parents now that Kearn had supposedly gone. Lady Mandy, watching her, saw her face change in the light from the screen.

'Oh God. What now? There's nothing left to leak any more.'

Wyatt shook her head. 'It's from Kearn. It's all happening in Fore Street, apparently.'

'Well, what's *he* doing there?' Lady Mandy demanded. 'He's supposed to have left the area. Which was the least he could do, after the damage he's caused.' Her voice, in the dark, tightened with fury. Kearn, architect of every disaster that had assailed her.

Wyatt felt all sympathy for the beleaguered thespian drain away. Pompous old bat. 'He had nothing to do with any of the leaks,' she said sharply, wondering whether to reveal who had.

But from what she could gather from Kearn's message, everyone would know soon anyway.

'Come on!' Wyatt grabbed Lady Mandy's wrist.

In Great Hording's main street, slung across the cobbles outside the bookshop, were several vehicles. One was an Ocado van. Typical, Lady Mandy thought. The same lost East European driver seemed to spend his life circuiting the village. One might almost think he was keeping an eye on it.

Another was a huge gold Rolls Royce and the other the massive black limousine that looked, Lady Mandy thought, like the one Lulu habitually went around in, driven by that peculiar, silent butler of hers.

'How infuriating,' the grande dame of Great Hording sniffily observed to Wyatt. 'It seems that our dear Glass Slipper, not someone one imagines reads much, was suddenly seized by the urge for literature and came to the bookshop instead of the pantomime.'

'I'm not sure it was that which seized her,' Wyatt replied, just as two figures suddenly raised themselves from behind the Rolls Royce and the limousine. One, Lady Mandy saw, was Lulu's peculiar butler, impeccable as ever in bow tie and cutaway coat. The other, even by Great Hording standards, was an extraordinary sight. He was huge, black and wore a gold leather biker jacket entirely covered with crystals. These blazed under the streetlights, flashing off the lenses of some enormous gold-rimmed sunglasses. As, now, he opened his mouth to roar, light shot from a ruby in one of his huge white front teeth. '*Get the motherfuckin' fuck outta there!*'

'My God,' said Wyatt, starstruck despite the circumstances. 'It's South'n Fried!'

'I don't know how it's cooked, but it's certainly foul-mouthed!' Lady Mandy exclaimed. 'Such language! And he's carrying two guns!'

Actually, they were a ball-bearing gun and a plastic AK47, grabbed from the Great Hording toyshop. But, as befitted an establishment selling to the oligarchs of tomorrow, they had a highly convincing appearance.

South'n Fried gestured with his BB gun. 'Come on out, you bums! Or I shoot!'

The gestures were, Lady Mandy now saw, aimed at the empty first-floor windows of the bookshop. 'Poor Peter!' she gasped. 'Is he in there, do you think?'

'He's not actually Peter,' Wyatt said. 'His name's Andrew Redgrave and I wouldn't be too sorry for him. He's a master spy.'

'Redgrave!' Excitement made Lady Mandy ignore the last sentence altogether. 'Is he a relative of dear Vanessa? Oh my goodness, what's happening now?'

The form of Peter Delabole had appeared in the first-floor window. Lady Mandy screwed up her eyes. He was holding someone. Bless him, he was actually holding her missing Slipper. Lulu had been found. The show could go on, after all.

'Peter!' Lady Mandy waved. 'You're just *too* marvellous! Is it true,' she went on as Wyatt goggled at her, dumbfounded, 'that you're a relative of—' The sentence was never finished.

Wyatt rugby-tackled the grande dame of am-dram. 'Get down! He might have a gun!'

Cheek pressed against the cobbles, Lady Mandy stared at Wyatt in amazement. 'Was that really Kiki in the other window? With Pavel? I must say I'm surprised. Never a good idea to sleep with the staff, in my view.'

Wyatt, crouching behind the limo, could see nothing of the action now. She could only guess at what was happening. Hopefully Special Forces were in the building, about to make arrests. But where was Kearn? She hadn't seen him for what seemed hours, when he had left Riffs, as he said, to meet someone.

Who was that someone? Had it been a trick? Sickening fear now rose in Wyatt's throat. There had been so much dealing and double dealing. Kearn had unpicked so much of it, but had he been trapped himself at last?

There was a lot of shouting, and the sound of sirens. The police, it seemed, had arrived. As ever, slightly late. More cars, the slamming of more doors.

A megaphone. 'This is the police. We have you surrounded. Armed officers have entered your building from the back. Surrender now, and release the prisoners.'

'Never!' screamed Peter Delabole. Wyatt, her fingers crossed, raised her head just enough to see over the bonnet of the limo. At that exact moment Lulu, who had evidently been awaiting her chance, slipped out of the master-spy's grip, bent him over and wrenched his arm back in a half nelson. 'Ow!' screamed Delabole, while Vlad, below, nodded approvingly.

Only now did Lulu spot who stood below in the Georgian street flashing with the revolving lights from police cars.

'South'n Fried!' She leant so far out of the window in her excitement she just avoided falling out. 'You have bust ass?'

'I came straight from the tour, baby! Wanted to give you a surprise!'

'Is *big* surprise!' Lulu screamed back, right by Peter's ear. 'Is *good* surprise!'

'So will you take me back, baby?'

As everyone was following the intensity of the drama, Kiki seized her moment. Filled with wild rage at all the injustices Fate had dealt her, of which being bundled into an Ocado van and made to intercept Lulu at the village hall entrance was only the latest, she summoned all her strength and delivered that rage straight into Pavel's unsuspecting teeth. 'That's for leaking the picture of Jolyon Jackson!' she hissed.

The lanky waiter/assistant master spy toppled backwards into the room. There was a huge crash, followed by the slithering and bumping of what might have been hundreds of books.

Only now did Laura and Harry, having been caught in a five-way traffic light on Great Hording's outskirts, come tearing into Fore Street. They were just in time to hear Lulu say, 'Yes!'

EPILOGUE

'I'm not sure it's quite me,' Harry said, adjusting the foraged buttonhole in the lapel of his loudly striped Gucci blazer. 'It's too small and tight.'

'It's supposed to be small and tight.' Laura grinned. All the groomsmen were wearing couture menswear. Harry had particularly objected to handmade rose-gold brogues with no socks. 'At least you're not mismatched and distressed,' Laura reminded him. The bridesmaids were all channelling the boho-vintage vibe in pre-loved floaty flower-print dresses.

Secretly, she thought Harry looked amazing. His chiselled face and tumbling hair looked completely new season Burberry, as South'n Fried had said. Harry had had no idea what he was talking about. But Laura's heart swelled with pride whenever she looked at him. Having him back was so wonderful, even though she knew it would not be for long. It never was.

She and Harry were getting wedding-ready in one of the enormous suites at Riffs. While it still bore traces of Roger's exuberant reign, Lulu had done her best to tone things down and boho them up. Their room had a baroque sleigh bed and its own wood-burning stove complete with piles of logs whose sawn-off ends were painted neon pink, orange and green. In the bathroom were a brass-bound sea chest, a telescope and a roll-top bath. 'All we need is a parrot,' Harry had drily observed.

This whimsical romantic style should have sat oddly with South'n Fried's more contemporary aesthetic. He had installed mouthwash-blue leather banquettes all over the house and hanging lamps featuring red and blue DNA atoms in coloured glass double helixes. A display of single trainers in Perspex cases greeted visitors in the entrance hall. But strangely, this extreme mixture of styles seemed to work.

Laura looked anxiously at her dress in the mirror. As chief bridesmaid she was boho-exempt and condemned to a shimmering close-fitting sheath accessorised with vast, dangling diamond earrings whose cost she daren't think about. At the very least they flouted Mimi's maxim that *if your personality sparkles, there's no need for anything else to.*

'Not now,' she murmured, as Harry took her in his arms again. 'Lulu will be here in a minute.'

He smiled lazily at her as, once more, he pushed her gently back on the bed. 'You know her. She's always late.'

The bride was arriving under her own steam at Riffs' Victorian Gothic chapel. Her entry was to be a surprise, although not to Laura. Kate Threadneedle, as her parting act, had been more than helpful about lending a horse pale enough to be coloured with vegetable dye and submissive enough not to mind having a cardboard cone on its forehead. Both had been applied by Dung Spaw, as her contribution to the wedding. In short, Lulu was entering married life on the back of a blue unicorn.

Harry was unzipping her dress when his mobile phone pinged. Glancing at the screen, he groaned.

'South'n Fried?' guessed Laura.

Harry nodded, sending another wavy lock of hair tumbling forward. 'He's so nervous. You'd think when someone had played stadiums all round the world, getting married wouldn't bother them.'

'Maybe it's Lulu's father,' said Laura. 'I'd be nervous of him.'

Her friend's mysterious parents had not been a disappointment. Lulu's father was vast, cigar-smoking, exotic and silent while her mother was fluttering, petite and decked in head to toe Chanel, new season. No vintage for her, unless you counted the diamonds glittering from every exposed piece of skin. '*Society* is my favourite magazine,' she had told Laura the night before. 'Lucille-Irmintrude never told me you were the editor!'

'Oh yes,' beamed Laura, sidestepping the situation's complexities. All that mattered was that Christopher Stone had returned her to the editor's chair. For the moment, anyway.

Clemency had been strongly encouraged to resign due to 'exhaustion', and Carinthia claimed to be retiring from glossy magazines to pursue a career in the care sector. 'I've led such a privileged life,' she had told *Media Guardian*, 'and I feel that now I ought to help those less fortunate than myself.' It was this that made Laura certain that the spa leave was yet to work its magic and Carinthia was still getting hold of the vodka somehow.

But for the moment, Laura was riding high. The 'Spy Village' piece, which was how the 'HNI Hamlet' angle had ended up, had rocketed the circulation into the stratosphere. Great Hording was no longer an HNI hamlet anyway. The fallout from the scandals and Laura's sensational exposé had seen most of the high and mighty move on to pastures new.

Jolyon Jackson, who had, after all, lost his seat in the recent election, had been moved to the Cotswolds by his wife. Banished to the packing department of Nanny Knows Best, he now spent his days wrapping smocked dresses and sailor suits in cellophane. Tim Lacey, meanwhile, had left the Hollywood Estate for the actual Hollywood, California, where he was directing Justin Bieber in *Les Misérables 2: Electric Bugaloo*. 'Country life had gotten a little quiet for me,' was how he disingenuously explained the move to the *Hollywood Reporter*. 'I wanted to be back where the action is.'

The villagers who remained had all been invited to the wedding. Some were directly involved with it; Kiki, a changed woman since, backed by Lulu, she had bought the pub freehold from Jonny Welsh, was masterminding the catering. Lady Mandy was putting her thespian talents to good use by rehearsing the bridesmaids' flashdance to within an inch of its life. Anna Goblemova was helping Vlad with the bridal hair and facial contouring, while Edgar was manning the decks at the disco. Dame Hermione had graciously presented a signed set of her Saddle-Saw series to the happy couple and Zeb Spaw had designed the wedding invitations, which took the form of a handful of soil shoved through people's letter boxes. 'It symbolises symbolism,' was the great artist's cryptic explanation.

'My mother does know you are editor!' Lulu hissed, dipping by on her rounds of the pre-wedding party. 'I tell her but she never listen.'

'Never mind that,' Laura teased. 'What about Lucille-Irmintrude?'

Lulu groaned. 'My real name is state secret, hmm? And will stay that way now MI6 not here any more?' Both Sir Philip Peaseblossom and Richard Threadneedle had returned to London in a last-ditch attempt to save their jobs. When you considered the effect of the Russian hacks overall, Laura thought, it was tempting to conclude that, far from bringing British society to its knees, in Great Hording at least they had improved things.

The trial of the Russians began in a couple of weeks. Ellen, who Laura had earlier spotted downstairs drinking champagne with Sergei Goblemov, would be reporting on it for *The Sunday Times*. It was Sergei's first post-accident appearance and they seemed to have a lot to talk about; no doubt he was giving her a few pointers for her story. Laura felt a surge of pure satisfaction about having got in first with the whole thing. She, the glossy mag editor, had beaten the serious journalists at their own game! Even Harry had had to give her credit for that.

A knock at the door and Wyatt entered wearing a top hat and frock coat in plum velvet. With her was Kearn, another groomsman, in a Savile Row suit worn with brilliantly new white trainers. He was also showcasing, as the Ivys commentators would have said, a black diamond earring and a huge status watch.

Wyatt's fingers were neon at the tips, Laura saw. Hers

too. Along with Kiki and Lulu, the two of them had spent every night the previous week preparing the handmade touches Lulu wanted for her wedding. Vintage cutlery had been sprayed in vibrant colours to make the table 'pop', and to make wedding favours. Home-made jam had been poured into tiny Kilner jars and given hand-stamped luggage labels.

'Come and look at this.' Harry was at the window. A small plane was flying towards the house. As it neared, it turned and a banner streamed out behind. 'CONGRATULATIONS ONE AND ALL FROM CASPAR AND SAVANNAH. SO SORRY THAT FILMING THE NEW BOND "KIEV CHICKEN" MEANS WE CAN'T BE WITH YOU.'

'Such a shame they couldn't come,' Wyatt said longingly. 'I love Caspar Honeyman. After you, of course,' she added hastily, as Kearn looked hurt. 'Amazing they're back together though, isn't it?'

Laura nodded. Of all the consequences of the amazing Ivys evening, it had been the least anticipated. But Caspar had come round from his self-imposed blackout with no memory of anything that had happened during the last two months, a fact Savannah had been swift to exploit. Her new role, as Bond Girl Happy Ending, promised a return to the sunlit uplands of extreme fame and Laura had read that there was a part for the dogs as well. Che, Mahatma, Pankhurst and Mandela had been cast as the secret death weapon of a new Bond baddie who threw his enemies into their kennel to be savaged.

But Laura could not blame Savannah for any of this. On the contrary, she now felt almost warmly towards her.

According to a recent interview, the first thing Savannah

had done after their reunion was take her scissors and snip off Caspar's man-bun.

You had, Laura thought, to give her credit for that at least.